BABY

ON BOARD

AND

THE ONE
THAT GOT AWAY

BY
JAMIE SOBRATO

MILLS & BOON

Dear Reader,

Having written about two fantastic brothers who find love with two equally wonderful heroines, I sat down to write *Baby on the Ranch* knowing the heroine I paired with strong, determined, super-sexy Cade was going to have to be quite a woman.

First, she'd have to be gorgeous, just to catch his eye. But, casual as Cade can be sometimes, he's also a widower. Absolutely positive he's already lost the love of his life, he won't be swayed by just any woman.

So I created beautiful Suzanne Caldwell, a lonely single mum, only to discover that she owns the final one-third share of Andreas Holdings that Stephone Andreas gave to his first secretary for sticking with him through the tough times. And Darius tells Cade it's up to him to keep Suzanne happy until they can pull together the cash to buy her out.

Though sparks fly when the charming rancher meets the very wary, very broke single mum who must sell her stock now or go hungry, it takes more than attraction to build real love. Sorting through their bad pasts could be enough to send secretly heartbroken Cade scurrying away.

This was, without a doubt, one of the most fun books I've ever written. I hope you'll fall in love with Cade in a heartbeat, and find yourself rooting for desperate Suzanne who really only wants a home.

Susan Meier

BABY
ON THE RANCH

BY
SUSAN MEIER

Susan Meier spent most of her twenties thinking she was a job-hopper—until she began to write and realised everything that had come before was only research! One of eleven children, with twenty-four nieces and nephews and three kids of her own, Susan has had plenty of real-life experience watching romance blossom in unexpected ways. She lives in Western Pennsylvania with her wonderful husband, Mike, three children, and two over-fed, well-cuddled cats, Sophie and Fluffy. You can visit Susan's website at www.susanmeier.com.

First published in Great Britain 2011
by Mills & Boon, an imprint of Harlequin (UK) Limited,
Eton House, 18-24 Paradise Road, Richmond, Surrey TW9 1SR

© Susan Meier 2011

ISBN: 978 0 263 88895 9

23-0711

Harlequin (UK) policy is to use papers that are natural, renewable and
recyclable products and made from wood grown in sustainable forests. The
logging and manufacturing processes conform to the legal environmental
regulations of the country of origin.

Printed and bound in Spain
by Blackprint CPI, Barcelona

CHAPTER ONE

SUZANNE CALDWELL SHOVED against the spot in the door of the Old West Diner where the Waitress Wanted sign filled the glass. The scent of fresh apple pie greeted her, along with a rush of noise. Though there were no more than ten people at the counter and in the booths, the place was as rowdy as a party. Women wearing jeans and tank tops sat with men dressed in jeans, T-shirts and cowboy hats.

She didn't get two steps into the room before the noise level began to drop. As if noticing the stranger, people stopped talking midsentence.

She clutched her six-month-old baby, Mitzi. There was nothing like walking into a roomful of staring strangers to make you realize how alone you were in the world. And she was definitely alone. She'd run out of gas about a mile out of Whiskey Springs, Texas, and, literally, had no one to call for help.

No family. Her grandmother had died six months ago and her mom had died when Suzanne was six. Her dad, whoever he was, had never acknowledged her.

Her mom and grandmother were both only children, so she had no aunts, no uncles, no cousins.

And no friends. The wonderful sorority sisters who'd vowed to be her ally for life had dumped her when she got pregnant by a popular university professor. It was her fault, they'd said, and had accused her of trying to ruin Bill Baker's career. As if. The guy had gone on a campaign to seduce her and had wormed his way into her life because of her grandmother's fortune. When Martha Caldwell made some major mistakes in money management and lost the bulk of her wealth, Professor Baker suddenly didn't want to see Suzanne anymore. And he most certainly wanted no part of their baby.

So, yeah. She was alone. Alone. Broke. Desperate to make a home for herself and her baby. And she'd left Atlanta bound for Whiskey Springs, hoping to find some help.

But after walking the last mile on a hot June day, her heels ached in her black stiletto boots. Mitzi squirmed in her arms. Her heavy diaper bag was dislocating her shoulder. Still, she kept her head high as she made her way to the first empty booth. By the time she got there, the diner was dead silent.

A waitress shuffled over. "Help you?"

She cleared her throat. "I'd like a piece of the apple pie I can smell, a cup of coffee, a glass of milk and some pudding, please."

"What kind of pudding?"

She swallowed. Not one person had turned back to his or her coffee or food. They just stared as if she were a zombie or vampire or some other mythical creature they'd never seen before. "What kind do you have?"

"Vanilla or chocolate."

"Mitzi loves vanilla."

Without so much as a word of acknowledgment, the waitress scurried away.

"You're not from around here."

Knowing the man could only be talking to her, she

followed the voice and found herself staring into a pair
of the shrewdest eyes she'd ever seen. Cool, calculating,
so black the pupils were almost invisible, his eyes never
blinked, never wavered as they held her gaze.

Toto, we are not in Kansas anymore.

"No, I'm not from around here."

"What's your business?"

"None of yours." She turned away from the penetrat-
ing, unsettling eyes and shifted Mitzi on her lap.

To her horror, the man walked over and plopped down
on the bench seat across from hers. His full lips pulled
upward into a devilish smile. His dark eyes danced with
pleasure. "Now, see. That's not just a bad attitude. It's
also wrong."

She should have been scared to death. He was big.
Not fat, but tall and broad-shouldered. The kind of guy
who could snap a little five-foot-five girl like her in
two. But instead of fear, a very unladylike shiver of lust
rippled down her spine.

"Everything that happens in Whiskey Springs is my
business because this is my town."

Not at all happy with herself for even having two
seconds of attraction to an ill-mannered stranger, she
said, "*Your* town? What are you, the sheriff?"

He chuckled. The people at the counter and in the
booths around them also laughed.

"No. I'm Cade Andreas. I own this town. I bought
all the buildings last year. I lease the businesses back
to their proprietors, but I still own every square inch,
including the one you're sitting on."

Oh, good God. *This* was Cade Andreas?

Fear and confusion immediately replaced attraction.
Wasn't the Andreas family broke? She owned one-third
of Andreas Holdings stock and hadn't been able to sell

it because the company was on the skids. What was he doing buying a town?

"And I'd like to know what brings you to my town."

She raised her gaze to his face. A day-old growth of beard covered his chin and cheeks, giving him a sexily disreputable look. His lips were full, firm, kissable. His nose had been broken—undoubtedly in a fight—but it wasn't disfigured, more like masculine. Definitely not dainty. There was nothing dainty about this man. He was all male. One hundred percent, grade A, prime specimen sexy.

Finally, their eyes connected. Her chest tightened. Her breathing stalled. She could have blamed that on her unwitting attraction, but refused. A guy who bought a town had to be more than a little arrogant. Definitely past vain. Maybe even beyond narcissistic. And she'd learned her lesson about narcissistic men with Mitzi's father. It would be a cold, frosty day in hell before she got involved with another self-absorbed man. So she refused to be attracted to Cade Andreas. Refused.

But she still needed a job. She might own stock worth millions of dollars, but nobody wanted to buy it. Potential didn't sell stock these days. Dividends did. And in the past two years Andreas Holdings hadn't paid any. So she was hoping that since she owned one-third of the company they could at least let her work there. The choice to approach Cade Andreas, the youngest of the three brothers who owned controlling interest of Andreas Holdings stock and ran the company, was simply a matter of practicality. Texas was driving distance. New York City, the headquarters for the corporate offices, wasn't. Still, if they gave her a job, she'd get there somehow. She'd go anywhere that she could put down roots and make a home. Maybe find some friends.

"What brings you to my town?"

This time the words were harsh. Not quite angry, but definitely losing patience.

She glanced at the waitress who stood behind the counter, balancing a coffeepot and Suzanne's piece of pie, obviously holding them hostage until she answered Cade.

She looked back at him. His already-sharp eyes had narrowed in displeasure, and she had the sudden, intense intuition that if she told him who she was—in front of his adoring friends and the frozen waitress—he would not jump for joy. She would bet her last dollar that none of these people knew how much trouble Andreas Holdings was in and Cade would not be happy with the person who announced it.

There was no way she could say who she was and why she was here without talking about something he would no doubt want kept private, and no way she could explain her presence in this two-bit town so far from a major highway that no one was ever just passing through.

She glanced around, saw the sign in the door advertising for a waitress and grabbed the first piece of good luck that had come her way in over a year.

"I heard about the job for a waitress, so I came."

"In your fancy boots, with your baby all dolled up?"

"We put on our best stuff," she said, making herself sound as if she fit the part of a waitress. She regretted the deception, but if anybody ever deserved to be played, this guy did. Owned a town, huh? She potentially held the future of his family's company in her hands just by choosing whom to sell her stock to, yet he'd never once considered that she might be somebody worthy of his time. "For the interview."

A short, round dark-haired woman wearing an apron scampered out of the kitchen. "You're looking for a job?"

"Yes." The truth of that brought her back to reality. Her purpose for coming to Whiskey Springs *had been* to get a job—from Andreas Holdings. Now that plan was on hold. She wasn't exactly here to be a waitress, but money was money. And she needed some. Now. Today. She had enough cash to pay for her piece of pie and even buy extra milk for Mitzi, but after that she and Mitzi were sleeping in her car.

"I'm Suzanne Caldwell." Because her grandmother had held the stock in a trust, her name wasn't mentioned on any documents, so she could give it without worry. "This is my baby, Mitzi."

Mitzi picked that exact moment to cry. The little brunette scrambled over. "I'm Amanda Mae and if you want a job, you've got it." She shot Cade an evil look, causing Suzanne to immediately love her. "Real men don't make babies cry."

Cade held up his hands innocently. "Hey, I was on my own side of the booth the whole time. I didn't touch her."

"You're threatening her mama."

His face fell. "I never threatened her!"

"Just your voice is threatening."

He sighed. "Yeah. Right. Whatever."

She took the baby. "Would you like a bottle, little Mitzi?"

Suzanne said, "I ordered some milk and pudding for her."

Amanda Mae looked horrified. "June Marie, where are you with this baby's food?"

The waitress hustled over, set Suzanne's pie in front of her and poured her a cup of coffee before she rushed away and got both the pudding and the milk.

Eyes narrowed, Cade studied the woman across the booth from him. She was a pretty little package. Eyes so blue they bordered on the purple color of the wildflowers that grew on his pasture in the spring. Black hair cut in a straight, blunt line at her chin, giving her a dramatic look that didn't fit with a woman who needed a job as a waitress. And those boots. Black stilettos. The kind a man envisioned on his chest, pinning him to a bed.

He stopped those thoughts. She might be a pretty with her perfect nose and full, tempting lips, but he wasn't interested.

Still, he had no doubt that he had to keep an eye on her. Something wasn't right with her. It wasn't just her city-girl clothes. Her demeanor didn't fit. Waitresses didn't have smooth hands, perfect posture, an unblinking stare.

He rose from the booth. "Well, seeing as how you seem to have gotten the job you wanted, I guess we'll be running into each other from time to time."

She only smiled. A cool, remote smile that heated his blood and all but challenged him to turn on the charm and see how long it would take to get that smile to thaw. Luckily, he was smarter than that.

Amanda Mae said, "Do you have someplace to stay, honey?"

She faced the diner owner. "I— No. Actually, I need a place to stay."

"Hotel's in the next town over," Cade said, striding back to his seat at the counter and his now-cold coffee.

Amanda Mae shot him another evil glare. "Or she could use the apartment upstairs until she gets on her feet."

"I'd like that." Suzanne pressed her fingers to Amanda Mae's hand in a gesture of appreciation that stopped Cade cold. Maybe she was in need of a little help? Her crisp white blouse and fancy jeans could be the last good things she owned. He hadn't heard a car drive up. He glanced out the big front window into the street. He didn't see a car. She could be dead broke—

Nope. His business sense wouldn't accept that. Something about her screamed money. Big money. If she was pretending she didn't have any, there was a reason.

Damn. He was going to have to keep an eye on her.

Immediately after Cade left, Amanda Mae took Suzanne upstairs to look at the little furnished apartment.

"One of the waitresses always lives here," she said, leading Suzanne into the tiny bedroom that barely had enough space for a crib and a double bed. "So we keep it furnished."

Gratitude weakened Suzanne's knees. At least they wouldn't have to sleep in her car tonight. She turned to Amanda Mae with a smile. "Thanks. I appreciate it."

Amanda Mae stuffed a few bills into her palm. "And here's some money to go to the secondhand store down the street and buy some sheets and towels."

Her face reddened. This time last year she was telling her grandmother she was three months pregnant and that her baby's daddy wanted no part of her. Her wonderful, loving grandmother had taken her hand and told her not to worry. That everything would be okay. Even though she'd made some bad investments, they still had the Andreas Holdings stock.

A couple of months hadn't just changed everything; they'd taken away her home, her only family. Instead of being a well-loved granddaughter, she was a broke single mom. So alone her only contacts had been lawyers and accountants, until her grandmother's estate was settled. Then even they didn't call.

Tears welled up. She caught Amanda Mae's gaze. "I'll pay you back."

Amanda Mae squeezed her hand. "In good time. For now, I'm just happy to have some help for the breakfast crowd."

Driving back to his ranch, Cade speed-dialed the number for his assistant.

"Hey, Cade."

"Hey, Eric." He'd hired Eric right out of grad school because he was sharp and educated, but also because he had total recall. If someone mentioned an aunt, cousin, sister, brother or long-lost friend even once in a conversation, Eric would remember him or her. "Have you ever heard of Suzanne Caldwell?"

"Can't say that I have."

Damn.

"Who is she?"

"Just a woman who came into the diner today. She took the waitress job, but something just didn't seem right about her."

"Ah. I'm guessing your business sense kicked up."

He scowled at the phone. "Don't poke fun at my business sense. It's made me rich enough that I'd never have to work another day in my life. While you, on the other hand, still work for me."

He disconnected the call. But when he thought of Suzanne, the hair on his nape snapped up. Damn it! Why would a waitress activate his business sense? And why was he going back to his ranch when his instincts were screaming that he should be checking into this?

Slamming on the brakes, he manipulated his truck through a fishtail and headed back into town. He pulled it into a parking space at the diner, but when he walked by the huge front window, he saw that the new waitress wasn't inside.

His instincts calmed, his intuition quieted and he cursed himself for being the suspicious fool that Eric hinted he was. But before he could turn around and go back to his truck, he saw Suzanne coming down the outside steps from the second-floor apartment, carrying her baby.

A hot rush of desire whooshed through him. Luckily, the hair on his nape also prickled the way it always did right before a negotiation went sour. The first reaction might have been attraction. But the nape prickle? That was what told him he was about to get into a fight. Not a fistfight, but a disagreement, or maybe a battle to protect what was his. He slid into the alley between the general store and the hardware and watched her head up the street.

Unfortunately, the view from behind was every bit as stunning as her front profile. Her straight black hair fringed the collar of the crisp white blouse that hugged a trim, toned back. It slid along the indent of her small waist to an absolutely perfect behind that swayed ever so slightly with every step of her long legs—legs made to look longer and sexier by her stiletto boots.

Attraction hit him like a warm ocean wave and left him drowning in sensation. This time he had to admit it was only attraction. He tried to blink it away but failed. There was just so much about her that was geared to appeal to a man. No male alive could resist that kind of shapely body. Especially when the pretty little package had a face to match. Dramatic hair. Eyes that could very well glow in the dark.

He shook his head to clear the haze. Fantasizing would not do either one of them any good. He needed to figure out why she set off his business alarms or it would drive him crazy. Yes, that might make him a control freak. But he was a rich, successful control freak. And if his business sense said jump, his answer was always how high.

When he was sure she was far enough ahead that she wouldn't see him, he followed her. When she ducked into the secondhand store, he stopped. He waited for her to get deep enough into the building that she wouldn't notice him hovering beyond the display in the big glass front window.

Judy Petrovic, proprietor of Yesterday's Goods, ambled over to her.

Suzanne turned and offered her a sweet, sincere smile, which nearly knocked Cade off his feet. He'd never seen her smile. Well, he'd seen her sassy imitation smile, but never a genuine smile until now. And he was glad. Had she smiled at him like that in the diner he worried he would have stuttered.

She handed her baby to Judy, then her heavy-looking diaper bag. Judy bounced the little girl as Suzanne dipped down and rummaged through a table of what looked to be sheets, maybe towels. Walking back and forth from the display to the cash register, she made a pile of linens before she grabbed a pair of secondhand jeans and a T-shirt, and several things for her baby. After Judy rang up her purchases, she paid with crumpled-up bills that she'd been clutching in her left hand.

Cade pulled back and slid around to the side of the building, his chest tightening with regret. She'd said she'd come to Whiskey Springs for the job as a waitress and she'd asked for it without a hint of regret. Now she was buying somebody's old, worn sheets to fit on the old, worn mattress on a bed that had seen more years than most of the people in this town.

She really was broke.

And here he was spying on her like some old goof.

He was a goof. The truth was he wasn't entirely sure that his sixth sense about her really was his business sense. It could be nothing but attraction. Lord knew it had been so long since he'd been naturally overwhelmingly attracted to a woman that he might have forgotten the signs. He'd botched his first marriage so much that he stayed away from any woman who might inspire anything more than lust. And a woman with a baby wasn't somebody a man should be fooling around with. Since he didn't want to be attracted to Suzanne, he could be trying to kid himself into thinking it was his sixth sense. Rationalizing so he didn't have to admit to anybody that he virtually tripped over his tongue when he looked at her.

A dry dusty breeze swirled around him, reminding him that he was hiding in an alley, spying on a waitress.

Good God. What was he doing?

CHAPTER TWO

CADE RAISED HIS ARM TO WAVE hello, but it slid across silk sheets, and the wonderful dream he was having burst like a bubble.

He bounced up in bed and scrubbed his hand across his mouth. It was the same dream he always had. It began with him riding up to the main corral, watching his deceased wife, Ashley, as she tended the long strip of flowers she'd planted along the road to the barns, stables and corrals. No matter how many times he'd told her that barns did not need flower beds, he'd never been able to get it through her head.

But when he had the dream, the chance to see her, he didn't want to argue about flowers. Even in sleep, his heart knocked against his ribs, and he wanted to hold her, to kiss her, to tell her how much he missed her.

He squeezed his eyes shut. He didn't get the chance to do any of those. Just like always, he hadn't even gotten to say hello. His subconscious wouldn't even give him hello, forget about a hug, a light kiss....

Knowing he couldn't give in to the sadness, he tossed back the covers and headed for the shower. He'd gotten beyond losing Ashley. She'd died two years ago and he wasn't an idiot. She was gone. He couldn't deny that there was a hole in his chest where his heart should have been, but that part of his life was over.

He ducked his head under the spray and let the water beat down on him, remind him he was real, remind him he had satisfying work, a huge ranch, oil wells, a town that depended on him. There wasn't a man in the state of Texas more fulfilled than he was.

It was enough.

He shoved his legs into jeans, wrestled a T-shirt over his head and jogged downstairs. Though it was only 4:00 a.m., Mrs. Granger, the cook, would have coffee in the kitchen. Still, he didn't turn toward the warm scent. He also didn't go to his office. It was hours before the New York Stock Exchange opened, so there was no point going to his desk. Instead, he found an old pair of boots, jumped in his truck and headed for the stables.

That was what he usually did after the dream. Not just because he needed something to occupy his mind, but because the dream left him hungry, angry, and he wouldn't inflict himself on anybody until he settled down.

He hadn't expected lights to be on in the long red stable, but he wasn't surprised to see his foreman and father-in-law, Jim Malloy, cloistered in his office.

"What are you doing up so early?"

Jim's chair creaked as he leaned back. "Me? This is my normal starting time. My guys will be here in an hour or so. I need to get caught up on paperwork. Better question is what are you doing up so early? Stock exchange doesn't open for hours."

He flopped to the chair in front of Jim's desk. Shrugged.

"You had that dream again."

Cade said nothing.

"Pain's probably never going to go away."

"I'm fine. I have my work."

"A lot of work," Jim said with a laugh.

They were quiet for a few seconds then Jim rose. "Coffee?"

"Is it fresh?"

"Come on. I haven't been here *that* long. Of course it's fresh."

"Then I'll have some."

Jim poured two mugs of coffee and handed Cade's to him before he sat on the edge of the desk. "You were a good husband to Ashley and you're still a good son-in-law."

Cade snorted in derision. His father-in-law had known about the time Cade had spent away from Ashley. The times business had taken him to other cities for weeks at a clip. It was kind of him to tell Cade he'd been a good husband, but Cade wasn't so easily buffaloed.

Jim patted his knee. "You *were* a good husband. Just because you don't get to talk to Ashley in your dream, it doesn't mean you're being punished."

Jim was wrong again. He'd been out of town the day Ashley died. Not with her. Not holding her hand, but sweet-talking an oil baron into selling his company. And Ashley had died alone. That, he believed, was what his subconscious was telling him every damn time he had the dream. Just as she hadn't gotten to say goodbye to him, his subconscious wouldn't let him say goodbye to her. Not even symbolically.

Still, he didn't argue with Jim. He took a sip of coffee then choked it out. "My God. Sludge tastes better than this."

"Oh, yeah? And when, exactly, have you tasted sludge?"

Cade laughed. Jim went back to his seat behind the desk. They occupied themselves talking foals and fences, the price of beef and which animals they'd breed. Seconds turned to minutes and minutes to an hour and with every tick of the clock, the tightness in Cade's chest loosened. The residual sadness from the dream receded. He'd never get a chance to say goodbye to Ashley. He had to accept that and move on.

Suzanne woke a little after five o'clock and actually showered before Mitzi even stirred. She dressed quickly in the little pink uniform Amanda Mae had given her for her first day as a waitress, then just as quickly dressed Mitzi. She grabbed her cereal and a fresh bottle on her way out the apartment door.

As expected, she found Amanda Mae in the diner kitchen, kneading a batch of bread.

"Make room on the prep table for me," she said, sliding Mitzi into the seat of the swing they'd set up in the corner. She and Amanda Mae had already decided Mitzi could be in the diner with Suzanne while she worked. When the diner got busy and the kitchen heated from all the cooking, they could move the swing and Mitzi to the little alcove between the dining room and kitchen. But now, the kitchen was a quiet, homey place, suitable for a baby.

"As soon as I feed Mitzi, I'm going to bake a batch of my grandmother's cinnamon rolls."

Amanda Mae's eye brows rose. "Oh, yeah?"

"It's my way of saying thank you for giving me a job."

"Hey, it's no skin off my nose. I know you're probably only temporary, but I need the help. I'm happy for any amount of time you can give me."

Even though Amanda Mae understood, guilt took up residence in Suzanne's chest. She had no idea how things would turn out when she actually spoke with the Andreas brothers about her shares of stock, but she hoped they'd give her a job. She needed to make a home for her baby and waitress pay wasn't as good as working for a shipping conglomerate.

So she fought through the guilt. Not only would she give Amanda Mae a good day's work every day she waitressed, but she'd found a tangible way to pay her back for her kindnesses. The Caldwell cinnamon roll recipe was a family secret, passed down from one Caldwell woman to the next. It was an honor to have it. But it was an even bigger joy to actually eat the cinnamon rolls.

She thought of Cade, hoping a good cinnamon roll might mellow him out, so she could confess who she was on day one of her charade as waitress. Then he could confess that his family didn't have the money to buy her out. So that she could ask for a job before Amanda Mae got accustomed to having her here. It was a long shot. But right now it was all she had.

When Mitzi was fed, she walked around the kitchen gathering the ingredients for the cinnamon rolls. Amanda Mae made room on the prep table for Suzanne and she went to work.

She began with warm water and yeast. When the yeast was ready, she added the other ingredients until she had a nice dough. As the dough rose, the first customers of the morning filtered in and back out again. But while the rolls were baking, the customers in the dining room began asking what was filling the air with the wonderful scent. Some waited long after they'd finished their breakfasts just to get one of the first rolls as they came out of the oven. By seven-thirty, over half were gone.

"Good Lord, girl," Amanda Mae said, staring at the second empty cinnamon roll tray. "We could sell three dozen of these a day."

"People will tire of them," Suzanne said, dusting her hands on her apron before she lifted Mitzi from the swing. She'd just finished putting the last pan into the oven.

"I'm not so sure."

Suzanne worried her bottom lip. "So you think they're good enough to soften a grouchy guy?"

Amanda Mae laughed. "Maybe. But if I were you, I'd try being nice to Cade instead of sniping at him the way you did yesterday."

"You noticed."

"Honey, two polecats fighting over table scraps make fewer sparks."

She winced. "I just don't know what it is about him, but he brings out the worst in me."

Amanda Mae laughed. "Or the best."

"Oh, come on. You're not saying we're attracted."

"Stranger things have happened."

"I can't be attracted to him."

"Figured as much. Figured you've got business with him. The only reason city slickers come to Whiskey Springs is because they have business with Cade."

She sucked in a breath. "I do."

"Then forget all about your hormones and be nice to the guy. At least until you get a chance to tell him what you need."

A little after eight, Cade was lost in work and didn't hear Eric come into the room until he said, "Have you even had coffee yet?"

Pulling away from the computer, he stretched his arms above his head and glanced at the clock.

"If you call the sip of the sludge I had in Jim's office coffee, then yes. But if you're talking about real coffee. No. I haven't even been to the kitchen yet. Did you get some?"

Eric waved a tall mug. "My first stop is always for coffee. But if you want, I can go back and get a cup for you, too."

He leaned back in his chair. "I'm fine."

Eric sat on one of the two chairs in front of Cade's desk. "So did you find out anything interesting yesterday from Suzanne Caldwell?"

He'd forgotten all about the waitress he'd met the day before. But now that Eric mentioned her, he was back to being curious again. She was too pretty, too sophisticated, too coolly elegant to be a real waitress.

Glad to have his mind off his failure as a husband, he rose from his desk and began to pace. "The thing is I have no idea how she got into town since she didn't have a car. Plus, she didn't have any luggage. Even a poor woman would have had luggage, if only one suitcase." He faced Eric again. "She could be running from something. Or someone. And that could be trouble."

"If this woman worries you so much why not go into the diner for breakfast? Maybe you can get some answers by turning on the charm."

The last thing he wanted to do was turn on the charm. He was way too attracted to her to tempt fate. Still, he didn't like people who kept secrets. His whole town was an open book. Everybody knew everybody else and they liked it that way. He couldn't tolerate somebody coming in and stirring up the pot.

That in and of itself was reason enough that he

probably should try to cuddle up to her a little. Show her he was a nice guy. A great guy. And maybe she'd tell him her story?

Convinced this was the right thing to do, he gave Eric enough work to keep him busy for the morning and jumped into his truck. He slid it into an empty parking space on Main Street and shut down the ignition. Oddly, he peered into the rearview mirror and checked his hair, which was sticking up on one side. He patted it down then scowled at himself.

What was he doing? He wasn't here to ask her on a date. He didn't want a date. He wanted information.

He rammed the truck door to open it and all but stormed into the diner. And there she stood. Order pad in hand. Pencil behind her ear. Crisp white apron covering the pink candy-striped waitress uniform Amanda Mae insisted that all her girls wear.

As the little bell above the door tinkled announcing his arrival, she glanced over at him. Their gazes caught. Her pretty violet eyes widened and his heart flip-flopped.

He held back a curse. Hadn't he already gone over all of this in his head? He'd had the love of his life, and he'd botched that relationship. So he wasn't interested in trying again. And even if he was looking for a fling, something discreet and purely for sex, Suzanne Caldwell was not the woman he would choose. She might be pretty. Very pretty. *Dramatically* pretty. But she had a baby and he was certain she was holding back information about herself. He was not interested, except to make sure she wasn't a threat to the peace of his people.

He ambled to the counter, slapped Marty Higgins on the back and sat on the stool next to him. "Morning, Marty."

"Morning, Cade."

He and Marty were the only two patrons left from the morning rush, but that might be good. In a quiet diner, the waitresses sometimes had nothing better to do than talk to the customers.

As casually as possible, he slid his gaze to Suzanne's again. "Morning, Ms. Caldwell."

"Good morning, Mr. Andreas."

"It's Cade," Marty corrected before he took a sip of his coffee.

Cade pulled out his most charming smile. "He's right. Everybody calls me Cade."

"Is that an order?"

His eyes narrowed. "It's not an order and it's also not a reason for you to be so prickly. Especially when I haven't even had coffee yet."

She pulled the pencil from behind her ear. "So you want a coffee."

"And eggs over easy, bacon, home fries, rye toast and two blueberry pancakes."

She stopped writing and glanced at him again. Her gaze rippled from his face down his chest and probably would have gone the whole way to his toes had he been standing.

"You got a problem?"

"You're awfully fit for a guy who eats like a horse."

Hormones bubbled up in him. He had always been proud that he was in shape as a result of hard work, not some sissy gym. But he didn't like the way his gut tightened or his hormones awoke like a bunch of cowboys at the scent of morning coffee. "Believe me. I'll use it all up before noon." He made a quick shooing motion with his hand. "Just go get it."

She smiled sweetly. "No reason to be prickly."

His hormones spiked. Damn she was sassy!

She turned and sauntered away and he watched every sway of her hips, cursing himself in his head for not looking away as he should have.

"She is a pretty little filly, isn't she?" Marty whispered, leaning in so only Cade could hear.

"Yeah, but she's pretty like a cactus. Nice to look at but a man had better not touch."

Marty chuckled. "See, now I hadn't even gotten to the thinking-about-touching stage. You must have it bad. Especially if you're coming into the diner for breakfast when you've got a damn fine cook at your ranch."

Cade glowered at Marty. "I'm here for information." He stopped himself. Why was he explaining himself to the guy who ran the hardware? Since when did he explain himself to anybody?

Marty slapped a five-dollar bill on the counter and rose. Leaning across toward the kitchen, he yelled, "See you tomorrow, Amanda Mae." He smiled at Suzanne. "You too, sugar."

Suzanne strolled back to the counter, pot of coffee in one hand, cup and saucer in the other. Placing them in front of Cade, she addressed Marty, "You leave me a halfway decent tip?"

Marty laughed. "Yep."

"Okay, then, you can go."

Marty left, chuckling to himself and shaking his head. Cade's blood pressure rose. The woman knew she could wrap most men around her little finger because of her looks alone. Well, he was not going to be so easy to manipulate as old Marty.

"Cream?"

"No. I drink my coffee black."

"Wow. Alert the media."

She turned to go, but he snagged her wrist. His fingers wrapped around skin so soft they felt pillowed by it. Her scent drifted over to him. Her gaze swung to his.

He fought the urge to swallow. Her eyes were so beautiful it was enough to stop a man's heart. But he was stronger than this. Smarter than to get caught in a woman's web. And he was also a man on a mission. Figure out who she was so he could get rid of her or just get rid of these odd feelings he had every time he was with her.

"How the hell did you ever succeed as a waitress with that attitude?"

She smiled sweetly. "Maybe I didn't? Maybe that's why I had to travel the whole way here to be able to find someone who'd hire me?"

It was the first thing she'd said to him that made perfect sense. He dropped her wrist and let her go. She returned a few minutes later with his food.

Just then her baby let out with a squawk. Seated in a swing set up in the alcove between the dining room and the kitchen, she slapped a rattle against the white tray.

Cade wasn't surprised that her baby was there. Whiskey Springs was a very laid-back town and Amanda Mae was a very sweet, helpful employer. But it had been so long since he'd seen a baby that curiosity overwhelmed him. Gino, his third half brother, had been six months old when their father had died and passed off Gino's care to the adult Andreas sons. But in the eighteen months that had passed, Gino had become a two-year-old, a toddler. He wasn't a baby anymore.

He peeked at the little girl with her big blue eyes and shiny black hair just like her mother's, and an achy pain circled his heart. Because he had black hair and Ashley had had blue eyes, he'd always imagined that at least one of their kids would have dark hair and Ashley's pale blue eyes. But he and Ashley couldn't have kids.

The reminder made his heart hurt a little more. Not only would he spend the rest of his years without the woman he adored, but also he'd never have kids. Being a father had been the one goal in life he'd wanted more than success. His own father had been a poor excuse for a dad and Cade knew in his heart he could do better. Lots better. If only because he knew exactly what a kid longed for from a father, because he hadn't had it.

He studied the little girl. Her plump cheeks. The spit bubbles she blew as she sputtered and chattered, trying to form words. She was so cute. So happy.

She *was* happy. That had to mean Suzanne was a good mom. But that only brought him back to the same question. Why would a single mom take her baby so far from home for a job that barely paid minimum wage?

When Suzanne walked back to refill his coffee, he caught her hand again. "What are you doing here, really?"

"Maybe I'm running?"

Cade scowled. Now she was teasing him.

But she sighed and said, "Look, I'm not trying to hide my past. It's just kind of embarrassing. I got involved with a college professor who took advantage of my innocence. I was a bit of a starstuck puppy."

Surprised by her easy admission, he leaned back and felt a tad foolish for constantly questioning her motives.

"When I told him I was pregnant, he told me he didn't want anything to do with me or our baby. Eventually I had to quit school. Then my grandmother died and now I'm alone and broke."

Foolishness morphed into regret. His father, the

great Stephone Andreas, had done the same thing to his mom—and him. Stephone had gotten his mom pregnant then barely acknowledged Cade's existence until he was eighteen. Then he'd sent a lawyer to offer the trust fund that became Cade's grubstake to make himself a very rich man. But through his entire childhood, his mom had busted her butt to make a life for them. He had a soft spot for single moms.

So why did he continually harass this one?

But before he could apologize, Suzanne caught his gaze and very quietly said, "Where I come from, people share. I just told you my big embarrassing secret. Seems to me you should reciprocate by telling me yours."

Any bit of sympathy he had for her disappeared and was replaced by a swell of annoyance. His biggest life secret was that he'd never gotten the chance to say goodbye to his wife. And that was none of Suzanne's business. Especially since he found her attractive. Ashley was the love of his life. She was a sweet, wonderful woman who would have never talked to him—to anyone—the way Suzanne just had, nosing into personal business.

"Hey, Cade!"

To Cade's complete horror, his mother, Virginia Brown—Ginny for short—walked into the diner and over to him. A tall brunette with sharp green eyes and a perpetual grin on her face, she took the seat Marty had just vacated.

"What are you doing here? Don't you have a cook?"

"Yes, I have a cook." He faced his mother with a warning glare.

She only laughed. "So why are you at the diner?"

She asked the question as Suzanne wiped down the counter in front of them, cleaning away Marty's crumbs.

Cade didn't have to reply because Suzanne said, "What can I get for you?"

His mother smiled, but she sniffed the air. "What is that wonderful smell?"

Suzanne straightened with pride. "Cinnamon rolls. I gave Amanda Mae my grandmother's recipe as a thank-you for hiring me."

Even as Suzanne spoke, Cade picked up on the scent himself. Because it had mixed in with the aromas of coffee and pancakes, he'd almost missed it. But the second he homed in on it, his mouth watered.

"I showed her how to make them this morning."

"Are there any left?" Ginny asked hopefully.

Suzanne shrugged. "Maybe a dozen or so."

"I'll have one of those and a cup of coffee."

Cade said, "And I'll have one to go."

Suzanne suddenly became very busy dusting a napkin holder. "Want another cup of coffee?"

"Yeah."

As Suzanne walked away, Ginny burst out laughing. "You don't have to answer my question about why you're here. I think I figured it out on my own."

"You figured wrong."

Ginny laughed again. "Really? Did you miss how she blushed when you said you wanted a cinnamon roll? I think she thinks the way to your heart is through your stomach."

With a deep breath for patience, he faced his mother again. Rolling his eyes in Suzanne's direction to let his mom know he couldn't talk in front of the new waitress, he said, "You've got it all wrong."

She laughed. "Really? You're here when you shouldn't

be and she's serving up old family recipes? If you don't see the signs in that then you're the one who's got it all wrong."

Suzanne didn't really hear the exchange, though she caught enough of it to ascertain that the woman sitting next to Cade was his mother. There wasn't much family resemblance. His hair was black. His mother's sable. His eyes were dark. His mother's pale. Their only common trait was that they were both tall and fit.

In his gray T-shirt and tight jeans, Cade looked especially fit. And that was why Suzanne had been thrown off her game and forgot to be nice to him when she waited on him. But she'd tried to rectify that by telling him about Mitzi. She'd even tried to get him to tell her about himself, hoping for an opening to explain she was the owner of the trust that held one-third of his family's company's stock.

But he hadn't bitten and now he wasn't alone at the counter anymore. Worse, he was taking his cinnamon roll out. He wouldn't eat it in the diner, swoon with ecstasy and be open to anything she told him. By the time he ate the thing, he could even forget who'd made it. She needed to come clean with him about who she was. If she could just get fifteen minutes of his time, in private, she could end this blasted charade.

One cinnamon roll in a take-out box and another on a dessert plate for Cade's mom, she walked over to the counter, poured Cade's mom's coffee and set a cinnamon roll in front of her. As she set Cade's take-out box in front of him, his mom very sweetly said, "I didn't catch your name."

Hoping to get him to stay, Suzanne refilled Cade's cup. "It's Suzanne. Suzanne Caldwell."

"I'm Ginny Brown. I used to be the town librarian, but since my son struck it rich, I now own the bookstore."

As Suzanne said, "It's nice to meet you," she noticed the burn of embarrassment crawl up Cade's neck to his face.

Ginny patted his arm. "He hates it when I mention his being rich."

Cade caught her gaze as if pleading for mercy, a move so unexpected that something soft and warm cradled Suzanne's heart. It was sweet that he couldn't be angry with his mom. But it was also curious that Ginny believed he was still rich.

Unless even she didn't know about the Andreas Holdings troubles?

Cautious, she ran the damp cloth along the counter again. "You should be happy your mom is proud of you."

"There's such a thing as being too proud."

She shrugged. "Maybe. But I think I would have liked to have known what that felt like. My mom died when I was six."

Ginny gasped. "I'm so sorry."

She shrugged again. "I had a good grandmother to raise me." Even as she said that, she glanced back at the kitchen. In a lot of ways Amanda Mae reminded her of her grandmother. Except younger. Probably about her mom's age. Ever since she'd arrived the day before, Amanda Mae had been nothing but kind. This morning's customers had accepted her, as well. And she liked them. If she didn't have other business to attend to, this would be a perfect place to make home.

But she did have other business.

She faced Cade and his mom. "Anyway, it's from my gram that I learned how to make the cinnamon rolls."

"Well, if they taste as good as they smell, the people of this town are going to love you forever."

Warmth filled her heart at the possibility. Wouldn't it be nice to have a whole town of friends?

Finished with his breakfast, Cade rose. He tossed a twenty-dollar bill on the counter and picked up his take-out container. "This should cover it and the tip."

With that he left, and she'd missed her chance to tell him who she was.

After about thirty seconds of staring at the door, Suzanne realized she'd watched him go. What female over the age of fifteen wouldn't? He had a strong, broad back, exquisitely outlined by his tight gray T-shirt. And a perfect backside in well-worn jeans. Add boots and a Stetson to that combo and the mouths of women in three states were probably watering right now.

"Could I have some more coffee?"

Shaking herself out of her daze, Suzanne smiled down at Cade's mother only to see that Ginny was smiling up at her. Shrewdly. Craftily.

"You know, we're having a party at Cade's ranch on Saturday night. I'd love it if you'd come."

CHAPTER THREE

BECAUSE CADE DIDN'T VENTURE into the diner the rest of the week, Suzanne knew she had to go to his party.

She had Amanda Mae drive her to her car to get her two suitcases on Saturday afternoon. The diner owner's eyebrows rose when she saw the powder blue Mercedes, but she said nothing. In the four days they'd worked together, an odd kind of bond had grown between the two women. Since her grandmother's death, Suzanne had felt alone, adrift, and she sensed Amanda Mae didn't often get close to people, either.

But though their growing friendship bolstered Suzanne's courage enough that she knew she could talk to Cade that night, she also realized that she was growing attached to Amanda Mae. If she stayed much longer and got a job at Andreas Holdings, she'd have to move away. Then she'd feel a real loss and so would Amanda Mae. Tonight had to be the night she talked to Cade.

That evening she dressed in the only cocktail dress she'd kept—a little red sheath—her grandmother's pearls and red stiletto sandals. When Amanda Mai's sixteen-year-old neice, Gloria, arrived to babysit, she gave detailed instructions on caring for Mitzi, then carefully guided herself down the outside stairway in the waning light.

Using the directions Amanda Mae had written out for her, she confidently drove to Cade's ranch. But maneuvering down the long lane that led to his house, she was so confused she nearly stopped her car. Though the house was huge, it was simple. Plain white with black shutters and a black front door with a silver door knocker. There was no valet parking. Cars had just stopped on each side of the lane, but even more cars had been parked in the grass of what should have been his front yard.

She frowned. This was different.

As she opened her car door, music greeted her, making her think the party was outside. Which was fine. She liked garden parties. She especially loved a gorgeous sit-down dinner outside in the early evening. The only problem was an outdoor party sort of screwed up her plan. Because she knew she had to tell Cade who she was, she'd decided to ask him for a few minutes alone. She'd envisioned him saying yes, then herself leading him to his office, where she'd explain who she was in that businesslike environment behind closed doors. First, so no one could overhear. Second, so his reaction would be more professional than personal.

She walked up the cobblestone sidewalk to the front door and rang the bell. But after two minutes and two more bell rings, no one had answered. She tried the silver knocker but that brought no one to the door, either.

With a sigh, she walked around the side of the house. If they were outside, she would just join them.

But when she rounded the corner, she stopped dead in her tracks. Long buffet tables were piled high with food. The music she'd heard was a country band playing a square dance. Couples moved around in a circle under the canopy of a gazebo. Lights circled a swimming pool where kids and teenagers were actually swimming. There were no lily pads decorating the pretty blue water. No careful row of flower pots strategically placed to preclude anyone getting to close to the edge. Nope. This pool was in use.

The urge to turn and run enveloped her, but before she could move, Cade's mom hurried over. "Suzanne! You look exquisite."

"Thanks." She took in Ginny's jeans and bright yellow T-shirt, her cowboy boots. "I didn't realize this was a—"

"Barbecue." Ginny winced. "Sorry. I just assumed you'd realize that in Texas *party* usually means *barbecue*."

Cade picked that precise second to walk over. Dressed in jeans and a chambray shirt with a bolo tie and a Stetson, he looked like a man who could own a town. Sleek, sexy, sharp and just country enough to remind a woman she was on his turf.

The crackle of attraction that raced through her competed with a rumble of warning. *Tell him. Get him alone and tell him who you are. Do not waste another second.*

Before she could utter a peep, though, Cade's eyes made a quick sweep from her sandaled feet up her dress to the top of her head and sent another burst of attraction through her.

He smiled slyly. "Come on. Surely you knew this was a barbecue. Everybody in the other forty-nine states knows barbecue is Texas's middle name."

But Cade wasn't one bit sorry she hadn't dressed for a barbecue. Her sexy little sheath was just short enough to show off her great legs. Her super-high-heel sandals sent the blood humming through his veins. The pearls gave her a classy, elegant look.

What if she'd dressed like this deliberately? Wanting him to notice her?

"Let me introduce you around before dinner." Ginny took Suzanne's arm and turned her to the crowd. "You've met most of these people at the diner. Still, there are a few you haven't."

"But I—" Suzanne protested, but it was as if his mom didn't hear. And just like that, Suzanne had been spirited away.

He watched them go. His eyes narrowed as his gaze honed in on the back—or should he say lack of back—in Suzanne's dress. It was literally open from her neck to her hips…another inch and it would have been illegal in some states.

But it wasn't. It was simply mind-numbingly sexy.

Eyes narrowed, he watched as his mother introduced her to Jeb and Caroline Hunter, the couple who owned the ranch next to his. She smiled politely and shook hands with Jeb, but her gaze wandered over to his.

Before he had a chance to react, his mom took her to Tom Calhoun, Bruce Murphy, Danny Jones and Joshua Turner. All four were recent university graduates. Tom worked at the bank with his father. Bruce had taken over the local car repair shop. Josh was a freelance certified public accountant and Danny was still looking for a job.

He stiffened a bit. Any one of those men was more suited to her. They were her age. Just starting out like she was.

But, once again, after shaking hands, Suzanne's gaze ambled back to his.

He smiled. Well. Well. Maybe she wasn't interested in men her own age? And maybe he'd been playing this all wrong. She might have a baby, but she'd been burned by that child's daddy. Maybe she wasn't interested in another long-term relationship? Maybe she wasn't interested in a relationship at all? Maybe she was a young, healthy, sexy woman looking for a little fun, a little romance.

And from the way her gaze kept streaming back to his, maybe she was looking for that fun with him?

His eyes never left her as his mother trotted her through the group, introducing her to all the guests. Even the kids in the pool. But every few seconds, her gaze would wander back to his and he'd smile.

Until finally, *finally,* his mother got her a glass of wine from a passing waiter and left her with Missy Jo Johnson and Amanda Mae. This time, when her gaze ambled over to his, he nudged his head to indicate she should break away, come to him.

It was a test. If she came over, he'd know she was interested. If she didn't...well, he had other guests to pursue.

Just as he expected, she excused herself and walked over.

Playing with her pearls, she cleared her throat. "Um, Cade, could you and I go somewhere private to talk?"

Sweet success sparked through him. He didn't mind leaving the party. His guests were entertained and probably no one would miss him. More important, no one would be so foolhardy as to come looking for him.

She glanced up at him hopefully.

He smiled down at her. In ten minutes the charcoal beneath the beef wouldn't be the only thing sizzling.

"Sure, sugar."

With his hand at the small of her back, he guided her through the French doors into the formal dining room. The velvet skin of her back tickled his palm with every step she made. Little beads of sweat formed on the back of his neck.

She peeked back at him. "Do you have a den?"

"Den?"

"You know, sort of an office. Someplace private?"

He'd intended to simply take her to his bed. But he wasn't about to argue over logistics. In the marble-tile foyer with the huge crystal chandelier, he pointed straight ahead. He let her get a few steps in front of him so he could take in the view of her gorgeous back, her nicely rounded bottom caressed by the soft material of her perfect red dress. He pressed his hand to his chest to still his beating heart. She was absolutely perfect.

Whoever said money didn't buy happiness was a complete liar.

"Second door down."

She stepped into the room ahead of him. He closed the door and locked it.

Apparently hearing the click, she turned and frowned at him. "You're locking the door?"

"Well, you don't want to get caught do you?"

She frowned. Her full lips turned down prettily, creating a dimple in her right cheek. Cade all but rubbed his hands together with glee.

"No. I don't."

She sipped her wine. Realizing she might be nervous, he didn't immediately pounce, but ambled to the bar and poured himself two fingers of Scotch. They might have to get back to the party, but the beef wouldn't be done for another hour. They had plenty of time.

He motioned to the black leather sofa. "Seat?"

She smiled nervously. "I think I'd rather stand."

His brow puckered. Confusion eclipsed the heat sparking in his blood stream.

"I…um…" She glanced down at her wine, then back up at him with a hesitant smile. "Well, there's something that I have to tell you."

That didn't quite compute. "Tell me?"

"Yes." She sucked in a breath. "I'm Suzanne Caldwell."

His eyes narrowed.

"You don't recognize the name because my grandmother never had her name on any documents. She held everything in trust."

His hormones stilled. "Held what in trust?"

She cleared her throat. Swallowed again. "The one-third interest in Andreas Holdings that your father had given her."

His hormones died. His muscles tensed and his brain went to red alert.

"*You're* the missing shareholder?"

She nodded.

Cade swayed a bit, downed his Scotch and fought the urge to fall to the sofa. "Well, this is a hell of a time to tell me."

"I couldn't think of a better time—or way. The times I saw you in the diner there were people around. I know your father's company has fallen in hard times because I couldn't sell my shares—"

His face fell in horror. "You tried to sell your shares?"

"What else was I to do? My grandmother's estate— furniture, art, everything—went to pay off debts I didn't realize Gram was accumulating. I have no money."

"At least there's one thing you weren't lying about."

She gaped at him. "I never lied at all! I told you the truth. I had come here to Whiskey Springs looking for a job. In fact, that's why I'm here right now."

"You want a job?"

"Why not? I own one-third of the company. Surely, there's something I can do at Andreas Holdings. Something that pays enough that I can support my baby."

He squeezed his eyes shut, counted to a hundred and still couldn't control his temper. He didn't know who he was more angry with, her for not telling him who she was the day she arrived, or himself for being such an idiot. Attracted to the enemy. Because that's what she was. Whether she knew it or not, she held more shares of his father's company than any of the Andreas brothers. Yes, united they owned controlling interest, but if they ever had a fight or came down on different sides of an issue with the company, *she'd* rule.

They needed to get those shares back. But even though he could afford to buy her out, his brothers couldn't. They were rich but didn't have that kind of money to spare. And he wouldn't buy her shares because, added to his own, they'd give him controlling interest. Then he and his brothers wouldn't be equals anymore. As it stood, everybody knew he had about ten times the money his brothers had. But when it came to owning their family's company, they were all equals. His buying her out would ruin that.

He took off his Stetson and tossed it across the room.

"I need time to think."

"To me there's nothing to think about. I need a job. I own one-third of a company. It's a no-brainer."

"No, it isn't. The company isn't here. It's headquartered in New York."

"So you're telling me you can't give me a job?"

No. He was stalling for time, trying to figure out how to arrange this so her stock didn't ruin the relationship that had finally been forged between the four Andreas half brothers.

He glanced over at her pretty, pouty expression and his hormones jumped again. This was so not how he'd expected to be spending the next hour.

"Do you have any skills?"

"I was an art history major. One semester away from getting a degree."

He groaned. Like Darius had any use for an art history major.

"My brothers are going to kill me."

She walked over, stood directly in front of him. The scent of her cologne combined with the shear force of her femininity and sent his hormones scurrying to life again.

"Why? I'm the owner of the stock, not you."

He scrubbed his hand across his mouth. "Greeks have a long tradition of killing messengers."

She laughed and he fought the urge to squeeze his eyes shut. He needed twenty minutes alone to think this through, but he couldn't send her back to the party unescorted. God only knew what she'd tell his guests.

"All right." He strode around the desk and flopped into the tall-back black leather chair. Whether he liked it or not, he could not make this decision alone. He pointed at the captain's chairs in front of his desk. "Sit."

She ambled to the desk. "What are we doing?"

"We're calling my brother."

"Ah."

Ah? Even the way she'd said that was cute. Sexy. He had to get rid of her. This was what he got for sniffing around a woman who, according to his very accurate business instincts, was trouble.

Dialing the number from memory, Cade sat back in his chair. Darius's house manager, Mrs. Tucker answered. "Andreas residence."

"Hey, baby. How's it going in the money capital of the world?"

Hey, baby? This was how he talked to staff?

Suzanne sniffed and tried to yank her skirt to a more proper place on her legs. Too late, she realized Cade would notice the action and that would only draw his gaze where she didn't want it.

She wanted to be taken seriously. Given a job. Yet this whole meeting had a weird feel to it, almost as if something had been going on that she'd missed.

"Can you get Darius for me?"

She pursed her lips. Straightened her spine. Tried to look like a woman with something to offer a huge shipping conglomerate. She knew her "almost" art history degree hadn't given her a marketable skill, but she could type. She could organize. There were a million things she could do. Plus, she wasn't picky, or proud. She'd take what she could get.

Just then Cade's gaze met hers. Intense heat filled her. He was so good-looking that for a few seconds there, when they'd found themselves alone, before she'd told him about her shares of Andreas Holdings, she'd wondered what it would be like if they'd gone to find someplace to be alone for an entirely different reason than business....

She swallowed. Oh, good grief. Now she got it. In those few seconds, he'd been wondering, too. Or maybe planning.

That's why he'd locked the door!

Oh, no! He might have actually thought she'd brought him to his office to seduce him.

Well, too bad. She needed a job more than she needed a boyfriend—no, lover. He'd never be anybody's boyfriend, but she'd bet he'd happily be her lover.

Heat filled her. Her insides constricted then blossomed.

She had to stop thinking about that.

"Hey, Darius, it's me. I've got good news and bad news." A pause. "Well, the good news is I've found our mystery shareholder. The bad news is she wants a job. I'm going to put the phone on speaker." He hit a button on his phone then replaced the receiver.

"Darius, our shareholder is Suzanne Caldwell. She's across the desk from me."

"It's a pleasure to meet you, Ms. Caldwell."

Darius's voice was deep and smooth and had the tone of someone accustomed to being diplomatic. With Cade Andreas as a brother, he probably had to be.

"It's a pleasure to meet you, too, Mr. Andreas. I'm sorry to be trouble, but my grandmother died only a few months ago and the estate was a mess. She had spent more money than was coming in for the past several years—"

"Probably because Andreas Holdings stopped paying dividends."

"Maybe," Suzanne agreed. She sucked in a soft breath. "Anyway, I have a child. A baby girl, Mitzi, and I—we—"

"Of course, you need money. Perfectly understandable. You do understand, though, that Andreas Holdings isn't in a position to buy your shares."

Cade leaned back in his chair. Crossed his arms.

Gave her one of those looks that could have melted butter.

Having realized where his mind had been when he locked the den door, Suzanne didn't get a shiver of fear from "that" look. Instead, her blood simmered.

She licked her lips. "I understand. I'm not approaching you to sell my shares."

Cade sat forward and leaned his arms on his desk. "She wants a job, Dar."

"As?"

Again Cade answered. "I know you can't drop her into a vice president position, but she's fairly smart."

Suzanne glanced up sharply. *He thought she was smart?*

"And," Cade continued, "I'm sure there are a lot of things she could do for us on an executive level. Something that would pay her enough to get a nice condo and a nanny for her baby."

Wow. He was being so kind. So considerate. So generous. Almost as if he liked her.

Her stomach filled with butterflies.

What if he liked her? What if this strong, sexy, smart man hadn't harassed her at the diner because he was the bossy overlord of the little piece of heaven he called Whiskey Springs, but because he'd been…interested… and his flirting skills were a little rusty?

She swallowed.

"There's got to be something she can do."

"Why don't you both fly up to New York City tomorrow morning so we can discuss it? You can be my guests at the house in Montauk Sunday night. Gino will be thrilled to see you, Cade. And Whitney loves company. Bring your daughter, Ms. Caldwell. It will be our pleasure."

With that Darius disconnected the call and silence reigned in Cade's office.

He leaned back in his chair. Rubbed his fingers across his forehead. Closed his eyes.

This wasn't at all what she'd had planned. And the thought that he might "like" her only added confusion to the mix. He was a gorgeous, sexy guy and she was attracted to him. But was she ready for anything to happen between them? After having been dumped only a little over a year ago?

No. She wasn't.

"I'm sorry."

"You didn't make the royal proclamation that we had to go to New York together. Darius did."

"I know, but your having to go to New York is my fault. I'd be happy to go by myself." She winced. "Except I don't have plane fare."

"I have an actual plane."

"Really?"

"Seven."

Her eyes widened. For a family that was broke, they certainly had more assets than she did.

"We'll leave at six. That should get us to the house in Montauk before noon, considering we'll have to drive from the airstrip."

He rose from the desk. "Now, I have guests to attend to."

He walked out of the den without another word. Suzanne folded her hands on her lap not quite sure what she should do.

She was about to fly to New York City with a man who'd thought she'd brought him into his office to seduce him. A man who plainly had been willing to be seduced.

And he'd left before they could clear the air about their feelings.

Could she have botched this any worse?

CHAPTER FOUR

WHEN SUZANNE'S CELL PHONE alarm woke her at four o'clock the next morning, she pulled the covers over her head. Explaining who she was to Cade had been a disaster. Now she had to fly to New York with him. That is, after she told Amanda Mae she couldn't work for the next few days—and might not be coming back to work at all.

Staying in bed sounded like a really good plan.

Unfortunately, Mitzi had heard the alarm, too, and her soft cries filled the room.

"I'm coming," she said, sliding out of bed. She fed the baby a bottle, dressed her in a happy yellow sundress with pink, blue and green ladybugs circling the hem, then took a shower and dressed herself in the blue suit she'd kept for interviews. Because, technically, she was going for an interview.

Ten minutes later, balancing a baby, a diaper bag, a suitcase packed with extra clothes for both her and Mitzi, and a car seat, she carefully walked down the outside stairway and into the diner.

Amanda Mae harrumphed. "What are you all dolled up for?"

She set the empty car seat on the floor. Walking to the cupboard where they now kept Mitzi's cereal, Suzanne avoided Amanda Mae's gaze. "I'm going to New York City with Cade Andreas."

She turned just in time to see Amanda Mae's big brown eyes pop and her mouth fall open. "What?"

"Oh, Amanda Mae. I am so sorry, but I have a confession to make."

"Look, honey, there isn't a woman in the world who could fault you for quitting a job as a waitress and running away with Cade Andreas. Even I'd let him put his boots under my bed and I haven't done the nasty in over a decade."

Thank God that made her laugh. "No. I'm not... He's not... We're..." She stopped. She had no idea what they were. He'd taken her part in the discussion with his brother. He'd made inroads with the company she couldn't have made for herself. And he was taking her to New York.

"Oh, come on. I told you I saw that spark between you. I think our boy Cade is sweet on you."

She swallowed, ignoring the heat that shimmered through her at the thought that Cade might actually feel something for her. Hadn't she thought the same thing herself the night before?

"We're going to New York to talk with his family. I own one-third of the company he and his half brothers inherited when their dad died."

Amanda Mae's eyes narrowed. "You're an heiress?"

Busying herself with preparing Mitzi's cereal, she said, "If you call someone who actually doesn't get any money from the estate they inherit an heiress, then, yes, I'm an heiress."

"You had an estate but didn't get any money?"

"My gram made some bad investments." She slid Mitzi into the swing and stooped down to begin spoon-feeding her. "Really bad. And she stopped getting dividends from the one company she thought she could always depend on." She didn't say from whom she stopped getting dividends to protect Cade and his brothers. "Three years went by with her losing money, but she never stopped her outrageous spending. So when she died I had to sell our home, our furniture, the art collections." She glanced down at her simple blue suit. "Even most of my clothes."

Crossing her arms on her chest, Amanda Mae said, "What does that have to do with going to New York?"

Scooping another spoonful of cereal into Mitzi's eager mouth, she cleared her throat. "I'm hoping that since I own one-third of their company, they'll give me a job."

Amanda Mae blew her breath out in disgust. "No matter how you slice it, you're leaving, and from what you're saying I don't even get any good gossip out of it."

"I'm not a hundred percent sure I'm leaving for good. They might not give me a job." She fed another bite to Mitzi as she continued in a rush. "So I may have to come back and continue working for you."

With a sad sigh, Amanda Mae turned away. "Yeah, well, I've still gotta call someone to come in to handle your shift this morning."

Suzanne's throat tightened. She liked Amanda Mae. There had been a click of something between them, an instant bond. It didn't feel right to be hoping to get another job. It felt even worse to have saddened her friend.

"I talked to your niece last night. She'll do the breakfast crowd."

The diner door opened and Suzanne's gaze swung

over as Cade walked in. He wore his usual jeans and T-shirt. But today, remembering Amanda Mae's comment that he was sweet on her, the little zing of attraction she always felt for him morphed into a breath-stealing whoosh. He could have any woman on the face of the earth. If he was interested in her, it was equal parts of flattering and confusing. She really wasn't ready for another relationship. But how did anybody turn down a man like Cade Andreas?

Amanda Mae glanced sideways and saw him, too. Still, she didn't turn around and face Suzanne. Her voice was gruff when she said, "Okay. Thanks for taking care of that. You scoot now."

Suzanne's heart turned over in her chest. Even with Cade waiting for her in the dining room, she couldn't get her feet to move. Still she had to follow through with her stocks. If owning one-third interest gave her enough clout to get her a good job she owed it to Mitzi to take it.

She scooped Mitzi out of the swing. "I'll stop in when we get back." She smiled ruefully. "To let you know if I'm still your waitress."

Amanda Mae didn't turn around. "Sure."

With that, Suzanne walked into the dining room.

Cade didn't say a word, simply motioned for Suzanne to follow him outside. At the door, he took the car seat and diaper bag from her and she carried Mitzi.

He opened the back door of his extended cab truck and slid the car seat inside. "I know this thing gets buckled in but I don't know how to do it." He held out his hands. "So give me the baby while you install it."

She slid Mitzi to him, careful to keep from accidentally brushing hands, and efficiently installed the car seat. When she turned to take Mitzi from him she noticed he was studying her. "Haven't you ever seen a baby before?"

He smiled ruefully and handed Mitzi to her. "Yes and no. Yes, I've seen a baby. But it's been a while." He paused, then added, "She's cute."

If that was a peace offering for leaving her in his office the night before, or a way for them to get back to a natural footing with each other, it worked. "Thanks. I like her."

He chuckled. "No kidding."

Once Mitzi was buckled in, he ushered her up to the passenger seat then rounded the hood and climbed in himself.

Emotionally confused after her talk with Amanda Mae and not wanting to break the fragile peace between herself and Cade, Suzanne stayed quiet. But the silence in the truck became oppressive, nudging her to say something—anything—to break it. Blessedly, his phone rang.

Wearing an earpiece, he didn't have to pick up. He said simply, "Hey, Eric, isn't it a little early for you and monster dog?"

As he spoke, her gaze strayed over to him. It wasn't often that he was occupied and she grabbed the opportunity to study him without worry. She took in the stretch of the denim across his strong thighs. The way his T-shirt hugged the well-defined muscles of his chest. His easy competence driving.

What would it be like to be dating this man?

Her breath stalled in her chest. The blood in her veins crackled to life. He was, without a doubt one of the sexiest men she'd ever seen. But date him?

Okay. It would probably be fun, since she guessed he'd never be boring. But she didn't know him. And she didn't even really know that he liked her. All she had were suspicions based on Amanda Mae's observation and the guess she'd made the night before that he thought she'd brought him back to his office to seduce him. That was trouble enough. She had to stop thinking there was more to it.

When they arrived at a private airstrip, she jumped out of the truck and immediately grabbed Mitzi and headed for the plane. Though she'd flown in private planes before, Cade's was one step beyond what she was accustomed to. Five butterscotch leather seats were arranged throughout the cabin. Two sat across from a shiny yellowish wood entertainment unit with a big-screen TV. Two sat by a bar made of the same shiny wood. One in the back was connected to a desk.

Cade strode to the one in the back and tossed a black leather briefcase on the desk.

Ten seconds later, the pilot jogged up the steps, followed by a female copilot.

"I'm Dave. This is Jenny." The pretty red-haired copilot nodded. "The weather looks good. We should be in New York in a few hours." He smiled at Suzanne. "Buckle yourselves in."

With that he and Jenny entered the cockpit. Cade pulled two files out of his briefcase, opened them and never looked up again.

She suppressed a sigh. She understood he was ignoring her. She supposed that could actually work to their advantage. If they were both on their best behavior, they wouldn't risk another misunderstanding. But, sheesh, it was going to be a long, boring ride if they didn't talk.

Hours later, Suzanne almost cheered when they landed. From the plane's window, she could see a man in tan pants and a white dress shirt standing by a long black limo, holding a toddler. A woman in capris and a frilly blouse stood beside them. All three wore sunglasses. The toddler squirmed.

The captain and cocaptain said goodbye as Cade walked down the three steps to the tarmac, then took the big diaper bag from Suzanne and caught her hand to help her down the steps. When his fingers closed around hers, their eyes met. The hot June breeze drifted around her. Warmth radiated from their joined hands.

Okay. He might be ignoring her but they were still attracted to each other and last night they'd both jumped to some bad conclusions. She had to do something about the awkwardness between them. And quickly before they weren't alone anymore.

"Look, I'm sorry I gave you the wrong impression last night."

Dropping her hand, he turned to walk to the limo. "What wrong impression? You own one-third of my family's company. No way I could get the wrong impression about a fact."

"So you're not mad about the other?"

He stopped and faced her, his expression shuttered. "What 'other'?"

Ah, so he wasn't ignoring her. He was pretending the beginning part of their conversation, the click of the lock on the den door, the hot look in his eyes never happened?

Actually, that would be one way for them to get beyond the awkwardness.

"I was just pleased you took my part with your brother last night."

He huffed out a breath, propped his hands on his hips and looked up at the blue sky. "It was the right thing to do. The fair thing."

Her pulse stilled. Her battered ego fluttered to life. Fairness might be commonplace for him, but she couldn't remember the last time anyone had truly treated her fairly. Except Amanda Mae. Still, there was no way to explain that to him without getting maudlin or too personal. And after her last attempt at a personal conversation with this guy—well, she knew better.

So she simply said, "Thanks. I appreciated it."

As they approached the limo, the man Suzanne assumed was Darius stepped forward. He took the diaper bag from Cade. "Nice to see you, brother." He turned to Suzanne. "And this must be Suzanne and Mitzi."

From his welcoming smile, it was easy for Suzanne to see Darius was a nice guy. With black hair and dark eyes similar to Cade's, he definitely had a family resemblance to his half brother. "Yes. I'm Suzanne Caldwell. It's nice to meet you."

"This is Whitney, my wife, and our son, Gino."

Whitney grinned and pointed at Mitzi. "Can I hold her?"

Suzanne laughed. "Yes. She gets a little heavy after hours and hours on a plane."

After a quick scowl at Cade, as if chastising him for not helping with the baby, Whitney took Mitzi. "Well, hello there, Miss Mitzi."

Mitzi immediately began to cry.

"I'll take her back."

Whitney returned the baby to Suzanne. "She'll get used to me, but now's not the time to force the issue."

"Cook has made lunch," Darius said, motioning for everyone to enter the limo when the driver opened the door.

When they were settled, they took off toward Darius and Whitney's home. Suzanne spent most of her time entertaining Mitzi, while Darius, Whitney and Cade made small talk.

Out of the corner of her eye, she studied their interaction. A brother and his wife, teasing another brother who gave as good as he got. He wasn't rude, the way he'd been the day she'd met him. He wasn't overbearing, as he'd been the day he'd come into the diner. He was nice.

Normal.

Huh! She almost snorted a laugh. Normal? He owned a ranch, a town and seven planes. And a big chunk of a shipping conglomerate. He might wear boots and jeans, but he was savvy, sharp. Sophisticated.

A sizzle of excitement sparked through her. She wasn't just attracted by his looks. She liked that he was smart. She liked that he was savvy.

She almost groaned. Being around him must be making her brain soft because it didn't matter if she liked him or not. She'd been burned by the last man she'd been involved with and now had a baby to raise. She needed a job. Those were the things she should be thinking about. Not how attractive he was. Or even how smart.

The "house" in Montauk was actually an oceanside estate. They stepped out of the limo to the sounds of waves crashing on the shore. Whitney showed Suzanne to the suite of rooms she would be using during her stay and then escorted her and Mitzi to the dining room where Gino ate macaroni and cheese and the four adults ate spinach salads with crusty homemade bread.

After lunch, Whitney suggested they leave Gino and Mitzi with the nanny for an afternoon nap, while she and Suzanne took a stroll on the beach.

Darius led Cade to the office, and he plopped down on a seat in front of Darius's desk. "Okay. So you've met her. What are we going to do?"

Before the question was fully out of his mouth, the office door opened and Nick, the other Andreas half brother, walked in. "Mrs. Tucker sent Michael to the nursery and Maggie to the beach where Whitney and Suzanne are walking," he said, referring to his fiancée and her nine-month-old son. "She told me the men were meeting in the office."

Darius gestured to the empty chair in front of his desk. "Take a seat. We're talking about shareholder number five."

Wearing cutoff jeans and flip-flops, Nick plopped down on the seat beside Cade. "Ah, the mysterious Suzanne Caldwell, the one who technically owns the most stock."

"Individually." Cade snarled. "Together we still own two-thirds."

Nick laughed and addressed Darius. "Touchy."

"Did you see Ms. Caldwell?"

Nick shook his head. Darius laughed. "Just wait. One look and you'll know why our brother is behaving like a bear with a thorn in his paw."

"I'm not behaving like a bear." Cade popped out of his seat and began to pace. "I'm just concerned. She tried to sell her stock. Nobody wanted it, but once our annual statement comes out and everybody sees profits are up, she'll get offers. And Andreas Holdings isn't in a position to be one of them."

"Cool your jets, Cade. Nick and I decided we shouldn't wait for the company to have enough money to purchase the stock. We should buy it as individuals." Darius leaned back in his chair. "We know you could have your share of the money tomorrow. Unfortunately, Nick and I aren't that lucky. It will take us some time to get that kind of cash together."

Cade turned. "How much time?"

"I think eighteen months. After you called last night, I called Nick and we ran some numbers and we both think we can have our portions in eighteen months."

Cade groaned. "That's not good enough. She's broke. Seriously broke."

"That's why we've come up with some other ideas. First, I think you should take a look at her finances. Maybe she has assets she doesn't know about?"

He shook his head. "From what she told me accountants and attorneys pretty much pillaged every asset in her grandmother's estate to pay debts. I don't think I'm going to find anything they didn't."

Nick shrugged. "Look anyway. You never know. Her grandmother might have put some things in Suzanne's name alone. Things that might not have turned up on a search of her grandmother's assets."

Darius picked up a pencil and tapped it against his desk blotter. "Second, because we won't be solvent enough to buy her out for at least another year, we're going to have to strike a deal to buy her shares eighteen months from now when we have the cash."

"What kind of deal?"

"We'd set the purchase price of her stock at its value the day her grandmother died. We'll offer a million dollars as a holding fee. Then in eighteen months we'll pay the balance."

Relieved, Cade nodded, but Darius continued. "The job of persuading her to take the deal falls to you, Cade. Nick and I are running the company. We never pushed you to do any more than what you could squeeze in. So it's your turn to step up."

Nick grinned. "Suzanne Caldwell is all yours."

"And you talk to her today," Darius said. "As soon as you get a private minute with her, so she can stop worrying and enjoy her time here."

Suzanne, Whitney and Maggie returned from their walk on the beach chatting like three long-lost friends. Whitney had explained that Gino was actually Darius, Nick and Cade's half brother and that their father had been killed in an accident with Gino's mother. So Whitney and Darius had adopted him.

Maggie had explained that she had been married to Nick at eighteen. She'd left him when the brothers' absentee father, Stephone Andreas, had offered him five million dollars to divorce her, and now they were back together, planning a wedding in four weeks.

Suddenly Suzanne's story of having been taken advantage of by a sleazy university professor didn't sound all that crazy. And when Maggie and Whitney gasped in horror then sympathized, Suzanne actually felt wanted. Normal. Just like one of the girls.

They entered the nursery talking about how much alike Darius, Nick and Cade were even though they were entirely different. Darius had grown up working for Andreas Holdings and had stayed on as CEO and Chairman of the Board after their father died. Nick owned a manufacturing plant in North Carolina. And Cade was a billionaire. He'd taken the five million dollars their dad offered and he'd made himself a very wealthy man. Knowing he didn't depend on Andreas Holdings for cash explained a lot about his life in Whiskey Springs.

Both women also admitted it had been Cade who'd more or less nudged Nick and Darius into seeing the truth about their relationships. Which struck Suzanne as interesting. For a guy who wasn't married himself, he certainly seemed to have a high opinion of marriage.

By dinnertime, she was totally comfortable—until she saw the seating arrangement, which put her beside Cade. She knew his family wasn't matchmaking. Darius sat at the head of the table with Gino's high chair at his right. Whitney sat across from him, at the other end of the table. Nick, Maggie and Michael took up the entire left side. With Mitzi in the nursery with the nanny, she and Cade were the only two people left and there were only two chairs remaining. Both on the right side. It was simple math, not matchmaking.

Cade politely pulled out her chair. She accepted with a smile.

But after only five minutes of sitting beside him, a little hum of attraction set up housekeeping in her bloodstream, if only because of proximity. He was so close she could touch him if she wanted. So close he could touch her.

She told herself it was ridiculous to be plotting an accidental elbow brush. Told herself to stop being attracted to a guy she shouldn't want. But the truth was, after hearing Whitney and Maggie talking about Cade that afternoon, she didn't believe he was half the narcissist she'd originally thought. And what was the deal with him encouraging his brothers to marry Whitney and Maggie? She'd thought for a sure a rich, handsome guy like Cade would push a playboy lifestyle. Not just for himself but for his brothers, so he'd have guys to go to Vegas with. The fact that he hadn't made him seem like a whole different person to her.

A likable person.

A person very different from the professor who had dumped her.

And maybe she shouldn't be as afraid of this attraction as she thought.

The dinner of honey-lemon rack of lamb and red potatoes, served with good wine and mocha cream pie for dessert, was delicious and the conversation pleasant. Nick was a charming Southern gentleman who loved horses and enjoyed a good story. Darius was a businessman to the core, but Whitney easily mellowed him out, got him to laugh and talk about things other than employee disputes and prospective customers.

But the entire time Suzanne was aware of Cade. His size. His sexy Southern drawl. The times he joined in the conversation. The times he didn't.

She'd never felt as curious about a man before. She knew the attraction was to blame. Still, no matter how many times she told herself to stop wondering about him, she couldn't.

When dinner was through, Darius tapped his knife to his wineglass and said, "I'd like to propose a toast, but you'll notice my wife isn't having wine tonight."

Suzanne blinked. She glanced at Whitney, who had pinkened endearingly and the realization hit her the same time that it hit Maggie. Both gasped and simultaneously said, "You're pregnant!"

Whitney clapped with glee. "Yes! I'd wanted to tell you this afternoon but Darius and I had decided to make the announcement to everyone at once."

From there pandemonium broke out. Nick congratulated Darius and kissed Whitney. Maggie and Suzanne continued talking simultaneously. Cade held back, but only for a second. *He'd* wanted a baby. He'd wanted a black-haired, blue-eyed little boy. Or a blond-haired, brown-eyed little girl. They'd never figured out if it was he or Ashley who couldn't conceive because they'd found her cancer as soon as her testing began. Not wanting to upset her, he hadn't even gone for tests. So he didn't even know if he could have kids.

Now Nick had a son and would have more children. Maggie was an earth-mother. She'd happily tend to six kids. Go to soccer games. Be a den mother for Boy Scouts.

Darius had Gino...plus a new baby on the way.

And Cade would probably never have kids. No sons. No daughters. He was the one who hadn't pretended to be a big, bad playboy, as his two older brothers had. He was the one who had married his high school sweetheart, tried to start a family, longed to be the dad Stephone Andreas never was to him. He'd had visions of coaching Little League, visions of watching his daughter dance in recitals, visions of rocking babies in the rocking chair his mom had kept in her bedroom until he'd built his big house. Then she'd given it to him as a housewarming gift. Only to have it sit empty in an unused nursery.

Still, he swallowed back the injustice of it all and rose. He walked over to Darius, slapped him on the back and said all the right things.

When the commotion died down, Darius and Whitney excused themselves to get Gino ready for bed, and Nick and Maggie drifted away. Cade knew exactly what they were doing. He'd been ordered to take Suzanne under his wing and tell her the brothers' plan.

Talking to her was the last thing he wanted to do. Were the choice his, he'd grab one of Darius's best bottles of whiskey, amble down to the beach and get himself drunk enough that he wouldn't care that all his plans for a family had been snatched away from him.

Instead, he had to handle Andreas brothers' business.

Knowing that Mitzi was in the nursery with the nanny, he turned to Suzanne. "How about a walk on the beach?"

She faced him with a surprised look.

Because that sounded a little too much like a romantic overture, he cleared up any misunderstanding. "My brothers want me to tell you what we've decided about your stock."

"Oh." Her eyes clouded with something he couldn't quite identify. Disappointment, maybe? "Okay."

Pretending not to notice the expression in her eyes, he led her out the French doors, past the shimmering pool and down the path to the shore.

"I'm so happy for Darius and Whitney," she said, facing Cade with a grin. "They're wonderful parents to Gino."

He sucked in a breath. The lonely, empty feeling of loss returned, but he shut that down and forced himself to be happy for his brother. "Yes. They're great parents."

"And little Michael. What a scamp! He crawls everywhere." She peeked over at him again. "I can understand why Nick and Maggie decided to wait a few months to get married." She kicked the sand with the toe of her sandal. "Not only is he big enough now to stay with Nick's mom while they honeymoon, but they really wanted a summer wedding. On the beach." She glanced at him again. "Nick lives at the beach, too. In North Carolina. They grew up together at the beach, you know?"

He and Ashley had grown up together, too, so, yes, he knew. He knew all about first loves and how wonderful they could be. But for once he wasn't thinking about Ashley. He was thinking about Suzanne. He'd never heard that lilt in her voice before. She'd obviously had a good time with Maggie and Whitney. And even as he wanted to wallow in misery, he felt an odd stirring in his chest. Almost as if he'd been hoping for her to be happy and now that she was it made him happy. Proud. As if he'd had some part in it.

He scowled. He did not want her happiness to matter to him. It was bad enough he was in charge of her welfare. He didn't want to be manager of her happiness, too. He might have been forced to help her, but he refused to get involved with her. She was a pretty, sexy thorn in his side. A temptation he didn't want nor need.

"Are you going to stop talking long enough for me to tell you what my brothers decided this afternoon?"

She stepped back as if he'd slapped her. "I was just making conversation."

Okay, now he'd hurt her. He hadn't meant to. He'd just wanted this over with.

He stopped, ran his hand along the back of his neck. "Some of this you're going to like. Some of it you might hate."

"Just say it."

The hurt that wobbled through her voice hit him right in the heart and froze it. He hated to see women hurt or, worse, cry.

He sighed. "Look, I'm sorry. I know I'm gruff sometimes. It's just the way I am. But the bottom line is we want to buy back your stock. We can't afford it now, but we're willing to give you a holding fee."

Her eyes widened, lit with joy, and his heart began to beat again.

"You're going to give me a holding fee?"

"Yes, a million dollars."

Her mouth fell open. "A million dollars!"

"The company is improving. Once our annual statement comes out, you'll have real suitors who will be after your stock. Which is why we intend to be able to buy you out in eighteen months."

"Eighteen months!"

"We'll pay you the prevailing price on your grandmother's date of death."

She pressed her hand to her chest. "Oh, my gosh!"

"So you won't have to worry about the holding fee. Though it will be deducted from the amount you get for the stock, it'll be a drop in the bucket compared to the hundred million dollars or so you'll get in the sale."

Her face lit with so much joy that he relaxed.

"A hundred million dollars! I can get a house! A new car. Not worry about—"

But suddenly the joy faded, her eyes narrowed and she frowned. "Wait."

"What?"

"Does this mean I don't get a job?"

"This means you don't need a job."

"The hell, I don't! You're telling me you 'believe' you'll be able to buy my stock in eighteen months, but you don't know. All the agreements in the world mean nothing if you can't get the money together when you think you will. *Nothing* in life is certain."

He couldn't argue that.

"So you can't tell me for sure you'll be buying the stock. Your holding fee is more of a hope that you'll be able to buy the stock in eighteen months."

"Why don't we cross that bridge when we come to it? A million dollars is a lot of money—"

"Yes. And I appreciate it. But I watched my grandmother lose *hundreds* of millions of dollars in a few short years when the stock market began to crumble and Andreas Holdings quit paying dividends." She sighed. "I don't trust easy money. I'd like a job. Then I'd have the security of earning a steady salary, no matter how long it takes you to pull together the cash for my shares."

"Yeah, well, you don't have a marketable skill."

"I can type! I can research. I could even be a receptionist. I'm not picky—"

Something inside of Cade snapped. As he watched her pretty mouth telling him things that didn't actually seem unreasonable—but had to be unreasonable because they were not the plan he and his brothers had worked out—his frustration combined with the futility of arguing with this woman, who was too darned pretty for his own good, and he totally lost his hold on common sense.

All he wanted was for her to stop talking, and the quickest route to that, his hormones assured him, was to kiss her. Before he really thought the plan through, his arm snaked around her waist and hauled her to him as his head descended until his mouth met her soft, sweet lips.

Every muscle in his body tensed. He'd intended to surprise her into silence, instead *his* breathing stuttered, *his* chest tightened, *his* gut squeezed. Her soft lips drew him in, causing him to forget his mission. Especially when her lips seemed to invite him to taste more, take more.

Temptation and desire met and merged. She wasn't stopping him. And she tasted so good. So perfect—

Perfect?

For what?

She was a single mom. A business associate now. A woman he couldn't love then leave.

He knew better than to kiss her.

He *knew* better!

He jerked away, breaking the kiss, and stepped back. Shocked by his behavior, he ran his hand along the back of his neck. Suzanne stared up at him with wide eyes and lips dewy from his kiss.

"Okay, look. I'm sorry. That shouldn't have happened."

She simply continued to stare at him. And he knew he'd given her the wrong idea. Romantic ideas. Damn. Why did he always behave like an idiot around her?

He took another step back, away from her. "Here's the deal. I was married."

She blinked, as if absorbing that, then said, "And she hurt you, right?"

"No. She died." He said it gruffly, angrily. He'd learned long ago that anger was the best way to keep the other, more dangerous emotions at bay. "But even before she got sick, I proved to both of us that I wasn't any great shakes as a husband. She was the love of my life and I treated her shabbily."

He sucked in a breath, wished she'd stop looking at him with big blue eyes that had gone from sharp with desire to soft with sadness. For him. God, he hated pity.

"Get any romantic ideas you might have out of your head because I'm not in the market for a relationship and you shouldn't want me."

When she only blinked, Cade knew he wasn't getting through, so he pushed harder. "Okay, let me tell you a few things that never made it to the diner gossip because they're things I don't tell anyone." He held up his index finger. "Number one, I spent the first two years of my marriage traveling to build my fortune."

His second finger snapped up. "Number two, you'd have thought that after she got sick I would have settled in, settled down, but no. I wanted Beacher's Oil so bad that I pursued it like the Holy Grail and one night while I was sweet-talking my way into a deal, she faded away. She was gone when I got back."

When he stopped, the salty air rang with the sound of the waves. He scrubbed his hand down his face, surprised he'd admitted so much, but knowing he'd had to to make it abundantly clear to her why she shouldn't feel sorry for him. Shouldn't feel *anything* for him.

"Cade, I'm so sorry."

At her soft apology, he realized that even his expanded explanation hadn't worked because now her big blue eyes were rimmed with tears.

"Forget it. Just understand I was no good as a husband and stay the hell away from me."

CHAPTER FIVE

HE TURNED AND BEGAN STRIDING up the beach. Suzanne watched him bound away, an achy pain squeezing her heart. He hadn't fooled her with the gruff voice and the straightforward proclamations. She could see from the tortured look on his face that his wife's death had been brutal on him. It was no wonder he behaved oddly around her. He was attracted to her and didn't want to be.

He stopped, faced her. His dark hair blew in the breeze off the ocean. His dark eyes bored into her. "Are you coming? I'm not going to stand here all night. If you want to walk up by yourself that's fine. But it's dark and I don't generally leave women alone in the dark."

She scrambled across the shifting sand to catch up with him, confusion warring with the sympathy she felt for him. Losing her grandmother had changed her life, filled her with grief, filled her with *anger*. She couldn't even imagine how hard it would be to lose a spouse.

At the French doors off the patio into the den, Cade paused, waiting for her to get to the door before he opened it for her.

They stepped into the dimly lit den only to discover Nick and Maggie sat on the brown leather sofa, Whitney sat on a wing chair and Darius was behind the bar.

"Drink?"

Suzanne's gaze swung back to Cade, as if looking for his preference, but he walked away without a glance in her direction.

"I'll have a beer and I'll get it myself."

Carrying two beers and a glass of wine, Darius walked to the conversation group. He handed the wine to Maggie and one of the beers to Nick then sat on the chair beside Whitney's. "Great. I love it when someone wants to play bartender. Suzanne, just give your request to Cade."

"I'm fine. Thanks." Not exactly sure what to do, she hovered near the door.

Whitney waved her over, motioning to the empty love seat. "Please. Sit."

Suzanne glanced at the love seat then back at Cade. The only seat left in the room would smash them against each other.

It didn't matter. He'd made himself perfectly clear. He wasn't interested. He'd had the love of his life. He'd been a bad husband. And after her ordeal with Mitzi's dad, she was also smart enough not to want to get involved with a guy who boldly admitted he wasn't husband material...

Except that kiss had been amazing. Her breathing had stopped and all her senses had intensified. He'd drawn her in, clouded her brain, liquefied her limbs with one soft press of his mouth to hers.

They weren't just attracted. They were smokin' hot attracted.

But they were also smart. Too smart to get involved. He was a bad bet as a romantic partner. With her life in total chaos, she wasn't exactly looking for a romance, let alone a guy who might be attracted to her but didn't want to be. They had more than enough motivation to stay away from each other, even squished together on a couch.

She ambled to the love seat. Cade slid from behind the bar with his opened bottle of beer. But he didn't come over to sit with her. He headed for the cold fireplace.

Really? He was going to be that petty?

But a little voice inside her head cautioned her not to be so sure he was being petty. That kiss had knocked her socks off. Surely it must have had the same effect on him.

What if he didn't trust himself to control himself?

What if *that* was really why he was angry?

"So, I'm guessing Cade told you about our plans for you."

Something about the authoritative tone of Darius's voice raised her hackles, but she told herself not to be so sensitive. Even though the Andreas brothers hadn't offered a job, their suggested holding fee had been generous and she needed to think it through. Though she'd popped off with Cade, she couldn't simply turn down a million dollars because it wasn't what she'd expected.

"I thought your offer was very generous, but—"

"But she's a bit miffed that we didn't pony up a job."

When Cade interrupted her, Suzanne could have sighed. His interpretation of her reaction might have been correct, but now that things were sinking in, she wasn't quite so adamant. Besides, she could speak for herself.

"I don't think *miffed* is the right word. *Cautious* is better. I never expected to be offered a holding fee and I need—"

"You were like a bull snorting fire out on the beach. You're not happy with our offer."

Suzanne scorched him with a look. She might not have been happy with the offer, but that was her gut reaction. Not a real decision. Plus, his way of shutting her up had been to kiss her.

How would he like her telling his brothers that?

Darius quietly broke into her stare down with Cade. "What concerns you?"

"I asked for a job because I want some security. What happens in eighteen months if the company doesn't rebound the way you think it should?"

"It will," Nick put in, as calm and serious as Darius. "But that doesn't matter. The company itself isn't buying your shares. We're buying them from our personal accounts. And we'll easily have the money in eighteen months."

"And once you get that money, you're back to being a very wealthy woman," Darius reminded her. "If we employ you, you'll need to move to New York. You'll have to get a condo and a nanny. And just when you have yourself settled, we'll have pulled the money together to buy you out and you'll have to fire your nanny and sell your condo when you move back to Atlanta. If you take the holding fee, you can simply go back now, reenroll in school."

He had a point. With a million dollars she could go back to school....

She frowned. The thought of returning to the same university where Bill Baker taught was not a pleasant one. But her old school wasn't the only university in the country. With a million dollars she could enroll just about anywhere.

She could finish her degree and then take a year

of more practical classes. Like accounting. Or maybe business management. This rough patch in her life had proven she needed to be employable. If nothing else, somehow or another at the end of these eighteen months she intended to have a job.

Nick smiled. "We won't let you down."

"Plus, you might just discover you're not as broke as you think," Darius added. "You could find assets you didn't know about when Cade takes a look at the big picture of your finances."

Her eyes narrowed. "Cade's taking a look at my finances?"

Darius smiled. "Your grandmother could have opened accounts for you that she forgot. Accounts that wouldn't show up when her estate ran a check because they'd have your name and social security number on them, not hers. So I've assigned Cade to look into that."

Just when things started to fall into place in her head, she somehow ended up connected to Cade again. She shifted on the love seat. "I don't want Cade poking into my finances."

Cade snorted as if the idea didn't please him, either.

Whitney shook her head, rose and sat beside Suzanne. "I'm going to apologize for my husband and his brothers." She caught both of her hands. "I know Darius has a tendency to bulldoze situations and I'm guessing Cade didn't explain this well." She glared at Cade.

He shrugged. "I actually never got a chance to make much of an explanation."

"The way Darius explained this to me," Whitney said, "Cade himself wouldn't be looking at your books. He's got a staff of accountants who would be examining the records, searching for lost accounts, that kind of thing."

"Maybe I should hire some accountants myself."

Cade huffed out a laugh. "Why waste money on accountants when I have them at my disposal?"

She licked her lips. That was true. She might be getting a lot of money eventually. But right now she was getting only a portion of that money and she couldn't be reckless. If she was careful now, in a few short months she and Mitzi would be financially secure.

"Okay."

Whitney's eyebrows rose. "Okay?"

"I'll take the money. I'll take the help of Cade's accountants. I'll spend the next semester finishing my degree and the year after that I'll take classes that might lead me to a real job."

From across the room Cade said, "You won't need it."

But she ignored him. Just as he'd said, he wasn't right for her. *They* weren't right for each other. Sure, they were sexually attracted, but she absolutely, positively did not want to be involved with him. She understood he was sad and angry about his wife's death, but why he thought he could take that out on her was a total mystery. If she ever got romantically involved again, it would be with someone who would really love her and appreciate her.

And Cade Andreas did not fit that bill.

A few minutes after midnight, Cade was running chalk along the tip of his pool stick when Whitney and Maggie pleaded tiredness. Suzanne had long ago gone upstairs to check on Mitzi and simply hadn't returned. But now Darius and Nick also said their good-nights and strolled off to bed with Whitney and Maggie.

Perfectly happy to have a few minutes by himself,

Cade decided to have one last beer before he went to his suite upstairs. Unfortunately, he only got halfway through before Nick returned.

"I thought you were all snuggled up with the future Mrs. for the night."

"She's showering." Nick ambled into the room and fell to the seat on the sofa beside Cade. "I think you and I need one of those little talks like the one we had when you told me I had to pick up my end of the slack for Andreas Holdings."

"Not hardly, bud. You and Darius already had your little talk with me about helping Suzanne for the good of Andreas Holdings, and you see how well that went over."

Nick went on as if he hadn't spoken. "Tonight when Darius and I were trying to persuade her to take our money, we dangled going back to school in front of her."

Cade shrugged. "It worked a hell of a sight better than the talk I had with her." He vividly remembered how that ended. With a kiss. His intention had been to get her to stop talking and all he'd done was awaken his own damned hormones. "Our offer might have surprised her at first, but now she seems happy to take it."

"Yeah," Nick said, drawing out the one syllable into a long, skeptical word. "The problem is Maggie has some concerns about Suzanne going back to Atlanta."

"Maggie has some concerns?"

"Apparently they had some long talks today. From the things Suzanne said, Maggie believes Suzanne returning to her old school isn't a good idea. Mitzi's father is a professor there and apparently he made her life miserable enough that she had to quit. The guy's a snake and

Maggie thinks it wouldn't be good for Suzanne to even see him."

"And you want me to…what?" For the love of God, had Nick not already noticed that he was *not* the person to talk to Suzanne?

"Pour on some of your rich Texan charm and persuade her to stay at your ranch with you. There has to be a university near Whiskey Springs that she can attend, somewhere she can transfer her credits."

He gaped at his brother. Now he knew Nick was insane…

Except Nick hadn't actually seen the discussion he'd had with Suzanne. He hadn't seen how Suzanne had gotten her back up. He hadn't seen Cade lose his head and kiss her.

And it would be a cold day in hell before Cade told him.

He snorted a laugh. "Right. We've already nudged her into thinking about going home. It's too late to change her mind. She wants to return to Atlanta."

"Maybe not. Just because that's where her school was, it doesn't mean she wants to go to Atlanta. She might have simply been happy at the thought of having a plan and somewhere to go."

"There are lots of good schools. In other cities."

"She has no family, Cade. Even if she stays away from the creep who fathered her baby and moves to another city, she's still got a boatload of problems. Who's going to watch Mitzi? Who's going to answer baby questions? At the very least, your staff could babysit while she attends classes." He shook his head. "It just doesn't feel right to send her off into the world alone. Not when she's one of us."

"One of us?"

"As long as she owns Andreas stock, she's one of us."

Cade sucked in a breath. If there was one thing their father's death had instilled in them, it was loyalty. With that reminder, he felt a brush of guilt. But just a brush because there was one very good reason Nick and Maggie's plan wouldn't work. "And how am I supposed to persuade her to transfer to a university near Whiskey Springs and stay with me? We might see her as 'one of us' but she barely knows us."

"You could tell her you need her close in case your accountants have questions."

The collar of Cade's shirt suddenly got too tight. That idea might actually work.

"She's one of us, Cade." Nick rose. "And Maggie believes she's lost. Alone. We want her to be comfortable. Not to be struggling through her last year of school with no one to help her with her baby, when you've got a whole town at your disposal."

He left the room and Cade flopped back on the sofa. He could picture having Suzanne living in his home. He'd vacillate between behaving like an angry bear and a hungry panther, slithering through his house, following her scent, itching to touch her. Hadn't that kiss on the beach proven he couldn't control himself around her?

Damn straight it had.

He was not—absolutely was not—inviting her to live with him.

Except...

What if she was alone? What if she really would be struggling to go to classes and care for her baby? What if she had no one to talk to? No one to call if Mitzi got sick. No one to even ask questions about raising her baby.

He told himself to stop obsessing. Suzanne was a smart, independent woman who would be fine. She *wanted* to be on her own. Hadn't she said as much at least three times?

Monday afternoon, after a round of goodbyes at the limo Darius had sent to take them to the airport, Suzanne and Cade made the ride to the airstrip in total silence. When they boarded the plane, Cade again sat at the desk in the rear, his head down, his focus on the papers in three open files.

Closing her eyes, Suzanne made herself comfortable on her seat. But after they were in the air, Cade's voice drifted over to her.

"I know this weekend didn't turn out the way you'd hoped. But my brothers are genuinely trying to help you. They're nice guys. Even if you don't like me, there's no reason to be suspicious of them."

She glanced at Mitzi, who slept in her carrier, then back at Cade. She hadn't been able to sleep the night before. Not just because she'd agreed to take a million dollars to hold her stock and now had a direction for her life. But because she'd begun to remember some of the things Whitney and Maggie had told her about Cade. Things that had caused her to see him in a different light.

Like how he'd helped his two brothers see they were crazy about Whitney and Maggie and it was time to settle down. After her little tiff with Cade on the beach, she now knew he'd done that because he'd been married and understood a little more about life and love than his older brothers. But that didn't diminish the fact that he'd come to Whitney's and Maggie's aid. Just as he'd come to her aid the night she'd told him she was the missing shareholder, explaining to Darius that she needed a job.

He loved Gino. He loved little Michael. He teased and bantered with his brothers and their wives, but in a fun, brotherly sort of way.

If it hadn't been for that little tiff on the beach and the way he'd treated her after, she'd probably like him right now. And not just as a friend, but...well, romantically.

"I'm not suspicious of your brothers."

"Really?"

She shook her head and laughed softly. "Why would you think that when I took their offer?"

"Because you're quiet."

She pointed at the open files on his desk. "Yeah, well, you have work to do."

"And I've got plenty of time to get to it. Right now, I just want to make sure you're clear about our offer. That you don't have questions. That you're okay with everything."

Before this weekend she might have thought he was goading her, or thought she was too dumb to understand a simple deal. Today she knew he wasn't like that. If he was asking, it was out of genuine concern. Her heart got a little tug, but she ignored it. He'd made himself perfectly clear. He wasn't interested. And she had too many things on her plate right now to regret his choice.

"I understand everything your brothers told me this weekend."

"Good."

"Good..." She paused. Actually, she might understand everything about their deal, but there was one little bitty thing she didn't get about the Andreas brothers themselves. It was none of her business, but the truth was, with all the nice things Cade did for his brothers, his one omission seemed odd, out of character.

"Actually I have thought of something I might need to have cleared up."

"Like what?"

Marshaling her courage, she said, "Like you probably have five times the money your brothers have—"

"More like ten."

"So why don't you just buy me out? If you're all so worried about my stock getting into the wrong hands, why not just buy my stock and be done with me?"

He didn't even hesitate. "Because you own one-third of the company. My brothers and I each own one-sixth. If I buy you out and add my one-sixth to your one-third, I own half the company. We'd no longer be equals. I won't do that to them."

She blinked. Wow. If she had any questions about how he felt about his brothers they'd all just been answered. Their bond meant more to him than the possibility of losing her stock. Their connection meant more to him than money.

Maybe his wife's death had taught him a lesson?

Silence reigned again. But in a few seconds, Cade cleared his throat, bringing her attention back to him. "There is one more thing you and I need to discuss."

His sudden nervousness didn't fit with the straight-forward conversation they were having and she tensed. "What?"

"Nick and Maggie think you should live with me at the ranch."

Positive he was joking, she laughed. "Right."

"Hey, I don't want you to. But I figured I'd better tell you just in case it somehow gets back to you that I was supposed to ask, but didn't."

Confusion wrinkled her brow. "Why would they want me to live at your ranch? What would I do so far out in God's country?"

He peeked over at her, clearly relieved that she thought the idea as crazy as he did. "Exactly." But when he caught her gaze with his sincere brown eyes, her heart stuttered a bit in her chest. "I mean, I'm sure we could find a university nearby…but you're probably eager to get on with your life."

She did want to get on with her life. She truly did. But something about this man called to her. It was more than sexual attraction. More than empathy for his loss and his suffering. A click of connection sparked in her every time she as much as looked at him.

But he didn't feel the same thing for her. And she had money now. Plans.

"I am eager to move on. I have to enroll in the next semester of classes." She paused. She'd already figured out she wasn't going back to her old school. There was no way she'd risk seeing Bill Baker. "Except I'm not quite sure what university I'll go to. With a whole country full of schools to choose from, it could take me months to figure out where I should go."

He skewered her with a look. "There is no perfect plan, Suzanne. But the bottom line to this is neither one of us wants you to live with me."

Considering how she'd begun to soften to him, he was right. It probably wasn't a good idea. She shook her head. "No. We don't."

"Okay, then don't overthink it."

She settled back in her seat, convinced they'd made the right choice. But the thought of living at his ranch lingered and then morphed into something she hadn't expected. It might not be a good idea to live with Cade, but she had to admit it would be nice to stay in Whiskey Springs. Nice to see if she and Amanda Mae could have the kind of close relationship she'd suspected from the day they'd met. Nice to see all the people she'd met at the diner again, make them friends.

Nicer still to have roots.

A place to raise her baby.

A home.

CHAPTER SIX

WHEN THEY FINALLY ARRIVED at Cade's private airstrip, he shoved Suzanne's diaper bag and suitcase into his truck while she buckled sleeping Mitzi's baby carrier in the rear seats and they headed to Whiskey Springs.

It was, at best, a fifteen-minute drive to her temporary apartment above the diner, but to Cade it seemed to take forever. First, he was eager to get to town. Because the land was flat, he could see Whiskey Springs off in the distance and tonight it had a weird red glow. Something he'd have to investigate once he got there. He couldn't believe one of the residents would be so foolish as to start a fire on a scorching hot June night in a drought. This time of the year, the land was sometimes so dry it was a wonder it didn't spontaneously combust. But there was no other explanation for the red glow. It had to be a fire.

Second, he needed to get away from the woman in the truck with him. He understood her desire to make her own way with her million dollars. To find a university, finish her degree, have a skill so she'd know she and her baby would never go hungry. Hell, he'd been equally determined to prove himself when he turned eighteen and his dad dumped five million dollars in his lap. He'd wanted the money—needed the money—but he'd wanted to be his own man, too. So he'd learned to invest, to build his dad's peace offering into a real pile of money he could use to make more money, and then more money and more money. Until his dad knew that even without the five-million head start, he would have made it.

So he and Suzanne were a lot alike. Enough alike that he realized he might be attracted to her for a little more than just her cute little butt. That's what had scared him the night he'd kissed her and why he'd been so determined to scare her off. He thanked God she'd decided to take her money and run. Otherwise, they might actually become friends.

He nearly snorted a laugh. Friends? If they spent more than an hour alone, getting along, he'd have her in bed. And that wouldn't do either one of them any good.

Mitzi squeaked, then moaned slightly before she burst into genuine tears and everything inside of Cade stilled. Since meeting Gino, he was accustomed to squeaking and crying and even an occasional mess. Like spit-up. Having a baby brother had acclimated him to kids. Plus, it had taken some of the sting out of his own childlessness. True, he'd had a moment of regret when he'd heard about Whitney's pregnancy, but he'd sucked himself back out of that black hole. He would not ever have a child of his own. Period. He accepted that.

But hearing Mitzi, up close and personal, did the strangest things to his chest. It tightened. It sort of tingled. He wanted to turn around and comfort her.

"Shh! Mitzi, sweetie. We're almost there. Then Mama will take you out of that tight little car seat, kiss your sweet cheeks and tickle your belly."

Clearly not appeased, Mitzi only cried harder.

"Please, sweetie." This time Suzanne's voice held a note of pleading that clenched Cade's gut.

"Don't worry about her on my account."

Suzanne peeked at him. "The fussing's going to get worse the longer it takes us to get into town."

"I know. But we only have another five minutes." And the red glow hovering around the town got redder the closer they got. "She's a baby. She's been strapped in that seat for hours. I don't blame her for being uncomfortable."

Suzanne turned from trying to entertain Mitzi. "I know that and Mitzi knows that. I just didn't think you did."

"What? I look like some kind of baby monster?"

"No, but you can sometimes be a grouch."

He leveled his best watch-your-step look at her and realized he'd just proved her point. "Yeah, well, when it comes to kids I'm a lot more understanding than I am with adults."

The red skyline finally caught Suzanne's eye. She pointed out the windshield. "Is that normal?"

He shifted uncomfortably on the seat. "No."

"Oh, Lord."

He levered his foot on the gas pedal, pushing it to the floor. With Mitzi screaming and Suzanne's gaze glued straight ahead, Cade barreled the truck into town. He got only a third of the way down Main Street before Bob Patterson stopped him.

Dressed in the heavy-duty gear of a volunteer fireman, he motioned for Cade to lower his window.

Cade didn't waste time on greetings. "What's going on?"

"I'm sorry, Cade. It's the diner."

Suzanne gasped. "Oh, no."

Bob blew his breath out. "Total loss. Amanda Mae is beside herself."

Suzanne shoved her door open. "Is she down there?"

"Yeah, crying her heart out."

Cade watched in amazement as Suzanne blinked back her own tears. She jumped out of the truck and fumbled with the door of the extended cab and the catch on Mitzi's car seat.

Cade stopped her by grabbing her hand. "I'll take care of Mitzi. You go to Amanda Mae." He glanced out his window at Bob. "You take her down there."

"Yes, sir."

He caught Suzanne's gaze again. "And you stay with him. It won't do Amanda Mae any good to have you getting hurt rushing to her side."

With that, Suzanne scooted around the truck. Oddly, she did exactly as Cade wanted for once. She paused by Bob, who took her arm and directed her through the gathered crowd.

Mitzi squawked.

He opened the door and then the back door so he could reach in, unbuckle Mitzi and pull her out.

Holding her at eye level, he said, "All right. Here's the deal. Your mom had to rush down there, but we're going to take it a little slower. It's not going to help matters if you continue to squawk."

As if understanding, Mitzi stopped crying.

There. See? Everybody made too much of this whole parenting thing. Babies loved him because he was straightforward and honest with them. And he loved babies. If only because they didn't try to con you. The way he understood it, that particular bad behavior didn't present itself until junior high.

He settled Mitzi on his arm. But a thought occurred to him and he spun her around, holding her at eye level again. "Are we okay in the diaper area?"

She only looked at him. Her blue eyes as bright as her mom's. Her dark hair sticking up in all directions.

"What? I'm trying to see if you need a diaper. If you do, I'll handle it."

She still only looked at him.

Since she wasn't giving him any hint, his options were to check—which was not at all appealing—or take his chances. Hoisting her to his chest, he decided to take his chances.

She snuggled into his neck, nuzzling in as if she planned to go back to sleep—or as if she liked him, trusted him.

Wonderful feelings bubbled up inside him. But he told himself not to be ridiculous. Babies trusted anybody who kept them warm and dry.

Still, he couldn't stop himself from kissing her cheek before he began picking his way through the crowd. Most stepped aside as he ambled through. A few offered their regrets for his loss, since, technically, everything in town was his. But he didn't give a flying fig about the loss of one building. He'd created his plan to buy all the buildings in town so he could give people like Amanda Mae a break. He paid the taxes, took care of repairs, did renovations. A little town like Whiskey Springs didn't support its own pharmacy or diner or Laundromat. Hell, they barely supported a convenience store. So he'd bought them all, subsidized them, so the people who worked on his ranch or for the corporate offices of his oil company had the things they needed without having to drive forty miles to the closest city.

But though the building was his, everything inside that building had belonged to Amanda Mae, and he hoped to heaven she had insurance.

The closer he got, the more chaos surrounded him. Firemen worked diligently to ensure the fire didn't spread, but the diner was engulfed. Red flames leaped from the roof. The windows had already exploded out.

When Suzanne reached Amanda Mae, the diner proprietor was sobbing softly. Tears immediately sprang to Suzanne's eyes. She raced over to Amanda Mae, who was surrounded by townspeople. But the minute Suzanne appeared, she stepped away from them and threw herself into Suzanne's arms.

"I don't know what I'm going to do."

Suzanne stroked her hair. "I'm sure Cade will come up with something."

She shook her head fiercely. "No reason for Cade to care about my equipment and supplies. That's my doing."

"Well, insurance will—"

"I let my insurance lapse…"

All Suzanne could say was, "Oh."

Suddenly, Amanda Mae pulled away. "Oh, my gosh! I forgot. All your things were in the apartment."

Suzanne shook her head. "I didn't really have much."

"Which makes it all the worse that you lost it!"

"Let's not worry about me," Suzanne said, sliding her arm across Amanda Mae's shoulder. Inside, her heart was breaking. Not only had Amanda Mae lost everything, but she had no insurance. God only knew how Cade would handle this.

As if thinking him made him appear, he stepped through the crowd and walked over. Miraculously, Mitzi was sound asleep on his shoulder. The tears rimming her eyelids spilled over. It was probably the sadness of the moment that had her thinking this way, but she couldn't help seeing how adorable Mitzi looked with a man. A father.

Where had that come from? He'd warned her he was a terrible husband, not because he'd felt the need to unburden himself, but because they were attracted. He didn't want her to get ideas. She'd agreed. He would really be upset if he knew she'd seen him as a father for Mitzi.

Patting Mitzi's back, Cade walked over. "I'm sorry, Amanda Mae."

After blowing her nose, she batted a hand. "Don't worry about me. I think this might be the good Lord's way of telling me it's time to retire."

Suzanne gasped, but Cade said, "You're too ornery to retire. You need the diner. It's your lifeline to the people of this town. I've got another building—"

"I don't want another building." Fresh tears sprouted in Amanda Mae's eyes. "I didn't have insurance, so I don't have the money to buy all new equipment. I'm old. I'm tired. I can't start from scratch."

"I have money."

The words popped out of Suzanne's mouth before the thought even fully formed in her head.

"It'll take a hundred thousand dollars at least just for the kitchen. Then there's the dining room. I'd need booths, tables, chairs, plates, cups—" She ran her fingers through her hair. "And supplies. Every piece of meat, every jar of mayonnaise, every egg is gone."

"I've got money to replace it all," Suzanne said, her

voice slowing down as she really thought this through. She'd wanted to finish her degree, but she could delay that. Especially for a friend. Plus, if she invested most of her money in the diner, she could also work there. Except not as a waitress, but a partner.

"We'll be partners."

Amanda Mae blinked. "Partners?"

"I'll put up whatever it takes for new equipment, etcetera. You provide the expertise."

Amanda Mae sniffed.

"Cade's said he's got a building—"

"Yeah, but where are you gonna live? Your apartment's gone."

She glanced over at Cade. This was the part where it got tricky. He'd said his family wanted her to live with him. But in the plane they'd more or less decided that was a bad idea. Still, Amanda Mae needed her and she didn't so much want to finish school as she wanted a job. A place. Some security. Surely she could find an apartment once everything settled down with the diner. She'd only need to stay with him a week or so…

"Cade's brother wants me to live at his ranch."

Cade's mouth dropped open in dismay.

Amanda Mae gasped. "You can't give me your money and go live with Cade!"

"Sure I can. Cade and his brothers gave me a holding fee to buy my shares of their father's company's stock. And they were generous." She pressed her hand to her chest. "I can afford to do this."

Cade's deep voice drifted into their conversation. "Suzanne, can I talk to you for a second?"

Suzanne faced Cade with a hopeful smile. "Sure."

He dragged her away from Amanda Mae, who was

immediately swallowed up in the comforting arms of the townspeople again.

"I thought the plan was to go find a school and finish your degree?"

"Look, I know what's really bugging you is that I told Amanda Mae I would stay with you. But I only said that so she wouldn't worry about me for the next few days. I won't stay with you long. As soon as we get the new diner started, I'll find a place and move out."

He rolled his eyes to the heavens as if seeking strength. "Suzanne, this is going to be a lot of work."

"I know, but I want to work. I also want to do this." She glanced back at the diner owner. "Do you know that in one month of being virtually homeless while I tried to figure out what to do, Amanda Mae was the only person who helped me?"

He sucked in a breath, patted Mitzi's back. "No."

"Even you ushered me out of town, suggesting that I go to the next town over for a hotel room."

He looked away.

"Nobody saw that I was struggling, putting up a good front but drowning, except Amanda Mae."

She caught his arm to get his attention, but sparks of electricity crackled up his biceps. And Cade knew exactly why it was a bad idea for them to live together.

Still, Suzanne kept talking as if nothing were amiss. "This is my chance to pay her back. I want it."

He squeezed his eyes shut. Technically, what she was suggesting made perfect sense. Plus, it would appease his brothers. But he knew in real life it was going to be a disaster.

Why did he have to be so attracted to this woman? What was it about her that made him forget that he wasn't interested? Because even if he was looking for a woman in his life, this particular woman needed a husband and a father for her baby. And he'd vowed he'd never marry again. Didn't his hormones realize he could not be a husband? He could not hurt another woman.

"Come on. It won't be so bad to have me and Mitzi around. Look how you like her."

His heart turned over in his chest. He did like Mitzi. In a matter of a few days, he'd come to adore this baby girl. But that was actually another problem. He'd be with this child twenty-four-hours-a-day some days. He'd grow attached. Maybe long for something he couldn't have. His own kids. His well-ordered life would turn into chaos. Not because a child made a mess of things, but because he'd remember those plans, those dreams he'd had with Ashley. A houseful of kids. Christmas Eves beside a fireplace with little girls and boys wide-eyed with expectation. Little League. Dance lessons. Being a proud papa in the audience when *his* little girl danced a solo.

He swallowed.

Those dreams were gone.

And this child would only make him long for things he couldn't have. She'd already more than halfway stolen his heart. Her pretty mom would make him think that maybe, just maybe, he should try again.

But that wouldn't just be a betrayal of Ashley. It would be a betrayal of Suzanne. He couldn't ever love as completely, as wondrously, as innocently as he'd loved Ashley. And anything less would be cheating Suzanne.

He handed Mitzi to her mom. "You have two weeks." He turned to go, but faced her again. "And while you're at my house you keep the baby quiet."

"I thought you said you didn't mind her fussing—"

"Driving in a car with a baby and living with one are two different things. Especially since my office is in the house. Keep her quiet and out of my way."

CHAPTER SEVEN

AT TEN O'CLOCK THAT NIGHT, Cade's mom volunteered to take the baby. Because his truck already had the car seat, he and Ginny decided to exchange vehicles. Suzanne listened to their discussion without comment as they walked down Main Street to Cade's truck and stopped at the driver's side door.

"Take Mitzi to the ranch and put her in the room with the crib."

Ginny raised one eyebrow in response, as if questioning that. But he said nothing, only handed her his keys.

She gave her keys to him, saying, "My SUV is on Third Street."

Buckling Mitzi into her car seat, Suzanne gasped. "Oh, my gosh! I forgot about my car. It could be toast!"

"Where'd you have it parked?"

"There weren't any spaces behind the diner, so I parked it about a block away."

Ginny winced. "You might be lucky."

Cade said, "We'll check up on it after the fire's out."

When Mitzi was settled, Ginny opened the driver's side door. "I'll see you when you're done here."

"I think it might be pointless to wait up. You might as well stretch out on the bed. We could be here all night."

Suzanne gave Mitzi one last kiss on the cheek. When she hesitated over the baby, Cade caught her elbow and pulled her away from the truck.

"She'll be fine with my mom. We need to make sure Amanda Mae is settled, and right now you seem to be the person she's listening to. *Partner.*"

She winced at his tone, but hustled with him over to Amanda Mae. At least three times the diner owner pulled herself together, then broke down and cried some more. When the fire was out, the firefighters told her they would stay behind to ensure no residual sparks reignited, but she should go home.

Cade and Suzanne walked her to her sister's house, where her niece Gloria met them at the door. Doc came by with something to help Amanda Mae sleep. Holding the two pills, she hugged Suzanne and Cade then excused herself to get a shower and go to bed.

Suzanne and Cade found her Mercedes, which, aside from a bit of soot, was fine. She drove him to his mom's SUV and then followed him to the ranch. In the echoing marble-floored foyer of his big house, he tossed his mom's keys to the cherrywood table beneath a huge mirror.

"Since my mom is in the suite I'd planned to give you, I'll show you to a room you can use tonight."

"I'd rather be by Mitzi."

"My mom's a light sleeper. She'll get up with Mitzi if she cries." He headed up the stairs. "But if it will make you feel any better, I'll put you in the suite beside hers."

"It would."

"Great."

She didn't miss the sarcasm in his voice. She knew he wasn't happy she'd told Amanda Mae she was staying at his ranch, but she didn't want Amanda Mae to worry. Plus, she would be out of his house as quickly as she could find an apartment. There was no reason for him to be snippy.

They walked the length of a long hall and he opened the door on a pretty blue suite for her.

"Thank you. It's lovely."

He said, "Peachy," then turned, took the three steps across the hall and opened the door.

"That's your room?"

"Yep. You're right across the hall."

Memories of their kiss on the beach trembled through her. Though she was absolutely positive he wanted nothing to do with her, she also knew they were attracted to each other. And though this bedroom was only for one night, the room he would put her into for the next week or so until she found her own place was only a few more feet down the hall. They weren't so close as to be able to hear the rustle of sheets, but they were close enough that, if temptation arose, either one of them could take a short walk to find the other.

A little crackle sparked through her bloodstream.

This was ridiculous. They didn't want to be attracted. Still, there was no denying chemistry. Look what they'd done on the beach. Shared a kiss so hot they could have raised fog off the ocean. It wasn't wise to tempt fate.

"Don't you have another room you can put me in?"

"Thought you wanted to be by the baby?"

"Don't you have another room to put me and the baby?"

He opened his door with a small shove of his shoulder.

"Nope. That's the only one with a crib. I'm not running a day care here."

With that he stepped inside his room and closed the door. Foreboding rustled through her like the wind rustles through leaves before a storm, but she straightened her shoulders and went into her temporary suite.

He might be attracted, but he wasn't interested. Except maybe sexually. But neither she nor Cade would be stupid enough to play with fire.

Still, she intended to be out of his house long before it became an issue. And while she was here she could simply downplay their attraction.

Tired from staying up past four, and without Mizti to wake her, Suzanne slept until nine o'clock the next morning. When she woke, she panicked until she remembered Cade's mom had Mitzi. She sprang out of bed to find them, but realized she had nothing to wear but the filthy, smoky clothes she'd taken off the night before when she'd showered.

After a quick search, she found a fluffy white robe in the closet, and, using the comb in her purse, she managed to tidy her hair.

But she didn't waste time on makeup. She raced from her room and knocked on the door of the suite beside hers, the room Cade's mom had shared with Mitzi. But no one answered. Realizing they were probably already up and about, she ran down the wide spiral staircase, through the echoing marble foyer and to the hall, where she stopped.

She had no idea where Ginny and Mitzi were. The house was huge and it wasn't the only place they could be. There were barns, stables, a swimming pool, ponds. They could be anywhere.

Still, going to the only room she knew—the big office where she'd had her fateful conversation with Cade—didn't seem wise.

Except, he'd probably know where his mother was with Mitzi.

With a deep breath, she strode to the office and found him sitting behind the massive desk. Color suddenly warmed her cheeks. Not only did she remember what he'd been planning the last time they were in this room, but also she was practically naked beneath this robe. And he would know that.

This was not the way to downplay their attraction.

A dark-haired man in a suit sat on one of the chairs in front of the desk. Seeing her, he rose.

Cade rose, too. His eyes made a quick trip down her robe-covered body. "Suzanne."

She clutched the collar more tightly together. "Where is everybody?"

"If you mean Mitzi," Cade said, pretending great interest in something on his desk, as if using his search as a way to keep his eyes off her, "my mom is feeding her breakfast on the patio by the pool."

She turned to race away, but Cade stopped her. "Hey, before you go, I want you to meet Eric."

She stopped, faced them again. "Eric?"

The young man in the dark suit nodded slightly. "Nice to meet you, ma'am."

"Eric is my personal assistant. I just gave him the rundown on your situation. He'll lead the search for accounts your grandmother might have set up for you that you don't know about."

She'd forgotten about that. "Oh."

"You authorized it."

She swallowed. "Yes. I remember."

"Don't scowl as if you've made a deal with the devil. Using my staff is just a way to save you some money." His voice shifted, changed, and laughter filled it as he said, "Money which you need, since you're now partner in a restaurant."

"Diner," Suzanne corrected, straightening her spine. Did he think she was going to bail? Or, worse, did he think she and Amanda Mae were going to fail? "And I'm fine with the promises I made last night."

"Then you'd better get a hitch in your get-along because I'm meeting Amanda Mae in an hour to talk specifics about a lease for the new building."

"An hour?"

"And it takes fifteen minutes to get into town." He sat behind the desk again, pointed at her robe. "By the way, I had someone get the suitcase you took to New York from the truck. It should be outside your bedroom door by now."

Suzanne spun around and headed upstairs. She dressed in jeans and a clean T-shirt then ran to the patio, where she found Ginny sitting at an umbrella-covered table with Mitzi beside her in the high chair.

Shielding her eyes from the sun with one hand, Ginny said, "Cade told me the two of you are going into town."

"Yes. We're meeting with Amanda Mae to talk about a lease for the new diner." Suzanne pulled Mitzi out of the high chair, hugged her and kissed her. "Hey, baby. Your mama's here now."

Drinking deeply of Mitzi's freshly bathed baby scent, she let her gaze fall on the high chair and her brow furrowed in confusion. Why would a single man have a room with a crib and a high chair?

Then she remembered Cade had a half brother. Gino.

The little boy wasn't Darius and Whitney's son. But a half brother.

She hugged her baby again. "Oh, gosh. I missed you."

Ginny laughed. "She missed you, too. She had a screaming fit at about five this morning."

"Why didn't you get me?"

"Because we were fine. And you'd probably just gotten to bed. She took a bottle. I sang her a lullaby and she went right back to sleep."

Reaching over, Ginny tweaked Mitzi's cheek. "You are a precious little princess, aren't you?"

Mitzi giggled.

Surprised, Suzanne caught Ginny's gaze. "She likes you."

"She adores me and we will be fine all day without you."

"All day?"

"You're going into town, remember?"

"Seeing the building and signing the lease shouldn't take more than two hours."

"Honey, there'll be insurance reports for Cade's insurance claim and investigators to deal with. Not to mention an internet search for the new equipment and then there's the time you'll spend with Cade and his lawyer."

She bit her lower lip. "I'd better get going."

She handed the baby back to Cade's mom, but before she could pull away, Ginny caught her hand. "You've never really left her for a whole day before, have you?"

She shook her head.

"We're fine." Ginny's voice softened. "Seriously. This is like a playdate for me, too."

Suzanne laughed and said, "Thanks," before she

walked into the house again. Today she couldn't take Mitzi with her. But pretty soon she would be able to. She already knew Amanda Mae didn't mind having Mitzi in a swing nearby. Plus, as half owner of her own business, she called the shots.

Realizing that if the Andreas brothers had given her a job she would have had to leave her baby like this every morning, she raced up the stairs, grateful that her initial plan had failed.

Maybe she wasn't a jinx after all? Things might go wrong in her life, but good things always seemed to come of them. Her affair with the wrong man had produced a beautiful baby. The Andreas brothers' decision to give her a holding fee for the purchase of her stock rather than a job had resulted in her becoming a business owner.

A business owner!

She had a place.

She belonged somewhere.

Cade kept the meeting at his lawyer's office cool and professional. Amazingly, when it came time to make any decisions, Amanda Mae deferred to Suzanne. At first, Suzanne hesitated. Then Cade watched something shift in her pretty lilac-colored eyes. Her shoulders straightened imperceptibly, as if she'd realized she had to be the stronger partner in her deal with Amanda Mae while she recovered from the shock of losing her business.

As a professional negotiator Cade could have balked over some of Suzanne's suggestions, but as an Andreas brother his priorities were different. He sent his lawyer a quiet signal that whatever Suzanne and Amanda Mae wanted, it was to be done—including that Cade would pay for the construction to turn the empty building into a diner.

Let Nick tell him he wasn't taking care of Andreas family business now. He'd all but handed Suzanne and Amanda Mae a sparkling new building. And—God help him—she was living with him. Just as Nick and Maggie wanted.

They returned to the ranch about three that afternoon and Suzanne headed upstairs to see Mitzi. He didn't follow her. Spending the day watching her eyes light with joy every time he met one of her conditions had turned his nervous system inside out. She glowed as she took the reins of her partnership with Amanda Mae. And every time she grew stronger, more confident, his chest tightened with a strange kind of happiness. Gooey, sappy, it spread from his chest and made him want to strut with pride for being able to help her.

It was just wrong.

Wrong.

He had no intention of getting close to her even though she was about to live with him for the next few weeks while she apartment or house hunted.

Knowing she could find his mom and Mitzi on her own, he walked back to the office where Eric was using his laptop for the search of assets.

"Anything?"

"Nothing so far. Even though I have her social security number, I hit the wall with the banks. I need to have Suzanne sign some releases. Then I'll go to the banks Martha Caldwell used most often, releases in hand, and we'll see what's what."

He fell to the sofa. "Sounds like a plan." But after only ten minutes of listening to Eric catch him up on things that had happened that day, he began to twitch, and he realized he was listening for Suzanne. Had she found the baby? Was the baby all right? Had his mom been okay watching her all day?

He sighed and hoisted himself off the couch. Convinced it was the good host in him that was making him feel odd that he'd simply walked away from his guest, he headed out of the office. Damn his mother for drilling manners into him.

"I've gotta go check on Suzanne."

Eric grinned stupidly. "Sure. Fine. The rest of this can wait."

He nearly sighed again. Did *everybody* think he had a crush on Suzanne?

Taking the steps two at a time, he scowled. Of course they did. Because he was acting like a ninny about her. And after that earth-shattering kiss he might as well admit it. He *did* have a crush on Suzanne. A stupid crush. *Crush.* Infatuation. Not serious emotional attachment. They hadn't known each other long enough for him to have anything more than a sexual attraction. Sure, he'd realized they had something in common when he recognized her desire to make something of herself matched his own, but that was just one thing. There were too many good reasons to stay away from her to fall victim to an itty-bitty attraction.

Of course, there was the weird happy feeling he'd gotten watching her that day....

He scowled again. Seriously. Was even he going to question himself?

When he reached her door, he knocked twice. Knowing there was a small sitting room before the bedroom—so he wouldn't inadvertently catch her naked, but also she might not hear his knock—he turned the knob and opened the door.

Suzanne was halfway to the door, smiling from ear to ear. "Hey."

"Hey." He nodded at the baby she held. "Everything okay?"

"Yeah. She's great." She hugged Mitzi to her. "She loves your mom."

He hovered in the doorway. "Room okay?"

"It's lovely. Perfect." She glanced around at the comfy yellow sofa draped with a white angora afghan, the big-screen TV that could be hidden in the cherrywood armoire, the plush Persian rug on the floor grounding the grouping. "Actually, it's huge. My grandmother had some fancy suites, but this one is spectacular. That bathroom is to die for. And a baby bath? Whoever thought of that was just a genius."

He leaned against the doorjamb, hating the male pride that bubbled up in him at seeing how happy she was, and pretending he didn't feel it. "Yeah, it's nice."

"It's like the nursery is part of the suite." She frowned and gave him a puzzled look. "Do you sleep in here when Gino is here with you?" Her frown deepened. "Oh, wait. He has a nanny who probably sleeps here...." She stopped again. "Gino's only two and this house is older than two years old." She glanced around, as if disoriented. "Was Gino even born when you built this house?"

He cleared his throat. "No. Putting a nursery in was just a commonsense thing at the time. If you're okay, I'm going to go back to Eric. We have tons of work to do. I eat at seven. If you want to join me, fine. If you want to eat sooner or later just tell the cook."

With that he left, cursing himself for being an idiot. Suzanne was a smart woman, who, as her confidence grew, was getting smarter by the minute. He could not have a crush on her. She'd figure it out…and then what? They'd be awkward around each other; that's what.

She had to live here for at least two weeks—maybe longer if she decided to buy a house and had to wait to take possession. He could not let her realize he was beginning to like her. So he had to get rid of the crush. Dismiss it. Pretend it had never happened. Because it was foolish. Ridiculous.

He was better than this, smarter than this, stronger than to fall victim to some idiotic crush.

Suzanne joined him for dinner that night, but Mitzi was fussy so she didn't get through the salad before she had to take the baby and run. Cade alerted the staff and finished his meal, but with every course he got more and more antsy. Mitzi wasn't a fusser. What if there was something wrong?

Telling himself he was simply concerned, he tossed his napkin to the table and made his way to Suzanne's suite. He hesitated. But knowing he wasn't about to walk away, he rolled his eyes and knocked on the door. If he didn't do this now, he'd just come up again later. Might as well indulge his curiosity and get it over with.

Within seconds Suzanne answered, holding naked Mitzi, who was wrapped in a terry cloth blanket.

"Everything okay?"

"Everything's fine." She turned and headed for the nursery. "Mitzi's a baby. She doesn't believe in any-body's schedule but her own. Right now she wants a bath and to go to bed. I don't get a say in it."

Following her into the bright green room with a matching white crib and changing table, and his mother's old oak rocker, he grunted. "What's with the blanket?"

"You mean the towel? Would you hold a naked baby without some protection against an accident?"

He laughed.

She paused and nudged her head in the direction of the baby's bathroom. "Come on. I'm serious. We have only seconds here before she does something we could potentially regret."

He followed. Slowly. For a guy who was determined not to have a crush on this woman, following her was equal parts of smart and stupid. It was stupid because every second he spent in her presence meant possible discovery. But smart because there was no room in this house that reminded him of his thwarted life plan with Ashley more than this suite. And maybe he needed a reminder of what a man was really supposed to feel for a woman. This sexual thing he had going for Suzanne was only part of a relationship. It would be wrong to make a fool of himself over a crush that was based on very little more than the fact that she had a hot little body.

His heart sort of hiccuped when he entered the bathroom that had been built off the nursery of the master suite—the bathroom his wife had designed—and everything fell into place in his head again. This room had been built for his babies. Having a stranger use it was a potent reminder that he'd never have a child. Especially not with Suzanne. Because he didn't love her. He *wouldn't* love her. He'd never again love the way he'd loved Ashley and he hadn't been a good husband to her, so how could he expect he'd treat Suzanne any better? She deserved more.

She *did* deserve more. She was a nice woman who had a baby who needed a daddy. Not some jaded old cowboy.

Suzanne lowered Mitzi into the waist-high baby tub that had been installed beside the sink. "I'm telling you, this place is a mother's dream."

Happiness swam through him at her praise, but at least this time he understood it. It wasn't wrong to be glad to see the bathroom put to good use. It was pragmatic. For the past two years he'd felt this part of his house was a waste. It was good to see a baby in the tub. Good to see the well-designed space making a mom happy.

Mitzi splashed in the water.

Suzanne gently tweaked her nose. "You love this, don't you?"

He cleared his throat. Now that he had his priorities straight, he could actually converse with her without feeling like his hormones were going to take him down all the wrong roads.

"Gino loves a bath, too."

"Oh, so you've bathed him here!"

"Actually, he's never even been to Texas, let alone to the house. I've had the honor of bathing him when I visit him in Montauk."

She laughed. "Ah, building memories with your little brother."

"That's what Whitney and Darius call it. I call it more like survival of the fittest."

"He's a splasher?"

"Yeah, he is."

She ran a small pink sponge along Mitzi's body as the baby slapped her hands in the water and babbled, not paying any attention to her mom. It seemed Suzanne was bathing the baby without Mitzi noticing.

Cade smiled. This was good. Really good. The little reminder that Suzanne deserved better than him seemed to have turned off all his unwanted feelings. He only felt positive, happy things.

He pushed away from the door frame. "Well, if you don't need anything…"

She peeked back at him. "We don't. We're fine."

"Okay, then I've got to catch up on the rest of what I missed today."

"Eric is still here?"

"No. He goes home at six. Sharp. Every day. He'll come back if I want him to. He'll work seven days a week if I need him to. But he's got a big dumb dog who has to be let out to pee at six-fifteen."

Suzanne laughed. The sound filled the bathroom like music. "That's adorable."

Panic fluttered in Cade's stomach. He wasn't supposed to love her laugh. "Dog's ugly as sin."

She shook her head and went back to rinsing Mitzi. "Those are the best."

He swallowed. Sucked in a breath. Reminded himself that getting involved with her would be cheating her, so he wasn't allowed to have these feelings.

It didn't work. One glance at her bathing the baby and the fluttery feeling in his stomach intensified.

So maybe it was time to suck it up and spend a few minutes talking, so he could grow accustomed to her voice, her laugh…everything. Then there'd be nothing new about her to resurrect emotions he didn't want to have.

"He named the damned thing Ostentatious."

For that Suzanne turned and grinned at him. "Eric named his dog Ostentatious?"

There. See? That wasn't so hard.

"He says the dog always makes a grand entrance, but I'm guessing what he makes are big messes."

Satisfied that his crush was losing some of its power, he turned to go, but Suzanne said, "Cade?"

He stopped, faced her again.

"Thanks. I know you did me and Amanda Mae some favors today."

He grunted. He had billions of dollars, using a few of those dollars to make sure two women got a chance with a new business shouldn't feel like a favor. It should be common sense. So why had his chest just swelled with pride once more?

"Don't mention it."

She smiled. And his heart did a silly flip-flop.

Damn it! The crush was still very firmly in place.

It looked like he had two choices. Option one? Ignore her. Now that their business was done and he knew her suite was adequate, he didn't even have to be in the same room with her.

Option two? Spend so much time with her that she stopped being special. Attractive. Unique. Fun.

Mitzi dropped the plastic ball she was gnawing on and it fell to the floor. Suzanne bent to scoop it up and Cade's eyes followed the smooth flow of her back and the rounding of her bottom as she reached to retrieve it.

He turned and scooted away.

For now, ignoring seemed like the better plan.

Though Cade avoided Suzanne all day Wednesday, the pull that night was too strong to defy. Still, he'd refused to go to her room. Instead, he asked Mrs. Reynolds, his house manager, if Suzanne had eaten.

"Miss Suzanne and Miss Mitzi ate around five-thirty. Mrs. Granger made a special pudding for Mitzi, which the baby gobbled up." She laughed lightly. "Then they played by the pool for an hour before retiring to their suite."

Hearing that stodgy Mrs. Reynolds hadn't been able to resist watching them either, Cade didn't feel nearly so foolish when he had to fight himself to keep from climbing the stairs to check on them.

What was it about babies and new moms that brought out the protective instincts?

God only knew. Not only were Nick and Maggie overly concerned about her, but his staff also had it bad. Mrs. Reynolds kept tabs on her. The cook made special food for them. If Eric started acting all sappy and mushy, Cade would know his entire household had gone around the bend.

He forced himself to stay in the family room, playing video football for two hours, absolutely positive Suzanne and baby would be asleep by the time he went to his room. But when he walked upstairs, the door to Suzanne's suite was slightly ajar.

He sighed.

Don't do it! Do not check on her! Every person on the staff has checked on her. Your own mother called to be sure they were okay. They are okay. You do not need to check!

Of their own volition, his feet wandered to her door. His knuckles tapped twice. The door creaked open a bit more, and there were Suzanne and Mitzi watching TV.

"Hey."

"Hey!" Suzanne rose from the sofa, bringing Mitzi up with her. "You have some timing. Last night you hit bath time. Tonight I'm just about to feed her a bottle and rock her to sleep."

"I was only going to ask how things went today with

Amanda Mae. I'm guessing the shock has worn off and reality is setting in. I wanted to make sure you were dealing okay." How he'd come up with such a reasonable explanation for his presence on such short notice, Cade didn't know. But he was proud of himself. "Seeing as how you're busy, I'll go."

"No." She motioned him to follow her. "I can talk while I'm feeding her."

"Won't that defeat the purpose?"

"What purpose?"

"Aren't you trying to get her to fall asleep?"

"She's already dead on her feet. Once she starts drinking her bottle, there won't be enough noise on the planet to keep her awake. One conversation won't bother her."

They talked about Amanda Mae while Mitzi guzzled her milk. She burped, then Suzanne let her have the bottle again. This time, she drank slower. Her eyelids drooped until she fell asleep.

When Suzanne glanced up, Cade was staring longingly at Mitzi.

The whole situation confused her. She knew Cade was attracted to her, but didn't want to be. His way of dealing with her seemed to be ignoring her. She'd decided that was as good a plan as any and she'd given him a wide berth. But this was the second night that he'd come into their suite.

To see Mitzi.

He'd told her that he wanted her to keep the baby out of his way, but he was the one who kept finding them because he clearly liked the baby. Which was so cute she couldn't really fault him for it.

"Wanna lay her in the crib?"

He caught her gaze. "I'll wake her."

"I told you. She's a heavy sleeper."

He swallowed.

Suzanne saw such raw emotion, such raw pain in his eyes that things fell into place for her. "You built this suite of rooms for yourself and your wife, didn't you?"

"It doesn't matter."

"Sure it does. I don't think you get this, but I can see you're drawn to Mitzi...drawn here. To this suite. I think because you're curious."

He turned away. "A bit."

"There's no shame in that."

He snorted a laugh. "Suzanne, let it go."

"No. Just give in to the feelings. Everybody loves a sweet baby and Mitzi's one of the sweetest. Why don't you let yourself admit you enjoy having a baby around?"

This time, when he faced her he was not laughing. "Let...it...go."

She laid Mitzi in her crib and walked over to Cade. "You think you scare me?" She snickered. "Seriously. Only a little over a week ago, I was facing the possibility of sleeping in my car. You're going to have to do a little better than scowl."

"Okay, how about this?" He stepped closer, so close she could feel the heat of his body. "The reason I keep coming in here is because I have a crush on you."

She blinked. "What?"

"A crush. The hots. Call it what you want but I'd love to sleep with you."

She stepped back. Cleared her throat. She already knew that. He'd warned her off the night he'd kissed her. She just didn't think discussing it would do either of them any good. Still, she had to say something. "So you're telling me you're not coming in to see Mitzi?"

"No. I'm telling you that everything in my well-ordered life has been tossed in the air because of you." He turned away. Ran his fingers through his thick dark hair, spiking it. Then he spun to face her again. "I accepted my wife's death. I accepted that I'd never have kids. That my fate was to take care of my town. The people. And then you popped up and now everything's confused."

Suzanne frowned, backtracking to the most important thing he'd buried in his rant. "You can't have kids?"

"Don't know. We'd just begun tests to see why Ashley hadn't gotten pregnant in eight years of marriage when we found her cancer." He turned away. "Never seemed to be a reason to get myself tested after that."

"So you might actually be able to have kids?"

He shrugged. "Maybe."

"So don't torture yourself. Go get tested."

He spun to face her. "I think you're missing the big picture here. It doesn't matter. I was a bad husband. I'm not going to remarry. And I'm certainly not going to have kids with no mama."

"Why does that makes you mad at me?"

He took her chin, lifted her face until she caught his gaze. "I want to look at you only as somebody to sleep with. Then I could deal with you. Then I could get you in my bed or decide against it."

Her eyebrow arched skeptically. "I have no say."

He laughed softly. "If I decided I wanted you in my bed you would be there."

His tone made her swallow.

"But you have a baby. A little girl who reminds me how much I wanted to be a dad. To have sons. Boys to teach. Children to leave my legacy. And I'm not clear about anything anymore. Ashley was the love of my life. The woman I wanted to be the mother of my children. Without her, these rooms aren't supposed to tempt me."

"Maybe it's not the room." She didn't know how she got so bold, but the answer seemed glaringly easy to her. She stepped closer, mimicking his movement when he'd tried to intimidate her, showing him she wasn't afraid. "Maybe it's the situation. Since I'm as tempted by you as you are by me, then I don't see your problem."

He gaped at her. "I told you. I was a crappy husband."

That made her laugh. "You know what? I'm starting to think that's just an excuse. You're a nice guy. I see it every day. You bought a whole town so nobody would have to pay property taxes. You gave me and Amanda Mae more than a couple of breaks on our deal and you won't one-up your brothers and buy my stock. Face it, Cade. You're a nice guy."

He took a step closer, putting them so close they were just about touching. "You wanna test that, little girl?"

Her voice shook the tiniest bit when she said, "Yes," because she'd seen his kindnesses not just to her but to Amanda Mae, and his brothers. And he liked Mitzi. Wanted to be a dad. No matter how he saw himself, he was a good guy. He might have been a crappy husband to his wife, but it appeared her death had changed him. "I like you and you like me. Why shouldn't we do something about how we feel?"

"Because I'm being kind to you. Smart in the way I treat you."

"What if I don't want you to be smart?"

"You'd better. I don't intend to ever marry again and

you need a husband. But if you push me, I might not be able to walk away from what you're offering."

Her breath stalled. No man had ever worried that he wouldn't be able to resist her. The mere thought sent a shiver of excitement down her spine, liquefied her knees. He stood so close that if she lifted her hand she could touch the stubble on his chin and cheeks. If she rose to her tiptoes she could kiss him.

Renewed boldness blossomed in her, along with an incredible need. What would it be like to make love with a man who desperately desired her?

Heaven?

Or maybe hell. He'd been very clear that he didn't intend to remarry. And just as he'd said, she needed more from a relationship than just sex. She wanted a husband. She couldn't get into a relationship with another man who didn't want forever. She needed someone to cherish her. Love her. Be her partner.

And maybe that was the real bottom line. She wanted a partner and he was offering a roll in the hay.

She stepped back, away from him. "You're right."

"Damn straight, I'm right."

He left quickly and Suzanne fell to her bed in dismay. Wonderful sensations still rumbled through her. Longing she'd never felt before. But fool me once, shame on you. Fool me twice, shame on me. She'd never again fall for a man who didn't want her.

Completely.

For good.

One Bill Baker was enough to last a lifetime.

CHAPTER EIGHT

THURSDAY MORNING AS SUZANNE drove up to the brand-new building that she and Amanda Mae had leased from Cade, everything about her new project suddenly became real for her.

She wasn't just a diner owner on paper. She was a diner owner for real. She sat in her car, staring at the building, with realizations knocking into each other like dominoes. By partnering with Amanda Mae she'd made decisions beyond offering money and agreeing to work. She was creating a life here, in this town. About to buy a house or find an apartment. About to interact with most of the people who lived in Whiskey Springs, if only because the diner was the only place to eat out. About to be an active resident of the town owned by Cade.

She laid her head on the steering wheel in dismay. No wonder he had been so skittish, so agitated when she offered Amanda Mae a partnership. She had, without consciously deciding to, edged herself into his world.

She pressed her fingers to her temples, thinking it through and decided it was too late to call back her choices. She would simply have to learn to coexist with Cade.

And he'd have to learn to coexist with her.

Once she moved out of his house that should be more

than possible. In the five days she'd worked as a waitress, he'd only come into the diner once. Surely, they could handle seeing each other once a week.

Shoving her shoulder against her car door, she got out, bounded into the building and discovered Amanda Mae was already inside.

"So, Joey, I want the kitchen to be right here."

A man Suzanne had never met jotted notes on a small pad of paper. Wearing a pair of brown coveralls and big work boots, he had to be a representative of one of the construction companies they'd chosen to ask for bids on the work required to turn an empty building into a diner.

Suzanne handed Amanda Mae a cup of coffee she'd picked up for her at the convenience store. "Is this one of the people who will be bidding on the renovations for the diner?"

The man looked up sharply, as if startled by Suzanne's question.

Amanda Mae popped the lid on her coffee. "He's the guy who'll actually be doing the work."

"I thought we'd agreed with Cade to go out for bids?"

"Yes, but my niece Jennifer's husband called last night saying Joey needed a job."

So many facts assaulted Suzanne that she didn't know which one to focus on. She understood Amanda Mae wasn't herself. Her entire world had gone up in smoke. She had a right to do things that were a little impulsive, even irrational. But they'd promised Cade they'd go out for bids, and after the conversation the night before, she did not want to cross him.

"But the agreement we signed with Cade—"

"It's irrelevant. I've seen Joey's work. He's the best in town. Cade will want the best."

Joey glanced at her and smiled sheepishly.

"I'm sure he will. But a bidding process—"

"Would be a waste of time since the guy who is the best is available." Amanda Mae turned to Joey. "So, how long will this take?"

"If I get the right crew, I can probably have this done in six weeks, maybe a month."

Amanda Mae gasped. "Six weeks! I can't go that long without an income."

In all the confusion, Suzanne had forgotten Amanda Mae needed money, so her rushing to get this moving faster made perfect sense. It was an argument she could give to Cade for why she'd broken their agreement. But more than that, Suzanne had a resolution for that problem, too.

She tapped Amanda Mae's arm. "Actually, I have an idea. In the city a lot of vendors provide breakfasts, lunches and snacks with carts. I thought we'd try our luck on the internet and see if we could find a cart for a reasonable price—"

"Or I could make you a small stand in front of the building here," Joey said. "No charge except for materials," he added, catching Suzanne's gaze, as if telling her he appreciated her letting him have the job. "And you could sell your things from that. Right outside the new building that you want customers to come to anyway."

Suzanne brightened. Not just because he was building it for nothing, but because he'd thought it through. Her confidence in the town's best builder grew. "That's great."

Amanda Mae was not quite so enthusiastic. "Yeah, but where are we going to cook the food?"

"We can't "cook" anything. We'll have to sell things like sandwiches that we can put together in the stand." She smiled at Amanda Mae. "Plus, I'm sure Mrs. Granger will let me use her kitchen to make a batch of cinnamon rolls every morning."

"Thought you said people would grow tired of them."

"Thought you said they wouldn't."

Amanda Mae sighed. "Okay."

Suzanne frowned. She might have agreed but her tone was dull, listless. Selling sandwiches from a stand outside the future diner was a fantastic idea. Amanda Mae should be jumping for joy. But she wasn't.

She glanced over at her partner, genuine concern squeezing her heart. If getting a substitute income from a sandwich stand hadn't perked her up, then Suzanne was going to have to think harder, be smarter, figure out ways to show her everything was going to work out.

They spent the rest of the day on the internet, using Gloria's laptop to begin looking for appliances, pots and pans and utensils for the diner, as well as supplies to equip their interim sandwich stand. Needing the things for the stand immediately, they ordered those items that day, and actually got an overnight delivery on most of them. It was expensive, but they would be back in business on Monday morning.

By the time Suzanne returned to the ranch, she was exhausted. But she knew she had to go to Cade's office to tell him she and Amanda Mae had hired a contractor.

With a deep breath for courage, she turned and walked down the hall. As always, Cade sat at the huge mahogany desk. When she knocked on his door frame, he glanced up.

"Yes?"

"We hired a contractor today."

Obviously annoyed, he put down his pen. "I thought you were going out for bids?"

"Joey Montinegro was available."

Cade picked up his pen again. "Oh, well, okay, then."

She took a step into his office. "I take it this guy is good?"

"The best."

"Thank goodness. Amanda Mae hired him this morning without telling me." She took another step into the room. She knew he wanted to avoid her, but he was the closest thing she had to a mentor and she was worried about Amanda Mae. Maybe he'd have some advice. "It was the weirdest thing. All day long she behaved oddly. Not like herself at all."

"She just lost her business. She's bound to have a few moody days."

"This went beyond moody. She seems really sad."

He sucked in a breath, but didn't look up. "She probably is. Creating a new diner and even having a partner are risky. She has to be worried that you guys could fail."

"She did mention not having an income until we open, but we're opening a sandwich stand right outside the new building. In a few days we'll have an income."

He busied himself with the work on his desk again. "Just give her some time. She'll rebound. People have nowhere else to go to eat but that diner. Soon she'll remember that and she'll be fine."

"Okay."

She waited for him to say something else, but he didn't. She tried to think of something else to say, anything to make her presence less awkward, and couldn't.

"Okay, then. I'll just go to my room and play with Mitzi."

She turned to go, but he said, "Suzanne?"

"Yes?"

"Will you be joining me for dinner?"

There wasn't one spark of anything in his dark eyes. No attraction. No recognition. No interest. He'd made up his mind, shored up his defenses. There'd be no more personal conversations, no getting to know each other. That was how he intended to coexist.

She could probably eat with him that night, but they'd be like two awkward strangers.

Her heart tweaked a little in disappointment, but deep down inside she knew it was for the best.

"No. I'll get something after I have Mitzi settled."

But Mitzi wouldn't settle that evening and the once-comfortable suite became unbearably cramped. Because she'd come home early, she'd already spent hours stuck in three rooms and suddenly she couldn't do it anymore. Glancing out the window, she saw a series of sidewalks and trails that led to stables and corrals off in the distance. She changed Mitzi's diaper, put on her scruffy tennis shoes and headed out for a walk.

Her "walk" ended up taking twenty minutes. By the time she arrived, she was breathless. Hindsight was always twenty-twenty, but she wished she'd thought far enough ahead not to sell her stroller in the big sale she'd had to earn money to pay off her grandmother's debts and taxes.

She paused, admiring the flower beds that skirted the thin concrete road, pleased that someone had taken the time to make the place pretty.

"See these?" she said to Mitzi. "They're petunias."

"Sweet Williams, up by the barn."

She glanced around, confused because she hadn't actually seen anybody as she walked up. She still didn't see anyone.

"Down here."

An older man, probably in his late fifties, rose from behind a huge flowering bush. "Jim Malloy. I'm foreman here. And you're—"

"Suzanne Caldwell." Because he'd pulled off his gloves, she extended her hand to shake his.

He shook his head and smiled broadly. "Hands are still a little too dirty for shaking. Can't say I recognize your name."

"I'm partnering with Amanda Mae Fisher on the diner. Cade's letting me live here."

"Ah, you're the heiress."

She snorted a laugh. "If that much gossip has reached you here back at the barns, then you also know I didn't inherit any money."

"But you did get a big block of stock." He grinned. "Andreas Holdings stock. That probably put a burr in Cade's shorts."

She laughed. It wasn't funny that her being a shareholder of Andreas Holdings stock made Cade angry, but she loved the slang of this area. It provided a vivid, probably accurate picture of how Cade felt. She also loved the people of Whiskey Springs. Warm. Friendly. Genuine. Sometimes painfully honest. But she'd had so much dishonesty in her life lately that, even painful, the honesty was refreshing.

He pointed at Mitzi. "So who is this?"

She proudly presented her baby. "This is my daughter, Mitzi."

"Well, aren't you just the sweetest little thing?" He glanced at Suzanne again. "How old?"

"Six months…heading toward seven. It's really hard to keep up with baby ages. At first we counted in weeks, which was a dilly to try to figure out. Now counting months is nearly as hard."

"Yeah, it is." He glanced down at his dirty hands. "Wish I could hold her."

The regret in his voice hit Suzanne right in the heart. With his gray hair and kindly weathered face, he looked and acted like a well-loved grandfather. The sort of grandfather she'd always dreamed about but never had. She'd been so happy to have at least one living relative that she'd never told anyone about her secret longing for a granddad.

But suddenly that dream morphed and took a different shape. Because she had no relatives, her baby wouldn't ever have a grandmother or grandfather. No cousins. No aunts. No uncles. No father. She wished for a grandfather just like Jim Malloy for Mitzi, then stopped herself. She had to stop connecting herself to Cade. This guy was his ranch foreman. For both of their sakes, once she got a house in town, she'd have to stay away from anything connected to Cade.

"I guess I'd better get back. If Cade comes up to my room to say good-night, he might worry if I'm not there."

"You didn't tell him you were leaving the house?"

"No. I sneaked out. You could say he's really not happy to have me underfoot."

Jim peered over at her. "It's not like Cade to be unhappy about having a pretty girl around."

"We sort of bring out the worst in each other." Feeling odd talking about Cade with one of his employees, she changed the subject. "It doesn't matter." She nodded at the flowers at their feet. "By the way, I think it was a great idea to pretty up the area with flower beds."

He sighed, looked skyward. "It wasn't my idea. It was my daughter's." He caught her gaze. "I tend them for her now that she's gone."

It took a second, but only a second, for that to sink in. "You're Cade's wife's father? Ashley's dad?"

His eyes narrowed. "So he told you about her?"

She cleared her throat, made a mental note never to walk to the barns again and quietly said, "He spoke very highly of her. He loved her...I think he still does love her. She must have been a wonderful person."

"She was."

Suzanne saw tears fill his eyes and took a step back. "I should probably return to the house."

He said nothing, simply knelt down again and went back to weeding.

Walking beside flower beds that wound along a road that led almost to Cade's house, she suddenly understood why he couldn't consider another relationship. Reminders of his deceased wife were all around him... and so was her father. A father who'd never move on from the death of his daughter. A father who would mourn the loss forever.

A father who might also remind Cade he hadn't been such a wonderful husband.

The following Monday, Suzanne woke early, made her cinnamon rolls and headed for the sandwich stand. This was the day they would open for business. After stocking the stand on Friday and Saturday, she'd spent all day Sunday at the ranch, avoiding Cade, so it felt blissfully wonderful to have somewhere to go.

When she arrived, Amanda Mae was already there. "Give me those beauties," she said, taking a tray of cinnamon rolls from Suzanne's hands. "People are lining up."

Suzanne laughed. "And you've been worried that we'd fail."

Amanda Mae sighed. "All right. I get it. I know I was a bit of trouble last week, but I'm okay now and we need to get selling. So I'll say I'm sorry I was a grouch and we can get to work."

She turned to leave but Suzanne caught her arm, refusing to let her go without really talking this out. "You weren't a grouch. You were concerned about the future. I understand. I've been through a loss or two myself. I'm guessing I was probably a little hard to get along with after my grandmother died. Maybe even when I first came to Whiskey Springs."

Amanda Mae chuckled. "So, we're even?"

Suzanne smiled. "I think we're better than even." But as Amanda Mae carried her tray of rolls to the stand, Suzanne said, "Actually, I could use your help with something else."

Setting the tray of rolls in the front of the display case so everyone could see them, Amanda Mae said, "What?"

"Finding someplace to live."

For that Amanda Mae turned around. "You're leaving Cade's?"

"I was only supposed to stay there until I found a place. But we've been so busy I haven't even started looking for a house or an apartment. Now I've got to get moving."

"You have any money?"

"They gave me a nice chunk of change to hold my

stock. Lots of it went for diner equipment and things for this stand. Lots more is going for taxes. But I have a bit left. As long as I don't get carried away, I'll be fine."

"And pretty soon we should be making enough that we can both take a salary."

"Yeah. That's right. Pretty soon I'm going to get a salary!"

Amanda Mae laughed. "Okay, then I'll make a few calls."

Cade left the office that afternoon at three. He was tired of working, and one of the perks of being rich was that if he didn't feel like doing anything, he didn't have to.

He headed outside to the pool house, intending to change into trunks and enjoy what was left of the gorgeous day. The sky was blue. The sun was hot. And he owned a swimming pool he rarely used. So today was the day.

But when he stepped onto the patio, he found his mom and Mitzi. He'd almost forgotten about them.

He ambled over. "Hey."

His mom peered up at him over her sunglasses. "Hey. What are you doing out here?"

"Don't feel like working." He stooped down in front of Mitzi who sat in a pack-and-play under a huge umbrella. "How's it going for you today, kid?"

She gurgled a laugh.

"Does she go into the pool?"

"She loves the pool." She pointed to a small box past the pack-and-play. "See, she has two floaties and a turtle."

"What the devil is a turtle?"

"It's a one-piece suit that's a life jacket for a baby. I saw one on the internet and couldn't resist buying it."

She held up the garment that looked like it was stuffed with foam blocks. "See? It's padded enough and covers so much that it sort of looks like a tortoise shell when she puts it on."

He laughed. "Great. Give me two minutes to change and I'll take her in the pool with me."

"Actually, Cade, I'd appreciate if you could finish watching her for the day. I made dinner plans with Mary Louise Marks and I'd sort of like to slide by the beautician for a trim before I go."

Cade laughed. "Let me change into a suit and I'll give you your freedom."

He ran to the pool house and put on trunks. By the time he came out, his mom had not only stuffed Mitzi into the one-piece swimmer, she'd also gathered her things and was ready to go.

"You're not getting tired of this, are you?"

"No. But I have been neglecting the bookstore. Babysitting for Suzanne came up so quickly I never had time to look at my calendar. There may be more days I can't babysit."

Cade waved a hand in dismissal. "We have a staff here. You don't need to be here every hour of every day. From now on, just come and go as you want. The staff and I will work it out."

"Thanks." She kissed his cheek then scampered off.

He carried Mitzi toward the shallow end of the pool. "You know that outfit makes you look fat, right?"

Mitzi giggled.

He grinned. "Finally, a woman who doesn't obsess about her weight."

Mitzi laughed again.

Cade waded into the pool, then, holding Mitzi

under the arms, he skimmed her over the surface of the water.

She giggled with delight. A fluffy feeling invaded his chest. He let her dip a little deeper and she screeched.

He pulled her out of the pool and examined her face. "Is that good or bad?"

She giggled.

"Okay. Good."

He dipped her again. They played in the pool for at least an hour then Cade took her out and sat down with her on the chaise lounge. She was so small, so soft and so sweet. Part of him couldn't help longing to take care of her. To be the one to teach her to ride a pony. To be the one to teach her to swim. To be the one to pace the floor when she went on her first date.

But he couldn't. He knew he couldn't. Soon Suzanne would move out, taking Mitzi with her.

Still, he cuddled the baby closer. What was the harm in enjoying the few minutes or days he might get with her? None.

Mitzi fell asleep on his chest and he slid his arm over her, making sure she stayed put, before his own eyelids began to droop.

And that was how Suzanne found them. Her baby girl cuddled up to Cade, sleeping soundly. For several minutes she just stood staring at them, her own wishes and yearnings floating through her. It was so hard to believe Cade thought he was a bad person that at times like this she wanted to shake him silly and make him see he wasn't. But she also knew herself. She sometimes saw the good in people when there was none. And she couldn't be fooled a second time.

Still, he looked so cute with a baby. And Mitzi looked so cute with a daddy.

With a sigh of longing, she walked over to the chaise and as carefully as possible lifted Mitzi from his chest.

He immediately woke. "Hey—" He blinked, recognized who she was and said, "Sorry about that."

"What? I'm the one who should be sorry for not being here with my own child." She glanced around. "Where's your mom?"

"She had an appointment this afternoon. So I took over the job as babysitter."

Suzanne gasped. "I'm so sorry!"

He shifted on the chaise. "We have a staff. It's not like you're putting anybody out. In fact, my mom told me today she has a few things she needs to do at the bookstore and I told her not to worry. We'll handle Mitzi."

She caught his gaze. "You don't mind?"

He nonchalantly rose from the chaise. There was no way he'd let her see how much he'd enjoyed the afternoon. He didn't want her to get ideas again. He'd play this off as a duty. A task he could assign to his staff. "No. We'll be fine. You just go to work at your regular time and I'll instruct Mrs. Reynolds to be available if my mom needs her."

Wide-awake now, Mitzi squirmed. Full of energy she leaned toward the pool, screeching as if demanding to go back in.

Cade winced. "That's my fault. I let her play in the pool until she pooped out. Now that she's rested, it looks like she wants in again. Sorry."

But Suzanne laughed. "You're sorry you got time to take my little girl for a swim? Right about now I envy you."

She chuckled and headed for her suite, and he ran his hand down his face. She might envy him his free time, but he envied her more. Even with a job that took most of her day, a partner struggling to regain her footing and no home, Suzanne had everything he wanted.

CHAPTER NINE

THE FOLLOWING DAY, SUZANNE came home to find Ginny with Mitzi as usual. Ginny told her about the dinner engagement and needing to go to the beautician and Cade's offer of staff to take care of the baby.

Grateful to both Ginny and Cade, Suzanne said, "Thanks."

But Ginny brushed off her thanks. "We love her, Suzanne. The staff actually groans when I come in and take her."

Confident that no one felt put-upon taking care of Mitzi, Suzanne didn't worry. The following two nights she came home to find Mrs. Reynolds with Mitzi. But the Saturday evening, when she returned home a little later than normal and a lot more tired because there had been an unexpected rush for sandwiches for quick suppers, Cade was walking down the foyer stairway with Mitzi. In spite of her exhaustion, she couldn't help noticing how adorable they looked. The gorgeous dark-haired man with the adorable dark-haired baby. They could be father and daughter.

Longing tightened her chest, twisted her heart. She knew it had to be exhaustion that caused that slip, so she ignored it. "Hey."

"You look like hell."

After fourteen hours making sandwiches, she probably did. She wanted desperately to toss her purse to the foyer table and collapse on the floor. Her second-best desire was to go upstairs, shower and collapse on the bed.

Instead, she clapped her hands to Mitzi. "Come to Mama."

Cade held her away. "I'm serious. You look like hell. When was the last time you slept?"

"Last night."

"Don't try to buffalo me. I know she gets up at night. And I know you set your alarm for five every morning to make cinnamon rolls. When do you sleep?"

The urge to collapse against him and whine nearly overtook her. She'd been a spoiled college student when her grandmother died. Now suddenly she was a single mom, half owner of a diner, and she felt like she was drowning.

But he was not the person to tell. He didn't want to get involved with her. But his kindnesses to Mitzi sometimes had her forgetting that.

"I'm fine." Embarrassed, she took Mitzi from his arms. "I can be a mom and work. Millions of women do it." She shifted to the left, so she could walk around him up the stairs.

"Suzanne—"

She turned, tears pooled in her eyes. She wasn't just tired, she was beginning to see him in ways that weren't right. A father for her child. A confidant for herself. He might think he was a bad person but every day she saw evidence that he wasn't and she was beginning to like him. A lot.

"I'm sorry. I didn't mean to insult you. I was just saying I could keep Mitzi a while longer."

"I'm fine."

But she wasn't. She was tired and swimming in confusion. But she couldn't tell him that. She didn't want to get any closer to him than she already was, like him any more than she already did. And that's all talking would do. Make her like him even more than she already did.

Not wanting to spend another Sunday avoiding Cade, she packed Mitzi in her car. They took a long drive, and eventually drifted over to Amanda Mae's house. She made hot dogs on a grill and they sat on lounge chairs under a tree.

"So are you going to tell me what's bothering you?"

She couldn't really tell Amanda Mae she was exhausted. The woman was twenty years older than she was and not even slightly winded by the amount of work they were doing. Besides, this was her first job and they'd only been working a few weeks. Surely things would get better?

"Nothing. I'm fine."

"No, you're not." Amanda Mae studied her face for a second. "Okay, now I'm gonna go to meddling, but since we haven't been able to find you an apartment I think I know what's troubling you." She paused, sucked in a breath. "I've seen this thing that's been going on between you and Cade."

Suzanne stiffened. "There's nothing going on between me and Cade."

Amanda Mae laughed. "I saw your chemistry with the guy before you did." She laughed again. "Anyway, I'm guessing that has something to do with your sudden appearance at my house today."

Since that was the truth, she couldn't deny it. "Because I'm gone so much, he spends a lot of time with Mitzi." She swallowed. "He's awfully cute with her and she loves him." Her throat suddenly became unbearably tight, but she trudged on because it felt good to finally be able to admit some of this. "After I see them together, I get weird feelings. Like how he'd make a really good dad. But even though he likes me, he's said he doesn't want anything to do with me. So now, when we're both home, I feel like I have to hide from him."

Amanda Mae's face softened. "Oh, honey. Don't take it personally. He was so in love with Ashley. So young when he met her and so young when he married her. I don't think he even dated anybody else. After she died, he dated a bit for fun and company, but not looking to replace her. He can't replace her." She shook her head. "No, he *won't* replace her. And there's a bunch of us in town who respect that. But—" she sucked in a breath and caught Suzanne's hand "—that doesn't help you. Especially when we can't seem to find you an apartment so you can move into your own place."

"I'll figure something out."

Amanda Mae shook her head. "Actually, I've thought this through and I don't want you to stay in Whiskey Springs because of me. I appreciate you sticking by me through my sulk over losing the diner, but things are going well now. I ran the business myself before our partnership. I can run it again. If you think you need to go, go. Take a week, take a month, take a year. Just know that I'd like to see you come back." She shrugged. "You know. Be my partner. There's no man worth losing a friend over."

Suzanne's throat tightened even more. Amanda Mae might have run the diner, but she'd had help. Waitresses.

Busboys. The sandwich stand was a totally different animal and Suzanne couldn't abandon her. "Thanks, but I'll be fine."

Amanda Mae considered that. "And if you're not?"

"Then I'll take some time." She caught Amanda Mae's forearm. It had been so long since anybody really cared about her that she swallowed back a bucket of tears. "Thanks."

Amanda Mae groaned and batted a hand. "Don't go getting all mushy."

Suzanne laughed, as she fought her tears. She and Amanda Mae really had formed a bond. That was why she didn't want to leave. Whiskey Springs was the home she'd always wanted. Amanda Mae was quickly becoming the stand-in for her mom, who had died too young. The only fly in the ointment was her longing for a man who didn't want her.

It was dark when Suzanne returned home, but she felt better. Relaxed. But Wednesday night she was exhausted again. There was another rush on the stand just before supper time. Apparently, no one in Whiskey Springs felt like cooking on Wednesday and Saturday nights.

Done in, she melted onto the seat of her Mercedes, drove the fifteen minutes to Cade's ranch, rolled out of the car and went in search of her baby. When she found no one in the nursery, she groaned. She'd hoped only to have to walk up the stairs, bathe the baby, feed her and then shower herself before she could fall into bed.

But no such luck.

At the top of the stairs, she was so tired she considered folding herself into a ball and rolling down rather than walking. But she managed the steps, a trip to the kitchen—which was empty—a trip to the office—equally empty—and finally she found Cade and Mitzi in the pool.

"We just got in," Cade said as she walked across the patio to them.

"Oh. I was kind of hoping to take her upstairs and get her ready for bed."

"And I was thinking some time in the water might make her sleepy."

He was suddenly very knowledgeable about the baby, but she didn't have the energy to dwell on that or even out-and-out ask him why. Instead, she headed for the chaise lounge, hoping she didn't fall asleep while she waited for them to come out.

Cade played with the baby for another minute or two then he said, "Why don't you come in, too?"

"I don't have a suit."

"We have at least thirty in the cabana. They're all new. Once someone uses one, we tell them to take it home."

After standing out in the Texas sun for twelve hours, her sweaty body almost wept at the thought of diving into the cool water. But that would mean spending time with Cade—with both of them half-naked. Not wise. "I don't know."

Holding Mitzi securely with one hand, Cade skipped the other along the water, sending a cold spray over Suzanne. Sputtering, she bounced off the chaise.

"Hey!"

"Now, you're wet. No reason not to come in."

Sighing, and too tempted by the prospect of a refreshing dip to refuse, Suzanne walked into the cabana. He'd made his feelings plain and she'd already decided not to be stupid. She might like him a little more every day. But he did not like her.

As Cade had said, there were plenty of swimming suits, all with tags. She found her size and cringed at the tiny bikinis. There was no way in hell she'd go prancing out to the pool in a little red two-piece number. She rummaged along the rack until she found a pretty aqua one-piece. It not only fit, it also covered everything but a spare inkling of cleavage.

It was fine.

Really.

A little self-conscious, she walked out of the pool house and ambled over.

Cade made a big deal out of not watching her walk to the pool. He admitted to a bit of disappointment that she'd chosen the one-piece suit, until he saw how pretty she looked. The color suited her dark hair and creamy skin. Plus, covered or not, her curves were very nicely outlined.

Still, knowing she was off-limits, he focused all his attention on skimming Mitzi along the top of the water as Suzanne dived off the diving board.

When she surfaced, water ran from her hair along her shoulders down the crevice between her breasts. It was everything he could do to keep from staring. So he skimmed Mitzi along the water again, making her giggle, taking his attention away from Suzanne.

"Come on, baby. Want to come to Mama?"

Cade skipped her along the water, out of Suzanne's reach. "We're okay."

Mitzi giggled and Suzanne said, "I see that."

"We actually go to the pool every day."

"Really?"

Because her voice vibrated with concern, he added,

"I love to swim, but laps can get boring. She gives me a reason to be out here."

Suzanne's eyes softened. Their pretty blue color always fascinated him but this evening's softness filled him with trepidation. He'd lured her out to the pool to relax because he'd been worried about her. Now he not only saw the flaw in his plan, he also remembered why he'd been ignoring her. She was gorgeous. And he was tempted.

"That's actually kind of cute."

Trying to bring back the light mood, he snorted in derision. "Yeah, well, don't go telling the people in town. I have a reputation to maintain."

She laughed and everything inside of Cade responded, except not out of attraction, out of something else, something stronger, something warmer. Pleasure. Though he knew he was skirting a dangerous line, something pushed him to keep going, to make her laugh again, to make her happy.

"I'm serious. Something like this gets out, every woman in a three-mile radius will be bringing her baby over."

She laughed, slid her hand through the water. "You'd love it."

His heart stumbled. His chest tightened. Lord, he loved it when she laughed. Groping for something to bring them back to normal, he said, "For about a day and a half. Then it would get old. Let's just let Mitzi benefit from this."

"Yeah. She deserves it." She skimmed her hand along the water again, suddenly avoiding his gaze. "I feel really bad that she doesn't have a daddy."

So did he, but he also knew the truth. Pretty girl like Suzanne wouldn't be alone long. Though that thought squeezed his chest even more, he softened his voice and said, "She will. Someday."

"I have every intention of being a good mom, a great mom. But I know what it's like not to have a daddy." She shrugged. "Or even a granddaddy. I know it's a longing she'll always have. I have to fix that."

He swallowed. "You will."

She finally glanced over at him. "I hope. Otherwise it will be the great failure of my life."

He sniffed a laugh, glad to be reminded of why she had to be off-limits for him. *His* great failure. "We all get a great failure in life. Why should you should be any different?"

"Because mine involves someone else. A baby who doesn't deserve to do without because I was a poor judge of character."

"And my wife didn't deserve to be the one to suffer because I spent so much time away." He shrugged. "Lots of life isn't fair." Knowing they'd already been over his feelings about his first marriage and not wanting to tread that path again, he changed the subject. "So how was work today?"

She didn't hesitate. "Exhausting. I had no idea fifty percent of the population of a small town could want sandwiches for supper every Wednesday."

"Your cash registers must be singing."

"Amanda Mae is in her glory."

He laughed. "But you're just tired."

"Don't make a big deal out of it. This diner is going to be the best thing that ever happened to me. Already, I'm making friends. I love this town. I love the people. I never would have met half of them had it not been for the diner."

He wanted to tell her that it wouldn't do any good to

know everybody in town if she died from exhaustion. But he said nothing because a little voice inside him reminded him that her love of the town caused another complication for him. All this time he'd envisioned her being out of the picture once she left his house. Instead, he realized that exactly the opposite would happen. As she made friends, she would be invited to barbecues, baptisms, weddings, swim parties...everything he would be invited to.

She was in his life for good now. Permanently.

And he was going to have to watch when she found the daddy she so desperately wanted for Mitzi.

Because Cade agreed with Suzanne—her baby did deserve a dad—he knew he couldn't be hanging around, playing with her baby, trying to make her smile, clouding the issue for her and himself. So he avoided Suzanne after that and let Mrs. Granger and Mrs. Reynolds care for the baby when his mom couldn't.

But two Thursday later he still couldn't quite put them out of his mind. He returned from a meeting at the bank and walked back to his office to find Eric happily occupied at his desk in the room next to Cade's, and his messages neatly stacked beside his phone. But he didn't care one whit about returning those calls. The urge to find Mitzi or drive into town to check on Suzanne was so strong he had to fight himself to plop down on his chair.

Then his phone rang.

Glancing at caller ID, he saw it was his brother, punched the button and said, "Hey, Nick."

"Hey, Cade. I've got you on speaker. Darius is with me in my office."

"What's up?"

"Maggie wants you to invite Suzanne to the wedding on Saturday."

"Are you serious?"

"Dead serious," Nick replied. "You're coming anyway. It shouldn't matter if you fly her over with you."

Cade groaned. After two weeks of not talking to her, he still thought about her way too often. Now they'd be alone for a three-hour plane ride. Then there was the twenty-minute drive in the limo to Nick's house. They'd be at the same table for lunch and dinner on Friday, as well as breakfast, lunch and dinner on Saturday. Not to mention the actual wedding itself. He wouldn't survive that.

"I'm not even sure what time I'm leaving."

"You can work that out with her," Nick said. "Come on, Cade. Maggie likes Suzanne. She wants her there. She's afraid she's lonely."

"And Whitney thinks she needs family," Darius added. "After her visit here, Whitney had expected her to call and chat but she hasn't. So Whitney called her cell phone but she didn't answer."

"She's busy all day with Amanda Mae's diner."

There was a pause. "Amanda Mae's diner?"

"Suzanne made friends with Amanda Mae, the local diner owner. So when we saw the diner burning the day we got back from Montauk, she got caught up in the moment and offered Amanda Mae as much money as she needed to get the diner up and running again."

Another pause.

Cade slid his hand across the back of his neck. "I know you probably think this is insane, but she's busy and I know she's happy working at the diner—even if she is exhausted. Plus, because the apartment she was using also burned, she's forced to live with me until she can find a house or a condo."

"Well, that's something," Darius said. "But it sounds like she could use a weekend off. Bring her to the wedding."

"Yeah," Nick said. "It's going to be great. Ceremony on the beach. Big reception afterward. She'll have fun."

"Plus," Darius chimed in, "Whitney will hound me to death if she thinks 'one of ours' is being left out. So bring her."

They talked only another minute before Darius and Nick clicked off. As Cade hung up the phone, the antsy, hungry feeling he usually had around Suzanne was superseded by real concern. He rose from his chair and paced to the window, scrubbing his hand across his mouth.

He couldn't stand to think of Suzanne as alone, but now that his family had forced him to see it, he realized she'd basically set it all out for him. Her mom had died. Her gram had died. Mitzi's father had dumped her.

She'd come to a town where she knew absolutely no one, looking for a job, and Amanda Mae had given her one. Now she and Amanda Mae were friends and she was also making friends with the locals. But he understood what concerned Maggie and Whitney because it suddenly concerned him, too. She had no family.

No one. She might have friends and customers and people to talk to on regular days but what about holidays? Days when the diner was closed? In the times when a person needed a family, she'd always be alone. That's what Whitney and Maggie sought to prevent.

He couldn't let his attraction to her stand in their way.

* * *

Suzanne was surprised to find Cade waiting for her in the front foyer when she returned to the ranch house that afternoon.

"You and I need to talk."

"Now? I haven't even seen Mitzi."

"She'll be fine with my mom for another few minutes."

Tired and sweaty from a day of selling sandwiches, cinnamon rolls and drinks, she wanted a shower and twenty minutes alone with her baby. But she knew determination when she saw it and right now it was written all over Cade's face.

"All right." She crossed her arms on her chest. "Let's get this over with."

"You're not going to the gallows."

"I know but I'm tired."

"Getting up at five-thirty to be in town by eight every day will do that to you."

She rolled her eyes. "Haven't we already been over this?"

He sighed. "All right. You're right. Let's just get to it. Nick and Maggie would like you to come to their wedding on Saturday."

Her heart stuttered. It was equal parts of wonderful and confusing to be invited to the wedding of people she barely knew.

"Please don't tell me you don't want to go."

"I do want to go." Desperately. She liked Whitney and Maggie. She'd thought they'd made a connection. True, she was making friends with people in town every day, but she had a different feeling around Maggie and Whitney. Almost like what she imagined having sisters would feel like.

"We're leaving Friday morning. We'll stay that night

and Saturday night and return Sunday afternoon. Can you leave Amanda Mae alone Friday and Saturday?"

She chewed her lower lip. "I suppose she could get Gloria to help her at the stand."

"Good. You need a break."

She couldn't argue that.

Cade took a step closer. "You and Amanda Mae also need to work out a plan for this stand of yours. It might be time for a new schedule or maybe even time to hire an employee or two. You can't go on like this. You're exhausted."

He was the only person who seemed to care about that. Even Amanda Mae didn't see that by the end of every day she was dragging. The fact that he did, coupled with his nearness, caused her to swallow hard.

"I know neither one of you wants to be doling out money right now, but—" his voice softened unexpectedly "—you have to think of your health, Suzanne."

A shiver of attraction worked its way through her. He didn't seem to notice how close they were standing or that he was worried about her, being kind to her. It amazed her that he didn't see himself as a good person. Because ever since their trip to Montauk all she saw was goodness in him.

Unable to help herself, she looked up, caught his gaze. "We'll work something out."

"I hope so."

She smiled in response, and though he didn't return her smile, he did hold her gaze. Silence stretched between them. She thought about their time in the pool—when he looked so cute with Mitzi, when he talked to her about getting a daddy for Mitzi—and wondered how he couldn't see that she didn't want just anybody to be a father for her child. She wanted him.

She *did* want him. In spite of the way he kept warning her off, she was falling in love with him. And he'd also shown her signs that he liked her more than he wanted her to believe. Maybe even more than he let himself believe.

Which meant, if she wanted this, then maybe she'd have to make the first move.

She rolled to her tiptoes and brushed her lips over his. Need tingled through her, along with an amazing power. He hadn't moved. He barely breathed. But he also hadn't run, stepped back, told her no.

Her heart jumped to her throat. He was actually giving her a chance.

She rose a little higher on her tiptoes and, balancing herself with her hands on his shoulders, pressed her mouth to his.

She expected at least a bit of resistance, so when his mouth relaxed under hers and his hands dropped on her hips, a swell of feminine hunger shot through her. The time for pretense was over. He was everything she wanted and if he wanted her, she wasn't going to let him pretend otherwise. She deepened the kiss, but he quickly took control, opening his mouth over hers, forcing her to open hers to him.

Time spun out as his mouth seared hers in a hot, passionate kiss. Achy needs rose like wildflowers. Everything she knew or thought she knew about passion redefined itself in one blistering kiss. Her bones liquefied. Her blood shimmered.

And then suddenly he pulled away and stepped back. Raking his fingers through his hair, he squeezed his eyes shut.

She worked to steady her trembling limbs, her thundering heart, her weak knees. But it was no use. If he'd been pleased with her kiss, his reaction would have been very different. No guy who was pleased to have been kissed would squeeze his eyes shut.

Oh, lord. What had she done? No matter how much she wanted him, she knew he didn't want her. Yet, she couldn't stop herself from forcing the issue.

Mortification replaced desire. She turned on her heel and raced up the stairs.

The drive to the airport for the trip to North Carolina was made in complete silence. For the better part of the night before, Suzanne had actually considered not going to Maggie and Nick's wedding, but in the end she couldn't stay away. She couldn't turn down the possibility of making friends of Whitney and Maggie. She'd liked them too much to let a little thing like personal humiliation keep her home. God knew, she and Cade had ignored each other for two weeks, they could certainly ignore each other for a three-hour plane ride.

The pilot and copilot said good morning and disappeared into the cockpit to start the engines.

As the plane took off, she put her head back and closed her eyes. She heard the sounds of Cade moving about, then his voice when he said, "Juice?"

Surprised by his consideration, she quietly said, "No. I'm fine."

He opened his juice with a quiet pop. "So are we going to talk about this or what?"

She remembered their last plane ride, how Cade hadn't wanted to talk about what had happened in his den before she told him she was Andreas's Holdings' missing shareholder, and decided to take a page from his book. Rather than face her humiliation, she would simply refuse to discuss it.

Not opening her eyes, she said, "I don't think we have anything to talk about."

"I shouldn't have kissed you—"

Unfortunately, she couldn't let him take the blame. "You didn't kiss me. I kissed you."

"I seem to remember being a party."

That almost made her smile, but she still didn't open her eyes. "Now you're just trying to make me feel better."

"Yeah, I am." He paused, then added, "I can't take you to Nick's house all quiet like this. The women will skin me alive first and ask questions later. We have to deal with this."

For that, she opened her eyes. Sitting in the back, with his boot-covered feet on the desk, Cade didn't look a thing like a billionaire businessman, though he did look like a man prepared to discuss a problem.

But her problem wasn't that they'd kissed again. It was that she was falling in love with him and he didn't want her, so there was no way she would discuss it. And if she'd stop wallowing in her misery he'd probably let her alone. "We're fine."

"Really?"

"Yes."

"Well, it's a long plane ride. If you change your mind, I'm here."

Cade took his feet off the desk and prepared to work, proud of himself. He might not have gotten her to talk, but he'd made the offer and now they were at least polite enough that they wouldn't raise any suspicions when they got to Nick and Maggie's.

He shouldn't have kissed her the day before, but this time he'd recovered more quickly than he had from the last kiss. He was proud of the fact that he was able to talk to her. To treat her like any other person. To forget she was gorgeous. Toss wanting to sleep with her to the back of his mind. Now, when they arrived at Nick and Maggie's they would be normal.

Still, what pleased him the most was that even after that blistering kiss, he could relegate his sexual feelings for her to the back of his brain and not let them rule him.

He opened a file to get a little work done, but his gaze wandered over to Suzanne. Her eyes were closed, her head back. Her long neck was exposed. Without warning, visions of nibbling that long slim throat filled his brain, his hormones awoke, his body tensed for action.

He banished the visions, subdued his hormones and told his body to settle down. His family considered Suzanne one of theirs. And though he might not have agreed at first, discovering how alone she was, he knew it would be selfish of him to keep her away from Maggie and Whitney when she needed a family. So he could not nibble her neck. Slide his hands along the sleek curve of her waist. Press her into a mattress with the entire length of his body...

He squeezed his eyes shut.

Damn.

Just when he thought he was doing so well.

He leaned back against his seat, mimicking Suzanne. This sexual thing he felt for her wasn't going away. He should have realized that when he couldn't turn away her kiss the day before. Even if he had been able to control himself, and he hadn't, now Suzanne was having trouble controlling her reactions to him. But that was only part of it. He didn't just have a sexual thing for her; he also didn't like to see her sad. He hated the idea of her baby needing a daddy and hated even worse that someday some other guy would be that daddy because that meant someday some other guy would be Suzanne's lover.

So maybe it was time to start thinking of alternatives?

He couldn't marry her. He wouldn't tie another woman to him. But he cared enough about Suzanne and was attracted enough that he knew this wasn't just going to disappear because they wanted it to. He had to fix it, even if it was with only a partial solution.

Carrying Mitzi, Suzanne stood behind Cade as he opened the front door of Nick's house without knocking. They stepped into a foyer that rang with the voices of people in the open-floor-plan family room and kitchen, and she glanced around in awe. The place was much bigger on the inside than it appeared from the outside. Pale orange tile led to a cherrywood staircase that spiraled up three stories, meaning there was plenty of space for family and she didn't have to worry about being too close to Cade.

It was cute that he'd wanted to talk in the plane. But that had only made things worse. He'd made her laugh when she'd wanted to crawl into a hole and die. He cared about her. He was attracted to her and she was attracted to him.

She just plain wanted to be allowed to love him and she wanted him to love her.

And as soon as her mind drifted in that direction, she knew she was in trouble. Luckily, Cade brought her back to reality by shouting, "We're here," as he set their suitcases on the floor beside the tall staircase.

When he didn't get an answer, presumably because

he hadn't been heard above the noise coming from the kitchen, he simply left their luggage on the foyer floor and walked into the family room off the kitchen.

"Daddy, you put in too much shrimp!" Maggie stood beside a man who looked to be in his fifties. With his red hair and green eyes so much like Maggie's, it was easy to see he was her father.

"There can never be too much shrimp in jambalaya." Maggie's dad noticed them standing in the door and grinned at them over a huge pot on the six-burner stove in the center island of a pale oak kitchen with black granite countertops. "Hey! Nice to see you, Cade."

"Nice to see you, too, Charlie." He nodded in Suzanne's direction. "This is Suzanne Caldwell and her daughter, Mitzi."

"Your missing shareholder."

Maggie came from behind the stove and hugged Suzanne. "I'm so glad you could come. Let me take Mitzi."

She slid the baby out of Suzanne's arms as Cade motioned to Mr. Forsythe. "This is Maggie's dad, Suzanne, Charlie Forsythe."

"Nice to meet you, kiddo."

"Nice to meet you, too, Mr. Forsythe."

"Everybody calls me Charlie."

Just then the French doors opened. Whitney walked in carrying Maggie's son, Michael. Liz, the nanny, walked in behind her, holding Gino.

"Is that Mitzi?" Whitney cried then she spotted Suzanne. "It is Mitzi!" She raced over and hugged Suzanne. "You're just in time for lunch." She released Suzanne and hugged Cade. "Darius and Nick are on the deck grilling. You might want to join them."

"First, tell me what rooms we're in and I'll take the bags up."

Charlie waved him out the door. "I'll take the bags up. You go see your brothers."

Suzanne followed Charlie as he took her bags upstairs and directed her to a bedroom with a crib and a bathroom. It wasn't a suite, but a simple, comfortable room with access to the gorgeous upstairs deck that looked out over the ocean.

"It's beautiful."

"Yeah, Nick's got good taste," Charlie said, grinning. "Lunch in ten minutes. You don't want to miss my jambalaya." With that he left. Suzanne took a minute to unpack a few things and wash her face before going back downstairs to the noisy kitchen.

Whitney and Maggie immediately bombarded her with questions about the diner. Suzanne answered them, only to be rewarded with another round, until her nervousness disappeared as it had on her weekend in Montauk with these two women. As they set the long table in front of a huge window with a view of the Atlantic, Suzanne remembered thinking that being with Whitney and Maggie made her feel like she had sisters, and for a few seconds she let herself wonder what it would be like to be part of this big, noisy group.

Considering that only family owned shares of Andreas Holdings, owning one-third of the company did make her family of a sort. As long as she owned her shares, she really was one of them. And maybe in the eighteen months it would take for the brothers to come up with the money to buy her out she really could make friends with Maggie and Whitney—then she'd always be a part of their group.

But even as she thought that, Cade came inside and

she knew that wasn't true. Every time he was nice to her, she grew to like him just a little more and pretty soon her feelings might not be so easy to hide. And then what? Every time Maggie or Whitney would invite her somewhere Cade would be there. And some of those times he'd probably have a woman with him. How could he not? He was too gorgeous to be alone. And some women wouldn't want what Suzanne wanted. They'd settle for a one-night stand or a weekend here or there....

She nearly gasped. Dear God. What was she thinking? That she should marry him? She'd only known him a few weeks!

But in her heart of hearts she knew she wasn't wrong.

She wanted to marry him. And he wanted nothing to do with her.

CHAPTER TEN

NICK AND MAGGIE'S WEDDING took place at two o'clock Saturday afternoon on the beach right behind Nick's house.

Wearing a white gauze sundress and a big white sun hat, Maggie came out of the beach house and descended the deck stairs. Charlie walked her down a short path to the beach, where—two feet away from waves that crawled ever closer to their flip-flops—Nick, Darius and Cade stood with the minister. All three of them wore cutoff jeans and a T-shirt.

Nick's mom, Becky, a pretty blonde, stood near them. Suzanne and Whitney's parents, a wealthy New York lawyer and his wife, stood behind Becky. To the left, wearing sundresses and floppy sun hats, Whitney and a friend of Maggie's served as bridesmaids. And in front of them was a small group of Maggie's friends and employees from the manufacturing plant she managed for Nick.

It was the oddest wedding Suzanne had ever seen, but she wasn't really experienced with weddings. Most ceremonies she'd attended had been held in churches. Most grooms wore tuxes. Most brides wore a gown. But Nick and Maggie wanted the beach. They wanted to be comfortable. To declare their love.

Just the thought brought tears to Suzanne's eyes. Their love story had been a beautiful one. It was wonderful to see Maggie walk up to Nick, take his hand, declare her love in front of the minister, then cry softly as Nick read the vows he'd written.

Suzanne's tears brimmed over, and her gaze strolled to Cade. He held himself casually, as if he were unaffected by this ceremony, but he wasn't grinning the way Darius was. The way a brother would be. And Suzanne understood why. Darius could be silly and make jokes about Nick losing his freedom because he was with the love of his life, too. Cade had found and lost the love of his life. The memories brought to him by this ceremony were probably bittersweet.

Tilting her head to one side, she studied him, amazed that a woman could inspire that much devotion in a man. But, getting to know his family, she was beginning to understand it. The entire Andreas family was loyal, but Cade was loyal to a fault. If he'd fallen in love it had been forever. For good.

It was part of why she loved him. Even though he hadn't wanted her around, he was good to her. Fairness and honesty weren't just words for him; they were a code to live by. After the way she'd been treated by her friends and Bill Baker, was it any wonder she admired those qualities? Any wonder she admired Cade himself? He was a good man, somebody she *desperately* wanted to love because he embodied all the qualities she would look for in the next man she gave herself to.

Halfway through Nick's vows, Whitney's mom handed a tissue to Suzanne who began crying in earnest when the minister pronounced Nick and Maggie husband and wife. They were a gorgeous couple who would be bountifully happy for the rest of their lives. It was a beautiful thing to experience.

Still, that was only part of the reason she wept. She also wept for Cade. For his loss. For her loss. Because of his past, he'd never want her the way she wanted him, and a man she considered to be just about perfect was lost to her.

She scrambled back to her room, telling Whitney that Mitzi needed a diaper change. She stayed there while Mitzi napped, taking a long bath before she dressed in her red cocktail dress for the semiformal reception being held at a hotel a thirty-minute drive away.

Just before she would have been ready to walk downstairs to join the group, there was a knock at her bedroom door.

Adjusting her grandmother's teardrop pearl earrings, she raced to answer, worried that she was behind schedule and Nick or Maggie had sent someone to get her.

When she opened the door to find Cade, she gaped in amazement. Accustomed to seeing him in jeans and a Stetson, seeing him in a tuxedo rendered her speechless. With his dark, shiny hair combed in a respectable way, he was so good-looking he could have posed for magazine ads.

Praying she wouldn't stutter, she said, "Hey. Am I late?" Then turned around and pressed her hand to her chest. He would tempt a nun out of the convent. So it was not odd or surprising that she was having trouble steadying her breathing and hoping her knees could support her.

"No. I was sent to make sure you knew which limo you were riding in." He ambled into her room. "We're sharing one, by the way."

They were sharing a limo? Lord, she hoped there

was another couple or even another person riding with them. Let it be Charlie. Or Whitney's quiet parents.

"I'm ready. I just need to take Mitzi downstairs to Liz."

Cade led her down the spiral staircase. After they deposited Mitzi with the nanny, and Suzanne fussed over her long enough to ease her guilt over leaving, he guided her to the only limo left in front of the house.

She turned around in horror. "I *was* late!"

"Only a bit." He put his hand on the small of her back, where there was no dress, and pin pricks of excitement danced up her spine. "We're fine. Ten minutes behind them at most."

He directed her into the empty limo and her heart galloped. She was so late there was no other couple to ride with them. They were alone! Alone! She was going to make a colossal fool of herself.

She sat on the sofalike seat, shifting over as far as she could, basically hugging the wall.

Rather than sit beside her, Cade sat across from her.

She wrestled back a sigh of relief, not wanting to embarrass herself. But she knew that he knew she'd worked to put space between them.

"Drink?"

"God, no." If she was this nervous and antsy now, imagine what alcohol would do to her. She'd probably drool on him.

The limo pulled out, started off toward the hotel. Suzanne pretended great interest in the scenery.

"Relax. I'm not going to eat you."

She swallowed and tried to laugh. The sound came out strangled.

"Although I have to admit, the first time I saw you in that dress I considered it."

She smiled shakily. "The dress is dramatic. I bought it for the effect."

"Well, you got your money's worth." He leaned back, unbuttoned his jacket and lounged against the seat.

Looking so tempting she could have happily snuggled up to him, he smiled. "You know when you asked me for a few minutes alone that night at the barbecue, I thought you were going to seduce me."

"I know." Dear God, had her voice actually squeaked?

He shook his head. "I had some plans for you that night."

That sent a shaft of heat directly to her womanhood. They had to change the subject or she'd start to shiver. "I saw the look in your eyes. That was why I didn't waste time before I told you about my stock."

He chuckled. The rich, warm sound filled the air around her and seemed to wrap her in the essence of him.

"Yeah, well, if you could have read my mind you probably would have run for the hills." He paused, cocked his head and smiled sexily. "Or maybe not."

After a few seconds' pause, he kicked the toe of her stiletto-heeled sandals and caught her gaze. "You wouldn't have been sorry."

"Now it sounds like you're propositioning me."

He shrugged. "Maybe I am?" He smiled. "We're attracted. And we can't seem to control our chemistry. Or ignore it. Or avoid it. Because we're normal, healthy people. But we're also adults who should be able to discreetly enjoy what's between us."

"I have a baby."

"I have a ranch. What difference does it make?"

"It makes a lot of difference and you know it. I've already told you I want a father for Mitzi."

"And you know I already love Mitzi. You know I would be a good daddy to her for as long as we would be together. We'd just avoid the mess of promises of happily ever after. We both know that doesn't exist. So if we don't get married, just—" he nonchalantly lifted a shoulder "—live together, and you get tired of me and my work schedule, you'd have a get out of jail free card."

"Get out of jail free?"

"You could leave. No hassle. No questions."

She sucked in a quiet breath, not liking his idea. She already knew she was in love with him. She'd never leave. Never. "And what if you got tired?"

He grinned. "Tired? Of making love to you?" He laughed. "I don't think you're going to have to worry about that one."

Just then the limo door opened. Suzanne hadn't even realized they'd stopped moving. Cade stepped out then leaned in again. Offering his hand to help her out, he grinned at her.

She sucked in a breath, urging her heart and lungs to function normally, but the second he grasped her fingers, both her pulse and breathing went haywire again.

He tugged gently and she stepped out of the limo, but she struggled a bit to get her footing and he steadied her with a hand at the small of her back.

Arousal exploded inside her. She fought to suppress a shiver.

He smiled, slowly, knowingly. "See? We'd be very good together. And we'd probably last longer than you think."

"But you don't love me."

"I wouldn't be asking you to live with me if I didn't have feelings for you."

But not love. He didn't say it. He didn't have to. He'd already told her he'd had the love of his life. If she took his offer she'd be second-best. Always second place in his heart and his life. But would that be so bad? They'd be together. He'd help raise Mitzi. She'd be part of his wonderful family.

He said, "Just think about it a bit," before he turned them in the direction of the hotel ballroom.

Nick and Maggie greeted them at the door. Wearing a tux like Cade's, Nick looked almost as handsome as his younger brother. Maggie was breathtaking in a floor-length ivory sheath. It was, after all, their second wedding. She hadn't wanted to wear white or something too youthful. So she'd settled for classy and looked the part of a millionaire's sophisticated wife.

Cade guided her to the table reserved for family. Throughout the meal, Nick's mom, Becky, kept them entertained with stories from Maggie's and Nick's past—especially how they'd loved each other from childhood—until Suzanne's heart swelled with longing. She glanced over at Cade. There was no doubt he was gorgeous. The kind of man who could sweep a woman off her feet in seconds, not even minutes. But the love Becky had described was so pure and so innocent...so perfect, that she knew that was what she wanted—no, it was what she needed.

If she agreed to what Cade was offering, he might always want her sexually but she'd never have the all-consuming, innocent, wonderful love that she wanted. The kind that would steal her breath, wrap her heart in warmth, take her through the rest of her life.

Could she live without it?

With dinner over, the band played a soft romantic song for Nick and Maggie. The way they put their heads together and whispered caused Suzanne's heart to squeeze. They were more than attuned to each other; they were a matching set, two halves to a whole.

And Suzanne had her answer for Cade. She so desperately wanted the kind of closeness Maggie and Nick had. No matter how much she loved Cade, he didn't love her. She couldn't settle for second-best.

When Cade asked her to dance, she rose automatically, but hesitated as they walked to the dance floor. She'd been falling in love with him since the day she met him, but he had not been falling in love with her. With his offer, he'd put all his cards on the table and she had no more excuses, no starry-eyed hopes. She knew what he wanted from her. And it wasn't what she wanted from him.

They reached the dance floor and Cade slid his hand to the small of her back. Tingles formed. Everything female in her responded. To his touch. His scent. His very presence.

He pulled her close and the desire to rest her head on his shoulder nearly overwhelmed her. So she looked away. Unfortunately she saw Whitney and Darius dancing. Saw the closeness. Saw the intimacy of their glances. The way they danced like people who knew each other's next move long before it was made.

Her heart stuttered.

She wanted that.

She so desperately wanted that. So what was she doing with a man who couldn't give it to her?

"Relax."

She swallowed and looked up into Cade's face. His eyes were bright, alert, like a cat waiting to pounce.

She had absolutely no doubt that he desired her. But she couldn't let that muddy the waters. She'd made up her mind. It was time to be strong.

She stepped back. "I think I need some air."

His arms dropped away, but he immediately caught her hand. "There's a patio." He nudged his head in the direction of open French doors. "Come on."

Oh, great. If they were going outside, alone, she might have actually made things worse.

But he didn't seem to notice her hesitation. He led her across the crowded dance floor to a slight breach in the crowd then guided her to doors that opened onto a patio.

She gulped in air as he pulled her along the stone floor to a cobblestone path that wound through a tropical garden. When they'd walked past the reach of the outdoor lights, he stopped.

"Is this air enough for you?" He slid his hands to her back and pulled her close. "I sort of like it out here myself."

She should have told him she'd thought about his offer and had decided to decline. Instead, instinct took over and she leaned in against him. He was solid and warm and very, very real. True, he could never love her, but she did love him. A chance to be with him like this would never come along again. She wanted this minute, this one minute, to at least be held by him.

His hands inched up her spine, along her bare flesh, raising goose bumps. When they reached her shoulders, he pulled her closer still, lowered his head and kissed her.

The bottom dropped out of her world. His lips moved over hers possessively, taking not asking, because they'd kissed before. Twice.

And she answered just as passionately because if this was her last chance to kiss him she was going to make it good. She might never have seen herself as being assertive, but she had changed. She owned half a business. She had good ideas. And maybe that was the problem. She was no longer the frightened young woman who winced and ran away. She stayed and fought....

Maybe she should be fighting to win him?

He pulled her closer still, bringing her body against his. Even through the folds of his tuxedo jacket she could feel the strong beat of his heart and thrilled to the realization *she* was doing this. His heart was beating for her.

He was everything she wanted. Sexy. Smart. Savvy. Strong.

But that was the kicker. He was strong. Much stronger than she was, even with her newfound confidence. He wouldn't tame easily. If he tamed at all.

And if she didn't step away now, she'd never step away.

With a sigh of regret, she pulled back. "Stop."

He chuckled. "I don't have to. You just did."

She sucked in a breath of air. "Okay. Here's the deal. I like you."

He put his hands on her hips and dragged her back to him. "I like you, too."

She shook her head. "No. I *like* you." She winced. This was not the time to be pussyfooting around. This was the time to be real. Honest. "I *love* you. You might be able to get involved like this." She motioned with her hand between them, indicating their physical relationship. "But I want more."

"That's why we're out here away from everybody."

Panic raced through her. "No. Not *that* more. I mean

more as in a relationship, a real relationship, not a tryst in the dark. Not a secret affair." She swallowed. If she was doing this, she had to go the whole way. "I want you to love me."

His hands fell to his sides. "Oh?"

She squeezed her eyes shut as disappointment flooded her. Deep down inside she'd almost hoped he'd say he did love her or, at the very least, that he believed that someday he could love her. Instead, he'd confirmed her worst suspicions. He wasn't interested in love. Only sex.

She licked her lips, savoring the taste of him, a taste she'd never get again, and stepped back. "Come on, Cade. I've been saying it all along. I have a child. I need a home. A real home. I'm just starting to build my life again and I want to do it right."

"And living with me would be wrong."

"What Whiskey Springs man in his right mind would ever approach me after we'd lived together? You employ nearly everyone. I'd be a pariah."

He combed his fingers through his hair as if he knew she was right.

She shook her head sadly. "Did you think we could live together for a few months or maybe even years with no consequences?"

"I don't know."

"There'd be consequences. They are always consequences." Like her currently shattering heart that still, God help her, held on to the hope that he wouldn't let her go.

He put another two feet of distance between them. "I get it."

And by the fact that he'd taken another step back, she

knew that he did understand. He wouldn't argue and give her false hope or make promises he couldn't keep.

She turned and walked away. Up the garden path alone.

Pain rolled through her in a trembling wave. Her throat closed. Still, she fought the tears. She had at least another hour of this reception and there was no way she'd let anybody know Cade had broken her heart.

She was done being the person everybody pitied. She'd do her crying in private.

She rode home in a limo with Darius and Whitney, silently packed her things and ordered a cab that took her to the airport, where she used her one-and-only credit card to get a commercial flight. She found a late flight and climbed aboard the nearly empty plane. When she arrived in Texas, she called Amanda Mae to pick her up and by noon next day, she was at Cade's gathering the last of her few belongings.

"So what are you going to do?"

Having already cried herself out on the dark plane, she shrugged. "Not sure."

"Where are you going to go?"

Longing for her grandmother tightened her chest, brought tears to her eyes again. "I think I'd like to visit my gram."

Amanda Mae frowned. "Oh, honey, you're sad enough. Don't go to the cemetery."

"No. No cemetery. I thought I'd spend some time outside our old house. Just soak myself in the memory of what it felt like to be loved."

"If you don't stop, you're going to make me cry."

"I just need a little bit of something to hold on to. I came here looking for a job and found friends." She squeezed Amanda Mae's hand. "But I think I might have let go of my past too soon."

"Because it sucked."

She laughed in spite of herself. "No. It's more than that. I was so wrapped up in meetings with lawyers and accountants that I never really mourned my gram." She sat on the bed beside her friend. "I wonder now if that wasn't part of why I was so quick to fall for Cade. So quick to see him as a husband. A daddy."

Amanda Mae squeezed her hand. "You saw what he is. A good man. Don't fault yourself. Fault him. He's the one who can't move on."

And with that, they left her suite, her pathetic suitcase in Amanda Mae's hand, Mitzi in her carrier. They said goodbye on the driveway of Cade's big house and Suzanne promised she'd be back soon. But she didn't think she would be. She'd rather entice Amanda Mae to visit in Georgia. Maybe start a bigger diner. Or a bakery. Or anything Suzanne wanted because in another seventeen months she'd be a very wealthy woman.

Still a sad woman…but a very wealthy one.

CHAPTER ELEVEN

MONDAY MORNING, CADE headed for the stables, resisting the urge to drive to town to check on Suzanne to make sure she was okay. He'd gotten the skinny from his staff that Amanda Mae had brought Suzanne home and they'd packed up her belongings. He knew she'd probably gone to Amanda Mae's to live. Which was fine. Probably for the best.

He'd made a fool of himself with her. He thanked his lucky stars no one had been within hearing distance in that garden at Nick's wedding because his foolishness was only his own personal embarrassment.

Oh, he got what she was saying. She wanted what he didn't. Marriage. But the real underlying sentiment was much simpler. She wanted him to love her, and he simply couldn't risk it.

So he'd let her walk away, let her go back to Nick's beach house in the limo with Darius and Whitney. When she wasn't around on Sunday afternoon he'd correctly assumed she'd taken a commercial flight back to Texas.

He stopped his truck in front of the main stable and jumped out.

Standing with one foot hooked over the fence and

his black Stetson shielding his eyes from the sun, Jim greeted him. "Hey, Cade. How was the wedding?"

"Great." That wasn't exactly a lie, but he certainly wasn't going to tell his father-in-law that he'd propositioned Suzanne and she'd rejected him. "Nick's house at the beach is a paradise. And it's always fun to jag around with my brothers, make 'em feel like losers for settling down."

Jim laughed.

Cade relaxed and continued on into the stable. This was what he needed. Not just a quiet trot around the ranch to check things out, but a little time with Ashley's dad to remind himself that he was doing the right thing by stepping away from Suzanne.

He pulled a saddle from the hook on the wall as Jim said, "Heard that little girl from Georgia went with you."

His face heated but he kept walking toward his Appaloosa. "I couldn't exactly leave a houseguest alone while I went off gallivanting. Besides, Maggie and Nick wanted her there."

"She's a pretty little thing."

"I hadn't noticed."

"So what's this? You blind now?"

Cade laughed. "All right. She's pretty. But you know I'm not interested."

Jim opened the corral door. "Cade, it's been *years*."

"Two. Hey, Sugar," he crooned, approaching his horse. "I think you and I need to spend a little quality time together." Sugar lifted his head and whinnied. Cade grunted as he hoisted the saddle to his horse's back.

"Two long years," Jim said, helping Cade cinch the saddle.

"What? You think I have no concept of the passage of time?"

"I'm just saying it seems odd is all. We all loved Ashley. Her mom and I talk about her every day. But you're young. You should be moving on."

"I have moved on. Hell, I've got more work now than I ever had. And more people depending on me." Which was what he wanted—association with people but from a distance. This way he didn't hurt anyone.

He led Sugar out of the stable and spent the afternoon riding the fence until it ended, and just plain exploring the land beyond that.

Now both Ashley and Suzanne were gone. And he would have to deal with it.

That night Cade didn't sleep. He went to his office where he spent hours poring over reports for the new division of his oil conglomerate, even though he didn't absorb a word he read. At seven Eric arrived, took one look and simply headed into his office without comment.

But two days later, when he still hadn't slept, Jim wasn't as polite as Eric. "You look like hell."

"I haven't been sleeping."

"Word got back from town that your little girl from Georgia hasn't been showing up at the sandwich stand."

His heart stopped. He'd thought she'd gone to Amanda Mae's, maybe slept on her couch. He'd thought she was working the stand, surrounded by people who were growing to like her. "Her choice."

"So where'd she go?"

"She didn't tell me."

Jim sighed, fell to a chair in front of Cade's desk. "Are you slow or are you just plain crazy?"

"What I am is tired. Say what you came in here to say then leave."

To his surprise, Jim rose from his chair and walked to the door that separated Cade's office from Eric's. He closed it.

"Okay, I'll say my piece then I'll be gone. Suzanne was a cute little gal with a heart of gold and a very good head on her shoulders. And you liked her. Maybe even loved her. Yet you chased her away."

"I did not love her!"

"Really? You're not eating. You're not sleeping. You didn't even behave this badly when Ashley died."

The reality of that hit Cade like a punch to the chest. He couldn't sleep. He couldn't eat. He couldn't even work. Even after Ashley died, he could work.

"Oh, God." He pressed his fingers to his eyes. He did love her. "This is so wrong."

"How can you say that?"

"Because I wasn't a very good husband to the last woman I married." He sucked in a breath. "You know as well as I do that I left her alone. Lots. It hurt her."

Jim shook his head. "You were building a business. She always understood. Besides, you were there when it counted most."

Jim might believe that but Cade didn't. He put a business deal ahead of his dying wife. He wasn't around when she drew her last breath. The very second she needed him the most, he was gone.

"Cade?"

"I don't want to talk about it."

"This is about you not being there when she died, isn't it?"

He said nothing.

"Oh, Cade. She'd rebounded. That morning she was

happy as a lark. As I recall, she shooed you out. Because you'd been there every day for weeks." He sucked in a breath. "How can you not remember this? How can you not remember the vacations? The long weekends? The days when you only owned stocks and the ranch...when every other day was a holiday for you?"

Cade swallowed. Every time he thought of his marriage, he only remembered himself leaving. He remembered all the times he wasn't home as if they ran in a long unbroken stream. He'd forgotten the weeks he'd been able to take long vacations with Ashley because he worked for himself. He'd forgotten the days he'd stayed home just because he could. He'd forgotten the two weeks before she died, when he hadn't left her side, when he'd slept on a couch by the hospital bed they'd set up in a room near the kitchen.

When Cade said nothing, Jim tossed up his hands in defeat. "All I'm saying is you're a fool to let a good woman walk away. A fool not to take a second chance when the good Lord decides to give you one."

He rose and headed for the door. "That's it. That's my piece. I said it. What you do with it is your business."

The first night after Suzanne left Whiskey Springs, she'd gotten a hotel room for herself and Mitzi. The second night, having arrived in Georgia, she got another hotel room and bought some newspapers so she could begin house hunting.

But the third night, even in the familiar hotel room, she felt alone and cold. So lonely she could have happily curled in a ball and cried for hours. But she didn't. She couldn't. She had a child.

So she called Amanda Mae. "Hey."

"Hey. It's pretty damned late to be calling a woman

who has to get up at five to make your cinnamon roll recipe."

"Sorry about that."

"I hate making those blasted things. Can't I persuade you to come home?"

Home. Whiskey Springs had become home, but she'd made the mistake of falling for Cade and she couldn't live there anymore. "I thought you said you were fine on your own."

"I thought I would be, but I'm not. I'm used to your company. Can't we just ban Cade from the diner when it opens next week?"

Just the thought made Suzanne laugh. Still, she didn't want to talk about Cade. Every time she even thought of him, her chest hurt. Her eyes filled with tears.

"You visit your gram yet?"

She sucked in a breath. "No. Maybe tomorrow. I'll sit outside the gates, look at the house, remember some things."

"Makes sense. Just don't stay too long or think too much."

"I won't." Because things were getting too sentimental, she changed the subject. "Amanda Mae, I think it's finally sinking in that in eighteen months I'm going to be rich."

"I know."

"And I have to figure out how to manage that money so I don't lose most of it the way my grandmother did."

"Personally, I don't think you should have sold the stock. You should have waited around for the company to rebound and then been a real thorn in the Andreas brothers' sides."

Suzanne laughed in spite of the pain that crushed her

heart when she thought of the Andreas brothers, their wives, their babies. People who should have been her friends. They were lost to her now. "I don't want to be anything to them."

"Of course you do. I think that's the problem. You'd be part of their family if that stubborn old mule Cade wasn't such an idiot."

Suzanne smiled at the motherly tone in Amanda Mae's voice, even as the tears in her eyes spilled over. This time she didn't try to stop them. Mitzi was finally asleep so she wouldn't hear. And maybe a good cry was what she needed to get herself out of this maudlin mood?

"Look. I've gotta go. I'm really tired."

Amanda Mae sighed. "I should take a piece of that boy's hide."

"No. Let it go, Amanda Mae."

Suzanne clicked off, but Amanda Mae's eyes narrowed. Everybody in this town kowtowed to Cade Andreas, but Amanda Mae Fisher had long ago realized a woman had to fight for what she wanted.

She shrugged off her robe and threw it to her bed before she put on blue jeans and a T-shirt. It might be late, but she was mad.

When his doorbell rang after eleven, Cade cursed. He stormed up the hall, thinking the blooming idiot ringing his bell would wake Mitzi. Then he remembered Mitzi no longer lived with him. Sadness seeped into his soul, but he stopped it. Regardless of what his father-in-law thought, he couldn't get over leaving Ashley the day she died. Couldn't drag Suzanne into his life when his past relationship had been such a disaster.

He yanked open the door only to find an angry Amanda Mae Fisher on his front step.

"You are a freaking pain in my butt."

Cade stifled a long-suffering sigh. "Look, I know you're miffed. I know you want your partner back but—"

"I don't give a flying fig about having a partner. I ran that diner alone for fifteen years. I can run it alone another fifteen. But I do miss my friend." She stopped, sucked in a breath. "Cade, you know I haven't got any kids. And she was like my kid. In here—" she patted the spot where her heart would be "—I felt a connection. You know what it's like to be alone. Why would you force me to live without the chance to be somebody's mama, even if it is unofficial?"

Cade squeezed his eyes shut then popped them open again. Everybody was blaming him for Suzanne leaving, but it had been her choice. And didn't anybody see he was suffering, too?

"I don't know what you want me to do—"

"Go after her," Amanda Mae said, not giving him a chance to make any of his excuses. "It's you she wants. Sometime tomorrow she's going back to the estate she shared with her gram. She can't get inside, but she intends to spend some time sitting outside the gates, thinking about her past, remembering her gram. That poor kid's been through enough. Don't let her go on suffering just because you think you don't want her here."

The truth of that hurt his heart. He did want her here. He did love her. He'd realized that talking to Jim. But things between him and Suzanne were not as simple or cut-and-dried as Jim or Amanda Mae thought.

He'd had a great love and he hadn't been there for her when she needed him the most. Despite Jim's kind reassurances that haunted him. Hurt him. Held him back. Who was he to get a second chance at love?

He didn't deserve it and Suzanne deserved better.

Cade went to bed that night feeling cold and lonely. He crawled under the covers of the big bed that had been his and Ashley's, the only thing he'd brought from the master suite into his new room after her death.

Because he hadn't been able to sleep since Suzanne had gone, he didn't think he'd sleep that night, either. But he laid his head on the pillow and didn't have another thought. He immediately drifted off.

But it was a fitful sleep. A sleep filled with worry for Suzanne. He didn't know how much money she'd spent on the diner. How much money she had left. He hoped she'd have enough for a house but what if she didn't? What if she could only afford to rent a shabby apartment in a run-down section of the city? She'd be in an area potentially filled with drugs and gangs. And it would be his fault. His brothers would kill him. His sisters-in-law would skin him alive when they found out.

In his dreams they yelled at him. In his dreams, he didn't blame them. He worried about her. Feared for her. Chastised himself.

Then suddenly he was on his Appaloosa, riding. The wind billowed around him. Sun beat down on him. He knew the dream, knew that Ashley waited on the other side of this ride.

He gently nudged Sugar, urging him on.

As he approached the corral, he could see Ashley tending the flowers. He wouldn't get to talk to her. He wouldn't get much more than a few seconds to see her, still he nudged Sugar to go faster.

At the corral, he slid off the horse and stopped. He

raised his hand to wave the way he always did, and this time he didn't feel the silk pillow case. He didn't awaken.

Joy trembled through him.

"Ashley?"

She turned and smiled. His heart tripped over itself.

"Cade."

The sound of her voice was nearly his undoing. Joy and sorrow buffeted him like a ray of sunlight and an angry wind. He wanted to see her, talk to her, but he knew he didn't deserve it.

He took two steps over, but stopped, worried that if he got too close she'd vanish.

She smiled again, a warm, gentle smile that reminded him of just how young she was. How young she'd been when they'd married. How shy. How timid. By now, Suzanne would have come over, asked him a million questions. Maybe even kissed him. Ashley stayed where she was.

He swallowed. There was a gulf between them. Not just distance. Not even life and death. A real gulf. He knew her. He loved her. But not the way he knew Suzanne. Not the way he loved Suzanne.

She smiled again. Her head tilted to the side as if she were studying him, figuring something out. Then she raised her hand and waved slightly. "Goodbye, Cade."

Tears filled his eyes. "No." He stopped. He couldn't keep her. He knew he couldn't keep her. He swallowed once. Then whispered, "Goodbye, Ash."

When he woke, his room was totally silent. His weary body was relaxed. His weary mind sharp, alert.

He'd finally gotten to say goodbye.

* * *

The next morning, Suzanne awoke determined to find somewhere to live. Hotel rooms weren't cheap and, though she had money, she knew she couldn't stay in a hotel room forever. She wanted a house.

She woke Mitzi, fed her, bathed her and dressed her for the day. After checking out of the hotel, she took her meager possessions, mostly secondhand things she'd bought while in Whiskey Springs, and drove to a department store.

In a few months, she'd be filthy rich. She wouldn't squander what she had but, by God, she and Mitzi could at least not look like refugees.

In the store, she bought clothes for Mitzi, a stroller, a walker and two teddy bears. She bought shirts and jeans, shorts, skirts, tennis shoes and flat sandals for herself. And some makeup. She even found a salon and was lucky enough to get a walk-in appointment to have her hair trimmed.

With her hair coiffed, she asked for directions to the ladies' room and changed into a stylish skirt with a ruffled blouse very much like the one Whitney had worn the day she met her. As fascinated Mitzi watched, she put on makeup, fluffed out her hair and headed out to the parking lot.

Her Mercedes sat waiting. She stuffed all the bags she'd hung on the handles of Mitzi's new stroller into the trunk. Then she buckled Mitzi into her car seat.

Her intention had been to head for a real estate office to begin her search for a house, but when she reached a familiar off-ramp for the Interstate, she took it. She'd told Amanda Mae she wanted to say goodbye to her gram. And this morning she would.

Three turns got her on the road to her grandmother's

estate and twenty minutes later, she sat in front of the locked wrought-iron gate, staring at it.

She missed her grandmother. In all the hubbub of straightening out Martha Caldwell's beleaguered estate, she hadn't taken the time to grieve her loss. Looking past the gate to the big house beyond the long, well-tended lawn and flower beds, she couldn't actually see the small front stoop, but she could picture her grandmother sitting on the rocker beside the front door.

She snorted a laugh as tears filled her eyes. Her grandmother loved her front porch rocker, even though she was too far from the street to see anybody or for anybody to see her.

God, she was alone again. And she didn't want to be. She also didn't want to live in Georgia. She wanted to live in Whiskey Springs.

A soft tap on her window brought her out of her haze. She glanced over to see Cade. She didn't know how he'd known where she'd be, but he had. Joy filled her, then sadness. He might have found her, but she guessed Amanda Mae had sent him because he'd made it perfectly clear that he didn't want her.

She wasn't going back to the town where the true love of her life lived...especially since he didn't want her.

"Open the window."

"Go home, Cade."

"I can't go home. Amanda Mae has murder in her eyes. She blames me for you leaving."

Since she couldn't argue that. She didn't. She stared straight ahead.

He groaned noisily. "Come on."

She refused to even look at him.

"Please. We need to talk."

She still stared straight ahead.

"I talked with Ashley last night."

One of her eyebrows rose. Her curiosity was piqued.

Given that Ashley was no longer with them, at the very least, this would be a good story.

With a sigh, she opened her car door. He stepped aside and let her out.

"We had a busy morning. Mitzi's sleeping. I don't want to wake her."

She closed the door softly and faced him. Bad move. Not just because every hormone in her body sprang to aching life. But because he looked awful. Instead of his usual T-shirt and jeans, he wore pleated pants and a dress shirt. He had no hat so his hair blew in the slight breeze created by the overhang of rich green trees that surrounded her grandmother's property. His eyes were dull. Listless.

Talking to a ghost must not be pleasant.

"So?"

He peered over at her. "So?"

"How does a man talk to a wife who passed away?"

He winced. "I had a dream."

Her eyebrows rose.

"You don't understand." He swallowed. "Ever since Ashley died, I'd have this dream. In the beginning, I had it every day, then every week, then once a month."

She said nothing, only studied him. Birds chirped on the quiet street. A rare car drove by, forcing them to step off the road and to the sidewalk.

"I had the dream again last night. And this morning I realized I hadn't had the dream the entire time you were in town."

"Oh?"

He forked his fingers through his hair. "And last night the dream was different. I got to talk to her."

Gazing at her grandmother's house, a wave of empathy for him washed through her. What she wouldn't give for ten minutes with her gram. Just ten minutes to be able to say I love you and maybe hear the words again herself.

"Every time I have the dream, I walk over to her, hoping to say hello." He cleared his throat. "Hoping to get to say goodbye."

Her senses perked up. Things about his grief began to fall into place for her. "You never said goodbye, did you?"

He turned to her, his eyes flashing. "Don't feel sorry for me. I traded the chance to say goodbye for a business deal."

"No, you didn't. At least not on purpose. There was no way you could have known she would die that day."

He dragged in a breath. "She'd rebounded. She was happy. She shooed me off, saying I needed to get out of the house."

"Sounds to me like she was a really great wife." She shook her head. "Also sounds like you were around a little more than you thought."

"Maybe. Jim says I was. But I'm still something of a workaholic."

She laughed, stepped closer, put her hands on his shoulders to comfort him. She knew none of this had been easy for him. And the important thing was he'd come after her. "You could always change. A person who has billions of dollars doesn't have to work 24/7. He could take a day or a week or maybe even a few months off now and again."

He laughed, draped his hands around her waist. "Maybe." He swallowed. "I used to. Jim sort of reminded me of that, too."

She smiled softly, stepped closer. He felt so good, so strong, so real. "Maybe? There doesn't have to be a debate about it. You should just say yes." She shook her head. "You are a bit of a stubborn mule."

"So Amanda Mae says."

"You're also high-handed. Bossy. Arrogant."

"You think you can handle me?"

She laughed. "I left you, didn't I?"

His hands suddenly lifted from her waist. Slid up her back. Fell down again. "Yes. You did."

"I'm not sorry."

He laughed. "I didn't expect you would be."

"But I am coming back to Whiskey Springs." She peeked at him. "I like owning the diner. I like having my own things. A place in the world."

"I thought you wanted a place with me."

"I thought you didn't want me."

He leaned in, bumped his forehead to hers. "I do."

"You do what?"

"I do want you around."

"Are you asking me to live in sin?"

His head snapped up. His eyes narrowed. "You'd forgive me that easily?"

"Depends on what you say next."

He laughed, yanked her against him. "You're a smart, sassy, sometimes bossy woman who I think I love."

"Think?"

"Who I definitely love. I don't think I can live without you." He frowned. "No. I don't want to live without you."

Her chest tightened. It amazed her that he recognized the nuance of difference in those two statements. He was choosing her. Not being forced or compelled to love her. But choosing to.

A light, airy feeling invaded her.

"You've gotta say the words, Cade."

He brought her a tad closer. "What words?"

"Fooling around will not get you what you want."

"Fooling around is what I want."

She laughed. "Say the words."

He sobered. "I love you. I do. I want to raise your daughter, have six more kids—"

"Six?"

"Maybe seven."

Realizing he was giddy, she laughed. "Amanda Mae will shoot me."

"Only if you force her to be the one to bake the cinnamon rolls every morning." He paused, but only slightly. "Marry me?"

Her eyes filled with tears. "Really? You don't want an adjustment period."

"I hear it takes over a year to plan a wedding these days."

"It does, if you want to do it right."

"I want to do it right."

She pressed her lips together as the tears in her eyes spilled over. "So do I."

Then he kissed her.

EPILOGUE

DARIUS HAD MARRIED WHITNEY in the ballroom in the mansion of the Andreas family estate on Montauk. Suzanne had seen pictures of the elaborate, but quiet, event. Nick had married Maggie on the beach. She'd been there with them. She'd seen the sandals. Raised an eyebrow over the cutoff jeans Nick had worn.

So it seemed only fitting in Suzanne's eyes that she and Cade have a big church wedding, with a minister, Nick and Darius as groomsmen, Whitney and Maggie as bridesmaids and Gino as ring bearer.

In the bride's room of the huge old gray-stone church that looked more like a cathedral with its vaulted ceilings and regal pillars, Whitney fussed with Suzanne's hair while Maggie straightened the long train of her frilly white gown.

Suzanne sucked in a breath. "How's Liz holding up?" There were four kids now. Three-year-old Gino and toddlers Michael and Mitzi. Plus a baby, since Whitney had given birth to Elizabeth. Dressed in a tiny tux, Gino sat on a fancy Queen Anne chair, his little legs swinging, the pillow for the rings sitting on the counter beside him. But Liz still had three kids to watch until the formal ceremony was over.

"She's fine. She's got plenty of help from Mrs.

Reynolds and Mrs. Granger. Cade's den looks like a day care. I'm sure they're having a high old time. Stop fretting!"

She pressed a hand to her stomach. "I can't help it."

Maggie eyed her shrewdly. "Nerves or cold feet?"

"Just nerves."

Whitney laughed. "Afraid of marrying a multi-billionaire?"

She groaned. "I'm more afraid of marrying somebody so good-looking every woman in the world is going to try to steal him."

Maggie chuckled merrily. "Right. Cade only has eyes for you."

As if to confirm that, Cade caught Suzanne's gaze the second she and Marty Higgins stepped into the doorway of the big church and the organist began the chords of "Here Comes the Bride." A longtime friend of Cade's, constant diner customer and now the man dating Amanda Mae, Marty had volunteered to walk Suzanne down the aisle. His request for the honor had been every bit as sweet and sincere as Cade's proposal.

But at this second, she only saw Cade. As her designer gown swished softly on the silk runner that led her to the altar, she held his gaze, loving the way his eyes first skimmed her possessively, then softened with love when they locked with hers.

As she neared the end of the aisle, she looked over at Amanda Mae just in time to see her sobbing into a dainty pink hankie. She glanced at Jim and Audra Malloy and Jim winked at her, a private, special signal and she smiled, then she looked at Ginny, who sat in the seat in front of Jim and Audra. Ginny flashed her a grin before she too burst into tears. Audra Malloy tapped her on the shoulder and handed her a pristine white handkerchief. Sniffing softly, Ginny took it.

Suzanne finished her walk, nervously taking the hand Cade extended. The preacher opened his book and said, "Who gives this woman to be married?"

Marty choked out, "I do," then bussed a kiss across her cheek before he turned and took his seat with Amanda Mae.

She swallowed back her own tears. She'd entered this town a homeless orphan, a woman with no family, no friends. Now, almost one year to the date, she had a partner who acted more like a mom than a business associate. She had two best friends in Maggie and Whitney, and Nick and Darius, who would become real family when she married Cade.

Cade. The love of her life. Her reason to breathe. Her life partner. The man who'd given her a family and who would soon give her more children. Their house would be a noisy, happy place.

She couldn't ask for anything more.

No woman could.

THE ONE
THAT GOT AWAY

BY
JAMIE SOBRATO

All the characters in this book have no existence outside the imagination of the author, and have no relation whatsoever to anyone bearing the same name or names. They are not even distantly inspired by any individual known or unknown to the author, and all the incidents are pure invention.

First published in Great Britain 2011
by Mills & Boon, an imprint of Harlequin (UK) Limited,
Eton House, 18-24 Paradise Road, Richmond, Surrey TW9 1SR

© Jamie Sobrato 2010

ISBN: 978 0 263 88895 9

23-0711

Harlequin (UK) policy is to use papers that are natural, renewable and recyclable products and made from wood grown in sustainable forests. The logging and manufacturing processes conform to the legal environmental regulations of the country of origin.

Printed and bound in Spain
by Blackprint CPI, Barcelona

Dear Reader,

I love stories of second chances. Whether it be a near-death experience, a love lost then found, a phone call that changes one's life forever—or all three, as is the case in *The One That Got Away*. Such events have the power to transform people. I very much enjoyed exploring how Ginger, Marcus and Izzy are changed by each other and the events that bring them together.

Marcus, especially, is a man who needs to grow. Throughout the writing of this story, I imagined how it would feel to wake up in the hospital, having escaped death, and realize that no one cares enough to rush to his bedside. How would this change the choices he makes the second time around?

I love to hear from readers. You can reach me at jamiesobrato@yahoo.com or via my website, www.jamie sobrato.com, where you can also learn more about me and my upcoming books.

Happy reading!

Sincerely,

Jamie Sobrato

To Annabella Sobrato, who reminds me every
day how to live life with joy and passion

Jamie Sobrato lives with her two children in a Northern
California town not so different from Promise, where
she is at work on her next book. She loves to hike and
read good books, but not at the same time. *The One That
Got Away* is her twentieth novel.

PROLOGUE

Berkeley, California
Fourteen Years Ago

ONE MORE DRINK, and she would tell him.

Just one more very stiff drink, and he would finally know how she felt about him.

Terror, like a knife, sliced through her. Which was ridiculous. Marcus Kastanos was Ginger's best friend. She was closer to him than she was to any of her girlfriends. Often she didn't even know what she felt about things until she'd talked them over with Marcus. She shouldn't be hiding her feelings from him now, when it mattered most.

Maybe she should switch from beer to tequila.

She tried to get the bartender's attention by waving her empty beer bottle at him, but it was the end of the school year and the place was busy. He was focused on pouring drinks for a rowdy group celebrating graduation at the other end of the bar.

Her last night on campus, Ginger thought. She felt a torrent of mixed emotions. She was ready to move on after four years at UC Berkeley. She had completed her Bachelor's degree and was excited about starting grad school in Iowa in the fall to earn her Master of Fine Arts; getting into such a prestigious program had been a dream come true. But she also had to confront the fact that she had no home to go back to for the summer.

Her grandmother Townsend, who'd raised her since the death of her parents when she was nine, had died six months ago, and Ginger had no close family left. Marcus was leaving, too, on a trip around the world. This was the first summer she would be truly alone, and that left her feeling empty and scared.

"You look like you need another drink," Marcus said as he sat back down on the bar stool next to her. He'd just returned from the jukebox, where he'd spent the past few minutes pondering music selections.

"I definitely need another," she said, holding up the third bottle of Corona she'd emptied in the past hour. "But I'm making the next one a shot of Don Julio. Care to join me?"

He looked surprised. Marcus knew she didn't do shots unless she was totally stressed.

"Damn straight I'll join you."

Ah, Marcus. She could always count on him to make her feel better. At least for the moment.

She watched as he caught the bartender's attention, and she felt a mixture of affection and annoyance that the man immediately responded to tall, good-looking Marcus while he'd ignored, plain, wallflower Ginger. But that's how it always was—Marcus turned heads, while Ginger faded into the background.

With his adorably shaggy brown hair, piercing green eyes and naturally beautiful body, he was by far the prettier of the two of them. He was the beautiful swan to her ugly duckling. But Marcus saw past her frizzy hair and the extra pounds she tried to hide under baggy sweatshirts. He knew who she was on the inside. In fact, she was convinced he was the only person who truly understood her.

Unfortunately, he was dating someone else.

No sense in dwelling on the negative, though.

Not when this was the night. After four years together, she'd finally found the courage to tell him about the longing—and yeah, lust—she'd been feeling for him for so long she couldn't even remember when it had started. And okay, he might be surprised, but she was sure she hadn't misread the signals he'd been sending her lately.

Hadn't he said just yesterday that she meant the world to him? That she'd made his four years of college the best years of his life? He had never talked that way to her before, and she'd felt something significant shift between them. Surely she hadn't misread his meaning.

No, she was pretty sure he felt more for her than mere friendship.

He glanced over and flashed her a dazzling, heart-melting smile.

Yes. He definitely did. She could see it in his smile. And just as soon as she downed that shot, she'd tell him.

He slid one of the tequilas the bartender poured for him across the counter to her, and she buzzed with warm affectionate feelings.

"To graduation," he said, lifting his own glass to toast.

Ginger raised hers in return, then downed the drink in one long, fiery swallow. Marcus did the same beside her. Thank heaven for the agave plant and whoever had figured out how to make it into a beverage.

The burn of the liquor in her throat turned into

an overwhelming sensation of well-being and invincibility. It was just what she needed.

She could do this. She could tell Marcus how she felt.

She was going to do it.

Right now. This was it.

She caught his eye and let her gaze linger.

"You know," she said, leaning in close, "I've never had the guts to say this before, but I really love you."

There.

She'd done it.

The words had come out so easily, so naturally, she could hardly believe she'd waited this long. And when his eyes warmed in reaction, and his calm, easy manner remained unchanged, she knew she'd done the right thing.

He really did feel the same.

Joy sprang up in her chest like a geyser, and she wanted to leap off her bar stool and throw her arms around him.

He grinned, affecting the wavering posture of a falling-down drunk. "I love you too, *man*." He slurred the words purposefully. "You're the best."

His teasing performance shocked her back into sobriety.

He thought she was joking.

He didn't get her true meaning.

Oh, God. He didn't get it.

Heat rushed to her face.

She was the world's biggest fool. They'd been friends for years, and she'd never once had the guts to tell him the truth. Then yesterday, when he'd spouted a few clichéd words of affection, she'd grasped on to them desperately, convincing herself they'd held a deeper meaning, when all he'd really meant was that he was glad he'd had her as his emotional sounding board throughout college.

She was a fool and an even greater coward, hiding her true feelings behind their friendship. And she was never going to be happy.

Ever.

"Marcus!" a female voice cried from right behind them.

They both turned to find Marcus's girlfriend, Lisette Grayson, standing there, hands on hips, pretty face contorted into a frown.

"Why didn't you meet me at the apartment like I asked?"

"Is it that late?" Marcus glanced at the Budweiser clock on the wall, confused. "I'm sorry. I didn't notice the time."

He stood up from the bar stool and fished his wallet out of his pocket, then tossed a couple of twenties on the bar. "I'm sorry to rush off, Gin."

"It's okay," she lied, trying to put on a carefree expression.

Lisette, who'd never bothered to say more than five words at a time to her, simply turned and marched out of the bar, knowing without a doubt that Marcus would follow.

How did she get such confidence?

Ginger supposed it came with blonde hair, blue eyes, perfect features and a size 4 body.

Marcus paused, flustered. "She's still pissed that I'm going off on a trip."

Ginger knew exactly how Lisette felt. She didn't want to see Marcus go traipsing around the world for a year, either. Knowing him the way she did, she suspected he'd never come back. He'd find a nice little spot far away from the complications of real life and live happy as a clam. She'd been foolishly hoping that confessing her feelings to him would keep him from going—or even more foolish, cause him to invite her along.

But this was Marcus she was talking about. Thanks to his world-traveling hippie parents, he'd learned never to sit still for long. They'd taught him that the best solution to every problem was to leave it behind and ride off into the sunset.

"I guess this is goodbye, huh?" he said.

Tears sprang to Ginger's eyes. She didn't want to cry, not now. She refused to be the kind of girl that clung pathetically to a guy as he walked away. It was time for her to learn from her mistakes. She was never again going to let herself want someone who didn't want her.

"I guess so," she said, then hid her misery behind a fake smile.

"My flight to Paris leaves at six in the morning."

"I could drive you to the airport," Ginger offered, kicking herself even as she said it. She already knew Lisette had claimed the job.

"That's okay. You sleep in. You've earned it."

"Write to me, okay?" She hoped she didn't sound desperate.

He smirked. "I'll try. I'm not such a great correspondent."

"Take care of yourself, and come back, okay?" She said, refusing to accept that this might be the last time she ever saw him.

"You're asking a lot."

She laughed, though it came out sounding

forced. "Okay, don't take care of yourself, and don't come back."

"I think I can manage that."

He leaned in and gave her a long hug. Ginger clung to him as if her life depended on it.

Don't go, she wanted to beg. *Don't leave me here alone.*

"Try not to embarrass all those losers at the Iowa Writer's Workshop, okay?" He gave her shoulders a light squeeze as he released her.

"Oh yeah, like that's going to happen."

His smile disappeared. "You're brilliant," he said, sounding more serious that she'd ever heard him before. "Don't let any of those smug bastards convince you otherwise."

Ginger fought to get words past the lump in her throat. "This isn't goodbye, right? We'll see each other again, so no goodbyes."

He kissed her on the cheek, smiled and walked away.

CHAPTER ONE

MARCUS KASTANOS SAT on the set of the British news talk show *London Daily,* sweating a little under the glare of stage lights as hundreds of eyes from the studio audience stared at him.

He didn't consider promotion fun under the best of circumstances—and these were anything but ideal—but he knew his book was good. The story he'd told was an important one that people needed to hear, and for that reason, he'd do everything he could to make sure it got the exposure it deserved. The critical acclaim he'd received was nice, but it meant little if readers didn't know about the book and buy it.

Of course, the death threats were just about the best book promotion money couldn't buy.

If anyone had told him five years ago that he'd be living with a death sentence hanging over his head, he'd have laughed.

He still had trouble believing it.

But checking the street before he stepped outside, triple locking his doors, keeping his curtains drawn at night and traveling with a bodyguard had all become second nature for him the past year, ever since he'd first received the threats.

This wasn't his first time appearing on TV to talk about the political fallout from his novel, but today he felt more uneasy than he usually did, and he couldn't say why. He'd looked out his hotel room window that morning at the gray London sky and felt a bleak mood settle over him along with a more familiar restlessness. Probably the black mood and the edginess were inherited from his father.

The terrorist attacks in London in the past year only added to the anxiety that niggled constantly at the back of his mind.

But no matter. He was here, and he had his book to promote. *Seven Grains of Sand* had just come out in trade paperback a year after its hardcover release, and he wasn't going to cower in fear. The story had to be told.

"And we're on again in five, four, three, two, one…"

"Today we're here with American expatriate author Marcus Kastanos, talking about his controversial novel *Seven Grains of Sand,* and the death threats issued against him as a result of the book's publication."

The host, a man named Liam Parkinson, paused as the live audience applauded. Then he turned to Marcus.

"Thank you for joining us, Marcus."

"Glad to be here."

"As I read your book, I found myself wondering what led you to write a story about a Muslim woman struggling to shed her family's traditions. I'm guessing the book wasn't inspired by personal experience."

Marcus forced himself to grin at the question he'd already answered a million times. "In a sense, it *was* personal experience that led me to tell this story. I was involved in my twenties with a woman whose life wasn't unlike the heroine's in my novel. Her story always haunted me, and I've never been able to shake the anger I felt on her behalf when I listened to her describe what she'd gone through as a child growing up with the painful effects of female circumcision."

"Ah, yes. One of the more graphic parts of the novel—your description of that brutal procedure. Did you do any firsthand research?"

"Most of my research came from my former lover, who encouraged me to write the book, and medical and journalistic articles. I also had several people more familiar with the process than I am read the book for accuracy."

"And what about the now famous death threats? How has your life changed since you first received them?"

Another predictable question, but one Marcus couldn't really answer without putting himself in further danger.

"I'm a bit limited in where I go and what I do these days. I've also scratched all plans to travel to certain Middle Eastern or African countries."

Uneasy laughter from the audience.

"And how do you feel about—" The host's question was interrupted by the sounds of a scuffle in the audience and raised voices.

Marcus peered in that direction and caught the glint of light off metal. This couldn't be happening. Before he could react, the first shot exploded. Then another, and another.

Searing pain in his chest registered only after he was thrown backward against the chair.

In the uproar that followed, his sense of reality became a series of fractured images.

A hand. A leg.

The overhead lights were too bright.

Hey. He was lying down? Why?

Shouting. People all around him were shouting. He had to get up. See what the noise was about.

Ouch. Moving hurt.

His chest, wet and warm. And so painful.

Had he been shot?

He closed his eyes. Yeah. That was better. The noise and pain faded.

He was a kid. Playing. But where? Right. The commune. Oregon. That was chill, man.

No. Not Oregon. Amsterdam. High school. He was so mad. Just so pissed off at the world and his useless father. Didn't get out of bed for days. Depressed. Whatever.

Bed. Bed… Nice. All those hot girls. Berkeley. Good times. Classes. Lit. All those beautiful words. Pulling him in. Inspiring him…

Pounding out that stupid novel. Hours at the freaking computer. Hated it. Every painful second. But he had to do it…even if it hurt.

No. His *chest* hurt.

And why was it so cold? So freaking cold, and the lights…

The stupid glaring lights…

He closed his eyes.

Just let him sleep.

"Mr. Kastanos? Mr. Kastanos? Can you hear me?"

The woman's voice was unfamiliar. A British accent. A cool hand on his arm.

Marcus opened his eyes to see a nurse staring down at him. "Mr. Kastanos, can you hear me?"

He tried to say yes, but only a faint croak emerged from his throat. He struggled to work his head up and down in some semblance of a nod.

"Good. You're at Queen's Hospital. You've received a gunshot wound, but you're going to be okay."

Received a gunshot wound?

She made it sound as if he'd been given an award for good behavior.

"Marcus, thank God you're okay," said a voice from behind the nurse.

A familiar face hovered over her shoulder.

Who was that guy? He searched for a name to attach to the face.

Graham?

Yeah, that was right. Graham something. The publicist his publisher had hired.

Was he okay? Marcus wondered, struggling to sit up.

It was hardly the word he would have chosen for the way he felt.

"Mr. Kastanos," the nurse said, pressing gently

on his shoulder. "I'll send the doctor in to speak with you in a bit. For now, please keep yourself supine and try to rest."

She exited the room, leaving Graham to stare down at him. After waking up in a hospital bed, Marcus really felt that someone he loved should have been hovering over him with a worried look. Not his publicist, a man with a bulbous nose and the ugliest tie Marcus had ever seen. He'd only met the guy a week ago.

Maybe if he pretended to be asleep again, the publicist would go away. He wanted someone else here.

But who would he even call? Who would come?

Annika?

Where was Annika? He tried to remember. As a foreign correspondent, she traveled a lot.

Oh, now he remembered. She was in Beirut.

Not likely she'd drop everything and come rushing to his bedside, especially if he was, as the nurse had said, going to be okay.

"That was a right close one, old boy. But the doctor says the bullet went straight through you, missed all the messy bits and came out the other side."

"The bullet?" he tried to say, but his voice was a croaky whisper.

"What's that?" Graham said, leaning in closer.

"What *bullet?*" This time his voice was slightly more audible.

"You do remember being shot, don't you?"

No. Well, maybe… The flurry of fragmented images in his mind started to make sense.

"Do you remember being on the set of *London Daily?*"

Marcus nodded.

"And do you recall anything that happened—"

"Yeah." He closed his eyes as the memories came hurtling back at him, bringing with them a wave of nausea.

"They caught the bugger, you'll be glad to hear. He's in police custody."

Marcus struggled to formulate the question. "How'd he get a gun…inside…with all the security?"

"Unfortunately, the station's security weren't using metal detectors, so it wouldn't have been difficult to conceal a gun."

"No metal detectors?"

With his public appearance and the death threats issued against him?

"Sorry, old boy. Salman Rushdie was here just last year without incident and has a fatwa on his head. I suppose that made everyone a bit lackadaisical."

Graham pulled up a chair close to the bed and sat

down, then made a loud snorting sound and cleared his throat.

Charming.

"Say, do you want me to call anyone?" he offered. "Family? Friends? Let them know what's happened?"

Marcus closed his eyes. He didn't want to lie here staring at Graham, but he didn't want to be alone right now, either. Yet he had no family, no wife, no girlfriend unless he counted Annika, and he wasn't sure she wanted to be counted. How could he have never realized before that their relationship was pretty much a long-distance sex-buddy arrangement?

He couldn't think of anyone who'd want to jump on a plane and hurry to his side. Sure, he had friends, but…

The reality was, none of his friends were close enough to stay by his bedside.

Not a one.

And he knew why.

He left people behind. It was what he did, what he'd always done. It protected him from ever getting too close to anyone.

And now he had exactly what he'd always thought he wanted—no one. No emotional ties.

He'd succeeded at keeping everyone who ever might have gotten close at an impossible distance.

For the first time in years, he wished he hadn't.

"It'll be on the news," he finally said. "Anyone who cares can see it there."

But who would care, when there wasn't a person in the world who would beckon him to rush to his or her side in a crisis? He supposed he should feel lucky he had his paid publicist to keep him company now. Graham was better than no one.

CHAPTER TWO

"WHAT YOU HAVE HERE is a complete teardown."

Ginger Townsend pinned the contractor with a suspicious gaze, not believing him for a second.

"Excuse me?" she said calmly.

"You got rotting window frames, termite damage, a fifty-year-old roof, water damage, a master bath that needs major work—"

"I'm aware of all that. I told you about those problems over the phone, and I also told you this house has a sound structure that I think is worth preserving."

"Not with them termites." The balding, sun-weathered man tucked the pen he'd been scribbling with in the front pocket of his white T-shirt, and tore an estimate sheet from his note pad.

"There's not a house around here that doesn't have termite damage," Ginger argued. "Mine is limited to parts of the structure that can easily be repaired."

"Far as we *know,* it is. I'm just saying, this ain't gonna be a cheap job by any means. You might be better off starting over at the foundation."

Was the man being honest, or was this just his shtick for seemingly gullible female clients with limited knowledge of home renovations, who'd then rush to pay a fortune for his services?

She looked from him to the house, and they both stood staring up at the slightly sagging roof of the 1920s cottage on Promise Lake that Ginger had bought six months ago. She'd spent her life savings on the little house that was long on charm and short on practical features like central heating and insulation. But there was no way she could finance a full teardown.

"Um, well, thanks for your professional opinion," she said, deadpan.

Thanks a freaking million.

"Just callin' it like I see it."

"What does that mean for my leaky windows?" she dared to ask, already wincing at the anticipated monetary hit.

"Here's my estimate, but like I said…"

Ginger glanced at the figure he pointed to on the sheet and resisted the urge to throttle the man in his Winchell's Contracting shirt. She gritted her teeth and nodded.

It was a moment before she could speak. "Okay then. Guess I'll have to give that some thought," she finally murmured.

"Let me know if you decide to go forward with the repairs. My schedule fills up fast, so I'll need at least a month's notice, maybe more."

When Ginger was alone, she tore her forlorn stare away from the house that had become a money sink, and turned toward the closest neighbor's house. She wanted to talk to Ruby right now to get a bit of perspective. Ruby had known this house for decades, first as the owner and then as a neighbor. She'd know if it really required tearing down or if Mr. Winchell was just trying to drum up big-money work from a new-to-town greenhorn.

Ginger crossed the yard and went through the gate of the white picket fence that surrounded her elderly neighbor's property. Reaching the front steps, she was surprised not to see the older woman already peering out the front door, nosy as ever.

"Ruby?" she called through the open living room window. "Are you there?"

No answer.

"Ruby?" Ginger called again as she knocked on her neighbor's door.

Normally, no more than a single knock was required. Ruby tended to hover near the window at the slightest sign of guests, ready to pounce at the doorknob. With all of her family either dead or living too far away to drop by for an impromptu visit, the older woman relied upon neighbors like Ginger and friends from town for companionship.

Ginger made a point of checking in on Ruby every other day or so if their paths hadn't crossed for some reason. Ruby had quickly become like a grandmother to her during her short time in Promise.

She could hear the TV in the living room blaring, but detected no other signs of life.

Ginger tried the front door and found it locked. She knew Ruby tended to leave the rear door standing open to let in fresh air, so she circled the house, peering in windows, a sense of dread growing in her belly. No sign of Ruby, but when she reached the back door, she could hear water running in the hallway bathroom. She peered through the screen door and saw that water was pooling on the hardwood floor of the hallway.

"Hello? Ruby?" she called, more urgently now, trying the handle of the screen door and finding it, too, locked.

Her heart pounded as she jerked at the flimsy plastic handle, willing it to release. Finally, she gave it a mighty jerk with all her weight, and the latch snapped open, allowing her inside. She raced through the kitchen to the hallway, stepping carefully over the pooling water and into the bathroom, where she could see Ruby sitting on the floor in a green terry-cloth robe.

She was conscious, leaning against the bathroom wall. Water flowed over the top of the tub and onto the white linoleum floor around her.

"Ruby, are you okay?" Ginger said as she stepped around her and turned off the water.

"Oh? Hmm?" Ruby looked up at her. "What are you doing here, Ginger?"

She knelt down next to the older woman, her throat tight and her heart pounding. "Are you hurt?" she asked. "What happened?"

"Oh dear." Ruby frowned, looking more annoyed than hurt. "What on earth are you doing here?"

"I was about to ask you the same thing. Did you fall?"

"It's just terrible getting old." Her neighbor sounded disgusted.

"Have you hit your head?" Maybe Ruby was disoriented from a fall. That would explain why she was just sitting there while water flooded her hallway.

"No, no. I forgot I was filling the tub for my

bath, and when I came in, my feet went right out from under me."

"Did you hit anything on the way down?"

"Only my tailbone. I've been sitting here trying to decide if I feel like getting up again."

"Let me get some towels and dry the floor first, okay?"

Ginger opened the bathroom cabinet and pulled out an armful of towels, which she scattered on the floor around Ruby. Then she began sopping up the water. Ten towels later, she had the bathroom and hallway floors dry and had created a mound of sopping-wet towels in the now-drained tub.

"Okay, ready to stand up?"

It was disconcerting to see Ruby, normally spry and energetic, sitting on the floor looking so vulnerable. It reminded Ginger far too much of the other losses she'd suffered in her life—her parents, her grandmother. She didn't want to lose Ruby on top of everyone else.

"Don't you dare tell anyone about this," the elderly woman said as she extended her hands for help.

"My lips are sealed." Ginger knelt, placed her arms under Ruby's and carefully lifted her. She was surprised at how light the woman felt.

"I'm soaked," Ruby grumbled, sounding a little more like her old self.

"How does your tailbone feel? Do you think you can stand unsupported?"

"Let's give it a try."

Ginger let go, keeping her hands close in case Ruby became unsteady again. But she was standing firm, trying to straighten her soggy robe.

"Okay, now let's find you some dry clothes."

Her neighbor waved away the offer of help. "I'm fine. You go make us some tea and I'll get dressed."

"I'd better walk you to the bedroom," Ginger insisted, not convinced she could manage on her own. But Ruby was already elbowing past her, unwilling to be treated like an invalid.

Ginger gave a sigh of relief. That was more like the woman she knew and loved. She followed her down the hall to find the bedroom door swinging shut in her face.

"Let me know if you need any help," she called, then went back to the kitchen. The living room television was still on, and could be heard throughout the house, blaring the latest headlines on CNN. Ruby claimed the noise kept her company.

Ginger checked the kettle for water and turned on the burner under it. Then she got out cups, saucers, sugar and milk.

A moment later, Ruby came into the kitchen, already dressed.

"I'm sorry I'm such a mess—haven't had a chance to do my hair yet." She patted at the unyielding white bob that appeared only slightly less kempt than usual.

"You look fine," Ginger assured her. "I want you to let me know if you start to feel bad because of your fall. I'll take you to the E.R. anytime you want, okay?"

Ruby waved a dismissive hand. "Would you stop fussing over me and tell me why you had that work truck in your driveway first thing this morning?"

"I had a contractor over to look at the house and give me an estimate on some repairs. He said I need to tear down the place and start over."

Ruby scoffed. "These contractors—they all want your money. That house is as sturdy as the day it was built."

"That's exactly why I came over—to ask you what you thought." Ruby had lived in the cottage as a child and had been its owner until she sold it to a family twenty years ago. The parents, as they'd aged, hadn't kept up with repairs, and Ginger had bought the house from them knowing it was a fixer-upper—or at least that's what she'd thought.

Now she knew the full extent of what that term meant.

Two months ago a leaky roof and window, a few weeks after that a burst pipe in the kitchen wall. Then the discovery of termites, and the most recent surprise—most of the wood floor in the bathroom and one closet was rotten and about to give way under the weight of the tub and sink.

But oh, how beautiful the house was. Its pale weathered wood siding and gingerbread trim had a charm completely absent from any other home she'd ever had, and she loved the place deep down, as if it were a family member. Which explained why she'd been so put off by the contractor. It was as if he were advising her to pull the plug on Grandma.

Before Ginger could thank Ruby for her reassurance, a familiar name blared into her consciousness from the TV in the living room. She perked up her ears.

…*author of the controversial novel* Seven Grains of Sand, *shot on the set of a London morning news show…*

Marcus? Had they just said Marcus Kastanos?

Her Marcus?

Shot?

That's exactly what the report had said.

The news ricocheted around her brain for a startled moment, before her heart began beating double time and the reality of the words sank in.

She swung around and hurried into the living room, where the TV assaulted her with more awful details.

Terrorist...death threats...book tour...condition unknown...

The television screen now displayed a photo of the only man she'd ever loved, while the reporter stated the facts so dispassionately, they couldn't be real. None of this could be true.

Marcus.

Shot by a terrorist.

Condition unknown.

Suspect in custody...

No.

No, no, no, no, no.

As if she were the one who had been shot, a fast-forward movie of her friendship with Marcus played in her mind. Poetry readings, lazy coffee shop Sundays, hiking Mount Diablo, laughing at episodes of *The Simpsons,* daydreaming about being great writers someday...

"Are you okay, dear?" Ruby said from what felt like miles away. "You look like you've seen a ghost."

But she couldn't reply. She'd been propelled backward into her early twenties, when she'd been a naive girl in love with an undeserving guy. Her love for him had been deep, and heady, but completely foolish. She knew that now.

"Ginger, dear? What on earth is wrong?" Ruby sounded seriously concerned.

"I know him," she murmured.

"What's that?"

Ruby didn't have the best of hearing, and Ginger hadn't spoken loudly enough to be heard over the TV. The anchor had now moved on to a report about the latest financial news.

"I know him," she said again.

Ginger's heart continued to pound double time. She had to get away from the noise of the television, so she walked past Ruby, back into the kitchen.

"You know *who?*" her neighbor asked, following her. "That fellow on the news?"

"Marcus Kastanos. We were best friends in college."

"Well, isn't that the living end." Ruby frowned sympathetically. "I do hope he's okay."

Ginger had known about Marcus's controversial first novel—she'd read it, and thought it was brilliant—and also about the threats. She'd been afraid for him, but she'd never imagined...

It didn't seem possible.

Marcus, whom she hadn't seen since college,

was frozen in time for her, still the laid-back man-child she'd known and loved. But they'd lost touch. Marcus had never come back to the United States from his postgrad trip, and Ginger knew little more about his life than what she'd read in the author bio on his book jacket.

She'd last e-mailed him a year ago, a brief congratulations on his new book, to which he'd sent her a friendly but cursory reply. It hurt to be reminded how far apart they'd grown, so she hadn't made any effort to keep up the correspondence. It was easier not to.

Her hands shaking, she pulled a chair out from the table and sagged into it.

"You just take a few deep breaths," Ruby suggested in a voice meant to comfort. "I'll get you some water."

Marcus.

What if he wasn't okay? What if he—

She couldn't finish the thought, and the rush of emotion she felt at the possibility that he might die surprised her a little. She'd experienced enough death in her life to know all too well how it felt to lose someone she loved, but she didn't love Marcus in any active way now. And yet here she was, reeling as if she'd said goodbye to him yesterday.

This was ridiculous. Had she been kidding herself to think she'd moved on? No. Definitely not.

But still, she had to believe he was going to be okay. He was going to live. There wasn't any way life would deliver such a blow.

Except…she'd received the worst of blows already—the deaths of her parents and grandmother. Ginger knew firsthand how disinterested Fate was in the impact its twists and turns had made on her individual life. If Fate had ever cared for her personally she'd still have the family members she loved. And the words *shooter* and *Marcus* would never have been uttered in the same sentence.

Numbly, she took the glass of water Ruby handed her. Drinking down the cool liquid, she recalled the last time she'd seen Marcus, on the night of their graduation from UC Berkeley.

She'd insisted that night couldn't be a final goodbye, that they would see each other again.

The teakettle began to whistle, and the older woman turned off the stove and started making tea.

God, she'd been so foolish, thinking Marcus had wanted anything but her friendship, Ginger recalled. It still embarrassed her to remember how badly she'd misread him.

"I know!" Ruby exclaimed out of the blue. "He's that fellow, isn't he? The one you said you were in love with?"

There was nothing wrong with Ruby's memory.

"Yes," Ginger said, cringing inwardly.

"The one you said you left your fiancé for, because he could never measure up?"

God, her actions sounded so pathetic when put like that. She'd left Leo for a ghost, for a fantasy, for a love that had never been real, because it had never been reciprocated. But she'd known it was the right thing to do, because she hadn't loved Leo the way she should have—the way she wanted to love a man. And even though she knew Marcus wasn't the right guy for her, she had to believe there really was someone out there with whom she could share equally passionate feelings, not the lopsided kind she'd experienced thus far.

"I'm sorry, Ruby, I'm going to have to take a rain check on the tea." Ginger stood up, still shaky, and placed her now-empty glass by the sink.

"You're not going to go so soon?"

"I need to make some phone calls and find out about my friend," she said, her voice nearly breaking.

"Why don't you wait until you've calmed down a bit?"

"I…I can't. I'll come back in a little while, okay? I'll get all those wet towels out of the tub and hang them outside for you."

"Now don't you worry about that."

"It's okay, I'll come do it. Just give me an hour." And with that she headed out the back door.

She hurried across Ruby's lawn and her own, trying to think what to do. What made the most sense? Who could she call? How could she get in touch with the hospital in London?

How many other people would be thinking the same thing she was?

It wasn't as if Marcus belonged to her.

He didn't. And her feelings were a lost cause, but…

Ginger had long ago accepted her calling as a warrior for lost causes. Her house was a prime example. Any sensible person would have taken one look at the sagging roofline and moved on to buy a nice new house in the suburbs. But Ginger, either too brave or too foolish for her own good, had seen the house's history, its quirky handmade shingles and its beamed ceilings, and she'd been unable to resist the project of reviving it to its former glory.

She had no common sense, her granny Townsend had always said. But Ginger's grandmother, a bit of a romantic like her, had told her she had something better—*uncommon* sense. She'd said she could see things other people couldn't, which made her daring enough to try things other people wouldn't try.

Ginger supposed that was how she'd managed to make her living as a writer and adjunct college instructor. But it was also how she'd ended up with a house that needed more repairs than she could afford.

In all these years, she'd never let herself hope that Marcus might love her back, and she'd forced her heart to let go of the idea. Yet man after man hadn't been able to measure up to him, and now, years later, here she was alone and reeling at the news that he'd been injured.

She wanted to talk to Marcus, to see him, to get some assurance that he was okay. And maybe then she could make sense of this tumult of emotions she was experiencing.

But was she kidding herself? Were her motives really so pure, or did she actually want to see if there was any hope of her love being requited?

She went inside the house and down the hallway, straight to her office. Sitting at her desk, she brought her computer out of sleep mode.

Dear Marcus...

She began composing an e-mail to him in her head. I could hardly believe the news....

She made a face. No. She should call instead.

This kind of event required a phone call. Even an in-person visit. Maybe she'd fly to London. No, no, she was getting way ahead of herself. That was a crazy idea.

She didn't even have his phone number anymore. But she had his e-mail address.

So it would have to be an e-mail, for now.

Dear Marcus, she began again. I was so worried when I saw the news....

CHAPTER THREE

MARCUS LOOKED OUT THE small window as his plane dropped from its cruising altitude and a brown landscape came into view down below. Dry hills, a scattering of tiny houses, the piercing blue California sky all around him for the first time in years.

He should be happy to be returning to the United States. He was alive after the worst ordeal of his life.

One bullet cleanly through. Thirty-two stitches. Two weeks in recovery.

More concerned phone calls than Marcus would have expected, and an in-box full of mostly unread e-mail messages bearing headers such as I'm so glad you're okay! and I heard the news....

He hadn't had the stomach to read his e-mail for a week after getting back home to Amsterdam, because one phone call in particular had left him reeling, and he'd known an e-mail with an attached photo would be waiting for him in his in-box.

And when he'd finally opened it and seen the picture, he'd known it was all true. The face, the spitting image of his own mother as a little girl, was painfully beautiful to him.

It had been surreal hearing Lisette's voice after all these years. But it hadn't been her voice at all. Only one that sounded like hers.

Like hers, but different.

Younger.

The girl had seen the news about him and felt she had to call. She wanted to meet him.

Her name was Isabel.

Isabel Dawn Grayson.

Izzy for short.

She was thirteen years old.

The facts all lined up in his head, neat and orderly, but that didn't mean they made sense. His brain hadn't assimilated the idea that he was a father, that there was a kid in the world with his blood coursing through her veins.

But that hadn't been the only shocking news. Her mother, Lisette, was dead. Died three months ago of ovarian cancer.

Marcus hadn't talked to Lisette in the fourteen years since their breakup after college. Hadn't known he'd left her pregnant with a child. Hadn't even been able to make sense of the hows and whys of it all until a woman named Nina, Izzy's legal guardian and godmother, had gotten on the phone after Izzy and cleared up some of the details.

So now he not only had a daughter he'd never met before, but was also a single father. All in one fell swoop.

The impact of the revelations had left him reeling ever since the phone call, and he'd already been in a state of shock at finding himself flat on his back in the hospital thanks to a lone nut job with a gun.

If Marcus had been the mystical, spiritual thinker his parents had raised him to be, he'd have believed the universe was trying to tell him something big. But one element of his parents' philosophy had gotten through to him: he did believe in Fate. And Fate had handed him not only a second chance at life, but a chance to know the daughter he might never have otherwise met. Fate had made him a father, and he was going to make the best of these new circumstances in his life, no matter how radical a change from his previous reality it all was.

Izzy had said she wanted to spend the summer with him.

Maybe longer.

And he was on his way to meet her and start being her dad.

She'd been living in San Francisco with Nina for the past few months, but she hated the city. She'd spent most of her life on the rural California coast near Santa Cruz with her mom, and she was intimidated by the noise and the hustle and bustle of people everywhere.

The plane touched down on the tarmac of San Francisco International Airport right on schedule, and Marcus's stomach pitched. He was terrified.

No, he couldn't focus on his fear. It was only going to freak him out. He needed to concentrate on the pleasant, comforting parts of returning to the country he'd left.

There was Ginger, whom he'd always regretted losing touch with. She reminded him of his days at Berkeley. Those four years were probably the happiest in his life, and if he hadn't been such a lousy correspondent, he might still have been able to call her his best friend. She'd been the most sincere, solid person he'd ever let himself get close to. She was far more solid than him. He had always felt a little like a dry leaf to her oak tree…as if he might drift away with a strong wind, whereas she was rooted and strong, and would still be standing tall a hundred years from now. He realized that he'd always taken her for granted. She wasn't an oak tree—she was a special person who deserved better than a friend who never called or wrote.

It would be great to see her and catch up on all that had happened in the last fourteen years. And they were going to have a whole summer to do it, since she was opening her home to him and Izzy. He'd felt a little uncomfortable asking if she'd mind letting them stay for a week or so while he looked for a place, but when she'd suggested they stay the whole summer, he was reminded yet again of what a good friend she was. He had ulterior motives: Ginger was the one person he knew who might be able to help Izzy make sense of her mother's death, since she knew what it was like to lose a parent.

Warmth filled his chest when he thought of Ginger's kindness, of how insistent she'd been that having two houseguests for the summer would be no trouble at all.

There. That's what he needed to focus on. Happy thoughts.

Hers had been the most welcome of all the e-mails he'd found waiting for him upon his return to Amsterdam after the hospital stay. He'd called her right away and, without thinking twice, asked her for that huge favor, never really doubting that she'd be willing to help. Now that he'd stared death in the face, he understood the priceless value of such a good friend, and he promised himself he would never take her for granted again.

So she was meeting him at the airport, driving him to pick up Izzy and taking them to her house for the summer.

Ten minutes later he was hauling his carry-on bag through the concourse, following the signs pointing to the baggage claim area.

Taking in the sights and sounds of America again for the first time in so many years overwhelmed Marcus with a rare bout of nostalgia. The orderly bustle of American travelers, the sounds of English being spoken… He'd been in San Francisco International Airport countless times, but this time felt different. It was as if he were running away from his old life and the dangers it held. No, not really running away so much as leaving behind an old life for a new one that Fate had insisted upon.

And perhaps more importantly, there was the feeling of anticipation of what was to come. His life as he knew it was about to be dramatically altered, not by a gunshot wound but a thirteen-year-old girl.

His stomach roiled at the thought. For the first

time, the decisions he made about his life, his career, would affect someone else as much as they affected him. His daughter's life was in his hands, and it was a responsibility he wasn't sure he knew how to handle.

Marcus tried to find solace in the wide-open faces of the Americans he passed. Faces of every color, they held a quality not found in the more cautious, businesslike expressions of the Dutch or other Europeans.

He passed a couple of airport shops and was bombarded by the shiny commercialism that also managed to top that of the Dutch by miles some-how. The products were more numerous, the food more varied, the magazines glossier, the women on the covers more unreal.

And then he was descending an escalator, and his nervous energy doubled. Ginger had said she'd meet him near the escalator outside the baggage area. He scanned the crowd, looking for her sig-nature curly auburn hair. When his gaze landed on a woman with exactly that hair color, for a mo-ment he glanced away, sure it wasn't his old college pal.

But the recognition he'd seen in her own gaze caused him to glance back. Impossibly, it was her.

She looked nothing like she had in college. This woman, this grown-up Ginger….

No, it couldn't be.

But she smiled and waved and called his name. "Marcus!"

It *was* her.

He flashed a confused smile and stepped off the escalator to find himself enfolded in the embrace of a woman he barely recognized. Hugging her back, he fought to overcome his shock at the change in her appearance.

All of a sudden she pulled away. "Oh! I forgot your wound. Is it okay to hug?"

He laughed. "Don't worry. My shoulder is mostly healed. There's still a bit of pain but nothing to mention most of the time."

"Wow," she said, taking a full step back to scan him up and down. "It's so good to see you! You look exactly the same."

"Liar. But look at *you*. I didn't even recognize you."

Ginger blushed. "Oh, well, I guess I finally lost the oversize sweatshirts and perpetual ponytail."

"And the glasses, and—" He stopped short, not sure what else to say except that she simply seemed…different.

She'd always been on the curvy side, and he suspected her generous breasts used to cause her a great deal of embarrassment—hence the bulky sweatshirts that hid her figure. But now she stood proud and tall, her chest lushly displayed in a stretchy green top and her rounded hips accented nicely by a fitted denim skirt.

Her hair, which she wore down, cascaded over her shoulders in luxurious waves, and something about her expression and her posture made it clear that she'd grown up a lot in the years since they'd last seen each other. Gone was the awkward coltishness of her early twenties. She now had the air of a woman who knew who she was and what she wanted.

She shrugged, growing a little self-conscious under his scrutiny. "It's been too long." She turned her attention to the baggage claim area, glancing at the nearest display screen of arriving flights. "Do you have any luggage checked?"

"Nope. I've got everything right here," he said, indicating his laptop bag and carry-on suitcase.

"Still traveling light," she said, laughing.

"Backpacking taught me that."

"And what time do you need to pick up your—" She faltered, probably as shocked as he was at the situation. "Your daughter? What's her name again?"

"Isabel. I told her I'd be there around noon."

"In the Marina District?"

"That's right. The house is off Divisidero. I've got the address in my pocket."

She glanced at the small silver watch on her wrist. "It's almost eleven. Plenty of time."

As they headed for the nearest exit, Marcus resisted the urge to pepper Ginger with questions about her life. He felt bad for not having stayed in touch with her over the years, but he also knew Ginger well enough to realize she probably didn't hold it against him. She knew he was laid-back—maybe even lazy, he admitted—when it came to relationships, but in college she'd easily accepted his shortcomings.

When they reached her car, a white Toyota Prius, she opened the trunk for him to stow his bags.

Once they were in motion, she posed the obvious question as she navigated through the parking garage. "So, how are you feeling about meeting Isabel?"

Marcus's mouth went dry. "I'm terrified, of course. What if she doesn't like me or…"

"Or you don't like her." Ginger filled in the blank.

That was what he'd always loved about her. She could see straight to his heart.

"I wasn't going to say that, but yeah."

She shot him a sympathetic glance. "It's a valid worry, I think."

"You don't have any kids yet, right?"

Ginger barked out a surprised laugh. "No, none for me. I'm pretty sure I'd have already mentioned them if I had any."

"I guess so," Marcus said, wondering if he should pursue the subject. But he'd never felt the need to hold back with Ginger. "I'm surprised. I always thought you'd make a good mom."

"I'm only thirty-five—I've got a few eggs left in me," she joked.

"So you haven't even gotten married, huh?"

"I came close a few years ago, but…" Her voice trailed off uncertainly.

"Who left? You or him?"

"It's hard to say." She frowned, her eyes focused on the road ahead.

"Why'd you break up, then?"

"We were trying to adopt a baby from China, and when we found out we'd have a better chance if we got married, I got cold feet. Then Leo got mad and decided he didn't want to be with me if I didn't want to marry him."

"Wow," Marcus said, his thoughts tripping over what different paths their lives had taken. "I'm sorry."

"It's okay. Better off finding out sooner than later that we weren't right for each other."

"And the adoption? Are you still trying to do that?"

Ginger shrugged. "I'd still like to, but I'm flat broke since buying my house, and foreign adoption is an expensive process."

Silence filled the car for a few awkward moments.

He would have to get to know Ginger all over again, he realized now. She wasn't the same idealistic girl he'd gone to college with. She had a lifetime of experiences that he didn't know about.

"Have you seen any photos of Izzy?" she asked out of the blue.

"Yeah, she e-mailed me one. She's pretty. Dark hair, dark eyes, pale skin. She looks exactly like my mom did at that age."

"Does she look like you at all?"

"She does. It freaks me out a little, I'll admit."

"You have every right to feel scared and freaked out and anything else right now. It's a big deal discovering you have a kid you never knew about, and it's an awful thing that Lisette never told you."

"I guess. I mean, at the time, I'm not sure if…"

He trailed off, ashamed to say the words aloud. He didn't even know if what he was about to say was true, anyway. What *would* he have done if Lisette had told him she was pregnant? Would he have had the courage to stick around and be a father when what he'd really wanted to do was travel the world and be responsible only for himself?

It was an impossible question to answer now.

"I'd like to think that if I'd known about her, I'd have been a good father, but I don't know."

"I'm sure you would have been, Marcus—I don't have any doubt," she said with far more certainty than he felt.

"But Lisette and I were finished anyway. There's no way we could have stayed together for the sake of a baby, and I'm sure that's why she didn't tell me, you know?"

"I know, but it was still despicable not to say anything—not to give you the option of being a part of your daughter's life."

"I guess she was scared. And angry. I got the *Reader's Digest* version of events from a friend of hers who's Izzy's guardian now."

"Sure she was scared, but still…" Ginger's voice sounded a little odd.

If Marcus hadn't known better, he'd have suspected she was uncomfortable with the subject.

As she navigated through traffic, he studied her profile, still stunned at what a beautiful woman she'd become. And yet it was hard to put his finger on anything profoundly different. There were simply a lot of subtle changes that added up to a profound transformation.

Forcing his gaze away from her so that he wouldn't be caught staring, Marcus took in the sights of South San Francisco. This area north of the airport had never been known for great character or charm, but he felt a little tight in the chest to be here again. His parents were bohemian drifters, so he'd grown up never spending too long in one place, but cliché as it sounded, his heart had always called San Francisco home.

And here he was again.

Once Ginger was cruising on the highway and could divide her attention between driving and talking again, she cast a glance at Marcus.

"So Lisette died of ovarian cancer?"

"Yeah." A new weight settled on Marcus's chest.

He no longer held any romantic feelings for the woman, but it hurt in an oddly distant way to know she was gone. What was more painful, though, was knowing he'd never be able to talk to her about Isabel. He couldn't ask Lisette about their daughter's childhood—what her first words were, or what she'd been like as a little girl, or whether she'd suffered not having a father around.

That was all lost to him, but he wouldn't lose any

more time with his daughter. Somehow, he had to find a way to fit this child into his life.

"I'm sorry," Ginger said quietly.

"It's weird, you know. If I hadn't been shot in London, I wouldn't have found out that Isabel exists. She wouldn't have contacted me if she hadn't seen the news."

"I'm sure she would have. Maybe not now, but eventually."

"Who knows how many more years I'd have missed out on."

"So it's kind of a weird blessing, what happened, huh?"

"Yeah, I mean, I never would have thought being shot could be a good thing, but in some crazy ways it changed my life."

There was a moment's pause, then Ginger said, "I guess I wouldn't have gotten back in touch with you, either."

"I'm glad you did." That was one thing Marcus had no doubts about. "It was scary, lying in that hospital in London and realizing I didn't have any next of kin to call."

She said nothing, and an awkward silence grew between them. Ginger was too kind to point out the obvious—that it was Marcus's own fault he was close to no one. He might not have had control over the fact that his blood family had dwindled over the years, but he had only himself to blame for not staying in touch with all of his friends.

"Who *did* you call?" she finally asked.

"My publisher—since the book tour had to be cancelled."

"Oh."

Another awkward silence.

"I'm sorry," Marcus finally said, surprised at the emotion in his voice. "It was my fault we lost track of each other, and I really appreciate your helping me out now, even though I don't deserve it."

"It wasn't your fault!" She glanced over at him again, this time incredulous. "I mean, there are two of us here and we're both capable of making a phone call or writing a note."

"Sure, but—"

"There's no point in assigning blame. I'm so glad you're safe and back in the U.S., I don't care what happened, you know?"

Her voice sounded so much like the old Ginger he'd known back in school that he laughed. "I do. There's nothing like a near-death experience to remind you what's important."

"And Isabel," she said carefully. "Do you think she's angry with you?"

"For what?"

"For not being around."

"But how could I have been?"

"That's how an adult would think about things, but a child might see things differently. She might feel betrayed anyway."

Marcus hadn't considered this, and it gave his stomach something new to cramp up over. "I don't know what Lisette told her about me. I guess some of it might not be so great."

"Perhaps. Or even if she didn't say anything negative, Isabel might have read between the lines in an unfavorable way. Who knows?"

"Yeah," he said weakly.

"I don't mean to be pessimistic," Ginger added. "I only want you to be prepared for possible difficulties. Probably things will be fine."

She guided the conversation toward more neutral topics, filling him in on the classes she taught at the community college, the writing she'd been doing, the whereabouts of their college classmates, sprinkling in interesting gossip whenever she had any to share. But Marcus was barely paying attention. He knew she was trying to distract him, to get his mind off more troubling matters, and he appreciated her effort, yet he couldn't keep his thoughts from dwelling on the daughter he was about to meet.

As the minutes ticked by and they made their way through the city toward Isabel, Marcus found himself paralyzed with anticipation and dread the likes of which he'd never experienced before.

Not even the price on his head had scared him like this, because of course, the death threat affected only him. But this—this fatherhood thing—meant that his actions from this point on really mattered, that whatever he did affected not only him, but a child who needed him. A child who'd just lost her mother.

The ride passed too quickly, and when Ginger pulled into the driveway of the address Isabel had given him, he shuddered. A three-story Edwardian row house loomed before them, inside of which his child was waiting.

Okay, deep breaths. In, out, in, out.

He could do this. He could meet her. He wouldn't run away this time.

It was too late now, anyway.

CHAPTER FOUR

Izzy watched the car pull into the driveway, and her stomach did that thing where it felt like it was turning inside out. Then she watched *him* get out of the car. He looked nothing like she'd imagined.

Which was weird, since she'd seen some pictures of him on the Internet. His author publicity photo showed only his face, though, and now, seeing him strolling up Nina's driveway, she realized he was much bigger than she'd thought.

Her mom's last few boyfriends had been small men who talked about wine too much and worried a lot about keeping their shoes neat and their clothes lint free. She'd started thinking that kind of guy was her mom's type or something. She'd started thinking her mom had bad taste in boyfriends.

But this guy…this guy who was supposed to be her dad, Marcus Kastanos—would she want to change her name from Grayson to Kastanos, even though it sounded weird?—he looked like the opposite of a guy who talked about wine and worried about his clothes.

She heard the knock at the door and felt like puking.

Oh, God.

This was it.

Ever since the first moment she'd realized other kids had one dad and one mom or two dads or two moms or a houseful of moms and aunts and whoever else to care for them, she'd desperately wanted to meet her own father.

Well, she'd wanted to and she hadn't wanted to. Her mom had told her stuff. She'd said he wouldn't be a good dad. That he wasn't that kind of guy.

And now he was here, coming to take her off for their own little summer getting-to-know-you party. Why had she even suggested it?

But if he wasn't a dad kind of guy, then what? Should she even go?

She couldn't do it. She didn't know this guy. He didn't know her.

This whole meeting thing was a terrible idea. Why had she phoned him?

She stood up, walked across the room and locked her door.

Then she went into her bathroom and cried.

She buried her face in Nina's thick gray towels to drown out the noise of her pathetic sobbing, she had a moment of totally hating that she was messing up her carefully applied eye makeup, but she kept right on crying.

She hated the guy downstairs for not having stuck around when she was born to get to know her, to find out what a great person she was. He'd just disappeared. He'd been sure he wouldn't love her and he'd taken off.

He was a loser.

Well, maybe that wasn't fair. He hadn't known about her, so she couldn't really blame him for not sticking around.

And she hated her mom for dying. This was the thing she'd never said aloud in her own head before. It was an ugly dark cloud that had been lurking in the back of her brain, waiting for the right moment to move in and make everything even more screwed up.

Izzy sank onto the floor, taking the towel with her. Her chest was doing this weird heaving, shuddering thing, and she needed to blow her nose, and she was drooling.

Not pretty.

She heard someone knocking on the bedroom door and calling for her to come out. It was Nina.

"Izzy? Are you in there? Can you open up, please?"

She didn't have anything against her. Nina was her godmother and her mom's friend, and she'd been nice to Izzy. Too nice, even. Since she didn't have any kids of her own, Nina didn't know what to do with a teenager who'd just landed in her house, motherless and devastated. So she had bought Izzy stuff and tried to soothe her by taking her out to fancy restaurants. She'd even suggested the two of them take a trip to Hawaii or Paris or wherever Izzy wanted to go.

But it was weird. Izzy didn't want anything, and she didn't want to go anywhere. She barely wanted to get out of bed in the morning, but she didn't think about her mother much, either. Whenever a memory of her mom slipped into Izzy's head uninvited, she'd force herself to think about something happy, like her dog, Lulu, when she was a puppy and so small she could fit in Izzy's palm.

Right now Lulu was downstairs in a pet carrier next to her suitcase, waiting to be taken on the trip. Izzy wished she hadn't corralled her in that stupid carrier already. She'd have felt a little better if Lulu was in her lap now, staring up at her with her brown cow eyes.

Why had she freaked out like this? Especially now, after all the other stuff that had happened.

Izzy figured that once a kid's worst fear comes true and her only parent dies, and she survives the pain of it, or at least is pretty sure she's surviving, she starts to think nothing can shake her. She starts thinking maybe she's invincible, like some starry-eyed superhero.

But maybe the opposite happens. Maybe when the worst of it is already over, that's when a person falls apart.

Izzy swiped at the drool on her chin with the towel. Her breathing was coming out all shuddery, and she was pretty sure her face looked so puffy it would take her an hour to get it back to semi-normal.

"Izzy…honey…please open up!"

The "honey" part of Nina's plea sounded a little awkward, because she wasn't the kind of person who called people things like that. Izzy figured that even shortening her name to Izzy, as she preferred, must test Nina's preference for formality. Nina had been good to her, but Izzy could tell her godmother was more comfortable bestowing love on the two cats who loathed Lulu's presence than on a teenager, and Izzy didn't really blame her, since Nina had no kids of her own to practice on.

"Izzy, please let me know you're okay, at least. I'm going to have to pick the lock if you don't."

Oh, God. She wasn't ready to face anyone.

"I'm fine!" she lied, but the weepy sound in her voice told the truth.

She could hear Nina talking to someone in the hallway, and then footsteps retreated down the wood staircase. Izzy knew she couldn't stay hiding out in the bathroom forever, so she pulled herself up and took a good hard look in the mirror.

Yikes.

She splashed cold water on her face, hoping to rid her eyes of some of their puffiness. Then she went to work on repairing her makeup. She didn't wear much—just a bit of mascara, eye liner and blush. Nina insisted she didn't need it, but Izzy thought it made a difference. She figured if she had to go to her own mom's funeral, she got to decide whether or not she wore makeup, and Nina seemed to sort of agree, even though she didn't like it.

There was still a shaky feeling in Izzy's belly when she was done, but she didn't feel quite as bad as before. She guessed she needed to let out some of the sheer terror.

But now…

Now she had to face *him*.

MARCUS HEARD THE SOUND of whimpering and looked down to see that there was something brown and wiggly in the pink duffel bag on the ground. Upon closer inspection, mesh panels revealed what looked like a small dog. He knelt down and murmured some soothing sounds to the dog. He suddenly recalled Izzy asking if she could bring her pet along, though in all the upheaval of the past few weeks as he'd prepared to leave Amsterdam, he'd managed to forget they would have a dog along on the trip.

Had he even asked Ginger if she'd mind having a dog at her house?

"That must be Lulu," Ginger said, her memory obviously better than his. "Do you think she'll bite if we try to get her out?"

"Maybe that's why Izzy has her in this travel bag."

Ginger knelt beside the bag. "She looks harmless enough."

"Famous last words," Marcus joked, in spite of his grim mood.

He could tell by Nina's tone as she called through the door that things weren't going well upstairs. And he had no idea what to do. He didn't know how to be a dad, and he wasn't technically anyone's dad except when it came to biology, so he was pretty sure going up there would only make things worse.

He'd opted to stay put for the moment.

When Nina came back downstairs a few minutes later, her expression twisted in a tense smile, Ginger rose from her perch beside the dog.

"Is she okay?" Marcus asked.

Nina sighed heavily. "I'm sure she's about as okay as she can be given the circumstances. I think she's just having a little bout of cold feet."

"Should I go try to talk to her?" he suggested. "Or maybe leave and come back when she's feeling better?"

"I don't have a clue."

The sound of a door opening echoed down the stairway, and a moment later a pair of feet clad in brown suede moccasin boots came into view. A tall, thin girl with a heavy curtain of dark brown hair descended the stairs. She resembled the photo in Marcus's e-mail in-box, but she didn't.

What took his breath away most was how much she looked like him. Like a small, wiry girl version of him in a purple tunic sweater and skinny jeans.

Big, sad brown eyes so like his own stared back at him, seeming to take in the same truth he'd just registered—that there was no doubt who was related to whom.

"Isabel—I mean Izzy," he said. "Hello."

His voice came out sounding stilted, too formal. Marcus wanted to kick himself. He'd rehearsed this meeting in his head at least ten different ways. He could hug her, or shake her hand, or hold back and see what she was inclined to do, or make a joke to ease the tension, or any number of other things, but not one of them struck him as the right thing to do at the moment.

Izzy solved the problem for him by eschewing contact entirely and kneeling beside the doggy travel bag. She unzipped it and withdrew the tiny brown mutt, which looked to be part Chihuahua and part something else. The dog shivered in her arms as it gazed up at her adoringly and licked at her chin.

"This is Lulu," she said.

Marcus reached out and stroked the dog behind its small, floppy ears, grateful for something to do with his hands. He watched the girl's expression relax as she focused on the dog. Then she glanced nervously at Ginger, the one person in the room she didn't know.

"This is my friend Ginger," Marcus said. "We'll be staying at her house."

Ginger smiled warmly. "It's nice to meet you, Izzy. I think Lulu is going to love playing at the lake. Does she like water?"

Izzy grimaced. "She's afraid of water."

"Oh, well, that's okay," Ginger said.

Nina jumped in to rescue the situation. "Maybe I could help you load bags in the car, Ginger."

The two women each picked up a suitcase and went out the front door, leaving Marcus alone with Izzy.

"I know this is hard for you," he said. "Do you feel okay coming with me now, or—"

"It's fine," she said tightly. "Nina has to leave on her work trip to New York, and she said I can't stay here alone. She wanted me to go with her, but I don't want to."

"I'm glad you found me, Izzy," he said, trying to make eye contact. "We're going to have a good summer getting to know each other."

She avoided his gaze by keeping her focus on the dog, but after a few moments of awkward silence she glanced up at him, and he could see the sheer terror in her eyes. Also a bit of defiance, and a healthy dose of sorrow.

How did he go about making the acquaintance of a hostile teenage girl who'd just lost her mother?

He hadn't a clue.

Perhaps he should have read a book, or consulted an expert, but now it was too late....

"Do you like animals?" she asked.

"Um, yeah, sure."

"Are you just saying that? Do you have any pets of your own?"

"I don't have a pet, no."

"Why not?"

"I guess, you know, it's a big commitment. I travel a lot. It would be hard."

"Kind of like having a kid would be hard?"

"Sure, but—look, I'll have to change my life around a bit, but of course I'm glad to. I want you to feel welcome."

"Nina doesn't like having a dog in the house. She's too nice to say so, but she doesn't."

"Izzy, I'm happy to have your dog live with us, okay?"

"You have to say that."

"I mean it."

He felt off-kilter due to the strong undercurrent in their conversation, not quite sure if they were really talking about whether the girl or the dog or both were welcome in his life.

She glared at him with poorly concealed mistrust, then returned her attention to stroking the dog. Lulu had stopped shivering and was resting comfortably in her arms. Marcus was overcome with a wave of inexplicable gratitude for the mutt's presence.

Ginger and Nina reentered the foyer, and Izzy seemed eager to get going.

"Um, well, we should leave, right?" she asked.

"I thought you'd stay and have coffee," Nina said, glancing nervously around the group.

"Can we just get this over with?" Izzy said. "Your plane leaves in a few hours and I'm going to puke if we have to stand around like this much longer."

Marcus silently agreed with her, but at the same time he didn't want to rush her out the door. It seemed such an abrupt transition from a familiar place and person, to a world of strangers.

Nina sighed. "I guess we'll all avoid the rush-hour traffic if we head out earlier rather than later. Are you sure?"

Izzy shrugged. "Whatever."

She and Nina hugged briefly.

"Call my cell phone anytime you want, okay? Anytime. I mean it."

"Okay," Izzy said, sounding listless.

"I want to hear all about Promise Lake. And if for any reason you need to see me, I'll fly you to New York, or I'll come up to Promise once I'm back, okay?"

"Okay."

They said their goodbyes and piled into Ginger's car, Izzy in the backseat with the dog.

This wasn't going the way Marcus had envisioned. He'd expected a bit more enthusiasm on Isabel's part, maybe a bit more warmth. He hadn't expected sullenness or hostility, which proved how far in over his head he was right now. He didn't know a damn thing about teenage girls, so why did he think he could be a father to one?

He didn't. He hadn't chosen this situation. Not exactly, anyway.

Ginger started the car as the dog whimpered in the backseat.

"Is it okay if Lulu rides in my lap?"

"So long as she doesn't pee all over my seat," Ginger said, smiling into the rearview mirror.

Her light tone was met with steely silence, then the sound of the pet travel bag being unzipped.

"Have you had lunch yet?" Marcus thought to ask.

"No. I'm not hungry."

"I'm famished," Ginger said. "Maybe we should stop on our way out of town?"

"Know anyplace good?" he asked.

"There's a great Puerto Rican place in San Rafael once we cross the bridge. Sound good?"

"Do they allow dogs?" Marcus asked.

"Hmm, I guess not. Oh, but I know a pizza place with outdoor seating. How's that?"

"Perfect." He turned around in his seat. "Sound good to you, Izzy?"

"I said I'm not—"

"I know, I know, but maybe by the time we get there you can force down a piece of pepperoni pizza."

"I'm a vegetarian."

"Cheese pizza?"

She sighed.

Marcus turned forward again and stared out the window. Why had she wanted to get to know him if she wasn't willing to make an effort? He tried to recall what it was like to be thirteen years old. He had some hazy memories of teenage angst and raging hormones, but nothing to anchor him to Izzy's reality.

Especially not after what she'd been through. His own childhood might have been a little chaotic compared to most, but he'd had both of his parents, and he'd always been secure in their love for him. Izzy, on the other hand, had lost her mother and only just met her father today.

Maybe she was worried about losing him, too. Maybe it was easier to reject him first rather than risk being rejected.

He didn't know how she felt, but Ginger might. That had been his primary reason for asking her if they could spend the summer with her. She'd lost her parents as a child. She'd walked the same sad path Izzy was walking now, and maybe she could guide the girl through it.

Maybe she could guide him, too.

Of all the people he'd ever known, Ginger was the only friend he had who might be qualified to help.

And the fact that she was willing…

He owed her the sun and the moon for that.

CHAPTER FIVE

ONE AWKWARD LUNCH AND two even more awkward hours of driving went by before Ginger pulled into the driveway of her Promise Lake house and killed the engine.

"Here we are," she chirped too brightly.

She had the distinct feeling everyone in the car was regretting having agreed to make this trip, and now here they were, about to shack up in her house as if they wanted to be together.

She'd made a horrible, terrible mistake. She didn't know Marcus anymore. She'd been a fool to think she could just invite him back into her life and everything would work out.

"This place is beautiful," Marcus said as they got out of the car. "How'd you find it?"

"Do you remember Soleil Freeman from college?"

He frowned. "I don't think so."

"She's the poet Anne Bishop's daughter?"

"Oh, right."

"Anyway, she went to school with us, and we've kept in touch over the years. I came here to visit the nonprofit farm she runs on the other side of the lake. She mentioned that she'd heard the local community college was looking for a writing instructor and, I don't know, things started falling into place. I got the job, and then soon as I saw this place I fell in love with it."

She popped the trunk and grabbed Isabel's bags. The girl had her hands full of dog and purse, so Ginger smiled and said, "Let me show you where your room is."

Izzy simply stared back, expressionless, then followed Ginger toward the front door. The girl was definitely depressed, Ginger decided, and she had every right to be, but it didn't make the situation any easier.

Ginger had been nine when she'd lost her own parents, and she remembered the listless, strange year afterward as if it was a bad dream she couldn't quite wake up from.

As she mused about how best to help the girl, Izzy let out a yelp from behind her.

"What is *that?*" she screeched.

Ginger turned and followed the direction of the

girl's gaze to the ground, where a fat slug was making its way across the porch.

"Banana slug," Ginger said. "They're harmless."

Izzy made a face. "They're disgusting."

"That, too."

"Are there many of them?" she asked.

"Nope. I've never seen one here on the porch. It must have lost its way in the woods. Oh, by the way," Ginger added, "there's quite a lot of wildlife around here. We'll have to keep a close eye on Lulu."

"What do you mean?"

"I just mean, you know, with hawks and coyotes around…"

Oh God, had she ever picked a bad topic.

Izzy hugged the dog closer and continued to glare down at the slug as if it might make a sudden attack.

Ginger felt like pointing out that they were surrounded by icky, slimy, unpredictable nature and the girl had better get used to it, but she figured she wasn't going to win any points with that kind of talk, so she kept her mouth shut.

Izzy deserved her sympathy, not her sarcasm. Besides, Ginger remembered exactly how awful it felt to be thirteen. She could only imagine how painful it would be to lose you mother at such a volatile age. Nine had been bad enough.

The girl had gone through hell, and Ginger vowed not to add any more grief to her life, no matter how crappy Izzy's attitude got.

Once they were inside, she led Izzy down the hallway, giving a quick tour as they passed the living room on the right and the bathroom on the left. "Down the hall is the kitchen and dining room," Ginger said. "And this will be your room."

She turned on the light in the smaller guest bedroom. Its pale lilac walls gave the room a soothing feel that made Ginger consider painting her own room the same color. The guest room was furnished simply with an antique white wrought-iron bed, a weathered white dresser and a cheval mirror.

"You'll share the hallway bath with Marcus. I've set aside some extra towels in the bathroom—the pink set is yours."

The girl stared vacantly at the suitcases Ginger set down next to the dresser.

"I'm going to take Lulu out to do her business," she said. "Is there a place to walk around here?"

"You could take the path through the woods to the lake."

Izzy said nothing.

"Just go out the front door and around the house and you'll see the path." Ginger pointed east as she spoke. "It's a short walk."

The girl pulled a leash out of her purse and headed for the door, the dog still in her arms. Ginger followed her out to the living room, where she found Marcus studying photos on the fireplace mantel. There was a shot of Ginger's parents, one of Ginger with her grandmother, and one of Granny Townsend when she was a young girl.

He started to say something to Izzy, but she was through the door before he could get a word out.

"She's taking the dog for a walk," Ginger explained.

Marcus gave her a look that reflected a mixture of frustration and sympathy. He didn't need to say a thing. She knew exactly how he felt—or at least she could take a good guess.

It was surreal to have him standing in her living room, larger than life, studying her family photos. He was in so many ways her fantasy come to life. But, she had to remind herself, the fantasy and the reality had never met up before. And he was here as a friend now, one who'd nearly lost his life. But he was safe and in one piece. That was what truly mattered.

The moment he'd asked her if she would have

room for two houseguests, she'd know she was going to say yes. She definitely wanted to help Izzy and Marcus, but just as much, she wanted to help herself move on.

"Your room is behind the kitchen. Can I show you?"

"That's okay. I already figured it out and put my bags in there."

"Would it be good if I got lost for a while tonight, so you and Izzy can have some alone time?"

He grimaced. "I'm not sure either of us wants that right now."

"It might relieve a bit of the pressure to have one less person in the mix."

"Maybe." He gave the matter some thought as he turned away from the mantel and strolled to the French doors that looked out on the deck and the backyard and, beyond that, the woods and lake.

He peered out the door into the fading light of late afternoon and changed the subject. "Do you think she'll be okay out there alone?"

"Sure. The worst she might encounter is an overgrown banana slug."

"No snakes? Scorpions? Hungry mountain lions?"

Ginger laughed. "Doubtful."

"I never took you for a back-to-the-woods kind

of girl. I thought you'd live out your life in the urban jungle."

Ginger sighed. "I guess the urban jungle wore me down."

"What do you mean?"

She shrugged, unsure herself what she meant. But then she opened her mouth and out came words she knew were true.

"I couldn't spend any more time being perpetually single and living in an apartment and feeling like something was missing."

"So you figured out that redwood trees were missing?" he joked.

She crossed the living room and opened the double doors onto the deck so that the early evening breeze could flow through the house. "I needed to get out of the city, and this place cast a spell on me. Well, it and Soleil's baby girl," she added, only half joking.

Ginger felt a little shy talking about the main reason she'd moved here.

"Oh?"

"I knew when I met Soleil's baby that I wanted to have a child of my own. I mean, I knew it before, but when I held her little girl, I felt the wanting somewhere deep down, you know?"

Silly question. Of course he didn't know.

"So your biological clock's ticking, huh?" He flashed a wry grin that somehow annoyed her.

"That reduces what I felt to a cliché, and it didn't feel like a cliché."

He sobered. "I'm sorry. It must be hard, wanting a baby and not being able to afford one." He added this last part as if it didn't compute.

And truly, it was an odd dilemma when she thought of his own problem—accidentally having a child he'd never thought he wanted.

Ginger shrugged. "It's an abstract problem at the moment. I've just been dealing with the more tangible problem of getting this house repaired, and the more I try to fix, the more I find wrong."

He smiled. "It's great to see you doing so well."

His tone was warm, but… But that's all it was. There wasn't any interest on Marcus's part about whether she had a boyfriend or a lover or anything else. Otherwise he would have asked by now. She'd known there wouldn't be, but given that the last time they'd seen each other she'd still been pining after him, she supposed old habits were hard to break.

This was good. She'd moved on in her heart, and now her subconscious was catching up to it. This was exactly why she needed to spend time with Marcus, so she could prove to herself that what she'd had with him was a lasting friendship, not a missed romance.

She was older now, more mature. She knew better than to get caught up in those old romantic feelings again, that misguided longing.

"So what about the man situation? Anyone special in your life?"

Okay. He was interested.

"Special?" she repeated.

His smile turned playful. "You know what I mean."

"No one," she said, shrugging.

She hoped she sounded casual, but she feared the truth had slipped into her voice. She didn't want him to know that she'd spent well over a decade finding out that one guy after another didn't measure up to her standards—standards that she'd based on him.

How could she have let so many years slip past her with such unrealistic expectations?

"So what about this guy you almost married. Who was he?"

"Can I get you a drink?" Ginger said, dodging the question. "Glass of wine, maybe?"

"That sounds great."

She led him into the kitchen, then retrieved a decent bottle of cabernet from the wine rack on the counter. "I was thinking of making a little spaghetti carbonara for dinner, but since Izzy's a vegetarian…"

"I'm sorry. It doesn't look like she's going to make anything easy." He pulled out a chair and took a seat at the breakfast table.

"It's okay. She's thirteen. She's just doing what she's supposed to do."

"She's supposed to drive everyone crazy?"

"She's supposed to start asserting her independence."

His shoulders sagged. "I'm so unequipped to handle this."

"I was thinking… There's a really good therapist in town. Maybe it would help to get Izzy into therapy with her. Or maybe both of you?"

"That's a great idea."

Ginger removed the cork and smelled it, savoring the spicy, oak-tinged scent of fermented grapes. She turned just in time to catch an odd expression crossing Marcus's face as he watched her. But as soon as their gazes met, the expression vanished.

"I'll find her card and give it to you."

"Do I get to hear the story of 'almost'?" he asked, grinning again.

"Oh." She shrugged as she retrieved glasses from

the cupboard. "I guess so. But first, how does pasta primavera sound? I think I've got enough vegetables to throw a decent dinner together."

"Perfect. Thank you so much for thinking of Izzy. I'll take her for a grocery shopping trip first thing tomorrow to make feeding her easier."

Ginger poured them each a glass of wine and brought Marcus's to the table.

"Cheers," she said, toasting. "To new beginnings."

"Cheers—to *you*," he said, and something in his eyes set her insides tingling.

It was almost as if he was looking at her flirtatiously, but that was the old Ginger thinking. The new Ginger knew better. The new Ginger was going to learn from the past and remember that there wasn't any reason to take Marcus's warmth or his gaze or his anything else as a sign of romantic interest. He'd already proved himself incapable of seeing her as a desirable woman.

Right?

Right.

She just had to figure out how to get all the warm tingly stuff to stop happening, since he was still the same ridiculously attractive man he'd always been.

She took a drink of wine and allowed the sharp

burst of flavor to distract her. Savoring the notes of plum, blackberry and spice gave her a few moments to decide how to explain her almost marriage.

"I was with Leo for eight years," she finally said as she set her glass on the counter and began rummaging around for dinner ingredients.

"Leo? You almost married a guy named *Leo?*" His teasing tone caused Ginger to smile, but she didn't give him the satisfaction of seeing it.

"It was short for Leonardo, if you must know. He was Italian."

"Why didn't you want to marry him?"

Because of you was definitely not the appropriate response at the moment. Nor was it entirely true. "I…don't know. He was great," she said, shrugging. *He just wasn't you.*

No, she had to stop thinking that way. She knew she'd been unable to marry Leo because she believed there had to be a guy out there who could make her feel the way Marcus had once made her feel—only this time the guy would actually return her interest.

She filled a pot with water for the pasta.

"I get it. You weren't ready. Believe me, I know how that feels."

There was no point correcting him. "The breakup

was inevitable. I can see now that I look back on it. I'm not sure my heart was ever really into it."

"If your heart wasn't there, where was it?"

This was the kind of poetically poignant question that had made Ginger fall for Marcus so many years ago. He saw right to the heart of things—well, most things and most people. But not her. He'd never quite seen her heart.

She sighed, willing herself once again not to blurt out any uncomfortable truths. "I don't know. I guess my heart was in hiding. Afraid of committing or whatever."

He laughed. "You? Afraid of commitment? That's supposed to be my line."

"Why are you the only one who gets to use it? How many committed relationships did you ever see *me* in?"

"There was that one guy—what was his name? Neddy?"

"Teddy."

She cast a glance at Marcus over her shoulder and caught him grinning wickedly.

"Right," he said. "You were with him for what? A year?"

"Yeah, something like that."

"But it doesn't matter how many relationships I

saw you in. The point is I know what kind of person you are. You're not afraid of intimacy. You're probably devoted to it more than anyone I've ever known."

"I am not," Ginger protested, but as the words left her mouth, she realized he was right.

She was devoted to the idea of intimacy, and she'd done a great job of finding it with her friends. It was in her romantic relationships that she'd fallen short. And maybe it was her devotion to some ideal intimate relationship that had tripped her up.

An ideal intimate relationship with the one guy she'd ever loved, the one sitting at her kitchen table. A man she now wanted only to be friends with.

But the mere fact that he knew her so well sent the unwanted tingly sensations in her belly into overdrive. Her grip slipped from the heavy pot of water, sending it clattering into the sink.

"Need any help there?" Marcus called as she cursed and began filling the pot again.

"No, thanks."

"So you're still thinking about adopting, even without the guy around?"

"I don't know. It would be a long shot. But I'm getting older, and I don't want to put off having a child until some man I might never find comes along, you know?"

"Of course you'll find the right guy if you really want to." There was firm conviction in his voice.

"You make it sound so easy."

"Look at yourself." Marcus sounded incredulous now.

She turned to him to make sure she hadn't misread his tone. "What do you mean?"

"You're amazing—beautiful, smart, funny, accomplished. What guy wouldn't want to be with you?"

What guy, indeed?

She bit her tongue. *Not now*. Not now.

This wasn't the time to castrate him verbally for his utter and complete inability to see why she'd managed to be a failure with men all these years.

But the fact that he'd called her beautiful...

That sent the warm tingly storm south, into dangerous territory.

Pathetic.

She was completely hopeless if this was how she responded to a mere compliment from the guy she was supposed to be over.

She knew she was an attractive woman. Over the years she'd shed the insecurity of her twenties, along with the extra fifty pounds she'd managed to carry around from her preteen years, and she liked who she was and how she looked. She wasn't perfect, but she was comfortable in her body.

So why did Marcus's approval make her feel so damn fluttery?

Old habits, perhaps.

Or maybe it was just that he was finally giving her a compliment she'd deeply craved once upon a time.

"Isn't the real problem finding a guy that *I* want to be with?" she said at last.

"Ah, good point."

Ginger poured olive oil into a pan, turned the burner on low, then began crushing garlic to add to it. "So what about you?" she said as she worked.

"I'm definitely not looking for the right guy."

"You know what I mean."

"I was dating someone. Long distance. You know me. Love to put a country or even a continent between me and my beloved. But we called it quits when I decided to move back here."

"Who is she?"

"Her name is Annika. She's Dutch. I met her in Amsterdam, but she traveled a lot for work. I saw her whenever she was in town, which was rarely."

Ginger couldn't help herself. "Just the way you like it?"

"I thought so. But when I was lying in the hospital after the shooting and the nurse asked me who I'd like her to contact about what had happened…"

His voice had changed before he trailed off. He'd sounded uncertain, or maybe unsettled.

Ginger dumped a handful of crushed garlic into the oil and turned to look at him. But his expression was inscrutable.

She began chopping vegetables as he continued.

"I realized there wasn't anyone it mattered all that much to contact."

"I'm sure your girlfriend cared that you were shot."

"Yeah, but we didn't really stay in touch when she was out of town. I knew she was off somewhere working on a story, and…I don't know. I guess it was the first time I realized she and I were actually more like friends with benefits than significant others."

"And you don't call your friends with benefits from the hospital after an emergency."

"Right."

"So who did you call?"

"No one."

Again she turned, just in time to catch the haunted look in his eye.

"I'm sorry, Marcus. It makes me wish we'd stayed more in touch, you know? I wish I could have been there."

"No worries. I was happy to get your message when I returned to Amsterdam."

"Is that when you heard from Izzy, too?"

"Yeah. She said something like, 'Hi, uh, this is, uh…Isabel Grayson. Uh, I'm Lisette Grayson's daughter. And, uh, you're my dad.'"

"I can't believe you have a kid. You, of all people…" Ginger shook her head, then glanced over her shoulder to smile at him. But her smile vanished when she saw the uncertainty in his eyes.

And for the first time, she glimpsed how he really felt about having a thirteen-year-old girl take over his life.

He was more than just afraid. He was lost. Wandering a planet he'd never visited before, somewhere on the opposite side of the universe.

CHAPTER SIX

ONCE THEY'D MADE IT through a semi-pleasant dinner and Izzy had gone off to bed for the night, Marcus suggested they take their third glass of wine and go for a walk around the property.

He could hardly believe how settled Ginger's life seemed. How grown up she was. Which was foolish. Of course she hadn't remained frozen in time as a twenty-one-year-old college student. Of course she'd moved on to become someone more than the girl he'd once known.

But what surprised him most was how appealing he found this mature Ginger. She wasn't as remote or sophisticated as the women he usually went for. She'd always been a warm, welcoming person, but it had been her sense of humor and her take on life that had made her his best friend. That part of her hadn't changed, and yet, somehow she was transformed.

"I'm hoping to revive this rose garden someday,"

she said, gesturing to a row of forlorn-looking rose bushes along the side of the house. "The previous owners were gardeners."

"I remember you having a bit of a green thumb back in the day."

"That one little window box outside my dorm window didn't really count as a garden."

"You grew basil."

She laughed. "Yeah, I still do. Anything I can eat, I grow. I'm just not good with flowers, but I'm going to get there."

They rounded the side of the house, and Marcus spotted a couple of raised beds filled with healthy-looking plants. "Ah, see? I know you better than you think I do."

She beamed as she knelt next to one box and lovingly propped a vine back against its supporting stick.

"Are those tomatoes?"

"Sugar snap peas. The heirloom tomatoes are over there."

"Wow." In truth, he didn't know much about growing vegetables.

He just knew that the sort of constancy and stability required to garden had never been his thing. Those very qualities had been part of what had attracted him to Ginger—and at the same time made him wary. That constancy also made her a great friend, but now that he was seeing her in her new confident and curvaceous glory, he realized that she was just the kind of loyal, reliable woman he was terrified of.

She was supposed to be the one woman he could be friends with without ever having to worry about sex coming between them.

But here she was now, a whole new woman. The same, but irresistibly different.

Give him emotionally unavailable women on different continents any day. He knew how to handle them. They were safe.

"I've been wondering," she said, "how are you doing since the shooting?"

"I'm healed up fine," he answered.

"No, I mean, how are you *doing?*" she asked as they continued along the path toward the woods.

"It's weird—ever since getting on the plane to come back here, I feel like the shooting didn't even happen to me. It's like it happened to someone else."

"Because you feel safer here?"

"I guess so. And maybe it's partly that I've been so preoccupied thinking about Izzy, I don't have time to worry about anything else."

"Now you have to keep yourself alive not just for yourself, but for her, too."

He winced. "Gee, thanks for reminding me."

"Anytime," she joked, but he knew she was right.

He had a huge responsibility now. He was a father. Impossible, but true.

"I guess it's the classic near-death-experience reaction," he said, knowing Ginger wouldn't laugh at him, "but I've had this sense that I'm supposed to drastically change my life somehow, ever since I first woke up in the hospital."

"You're supposed to make right all your wrongs?"

"Yeah, me and Ebenezer Scrooge. Actually, it's more like I want to experience things I haven't experienced before. I'm thirty-six years old, you know, and there's a lot I haven't done yet."

"Like what?"

They paused at a bench that looked out on the lake. Sitting up on a bluff, beneath some trees, it provided an expansive view. Ginger sat down, and Marcus followed suit.

"Like…I don't know. Be a father?"

"Box number one, check."

He chuckled. "Yeah, didn't even have to work at that one. It just fell into my lap."

"What else?"

"Um, you know, maybe settle down a bit?"

Ginger cast a shocked look at him. "Get out."

"No, really."

"I guess that sort of goes hand in hand with being a dad," she suggested.

"Well, I could do it the nomadic way, like my parents did, but I want Izzy to have a better life than I did."

"You sound as if you've given this some thought."

"Not really," he joked. "It's just that the wine is going to my head."

But that was only half-true.

He was having thoughts he'd never had before. He'd taken one look at Ginger's beautiful, decrepit cottage and felt for the first time that he wanted a home of his own. Not a place where he lived for a short time, but a real home, where he could put down roots and grow a life for himself and Izzy, and maybe someone else, too. Izzy would need a woman in her life someday, and so did he. Hell, he wanted to do the family thing all the way—get married, raise kids, take the hand Fate had dealt him, and play it through.

He hardly recognized the crazy thoughts he was having. But he felt so present, so thankful to be alive, that he wanted to run with each wild idea.

For instance, what would it be like to kiss Ginger?

Was she a good kisser? He had no idea. Was she warm and eager or cool and reserved?

He was hoping for the former as he stared at her mouth.

"The thing about a near-death experience," he said, "is that it makes you wonder what you're missing out on. It makes you want to live in the moment more, and do whatever the hell you feel like doing."

She looked at him curiously, her eyes luminous in the fading light. "Oh, yeah? What else do you think you've been missing out on?"

"You," he said.

He hadn't meant to say it, but he *had* drunk half a bottle of wine.

And it was true. Sitting here right now, he couldn't think of anything on earth he was more curious to experience than Ginger.

He slid closer, leaned in and placed a gentle kiss on her lips.

No sooner did he wonder how she was going to react than he felt her response. She was, as he'd hoped, warm and eager. After the initial shock, she kissed him back, her soft, pliant lips coaxing his into a deeper kiss.

Wow.

He pulled back a bit, looked her in the eyes and

smiled slightly. "That was nice," he said. "Can we do that again?"

The words were barely out of his mouth before she parted her lips, and he leaned in again. This time he lingered, explored, tasted.

His body responded with an eagerness the likes of which he couldn't recall having felt before. He shifted closer and put one palm on her waist. He was contemplating where it might go next when Ginger's own hand landed on top of his.

She stiffened and pulled back from the kiss.

"What's wrong?"

She sighed. "Where did that come from?"

He grinned. "My near-death experience? Carpe diem, right?"

"Seriously. I…we…we're friends. How would Izzy feel if she saw us out here like this?"

Right. Izzy. He was supposed to be thinking of her needs first.

The thought sobered him, and he slid back until a proper twenty-four inches separated them.

"Sorry," he said. "I'm still getting used to this thinking-of-the-kid-first stuff."

"Yeah, well, I just don't want to screw up the summer before it's even gotten started."

"Right, right, good thinking."

"And seriously. What on earth is going on, Marcus? You've never showed the slightest romantic interest in me before."

He sighed and ran a hand through his hair. "Yeah, yeah, I know. We're friends, and I don't want to mess that up. I've always wanted to protect our friendship."

It was a lame excuse in a way. Because of course he'd never thought of kissing her back in college. They'd both had to grow up for him to see Ginger's appeal. Now he was looking at her through the eyes of a grown man—and a father—rather than the selfish perspective of a guy on the run from everything and everyone.

"I know you're going through tough times, and maybe it's tempting to seek the closest—and most convenient—comfort."

"Right," he said. "I guess you're right."

It was true, he supposed. The comfort of a willing woman's arms sounded like a welcome distraction right now. Too bad that woman couldn't be Ginger.

MARCUS'S GREEN EYES WERE barely visible in the moonlight. The two of them paused at the back door of the house, both reluctant to go inside, to leave behind this crisp, quiet night and whatever crazy spell it had cast over them a few minutes ago. As Ginger looked at him, trying to think what to say, only one subject came to mind.

That kiss…

Dear God. Ginger was going to spend the rest of her sad little life replaying that kiss in her head. Wishing she'd said or done something different.

Wishing she'd had the guts to go for it even though she'd known it was wrong.

"I'm really sorry," Marcus began. "I didn't mean to make things awkward—"

She held up a hand to stop him. "Don't mention it. How about we just pretend it never happened?"

He shrugged, then nodded. But his gaze searched hers for something else.

Was he trying to decide if she meant what she said?

"I was thinking," he finally said. "You mentioned your house needs some work, right?"

"Yes."

"I'm a little rusty, but as you might remember from my summer jobs, I know my way around a construction site pretty well."

"Oh," she said, blinking in surprise at the idea.

"How about I repay your generosity in letting us stay here with my carpentry services?"

"I don't know." This was the last thing she'd

expected him to throw at her. "You'll need to be spending time with Izzy, getting her settled, getting to know her—"

"Sure, but I'll drive her crazy if I'm hovering around her constantly. She needs space, too."

Ginger gave the matter some thought. She couldn't afford to hire a contractor anyway, so in truth, she was thrilled at the prospect of free labor.

"Wow," she finally said. "I have to admit, I love the idea."

He smiled. "Great. I'll get started in the next day or so. We can talk about your priority list tomorrow and what needs to be done."

They said good-night, and Ginger went to her room, closed the door and flopped down on the bed, her body still buzzing with so much adrenaline from their kiss that she wasn't sure she'd ever be able to fall asleep.

She buried her face in her pillow and let out one of those silent screams her therapist had taught her to use when she was frustrated and in a place where real screaming would be inappropriate. It didn't help, though. She still wanted to scream out loud.

Flipping onto on her back, she did an inventory of all her tingling body parts and decided there wasn't any use denying it—she was in for a long, sleepless, lonely night.

But Ginger was no stranger to insomnia. She'd suffered from it on and off since her parents' deaths, and she got some of her best writing done in those long, sleepless nights. In a sick way, she almost looked forward to bouts of insomnia.

She rose from the bed, grabbed the laptop computer she kept on her nightstand for just such occasions as this, and climbed back under the covers. As the screen started to glow, her mind began to settle into the quiet rhythm of composition. She'd learned years ago at writer's workshops in Iowa that writing, for her, was a form of salvation. It wasn't about the glory or egotism of publication. It wasn't about the need to make her voice heard. It was about saving herself from her own demons.

No, that made it sound more negative than it really was. More than anything, writing brought her joy. And a sense of peace that nothing else did. Lately, she'd been writing quiet little short stories about quiet characters making their way through quiet lives.

She didn't write so much for others as she did for herself. Which partly explained why Marcus was the famous author and she was happy teaching at the local community college.

As Ginger opened up the document that held her latest work in progress, she found herself unable to concentrate. Instead, her thoughts kept returning to Marcus, to what he'd said about changing, wanting to settle down, and to that completely unexpected kiss. How was she to feel about any of it?

Marcus had just survived a near-death experience, and clearly that colored his actions now. Was he serious about settling down, or was it just his fear of death propelling him into a frenzy of change that he'd later regret?

She suspected the latter was true, and she would have to be vigilant against getting sucked into something they'd both later regret.

But what about that kiss…

What if he didn't regret it? What if he wanted to see where it led? What if she did? What if the two people they'd become as adults had a chance to explore a relationship that they'd never had in their younger days?

Such questions were far too dangerous for her heart to contemplate, so she forced herself to begin typing.

CHAPTER SEVEN

MARCUS WOKE UP THE next day with a slight head-ache from the wine, wondering if the kiss could have worked out differently. He didn't regret it, exactly, but did regret having made Ginger feel uncomfortable. Of course she would worry about his motives in pursuing her romantically. Here he was, a new dad, just back in the U.S. after having been shot, and he was throwing himself at her after a matter of hours?

He must have seemed like a lunatic. And maybe he was, but he also knew from experience that life wasn't going to stop and wait for him. He had to seize his opportunities. Maybe he would just have to bide his time and prove to Ginger that he wasn't acting out of desperation to find a mother for his kid. Instead, he was a new man, and what he felt was a growing attraction to a woman he'd always considered a friend.

The house was silent as he rose and went about his morning routine. It was only when he walked down the hallway toward the kitchen that he heard the faint click clack of fingers typing on a keyboard. He followed the sound to the door at the end of the hall and found Ginger there, sitting at a desk.

"Morning," he said. "How long have you been up?"

She turned in the swiveling desk chair and smiled. "Oh, all night pretty much. I had trouble sleeping, and I eventually decided to spend my time writing instead of tossing and turning."

She was already dressed for the day in a pair of jeans and a stretchy pink tank top that created a warm glow on her pale skin, contrasting with her dark red hair. She was so damn pretty. He forced his gaze from lingering on the rounded swell of her breasts, and looked around the office.

"I hope I wasn't the cause of your sleeplessness."

"Don't give yourself so much credit," she said in a teasing tone. "If you'll remember, I've always had insomnia."

"Oh, right." He entered the room, perusing the bookshelves that lined the walls. "So this is where you write."

"Sometimes. I have a laptop for when I want to be more mobile."

"What are you working on these days?"

"Nothing much."

"Nothing much that kept you up all night?"

She laughed. "Yeah, okay, it's a short story, but I'm not going to let you read it."

He spun around, assuming an expression of mock offense. "How can you not let me read it? You're the best writer I know and I used to be your favorite critic."

"False flattery will get you nowhere—and you haven't read anything of mine in years."

"Seriously, Ginger, that short story you wrote about the girl lost in the desert still gives me chills."

Ginger rolled her eyes and groaned. "Oh God, you remember that thing?"

"I still have a copy of it. I found it while I was packing for my trip here."

She pointed her finger at him. "Use it for kindling next time you need to start a fire."

"You should write a novel."

"Everyone who writes novels thinks I should stop wasting my time with short stories, and write a novel."

Marcus leaned against her desk, wanting very much to read what she had on the computer monitor. She minimized the document to keep him from doing so.

"So why don't you?" he said.

"If you'd stayed in touch, you'd know that I did write one, and it was an utter failure."

A stab of well-deserved guilt shot through him. "I'm sorry. But sales have little to do with talent. I want to read your book. I bet it's great."

"It's over there on a shelf somewhere. Help yourself."

"So why not write another one?"

"I'll leave the wordy tomes for talented writers like yourself."

"How about a book of short stories then?"

Ginger crossed her arms over her chest and peering up at him. "Is there some reason you're so interested in my writing efforts?"

He loved the intelligent, feisty spark in her eyes.

"Because it's a lot easier than thinking about my own writing?"

She laughed. "Fair enough."

He stood up and went to the bookshelves, scanning until his gaze landed on a book spine that bore the name Ginger Townsend.

"Spells for Lost Girls," he said, reading the title aloud.

"It's actually based on that short story about the girl in the desert."

He pulled the book off the shelf, his chest swelling with pride. He'd known that story was outstanding. He'd always told her so.

"Wow," he said. "I'm impressed."

"Don't be. It sold about five copies."

He quickly flipped pages to chapter one, eager to read the opening lines.

"Oh God," she said. "Don't read it in front of me."

"Okay, okay."

He closed the book and found himself staring at the back cover, which displayed a black-and-white photo of Ginger leaning against a brick wall, her wild, curly hair draped over her shoulders in all its glory, her face wearing a far-off, mysterious expression that was somewhere between knowing and searching. She didn't look into the camera, but rather into the distance to some dreamy place where no one could reach her.

"Just tell me you like it after you read it, whether you do or not," she said, and he knew she was quite serious. "I don't want any brutal honesty."

"Stop it. I know it's going to be brilliant, because you wrote it."

Her cheeks turned pinker, and she glanced down the hallway. "Izzy's still sleeping, I guess."

"I'll check on her. Can I get you something for breakfast?"

"I've already had some toast," she said, standing up. "Why don't I get you something?"

"No, it's fine. I'll—"

"I insist. You're the guest, and I'm sick of writing now."

"Thanks. I'll read your book tonight."

"I was thinking maybe I could show you guys around the area today. How does that sound?"

"I don't want you to go to any trouble."

"I'd love to. It's fun playing tour guide, and it'll help you both feel more independent if you know your way around."

"Okay, thanks. That sounds great." He stepped aside and followed her into the kitchen.

Gratitude for her generosity welled up, and he had to resist the urge to sweep her into his arms and kiss her again. Resisting went against his new philosophy to live life to its fullest, but he supposed a little self-restraint was in order at the moment.

How had he managed never to fall in love with this glorious woman before?

He went down the hall, forcing his thoughts away from Ginger, and stopped at Izzy's door. He knocked softly and heard the whimper of the dog from inside, then the scrape-scrape of little toenails on the floor. He eased the door open and let the dog out, then peered in at the lump in the bed with the mess of long dark hair.

"Izzy?" he called softly.

No answer.

He stepped inside and walked over to the bed as the dog took off down the hall toward the kitchen, probably in desperate need of a potty trip outside. Izzy's breathing didn't have the slow steadiness of deep sleep, so he sat down on the edge of her bed and waited for her to open her eyes. For the moment she didn't stir.

This girl he barely knew was depending on him to be the best father he could possibly be. Was he up to the task? He believed he was, and part of him was eager to prove he could be a good dad. But that made the responsibility no less daunting.

She was embarking on the teenage years, and the last time he'd known a teenage girl up close and personal...well, he'd been a teenager himself, doing things he couldn't imagine—and didn't want—this child ever doing. And part of her was still a child. That much was easy to see. She was straddling the easy innocence of childhood and the tumultuous issues of adolescence, with one foot more firmly in the latter.

She rolled over toward him and yawned. Her eyes fluttered open when her leg bumped against his hip.

"Morning, Izzy," he said.

"Um, hi."

"Did you sleep okay?"

"Yeah, I guess so. Where's Lulu?" she said, scanning the bed and the floor.

"Probably outside doing her business."

"What are you doing in here?" She sounded more curious than offended, and he was glad he'd made the effort to seek her out.

"I just thought I'd check in and see what you'd like for breakfast."

"Oh. Don't worry about me. I'm going to hang out in bed for a while and read maybe."

He was still holding Ginger's book. "That sounds nice, but Ginger wants to take us on a tour of the area."

"Oh."

"Did you know she's an author, too? This is her novel." He held it up for Izzy to see. "Maybe you can read it after I'm done with it."

Izzy frowned. "Isn't she your best friend? Why haven't you read her book before?"

"It, um…" Wasn't published in the Netherlands? Actually, he had no idea if it was, and he didn't want to lie. "I haven't been a very good friend," he admitted, vowing to change that.

"Why not?"

This whole honesty thing was going to be harder than he'd thought, and he had a feeling that Izzy and Ginger were going to push him for answers.

"It was just easier, I guess, living on the other side of the world." The excuse sounded lame even to him. "But I'm back now, and I'm going to make it up to her."

Izzy shifted and sat up. "I need to hit the ladies'. Do you mind?"

"I'll give you your privacy. We'll be leaving soon, so you'd better get dressed and come out to have a bite to eat, okay?"

"Yeah," she said, her voice flat.

Why had she been so eager to meet him and spend time with him, when she seemed so cool and disinterested now? It was weird.

Marcus left the room, went into his own bedroom and put the book on his bed for later. But he'd been honest when he'd told Ginger he wanted to read it. Suddenly too curious to wait, he sat on the edge of the bed and picked up the novel.

Ten pages later, he was utterly engrossed. Her writing was so beautiful, so lyrical, such a perfect expression of her personality on the page.... He wanted to stay there all day and finish the book. He recognized the main character as the desert girl from the short story she'd written in college, and everything that had been good about that story was in the novel, only more polished. Better.

Why was she not the darling of the literary world?

Well, he did know the business well enough not to ask such naive questions. Success had to do with so many factors out of the author's control… But still, she was a better writer than him, and he was going to insist she send her latest project to his literary agent.

"Marcus?" Ginger called from the doorway.

He looked up and grinned sheepishly.

"You're reading it already?" she said with a pained expression.

"How could I not? I love it. The first chapter is absolutely brilliant."

She rolled her eyes. "You're such a liar. Are you almost ready to go? Izzy's in the kitchen finishing a bowl of oatmeal."

"Oh, yeah. Thanks for feeding her. I'll be out in just a sec."

Alone again, he read the last page of the first chapter, and a warm glow washed over him. If this wasn't love, then he didn't know what was. If it was possible to fall in love with a woman through the words she'd written, then he'd just done it. But no, that wasn't entirely true. Because he already knew Ginger. He knew she was the best woman he'd ever met. He knew she was the personification of all the beauty she managed to create on the page.

Sure, falling for her could ruin their friendship, but not if she fell for him, too. He just had to figure out how to make it happen.

CHAPTER EIGHT

"IT'S JUST HERE, to the left," Ginger said, gesturing with her hand.

Marcus steered the Prius onto the gravel road marked by a sign that read Rainbow Farm. They'd made their way around the town of Promise, poking into the shops, stopping at a café for lunch and learning the whereabouts of all the key businesses. And they'd done a quick and dirty tour of the outlying areas around the lake, with Ginger pointing out trailheads and swimming spots along the way.

The area was breathtakingly pretty. It reminded Marcus a little of the commune in Oregon where he'd spent much of his childhood. The trees, the endless green… But the town of Promise felt stable and historic. It lacked the uneasy transience of commune life.

Now they were on their way to visit Ginger's friends Soleil and West.

"What is this place?" Izzy asked from the back-seat. She sounded suspicious. "You're not taking me to some back-to-nature program for bad teenagers, are you?"

Ginger made a little choked sound in her throat and shot a panicky glance at Marcus. "No!" she said, her voice too high. "This is my friend's farm. It's a really cool place I've been wanting to show you both."

"Oh." The response from the back of the car was unenthused.

"Well, I mean, actually, there *is* a program for teenagers here," Ginger amended as the car crunched along the gravel road through a wooded area. "It's an internship program for kids from Oakland. I thought you might enjoy meeting some other kids your age. You might want to hang out with them over the summer."

Izzy was silent. Marcus glanced in the rearview mirror and caught her expression.

"This is an organic farm, right?" he asked, to break the silence. "What do the kids do here?"

"I think they learn how to grow vegetables and take care of animals, so they can go back to the city and work in an urban garden project," Ginger explained.

"Why do they need to come all the way out here to learn that, if the project exists where they live?"

Ginger frowned. "I'm not sure. I think Soleil's background as a social worker has something to do with it. I'm sure she sees the program as more than just learning farming skills."

"You mean she counsels the kids, too?" Marcus asked, hoping Izzy didn't think that was the main reason they'd come out here.

"Not formally, I don't think. But I know she sees herself being a counselor above anything else."

They rounded a bend in the road and came into a clearing. Up ahead was a white Victorian farmhouse with a red roof, and spread out on rolling hills behind it was the farm itself.

"Beautiful, isn't it?" Ginger said.

"Yeah." Marcus took note of a group of kids playing a game of badminton off to one side of the garden. On the porch, a man stood overseeing a toddler unsteadily maneuvering her way down the front steps.

"That's Soleil's husband, West," Ginger said as if she'd read his mind. "And their daughter, Julianna."

"Are those *goats?*" Izzy asked, her tone vaguely horrified.

"Yep."

"Do I have to go in? I want to sit in the car."

Marcus turned around to look at her. "Don't be rude, Izzy," Marcus said.

Ginger peered at him, her expression inscrutable, then glanced back at Izzy herself. "You want to sit in the car? By yourself? For an hour?"

"Yes." There wasn't a lot of conviction in the girl's voice.

"Sure, go right ahead," Ginger said.

Marcus caught the doubt in Izzy's eyes as he glanced in the rearview mirror. She wasn't sure what kind of trap she was walking into.

"But I thought you wanted me to socialize or something?" she asked.

Ginger shrugged. "Not if you don't want to. I thought this would be fun for you, but if you're not interested, stay in the car."

He marveled at how calm and unbothered by Izzy's petulance she managed to be. He needed to figure out how to master that skill himself. It was part of the reason Izzy had seemed to respond so well to Ginger today as they toured the town, while she rebelled against Marcus's habit of always wanting to control the situation. How had he turned into an overbearing father figure so quickly?

He balked at the change in himself. While his own dad hadn't been a traditional father, with his radical politics and his laissez-faire approach to parenting, somehow Marcus had defaulted into the stereotype of a TV dad—his own *Father Knows Best* impersonation.

As they pulled to a stop in front of the house, the man on the porch swept the little girl into his arms and came toward the car to greet them. He was smiling tentatively, dodging the grabby hands of his daughter, who was trying to stick her fingers in his mouth.

Ginger and Marcus got out of the car, and she made introductions.

"How about the girl?" West asked, nodding toward Izzy, still sitting in the vehicle.

But before Marcus could explain his daughter's rudeness, she opened the door and got out as if nothing was the matter.

"This is my daughter, Izzy," he said, the words tripping awkwardly off his tongue.

It was his first time introducing her to anyone as his child.

"Hi," she said to West. "How old is your little girl?"

"Julianna's eight months old."

"And already walking—that's amazing," Ginger said.

"I don't think it counts as walking until she lets go of the death grip on my thumb, but yeah, she's a precocious one."

"Can I hold her?" Izzy asked. "I mean, do you think she'd mind?"

"She'll probably love it. She lives for attention." West handed the baby over to Izzy.

"She's so cute," Izzy cooed as she hefted the weight of the girl against her narrow hip.

"Don't let the cuteness fool you. The little demon never sleeps for more than two hours straight, and thinks flinging baby food is an Olympic sport and she's going for the gold." But his voice was softened by affection as he gazed at his daughter.

"Is Soleil around?" Ginger asked.

"Sure. You should come in. She'll be thrilled to see you."

"I should have called first, but we were driving by and I couldn't resist stopping in to show these guys the farm."

"Anytime you're always welcome," West said as they followed him up the steps and across the porch.

Inside, the house smelled of fresh-baked bread. Marcus looked around, admiring the gleaming hardwood floors and simple, unpretentious beauty of the place. It was much as he imagined Ginger's house would be once they got it fully renovated.

They?

Yeah, he was already imagining himself sticking around for the entire job...and beyond.

They followed West down a hallway to a large, eat-in kitchen, where a woman with a headful of springy black curls was explaining to a tall, gawky looking teenager how to properly slice bread.

"We've got some visitors," West announced.

The woman looked up, and a broad smile crossed her pretty face. "Ginger!"

The two hugged and turned to the group.

"You probably remember Marcus from college and this is his daughter, Izzy," Ginger said.

Soleil greeted them both, then gestured to the boy cutting the loaf of bread. "You guys are just in time to sample Omar's first effort at rosemary bread."

She introduced them to the youth, who looked to be maybe fifteen and was wearing a pink, flower-print apron over his baggy jeans and sports jersey. He grinned and said hello, and the smile transformed his dark brown face. Marcus watched as the boy's gaze landed on Izzy and lingered there, sparking with interest. Izzy, for her part, assumed a posture Marcus had never seen her take before, hair flipped over her shoulder, hip cocked to the side.

Okay, she was holding a baby, but there was no mistaking the change in her. She looked flirtatious.

As parenting challenges went, he wasn't remotely prepared for boys. His first instinct was to grab Izzy by the hand and drag her from the house, shuffle her back into the car and maybe drive her to the nearest nunnery.

She smiled a coy smile and said hello to Omar.

No, Marcus definitely wasn't prepared.

"Bread for everyone?" Soleil asked. "Omar, why don't you help me serve?"

"Ma!" the baby cried, reaching for her mother and trying to squirm out of Izzy's arms. "Mama-mamama!"

"I could help with the bread," Izzy offered. "I think she wants you."

"Thank you, Izzy. She's probably getting hungry."

Marcus watched as his daughter went to the counter with Omar and began putting slices of bread on napkins.

"Why don't you give Marcus a tour of the place, West?" Soleil suggested as she sat down at the large oak kitchen table with Julianna squirming in her arms. "He's never been here before."

She casually flipped up her shirt and began nursing the baby, causing Marcus a moment's embarrassment. Not since his days on the commune had he been around the family scene, complete with breastfeeding moms and fussy toddlers. Suddenly, traipsing around a farm sounded like a marvelous idea.

"Izzy, why don't you come, too?" he said as she brought him and West slices of warm bread.

"Oh, um, I guess."

"Omar could show her around and introduce her to the other kids," Soleil said. "Would you mind, Omar?"

As he passed slices to Soleil and Ginger, he nodded. "Sure, that's cool." His eyes lit up and he smiled. "Hey, you want to see the chickens? We've got some crazy-looking ones."

Izzy, who'd taken a bite of her piece, shrugged. "Um, yeah," she said once she'd finished chewing.

"This bread is great," Ginger said.

"Delicious, Omar. I think you've found your calling," West added.

The boy smiled and motioned for Izzy to follow him. Marcus couldn't think of any good excuse to stop them. Okay, he was being an overprotective father. Surely there wasn't any harm in two kids taking a tour of the farm. Still, he made a mental note to keep an eye on them. After all, he was responsible for Izzy now.

"Come on out back," West said, motioning to Marcus. "I'll introduce you to the goats."

Marcus followed him reluctantly, hoping they'd quickly find their way around to the chicken coop. Chickens he was familiar with, but goats?

"So you're new to town, right?" West asked once they were crossing the yard behind the house.

A gorgeous Australian shepherd mix came running up to them and nudged Marcus's leg for attention. "Hey, buddy," Marcus said, bending to pet the dog.

"That's Silas. He'll make you stay there all day rubbing his head if you're not careful. So, you're here for the summer?"

Marcus straightened. "Yeah, I'm here for the summer. I'm, um, getting to know my daughter."

"Oh, right, Soleil mentioned that. You must have had quite a shock finding out you were a father."

Marcus smiled, surprised at himself. The topic didn't feel as weighty as it had even yesterday. His growing feelings for Izzy and Ginger, he suspected, were making him feel more positive about the situation.

"It was a shock at first," he said. "For Izzy, too, I'm sure. But we're adjusting. I guess the scariest part is the lack of a crash course in how to be a father. Any tips for a complete novice?"

They headed toward the pasture Silas following along behind.

"You know, I didn't find out about my daughter until Soleil was already five months pregnant. We had a rocky start, but things worked themselves out."

"And you're happy now?"

West smiled, and he didn't need to say a word. "Yeah. Being a father is hard, don't get me wrong, but it's amazing, too. Every single day is amazing, even the rough ones."

Marcus felt that now familiar stab of regret. "I wish I'd been around for Izzy's baby years."

"Is her mom still in the picture?"

"No, she died a few months ago."

"That's rough. I'm sorry."

"We hadn't been a couple since college." Marcus explained. "But it's rough for Izzy."

"It's good you've got Ginger around. I can't imagine a better role model for a teenage girl. You thinking of staying here in the area?"

Marcus hadn't been before he arrived, but now… "Maybe," he said. "I suspect we're going to like it here."

"I guess my only words of advice about the fatherhood thing is, you know, you've got to find it in yourself to be a better man than you ever thought you could be. Because your daughter doesn't deserve anything less."

Marcus chuckled. "That's what I was afraid of."

"You can do it, man, don't worry. If I can, any-one can."

But as Marcus surveyed this farm, the house, the barns, the animals, all the stability and respon-sibility it took to keep a place like this running, he wondered…. Was he way out of his element?

And even more important, was he cut out to be what Izzy needed?

Her happiness depended on the answer to that question.

He felt the euphoria of moments ago slipping away from him.

"I'm not sure I know what to do with a thirteen-year-old," he admitted.

"You'll figure it out. And she's welcome to come hang out with the kids here anytime you need a break. We'll teach her some useful skills—how to pluck a chicken and such."

Marcus laughed. "She's a vegetarian."

West grinned. "Then we'll teach her how to pick a cabbage. How's that?"

"I appreciate it," he said, not voicing his preference to keep her away from boys until the age of thirty.

"And don't sweat it," West continued, as if reading Marcus's mind. "Soleil runs this place with an iron fist in a velvet glove. You don't have to worry about the kids getting into any trouble."

"Has having a daughter given you any gray hair yet?" he asked West with a wry grin.

"I'm finding new ones every day."

CHAPTER NINE

GINGER WAS SOMEWHERE on the edge of a dream when she heard a knock at her bedroom door. Before she could react, the door creaked open.

"Ginger?" Marcus whispered.

"What wrong?" she croaked. "Is Izzy okay?"

"She's fine. Can I come in?"

"Um, yeah," she said, glancing at the clock on the nightstand. It was nearly midnight.

She sat up, leaned over and switched on a light, wondering for a brief moment of panic if her hair was a mess or if she had any dried-up drool on her chin.

Stop that. She wasn't the same foolish girl who'd pined after Marcus. She was a grown woman who understood that they'd never be more than friends.

"I'm sorry," he said. "I woke you up, didn't I?"

"Sort of."

He entered, filling up the room with his oversize

masculine form. It was the first time she'd had a man in this bedroom, she thought with a hint of regret.

"I just finished your book," he said, smiling as he sat down on the end of her bed and faced her. "I couldn't wait until morning to talk to you about it."

"Oh," she said, stunned. "You already finished it? I just gave it to you this morning."

"I've been reading it all evening. It's so damn good, Ginger. And I'm not just saying that. The way you wove the stories of the three girls together, and the spells. Brilliant. I really mean it."

She glanced away, uncomfortable with the effusive praise, even if he was just saying it to be nice.

"Are you sure you didn't crack your skull when you got shot? Suffer a brain injury, too?"

He shook his head, looking incredulous. "I'm serious, Ginger. I don't understand how that book went unnoticed, but it's one of the best things I've read in years. You should be very proud of yourself."

It wasn't like Marcus to gush. At least not the old Marcus. But this new guy who'd arrived on the plane from Amsterdam—she wasn't sure she knew all the rules when it came to him. He didn't behave in predictable ways. He didn't act like the guy she used to know.

"Thank you," she said. "I don't know what to say."

"Do you think you could get together some short stories for a collection? Something we could send to my agent?"

"No way! That's really nice of you, but—"

"Don't tell me you're not interested in publication anymore."

She shrugged, the movement making her conscious of how thin her blue silk nightgown was. One strap slipped off her shoulder and she grabbed it and put it back in place.

"I mean, of course I could use the money."

"Good. Then why don't I help you decide which stories to send?"

"Marcus…"

The prospect of letting him peruse her unpublished works left her feeling far more naked than the nightgown did. He knew her better than most people. Or at least she used to think. He knew which parts of a story were from her own life and which were made up. He could see through her fiction to her truths, and maybe that's why she was reluctant to have him read her work.

Or perhaps she was giving him too much credit.

"I can choose them myself," she finally said. "And then you can read them and see what you think."

"Tomorrow?"

"I don't know when I'll find time to look through everything. How many should I pick?"

He shrugged. "Just put together a few hundred pages worth. You don't have an agent now, do you?"

"No, we parted ways a few years after my book was published. She wasn't interested in representing short fiction."

"And you weren't interested in writing any more novels?"

"No."

"You really should. I mean, someday. When you're ready. The world needs your voice."

She sighed, trying not to laugh. "Don't you think you're laying it on a little thick? You don't have to say nice things to get me to let you stay here. I've already said yes, remember?"

He placed a hand on her leg, just below the knee, and the contact, even with a sheet between them, sent a shiver through her. "All kidding aside, okay?" He was gazing at her so earnestly she had no choice but to nod.

"Okay."

"I'm totally in love with your book. I'm going to let Izzy read it next, if that's fine with you."

"Oh. Wow. Do you think she's ready for it?"

Ginger had written the book as an adult novel,

even though the three main characters were teen-agers throughout much of the story.

"I think reading it will be good for her, yeah."

"Okay, but just wait until I talk to her about it first."

The protagonist lost her parents at the beginning of the story, and while Ginger was reluctant to introduce the subject to Izzy, she knew it was one that needed to be dealt with.

She was all too aware of Marcus's proximity and an awkward silence fell between them. She caught his gaze straying to her chest, if she wasn't mistaken, and her treacherous body tingled in all the wrong—right—places.

"In the novel, what did you intend for the reader to think when you had Greta and Jane disappear?" he asked, his eyes intent.

Ginger could hardly believe Marcus was sitting here acting as thought her unnoticed little book was the most important literary work to come along since the Bible.

"It was the spell. It worked."

"That's what I thought." He smiled, apparently satisfied. "Hey, I'm sorry. I know I shouldn't have woken you. I was just so excited to finish the story and…"

"And what?"

"I'm not kidding. It's a beautiful book. Almost as beautiful as you."

With that, he stood up and headed for the door, leaving Ginger to ponder his words.

Just before he walked out, he turned and said good-night, and she murmured a faint reply.

As she switched off the light and tried to go back to sleep, she wondered again if this seemingly new attraction he had for her was the real Marcus talking or the heady aftermath of his near-death experience.

And what if it wasn't false? What if he meant it?

It didn't matter.

She wasn't a big enough fool to love him again.

GINGER INHALED THE pungent scent of redwood trees as she watched a hawk circling high overhead, silhouetted against the bright blue sky.

Where had Izzy gone? Down the path to the lake, most likely. She'd taken off to walk the dog, and that was generally the way they went. Three days since her and Marcus's arrival, and the girl already had a daily routine. She spent much of her time at the beach, sunning herself, swimming or just playing with the dog.

Ginger strolled past the grove of redwood trees,

past blackberry bushes heavy with ripe fruit, past the mighty oak that stretched its branches over most of her backyard, and down the sloped path toward the lake. Up ahead to the left, she could see Izzy sitting on the beach, Lulu prancing around her, begging for attention.

Izzy's attention was elsewhere, though. She was staring out at the lake, or maybe past it to the horizon, her expression dark. A gentle breeze caught her long, dark hair and sent it fanning out slightly over her shoulders. She wore a gray T-shirt stretched tight over her thin frame, with a pair of faded jeans and white flip-flops.

And she appeared not to notice Ginger's approach. When Ginger finally sat down beside her and Lulu focused all her efforts on getting the attention of her owner, Izzy responded by glancing at Ginger. It was easy to see that the girl had been crying. Her face was blotchy, her eyes red and still damp.

"What?" Izzy said as a greeting.

Ginger tried to remember what it felt like to be thirteen. All she could recall was the utter misery. Awkwardness, self-consciousness, lack of confidence… She hadn't truly recovered from those same afflictions until her late twenties or early thirties. But then, she hadn't been nearly as naturally graceful as Izzy.

"I've been wanting to talk to you," she said.

The girl exhaled, clearly not interested. Ginger gave Lulu a thorough tummy rub, and the little dog edged her way onto her lap, clearly in ecstasy over the attention.

"Did Marcus tell you why he thought I'd be a good person for you guys to stay with this summer?"

"No." There was no hint of interest in the single-word response.

Ginger had hoped for a friendlier start to their conversation. She'd hoped to ease into the things she wanted to say, cushioning them with kindness. But Izzy was having none of that, so she decided to get to the point.

"One reason he brought you here is that I lost my parents when I was a kid."

Izzy glanced over at her, her expression more hostile now. Then she looked away again, back to the horizon.

"I was nine when it happened." Ginger could tell the story now without getting knocked down by grief, but for years she couldn't speak about it.

For years she hadn't talked about it. She'd simply gone about her life, knowing that people whispered about her behind her back. She'd endured their pitying looks—reveled in them, at times—but on the rare occasions when she'd opened her mouth and tried to tell the story to some curious person who asked about her family, her throat would close up and she couldn't get a word out.

She didn't cry, though. People always seemed impressed by that, as if her stoicism was some kind of virtue. Actually, the opposite was true, she'd found out during therapy. She'd been unable to grieve for her parents as a kid because the loss had been too big.

It had taken a therapist to point out that the reason she couldn't get close to men romantically was because she hadn't grieved for her parents yet. And that had finally set her on the path to crying the river of tears she needed to release.

"You mean like they died or what?" Izzy finally asked, her voice barely audible above the lapping of the water against the shore.

"Yes, they died."

"How did it happen?" Again, the quiet voice, though this time it was slightly more audible.

"They were in a car accident. A drunk driver—a car full of teenagers on their way to a party after the prom. My parents had gone out for dinner and were on their way home, but they never arrived. I was woken up later by the babysitter and the police knocking on the door."

Ginger stared out at the horizon, too, her chest tight. She didn't usually go into any details when she told people this story, but she'd vowed to give Izzy as much detail as she wanted if it would help her.

"So, what happened to you? Did you have to go to a foster home or something?"

"My grandmother was still alive. She took me in and raised me."

Izzy sat silent for a while. Ginger focused on the little dog, who lay contentedly in the crook of her crossed legs. She stroked her light brown fur, paying special attention to her favorite spots behind the ears and at the base of her spine.

"I know this sounds weird, but…did you ever get mad at your parents?"

Ginger knew she had to tread carefully here. "For leaving me behind?" she asked.

"Yeah." Izzy sounded a little defensive, as if she were embarrassed now that she'd dared to ask the question.

"Sure," Ginger told her. "And then I'd feel guilty for getting mad, and then I'd hate myself."

"Yeah." Izzy gave a heavy sigh.

"That's normal, Izzy. It's totally normal. We

spend our whole childhood knowing it's our parents' job to take care of us, and it's hard to accept that they're not going to be around anymore to do it."

"It's stupid." Izzy sounded angry now. "It's not like my mom wanted to get cancer."

"No, she didn't. And she didn't want to leave you."

"But she never even thought of finding my dad for me before she died. That makes me mad, too."

It made Ginger mad, as well, but she would never tell Izzy that. "Maybe she did think of it, but figured he wouldn't be able to help."

Izzy rolled her eyes.

"How did Nina become your guardian?"

"She was my mom's best friend and my godmother. They thought since I knew her and grew up around her, I'd be okay with going to live with her."

"And were you?"

She shrugged. "I'm not okay with any of it."

Ginger wasn't quite sure what "any of it" referred to, exactly, but she didn't think now was the time to press for details. She would try another tack.

"It was brave of you to contact Marcus like you did."

"No, it wasn't," she said flatly.

"He's a good person," Ginger said, hoping to re-assure her, "but it's going to take him a little time to learn how to be a father."

"Are you, like, his girlfriend or something?" There was an edge in Izzy's voice.

Ginger, inexplicably, felt her face flush. "No, it's like he told you—we're old friends from college."

Izzy studied her closely. "You don't look at him like he's just an old friend."

Ouch.

Ginger's first instinct was to deny, deny, deny, but she didn't want to lie to Izzy. The girl would see right through her, and they'd never establish any kind of trust.

"Well, however you think I look at him, all we've ever been is friends."

"You like him," she said, and this time it was a clear statement of fact. "And not just as a friend."

Ginger laughed. The last thing she wanted was hostile, manipulative Izzy going back Marcus to report that Ginger had a crush on him. But the teenager had managed to back her into a corner, and she didn't see any way out. "Why do you say that?" she asked in as neutral a tone as she could.

"I'm not stupid."

Ginger shrugged, giving in to defeat. After all,

hadn't she invited Marcus to stay with her in order to get over her old feelings for him?

Lulu, spotting a small bird nearby, jumped up from Ginger's lap and pranced over to investigate.

What was she about to say to Izzy was probably too mature for the girl to understand, but she had vowed to be honest with her.

"Okay, well, here's the deal," Ginger said. "I have a long history of going for emotionally unavailable men. My therapist says it's my way of not having to get too close to anyone. Self-sabotage, basically. I fear abandonment, since my parents abandoned me in a sense. So I fall for men who won't ever fall for *me,* since that means they'll never get close enough to leave me."

"What's self-sabotage?"

"It's when your subconscious—the part of your brain that you're not aware of—leads you to do things that are in conflict with what your conscious mind thinks it wants."

Izzy scrunched up her forehead. "That doesn't make any sense."

"No, it doesn't. I agree."

"I guess it's the same for me—like, how being mad at my mom for dying makes no sense."

Lulu barked at something in the woods, and

Ginger turned to see that the bird she'd been pursuing a few moments ago had perched on a nearby tree branch, frustrating the dog.

"We all want to feel there's someone to blame for the bad stuff that happens," Ginger said, relieved that the conversation had neatly traveled away from her feelings for Marcus, and equally relieved that she'd managed to both distract Izzy from her sadness and chip away at a bit of her hostility.

"So you like Marcus because he's emotionally unavailable? What does that mean?"

Okay, so she'd congratulated herself too soon. Ginger sighed.

"In your dad's case, it just means that he's always seen me as a friend, not a potential girlfriend."

"But people can go from being friends to boyfriend and girlfriend, can't they?"

Marcus's daughter was certainly persistent. "Sure, it happens."

"So why couldn't it happen with you two?"

Ginger wanted to tell Izzy it wasn't any of her business, but she was scared of ruining the little progress she'd made in gaining the girl's trust.

"Good question," she said vaguely.

The wind was starting to pick up. At this time of day, the change of temperature often caused a strong breeze to sweep across the lake and chase away those who, like Ginger and Izzy, hadn't brought a warm jacket along for the evening.

When Izzy shivered, Ginger took the opportunity to change the subject.

"Would you like to come back to the house and help me make dinner?" she asked.

"I don't like to cook."

"Really? Have you ever tried?"

The girl shrugged. "I've made eggs, but I burn them."

"Maybe what you need is a little instruction so you can enjoy the process."

For a moment Ginger was sure Izzy would refuse, but instead the girl stood up and caught Lulu in her arms to put her leash back on.

"I thought we could make a few pizzas. Sound good?"

"Whatever. So long as they're vegetarian."

They headed back toward the cottage in silence until they reached the oak tree.

"When your parents died," Izzy asked, "did you have nightmares?"

Ginger stopped walking. "Are you having insomnia?"

The girl nodded, staring down at the dirt path.

"I did. I had horrible nightmares, and I had a hard time sleeping."

She chose not to add that they'd gone on for years, that even in her twenties she'd slept with the lights on because she was so scared of what awaited her in her dreams. But she made a mental note to talk to Marcus about making an appointment for Izzy to see a therapist as soon as possible. Maybe she could prevent Izzy's grief from warping her life as much as Ginger's had warped hers.

"What kind of nightmares?" Izzy asked as they began walking toward the house again.

Lulu, sensing familiar territory, tugged against the leash and Izzy released it so the dog could run up onto the rear deck and wait at the door. She pranced there in excitement, brown eyes cast back at them in eager expectation of dinner.

"One of the most recurrent dreams was that I'd be crossing a bridge on foot," Ginger began. "Sometimes it would look like the Golden Gate Bridge, sometimes the Richmond Bridge, sometimes the Bay Bridge—but there wouldn't be much of a bridge to cross. There'd just be a few rickety boards on metal supports, and I could see the water down below, and every time I moved, one of the boards would feel like it was giving way and I'd almost fall."

"Oh."

They reached the back door, where the rickety screen reminded Ginger of yet another repair that needed to be made on her money-sink of a home, and went into the house. While Izzy fed the dog, Ginger got out the fixings for dinner.

She hadn't thought about those dreams in at least a few years. Relatively benign as they sounded when she described them, they'd always made her wake up with a scream caught in her throat, her body drenched in sweat.

In real life, she had no fear of bridges, but in her dreams they were objects of sheer terror. And when she thought of Izzy, her young life caught in that same cycle of sleepless hell, Ginger vowed she'd do whatever she could to make things easier for the girl.

CHAPTER TEN

IZZY CAUGHT ON TO chopping vegetables. She liked
the fact that Ginger didn't fuss over her handling
such a sharp knife. She'd simply showed her how
to hold it safely, warned her to keep her fingers
tucked away from the blade and taught her how to
chop a green pepper.

Easy.

She worked her way through peppers and onions,
and was now chopping mushrooms for the pizzas.
She was happy that they didn't have to keep talking.
Ginger had put on some kind of African music that
made the house feel alive.

Izzy didn't really want to like Ginger. Most of the
time she wanted the woman to go away, which didn't
make much sense when she and Marcus were staying
at *her* house. But she kind of liked Promise Lake.

She wondered if Marcus might consider getting
them their own place here once the summer was

over. Or would he want to go back to Amsterdam? Or somewhere totally different? She didn't want any more changes, and she was terrified of asking him the most important question—what came next?

What came after this getting-to-know-you vacation?

She liked the name Promise Lake. It sounded soothing, somehow.

Hopeful.

Full of good things to come.

That was how Izzy wanted to feel.

And she liked the sounds of the forest and the lake—they were somehow more like quiet than noise. The birds, the bugs, the frogs, the rustling of the trees that reminded her of breathing—it all worked its way inside her and made her feel calm in a way she hadn't felt in Nina's house in the city, where everything had seemed cold and mechanical.

Izzy even liked this broken-down house, with its crooked floors and crumbling walls. The light that poured through the big windows felt quiet and happy, and the bright, pretty colors Ginger had painted the walls made every room feel as if it were welcoming her to come in.

Most of all, she liked sleeping in what clearly had been meant to be a girl's room. Ginger had told her that she hoped to someday adopt a child. Some stupid, stupid part of her thought maybe Ginger wouldn't need to adopt a little girl from China if she got together with Marcus. Then Izzy would be—

No.

Stop it.

That was by far the stupidest thought that had ever tried to form in her head, and she wasn't going to go there. It was the kind of ridiculous fantasy some girl in a Disney movie would have—thinking everything would work out hunky-dory in the end and everyone would live happily-freaking-after...*blah blah blah.*

Like her mother had told her in one of their talks after the cancer had gotten bad, life never worked out like the fairy tales and Disney movies. Well, except in one way. The mom really did die sometimes.

But Izzy really, really didn't want to like Ginger, even if that crazy part of her wished for something more. She couldn't stand to lose anybody else. And if Marcus was really the kind of guy her mother had said he was, the kind who didn't do settling down or family life, then where did that leave them?

Maybe she shouldn't have pushed Ginger to admit that she looked at Marcus like she was starving and he was a big fat steak. But Izzy hadn't been able to help herself. Some hard little part of her had wanted to get under Ginger's skin and find a place that would hurt.

But now…

Now that she knew about Ginger's parents…

Now what?

If Izzy believed in angels, she might think one had just swooped into her life to guide her out of this hell and into a better place.

Was that what Ginger was supposed to be? Did angels come with curly Muppet hair and outfits from Old Navy's two-years-ago collection? Maybe in kids' movies they did.

"Hey," she said, mostly to distract herself from more corny thoughts. "When's Marcus coming back?"

"Anytime now. He went to the hardware store in town to pick up some lumber and supplies to work on the house."

"I thought he was a writer. How does he know how to fix houses?"

"He used to work construction during the summers in college, and before that he was taught carpentry on the commune where he lived for a while with his parents."

"I thought his parents split up."

"They did, but they still lived on the commune

separately, until he was about fourteen, I think. Then he moved to Amsterdam with his dad for his high school years."

"Do you think he'll want to move back there?"

"With you?" Ginger asked. "No, I don't think so. But maybe that's something he should talk to you about, huh?"

"I don't want to go there."

"I think he wants to here stay in the U.S. The threats and all…"

How much would it have sucked if her dad had been killed? And only a few months after her mother died. Well, at least the universe wasn't *that* cruel.

Izzy glanced over at Ginger, who was rolling pizza dough into lopsided round shapes. The universe *had* been that cruel to Ginger.

Losing both parents at the same time? Unexpected tears welled up in Izzy's eyes, and she dropped her knife on the cutting board. No, she wasn't going to start bawling again.

Not now.

Except she was.

Swiping at her eyes, she hurried off toward the bathroom before Ginger could see what was happening. Once she'd locked herself into the cool little room, with its white tile floor and pale blue walls, she was aware that if she let any banshee sounds escape from her throat, they'd probably echo through the whole house, thanks to the acoustics in here.

So she buried her face in the nearest towel and heaved a mighty sob. Grief, her mom had once said, was like getting caught in a whirlpool, and Izzy thought she finally understood what that meant.

It wasn't like going from one place to another. Like, now you're sad, the next day you're a little less sad, and a little less, and then finally one day you're happy.

Instead, you went around and around, feeling the same awful feelings again and again—better, worse, better, worse, worse, worse and worse still. Down, down, she went. Down the toilet.

When the sobs had stopped racking her body, she was sitting on the floor. She could hear Lulu scratching at the door, trying to get in so she could do her tear-licking routine.

A soft knock sounded.

"Izzy?"

It was Ginger.

The last person she wanted to see.

Or…maybe not.

Maybe she wanted to see Ginger, who was living proof that someone could get through having her parents die before she grew up, right when they were supposed to be taking care of her. Ginger looked like she was okay, didn't she?

Izzy tried to shut her brain off to the bad feelings. She stared at the tiles on the floor, visually tracing the lines of white space between them as they made a zigzag pattern across the floor to the door.

"Izzy?" Ginger knocked again softly. "Can I come in?"

At least she knew not to ask stupid questions like, "Are you okay?"

The answer was always no, no, no, of course she was not okay. But Ginger would know that, because she'd been through it.

Maybe Marcus had been pretty smart, after all, bringing Izzy to Ginger's house. Maybe he was trying to take care of her…or pawn her off on someone who knew what to do with her…

She crawled across the bathroom floor and unlocked the door, then pulled it open before sitting back down on the towel. Lulu came barging in first and hopped on her lap, licking anything she could get her tongue on.

Ginger came in and sat down next to her, but she didn't say anything. She just sat there, silent, and Izzy felt some little frozen place in her chest crack open and start to thaw.

MARCUS PARKED IN GINGER'S driveway, his rented truck loaded down with lumber. He loved the way his body felt after a day of physical labor. It reminded him of what a sedentary life writing could be. He usually balanced it by going on long runs, grueling day-long hikes, riding his mountain bike over tough terrain, but all the leisure activity in the world couldn't equal a day of construction work.

He was exhausted, and he loved it, and he hadn't even gotten started on the real work of repairing the house yet.

He climbed out of the truck and crossed the gravel driveway, admiring the simple, classic lines of the house as he approached. No wonder Ginger had fallen for the place in spite of its many obvious flaws. He was happy to be helping her out in this way, giving her a more solid home in exchange for the immeasurable help she was providing him and Izzy.

He entered the house and went to the kitchen, where he was surprised to see the ingredients for making pizzas scattered about, yet no one was around.

"Hello?" he called.

Heading down the hallway, he glanced in each

empty room until he found Ginger and Izzy sitting on the bathroom floor. His stomach tensed at the sudden notion that something was terribly wrong. Izzy's face, red and puffy… She was crying.

They both stared up at him, blinking in surprise at his arrival.

"Is everyone okay?" he asked, knowing it wasn't.

"We're fine," Ginger said quickly. "Just, you know, working through things."

Izzy stiffened visibly, pulling her knees to her chest and crossing her arms over them as she stared at the floor. Marcus wished for the hundredth time that he had even the slightest clue how to help her, what to say, what to do.

So much for the sensitive male he'd always thought he was. All it took was a thirteen-year-old girl to unravel his self-image.

"Did something happen?" he probed, grasping in vain for the right thing to say.

Ginger shrugged. Izzy started shaking her head, but then her shoulders began to shudder and a mournful wail escaped her.

"Ginger's parents," she managed to gasp between sobs, "died…in a car wreck." Then she buried her face in the towel and collapsed in a despair so wretched it shook her entire body.

Marcus gaped at the scene, frozen in terror.

Okay, Ginger's parents had died, what—twenty-something years ago? Hadn't she made that clear to Izzy?

He stared at Ginger, hoping she could make sense of things for him.

She turned from him without missing a beat and directed her attention to comforting Izzy. "It's okay," she murmured as she smoothed the girl's hair back from her face. "Just let it out. Let it out."

The sobs got louder, more mournful, as Izzy lay on the floor shuddering and shaking.

Some part of Marcus split open, baring him to an unwelcome pain. He had felt affection for Izzy before, even the slightest bit of connection, a sense that she was his flesh and blood. But this…this was the first moment when he knew he loved her in a deep-down way that he'd never loved anyone before. And he couldn't bear to see her suffer.

The scent of the lavender bouquet on the bathroom counter teased his senses, and he realized he should be doing something besides standing there like an idiot. The bathroom was too small for him to wedge himself inside and get closer to his daughter. Besides, Ginger was doing a fine job of comforting her.

He opted to kneel down next to Ginger so at least he wasn't towering over them. He watched as her soothing hands and murmurs slowly calmed Izzy down from hysteria to quiet sniffles, and he wondered at the big, intense feelings that had been bottled up in such a slight body. How had she contained all that grief? And how much more was there for her to let out?

Marcus couldn't imagine.

He turned his focus onto Ginger for a moment. Her long hair was swept back into a messy knot, her strong but feminine back only half covered by a halter top. At that moment she was the most beautiful woman he'd ever laid eyes upon. And he was sure it wasn't just intense gratitude coloring his vision.

She turned to him, and he was struck all over again at how beautiful she was. Dear God. How had he never noticed this in college?

"Could you bring her a glass of water and maybe a cool washcloth?"

Marcus got up and retrieved a cloth from the basket on the counter, wet it with cold water and handed it to Ginger. Then he disappeared into the kitchen to get Izzy a drink.

By the time he returned, Ginger was walking Izzy to her bedroom. She took the glass from him and continued on, so he followed behind them, feeling awkward and unnecessary.

"She wants to lie down by herself for a bit," she said to him when they reached the door.

Lulu, who'd been in the bathroom next to Izzy, was now following at her heels down the hallway, and Izzy bent to scoop her up. She carried the dog to the bed and lay down next to her, the crying jag gone but the afternoon still evident on her blotchy face and in her slumped shoulders.

She'd lost something bigger than Marcus could even conceive. She'd lost the one person in her life who'd taken care of her, and he couldn't begin to imagine how he would fill the hole Lisette's death had left.

He couldn't, but maybe Ginger could....

Whoa.

The moment the thought formed in his head, shame washed over him. She'd been a better friend to him than anyone else ever had, and he couldn't ruin that with...with whatever these weird feelings were.

Ginger set the glass of water on the nightstand and placed the washcloth over Izzy's eyes. "This will help with the puffiness. I'll come back in a bit to check on you, but just give us a yell if you need anything, okay?"

The way she took care of Izzy…it must have felt incredibly soothing to the girl. Marcus himself had longed for someone to care for him when he lay in the hospital after the shooting. Occasionally, a nurse would come on duty who had such warmth he felt truly comforted, but for most of them, it was just a job, of course. And he had no one but himself to blame for the fact that the only person who'd attended his bedside was a publicist he barely knew.

As Ginger left the room, he gave her a questioning look. Should he go in? Do something?

She took him by the arm and led him out, then closed the door partway.

Once they were in the kitchen, she turned up the African music playing on her iPod speakers, and leaned in close.

"Let's just give her a little space, and then you can go in if you want to, in a while. But I think she probably just needs quiet right now."

"What set her off?"

"I talked to her about how I'd lost my parents as a kid. I think it brought up a lot of feelings that are just too painful for her."

Ginger began spreading tomato sauce on the pizza crusts.

"What can I do to help?"

"Shred cheese?" She nodded at a hunk of mozzarella and a shredder sitting on the counter.

Marcus got to work, but he kept his attention focused more on Ginger than the task at hand. "You never talked about your parents' death in college."

"No, I didn't."

"Just that one time."

She let out a short laugh, but it sounded hollow.

"The whiskey shots."

"Truth or dare."

"God, I can't believe we did that," she said, shaking her head, a half smile playing on her lips.

"Truth—what's the worst thing that's ever happened to you?" That was what he'd asked her, expecting to hear the kind of answer most people gave. "When my grandmother died," or "When I couldn't swim and my dad threw me in the lake." Not "Being woken up by the babysitter...the police at the front door...both parents killed...drunk driver..."

The image of that scene was forever burned in Marcus's memory even though he hadn't witnessed it. He could imagine Ginger as a girl, groggy from sleep, stunned out of innocence forever.

Or he could almost imagine. Because he'd never gotten close enough to anyone to experience such loss. Even his father's death didn't measure up, because they'd always had a turbulent relationship, and his dad had been so depressed for so many years that he'd already been partly dead to Marcus when it finally happened.

How pathetic that the first huge loss he'd felt was when he'd almost lost his *own* life last month. How very self-centered.

"I didn't talk to people about it, period. I just couldn't. Not back then."

"You avoided me for a week after you told me," he reminded her. He hadn't had a clue what to do back them.

"You never asked me about it again, though. I was relieved."

"I guess I got the hint that it wasn't a welcome subject."

And, of course, it had felt way too intimate, too close for comfort, all that revealing the deepest secrets of their hearts.

"You were the only person at school who knew."

"And now?"

"Now I can talk about it. I tell people if they ask. I don't tell them my parents are living in Australia or anything like that."

Marcus remembered that had been her old stand-by line to keep from having to answer painful questions about her parents.

"What do you think changed to make it easier for you?"

"Years of intensive therapy."

"Oh, yeah, that helps." He'd had a little therapy himself over the years.

"I was so confused after my last boyfriend and I split up, I had to try to understand what went wrong. It felt like the same things were always going wrong with me and men."

She had finished with the tomato sauce and was sautéing chopped vegetables in a skillet as she talked. Marcus had a pile of cheese that looked like enough to cover two pizzas, so he stopped and leaned against the counter to watch her cook.

"I still find it hard to believe you have any trouble with men."

She sighed. "I'm done trying to find Mr. Right. I think I want a kid more than I want a partner, you know?"

"I'm here to tell you, it's not all it's cracked up to be," he said, half joking and half serious.

"Give it a few months. You'll adjust, I bet."

"Have you thought about going the sperm donor route?"

"Yes, but I still wish…I don't know. I guess I have all these ideals when it comes to having a child, adopting a child, whatever. Some part of me isn't ready to just give in and head down to the sperm bank."

"Good," Marcus blurted.

What on earth was he doing?

She said nothing.

"Maybe you'll find another partner," he suggested. "That would make it easier."

Where the hell was he going with this?

He was trying to picture himself in that role. That's what he was doing.

She still said nothing in response.

"So what did you figure out in therapy?"

She looked up from the skillet and met his gaze for a moment, then turned away again. "I figured out that I avoid intimacy to keep from having to experience another big loss in my life."

"Sounds reasonable."

"And I figured out that I hold every guy up to an impossible standard."

"What standard is that?"

"The standard of my idealized version of the perfect man—the perfect love."

Marcus's chest went tight. He frowned, trying to make sense of her words. "What do you mean?"

She half sighed, half laughed, shaking her head. Then she stopped and looked at him. "You never had a clue. You really didn't have a clue, did you?"

He was genuinely lost here. "About what?"

"The fact that I was in love with you all through college."

CHAPTER ELEVEN

THE TIGHTNESS IN Marcus's chest moved up to his throat, and he sputtered, unable to speak.

"What?" he finally managed to croak.

Ginger almost looked bemused. "I was secretly pining after you all that time. I never had the guts to tell you how I felt, because I knew you didn't feel the same."

"Ginger, I...I never knew."

His thoughts became a senseless swirl. Did this mean they might have a chance at— At what? What did he want? He panicked at every idea that formed in his head. Ginger had loved him back then? What about now? What did she feel now?

And what about their priceless friendship?

Looking self-conscious, she turned off the burner on the stove and drained the excess water from the pan. The onions, peppers and mushrooms were nicely browned, beginning to caramelize. She set the pan aside on the stove and took a deep breath.

"I finally figured out that I had fallen for you partly because you were so inaccessible to me. I knew you wouldn't return my feelings, and I knew I could keep you close but not too close. And then for years after, I used those feelings as a barrier to prevent me from getting close to anyone else."

"Wow," he whispered. How had he missed all of this back at school?

"No one else could measure up to a fantasy love that didn't really exist. I mean, I could make you as perfect a lover as I wanted, since you weren't around to upset my fantasies with reality."

"I wish I'd known. I'm sorry I was so…dense."

But was he? a little voice nagged in the back of his mind.

Was he sorry, or relieved? He would never have stuck around as a friend if he'd known how she felt. He'd have run, just as he did from every other woman who'd ever loved him.

"It's better that you didn't know, don't you think?" she said, a wry smile playing on her lips.

What did he say to that?

"Anyway," she continued. "I'm only telling you all this to get it out in the open. I'm in a much better place now, and I value our friendship far too much to mess it up with any weirdness."

"I, uh, I appreciate your telling me all this."

But the feeling growing inside him…he didn't know what it was. It wasn't good, though. Not good at all.

"When I heard you'd been shot, I knew I needed to see you again and reestablish our friendship. But I also had the selfish need to set things right between us so that I could move on with my life and maybe eventually have a healthy, romantic relationship with someone."

"You mean without having to compare them to me?"

"To my idealized version of you, right."

He forced a smile. "Happy to oblige. I can behave like a bigger jerk if that helps."

"No, no, your normal level of jerklike behavior will suffice," she said, not a hint of joking in her tone.

Then she looked up and caught his hurt expression.

"Kidding! I'm kidding," she said, laughing. "I swear."

He laughed along with her, but he felt as if she'd just smacked him in the head with that skillet she was holding.

If he valued their friendship so damn much, why

had he kissed her on his first night in Promise? And why did it feel like a loss to hear she was ready to move on and be nothing but friends?

GINGER WATCHED THROUGH the door for a moment as Marcus sat on the edge of Izzy's bed and talked to her. She didn't want to intrude on them, though, so she slipped quietly down the hallway and into the kitchen.

A half-empty bottle of merlot sat on the kitchen table. She grabbed it, along with her empty wineglass, and went out on the back deck.

The sun was setting, and it was almost dark. The air had taken on the first hint of an early evening chill, but the day had been hot, and was still warm enough for her to sit for a while without needing a jacket. Crickets chirped in the growing darkness, lulling Ginger into a meditative state.

She wanted to escape her thoughts. She didn't want to analyze her conversation with Marcus, what he must be thinking of her now. He must have been freaked out by her admission. She hadn't planned to tell him like that, but it had just come out. Perhaps she'd been keyed up after her talk with Izzy and the girl's subsequent meltdown.

Or perhaps inspired.

Unlike Ginger, Izzy was busy experiencing her

feelings. She was immersed in grief. She walked around with it in her heart every moment of every day, and that had to be healthier than the way Ginger had run from her own grief as a child. Not that she'd had any other option. Like all children, she'd simply been doing what she had to do at the time to survive.

But she didn't want Izzy to go through what she'd gone through as an adult, discovering her unexpressed grief so late in life, a wound that had never been allowed to heal.

Ginger sat in one of the two Adirondack chairs on the deck and propped her feet on the matching ottoman. She poured herself another glass of wine—it would make her third for the night, and she knew she needed to stop there. Any more and she'd risk doing or saying something stupid. Although she'd pretty much dealt with her previous feelings for Marcus, they were still a habit she knew she could fall back into easily if she wasn't careful.

Especially after the kiss…

Footsteps approached from the living room, and she heard the French doors open and close. "Looks like you found the best seat in the house."

"There's another one waiting right here for you," she said, gesturing to the empty chair next to hers.

He'd brought out his wineglass, too, and he sat down and filled it, then lifted it in a toast.

"To you," he said, his slight smile inscrutable.

She wanted to know his thoughts and at the same time didn't want to know them. What did he think of her now?

"To you and Izzy," she said, clinking her glass to his before taking a drink.

"Dinner was great," he said, sounding just the slightest bit awkward.

They'd made it through the meal without much tension. Izzy had provided a welcome distraction. She'd emerged from her bedroom, claiming to be ravenous, once the smell of cooking pizza filled the house.

And true to her word, she'd eaten enthusiastically and appeared to have totally recovered from her meltdown. They'd talked pleasantly, and Ginger had found herself marveling at the ease with which the three of them interacted in spite of the day's drama…or perhaps because of it.

It said a lot for Izzy that she could move past her negative feelings. The day before, she'd been a grumpy, sullen teenager. Now it was as if the dark skies had cleared to reveal bright blue sky.

Maybe it wouldn't last, but it was refreshing to

see a glimpse of the happy girl she must have been before her mother's death.

"Can you believe that?" Marcus said out of the blue.

"Believe what?"

He leaned in and whispered, "Her transformation."

"I'm as amazed as you are."

"It's all thanks to you."

She ignored the compliment. "I think she's starting to relax with both of us."

"Just now, in the bedroom, she was asking if we could stay here past the summer."

Ginger caught his guarded expression. "What did you tell her?"

"I told her I didn't know what would come next, but that we'd figure it out soon."

"You're welcome to stay here with me as long as you want," she said, knowing he was too polite to stay longer than the summer.

"When I left Amsterdam, I knew it was for good. I mean, I knew I was coming back here for Izzy, but I had no idea where we'd be living."

"You didn't give any thought to where you wanted to live?" That shouldn't surprise her, Ginger thought. Marcus had never been much for long-term planning.

"I guess I considered San Francisco, or maybe Santa Cruz since that's where Izzy spent a lot of her life before her mom got sick, but... I don't know. Other times I thought maybe we'd both need a fresh start someplace new, maybe Seattle or San Diego."

"Is your mom still in Seattle?"

He nodded.

"It might be nice to have her help."

"I don't know. She's not really a kid person. Even adult kids apparently, since she hasn't made any effort to see me in years."

"What about Nina? Do you think she has any feelings about custody?"

"Izzy's old enough to choose who she gets to live with, and Nina's fine with that."

"So she's choosing you?"

He shrugged. "She seems to be for now. Who knows what she'll think once she's in the throes of adolescence."

"I hate to break it to you, but I think you're already there."

Ginger sipped her wine, glancing over at him to sneak a quick peek at his profile. But he turned to look at her and their gazes locked.

"I don't know if I can do it," he said, his voice unexpectedly solemn.

"Do what?"

"Raise a teenage girl—alone or even with help. Moments like this afternoon make me realize that it's going to be hard. And it's not like I'm equipped for the job."

"I don't think you have a choice, Marcus," she said carefully, horrified at the notion that he would even contemplate abandoning Izzy after all she'd lost.

"I hate to admit this, but I wonder every day if she'd be better off with Nina. That's who Lisette chose to be her guardian, after all. She didn't choose me."

Fury unexpectedly filled Ginger, and she had to fight to keep her voice even. "That's a cop-out and you know it. She never even gave you the option of being involved in Izzy's life."

"For good reason," Marcus said, almost to himself.

Ginger's hand began to shake, and she slammed her wineglass on the side table too hard, causing it to shatter. She stared at the broken glass and spilled wine as if they made no sense.

"Hey!" Marcus leaned back from the table.

"Don't do that, Marcus." She could barely get the words out, she was so angry. "Don't. Do. It."

"What?"

"Don't run away again," Ginger said through a clenched jaw. "Don't do that to her,"

Shocked by the fury in her voice, he seemed to be struggling not to run away at that very moment. It was what he did when the going got tough, and she saw now why she could never, ever allow her fragile heart to love him as more than a friend.

"I'm not running away," he said, sounding too defensive. "I'm just…just trying to work out what makes sense for everyone involved. And you tell me—what makes more sense? A girl being raised by a strange guy who has no experience with kids, no home, no established connections in this country, or a girl being raised by someone she's known all her life, who loves her and has a home for her and who was chosen by her mother to take care of her?"

The sound of a slamming door caused them both to jump and turn in the direction of the house. Izzy was standing on the other side of the French doors, staring at Marcus as if he were pure evil.

"Izzy," Ginger cried, as she jumped up from her chair and went for the door.

The girl turned and ran through the house, with both Marcus and Ginger chasing after her.

At the front door, she scrambled to unlock it.

"Leave me alone!" she cried as they came up behind her. "Leave me the hell alone! You're a liar and a fake! You're just keeping me here until you can figure out a good excuse to dump me off with Nina again! I hate you!"

Ginger didn't think it would be safe to let her go out into the night, not now, not in this state.

"Izzy, that's not true—you need to calm down," Marcus pleaded, trying to block the door.

Before he could do it, though, Izzy had the door open and was tearing across the front lawn toward the woods. Lulu, upset by the commotion, was standing on the porch barking after her, less brave than her owner when it came to dark forests at night.

"I'll go after her," Ginger said to Marcus. "She's not angry at me."

"But…" He stared at the woods, where Izzy had disappeared.

"Just wait here in case she comes back," Ginger said firmly, then took off after the girl.

She ran as fast as she could, taking care not to trip on any roots, and wishing the whole way that she'd brought a flashlight. "Izzy?" she called. "It's me. Please stop."

That was the problem with troubled girls. They ran. They didn't stick around where they thought they weren't wanted. They ran away.

Ginger's passed a circle of redwoods, and to her surprise found Izzy standing just to the side of the path, staring up at the moon peeking through the trees.

Ginger stopped, breathing hard. "Thank God. Thank you for stopping."

"I heard what he said." Izzy's voice was quiet. "The door was standing partway open, and I could hear. I was just coming out to get another glass of water when I heard my name. I wasn't trying to listen in."

"It's okay. We probably shouldn't have even had that conversation without you there."

"He's going to leave me with Nina, isn't he?" she said, her voice thick with grief.

Ginger swallowed, tried to think of an honest answer that wouldn't condemn Marcus, but she couldn't. She was disgusted with him at the moment.

"He might," she finally said. "I don't know."

"My mom was right about him. He's too selfish to be a father."

Ginger studied Izzy's profile. She could see so much of Marcus in it. She bristled at the idea of Lisette saying such a thing about him, even if it might be true.

She didn't want it to be true, and neither did Izzy. Ginger wanted to believe something big had changed Marcus, that the death threats and the shooting had jarred him out of his easy life and made him wake up to the possibilities he was missing out on. Wasn't that what his return to the States was all about?

Or was it about fear?

Was it about Marcus running away again?

Izzy turned toward her abruptly. "Could I stay here in Promise and live with you?"

Ginger blinked, stunned. "You want to live with *me?*"

"You're the only person I know who understands what it feels like to have your parents die."

"Marcus's father died, you know," she said gently, trying not to sound as shocked as she felt.

"It's not the same. He was already grown up when that happened."

"You're right. It's not quite the same." She reached out on impulse and ran her hand down Izzy's long curtain of hair, smoothing it from her crown to the middle of her back.

"So can I?"

There really wasn't any reason for her to say no. She was already starting to love this girl, and it terrified her. She didn't want to think of how it would feel to have her leave.

"I would be happy to have you stay with me for as long as you want, but it's not my decision."

"It's my decision," Izzy said, "and this is where I want to be."

"What about your school in San Francisco? Won't you miss your friends?"

Izzy shook her head. "I wasn't there long enough to start school. I didn't have any friends in the city. While my mom was being treated at Stanford and we were staying with Nina, I was doing independent study. That's what my mom wanted, so she could spend more time with me."

"How about Santa Cruz? Do you miss being there?"

Another head shake. "I don't want to go back. It would be too sad to be there without my mom."

Up above, an owl hooted from a branch. They both looked up and saw the bird in a nearby bay tree, illuminated by moonlight, staring down at them with its strange eyes.

"Wow," Izzy whispered. "I've never seen an owl before."

As they watched, the bird took off, soaring on broad wings away from them into the night. With its departure, Ginger noticed that the rise and fall of the crickets' song seemed to surround them in stereo sound.

Izzy was staring at her intently in the dark now.

"I don't care where my dad goes. I'm staying here. This is the first place I've been that feels like home."

"I'm glad you like it here," Ginger said gently. "When I first came here, I was really sad, too. I think living here helped heal me."

"What were you sad about?"

"I had broken up with my boyfriend."

"How come?"

Ginger already knew that Izzy deserved her honesty. "He asked me to marry him, and I didn't want to."

"Because you want to be with my dad?"

"No, not exactly. I was afraid. Just like Marcus is now."

"What were you afraid of?"

"Getting too close. Losing my parents made me want to keep everyone away, so my heart couldn't get so hurt again."

"But you wanted to adopt a little girl, right? Why weren't you afraid of that?"

Ginger shrugged. "I don't know. I think I saw it as a chance to heal—to love a child the way I'd wanted to be loved after my parents were gone, you know?"

Izzy said nothing for a moment, but continued to stare at her. "That's why I want to stay with you, see? You could adopt me instead of some girl from China."

Tears sprang to Ginger's eyes. Of course. That was the way a child would view the matter, and Izzy was straddling the line between child and teenager, still able to see things through the lens of innocence.

Ginger couldn't bear to point out all the practical reasons why Izzy's idea might not be possible. Marcus. Nina. Reality. Not right now. Izzy had had enough disappointments for one night.

Instead, she wrapped her arm around Izzy's shoulders and pulled her close, giving her a squeeze. "We should go back to the house. Marcus will be worried."

"I don't want to talk to him tonight," Izzy said when they started walking.

"That's okay. Soon, though, maybe tomorrow, you two need to talk. I can't keep playing the go-between, because the point of this summer is for you to get to know your dad, right?"

"I already know everything I need to know about him."

The cynical adult comment, coming right after Izzy sounding so innocent, nearly caused Ginger to laugh in shock. She wished she had known the girl before tragedy had struck. She imagined Izzy being a confident, sassy thing who knew how to get what she wanted. She'd probably been one of the popular girls at school, which was a world apart from Ginger's own awkward childhood.

But her mother's death had changed Izzy profoundly, Ginger was sure. She herself had gone from being a bookish but confident girl, secure in her happy family, to a sullen child, never quite in step with her peers, never able to fully join in their carefree concerns. And being raised by her grandmother, a sweet little worrywart who dressed her badly and fed her too much, didn't help matters. Ginger ate to soothe herself, and she'd gained weight.

She hoped she could steer Izzy away from the lonely kind of life she'd had, but she also hoped Marcus would find it in himself to give the girl what she needed, too.

"You know," Ginger said as they reached the edge of the woods, "your dad might surprise you. Don't make up your mind about him yet, okay? People never know what they're capable of until a crisis strikes."

"What do you mean?"

"Well, Marcus getting shot, and then learning about you—this is his first chance to prove himself."

Izzy said nothing, and Ginger didn't want to make any hollow promises about what she was sure Marcus would do. She wasn't sure. She had no idea if he'd ever be anything more than the man he'd always been.

So far, he hadn't impressed her.

Marcus was waiting on the porch when they reached the house. He said nothing as they opened the front door to go inside, but he gave Ginger a questioning look. She motioned for him to come in. They followed Izzy to her bedroom, Lulu scampering at their feet. Izzy bent to pick up the dog, avoiding her father's gaze, and Ginger seized the moment to mime that Izzy was going to go to bed and that they should say good-night and leave her alone.

But there she was, playing the gatekeeper again. She needed to get herself out from between Marcus and Izzy. Otherwise, they might never truly connect.

"Good night, Izzy," she said from the doorway as the girl placed the dog on her bed and slipped off her shoes.

"Night," she replied, without looking up.

Ginger started to close the door, but Marcus stopped her. "I need to talk to Izzy," he said, and she resisted intervening.

She simply forced herself to nod and walk away. Izzy was his daughter, after all. Sooner or later he was going to have to learn how to deal with her.

"I don't want to talk to *you*," Izzy said, her voice

rising to a near yell. "Ginger, I told you I don't want to talk to him!"

Ginger sighed and forced herself to go to the kitchen, out of their way.

This wasn't her battle. She had to keep reminding herself of that.

CHAPTER TWELVE

"Go away."

Marcus stepped into the bedroom and closed the door. He probably should have just done as she'd asked, but at least now he had her where he could talk to her, and unless she knocked him down or climbed out the window, she didn't have any means of escape.

"I'm sorry for what you overheard earlier," he said.

She glared at him, then flopped down on the bed and rolled over so that her back was to him.

"Izzy, I only said what I said because I'm afraid I don't know enough about what you need to be a good parent to you."

Silence answered him. Lulu let out a soft whimper, then nestled in beside Izzy.

He had a feeling he was saying all the wrong things, but he was pretty sure there weren't any right things to say, either.

"I want you to help me in the morning," he blurted, recalling that he'd learned carpentry at Izzy's age.

Of course, she looked about as much like a girl who wanted to learn carpentry as he looked like a guy who wanted to wear a pink boa. But still. He had to try something. And he didn't know what else to do.

She gave no reply.

"I want you to do your part to repay Ginger for her generosity in letting us stay here, so you can start working as my assistant first thing in the morning. We've got windows to repair."

He took note of her expensive-looking designer jeans and flimsy halter top. "Oh, and make sure you wear something you can get dirty in."

Finally Marcus started to open the door, but then he paused. He was doing this all wrong, he knew. She didn't want some guy standing in the doorway barking orders at her. She wanted love and understanding. She wanted a shoulder to lean on. That's why Ginger appealed to her and Marcus didn't. He'd been behaving about as warmly as a rock.

He turned and looked at her again, stretched out on the bed, her back to him. He should go to her bedside, he thought. Sit down, put a hand on her shoulder, tell her he loved her.

But even thinking the words made his throat tighten to block them. Saying them aloud…there wouldn't be any taking them back. They'd lay down a world of expectations before him.

He willed himself to go to her and say something loving—anything—but he remained frozen in the doorway, unable to choke out even a simple "good night." Instead he turned and walked out the door, closing it quietly behind him.

He looked around the house for Ginger and found her bedroom door standing ajar, soft lamplight pouring out.

"Hello?" he called quietly. "Can I come in?"

"Yes."

He went into the room and found her standing at the window, looking out into the darkness as she unbraided her hair. She turned to face him. "How did it go?"

He shrugged. "I talked. She gave me the silent treatment."

"I guess that's better than her screaming and throwing things at you." She flashed him a faint smile, but something about her demeanor suggested she was still angry over what he'd said on the deck.

He hated the thought of her being disappointed in him. And as she undid the last part of her braid and her hair fell about her shoulders, he felt as if something important was unraveling before him, something ephemeral and impossible to name. A weight settled on his chest.

"I told her she has to start helping me tomorrow with repairing the house. I thought maybe I could teach her some carpentry."

Ginger laughed unexpectedly.

"What?"

"I…I think that's a great idea. It's just…those fingernails she spends so much time keeping perfectly painted and filed are going to get destroyed."

"That's probably a good thing."

She laughed again, and Marcus breathed a sigh of relief that the tension from a moment before was dissipating.

"You know," he ventured, feeling braver now. "About what you told me earlier, about how you feel, or used to feel about me?"

She nodded, her gaze searching his. "Yeah?"

"I'm flattered."

He'd planned to say more, but the words escaped him. So he crossed the room to where she stood and pretended he was interested in the full moon outside.

"Beautiful tonight, isn't it?" she murmured.

He turned to face her. "You're beautiful, yes."

"Marcus…"

All the latent desire that he'd been working so hard to ignore since their arrival, and then that delicious kiss, came rushing up inside him. He reached out and traced his finger along the delicate line of her collarbone. It was an oddly intimate gesture, probably the most intimate way he'd ever touched her, and he could see gooseflesh popping up on her skin.

His gaze lingered on her chest, on the curves of her breasts that rose slightly above the stretchy fabric of her white top. He could see that she wasn't wearing a bra, and the outlines of her nipples became obvious as her body responded to his touch.

She still wanted him. The evidence was written all over her. And she wasn't pushing his hand away, wasn't backing up. Her lips were parted slightly, and her breathing had quickened.

Of course he knew the signs of a woman's desire, but he didn't know how to navigate this new territory they were traveling, the space between friends and lovers.

A nagging fear tugged at him. He was taking advantage of her. He knew her weakness now, and he was using it against her. For good reason, perhaps. He wanted the best for Izzy, didn't he? Would he have any chance at all of raising her without Ginger's help?

Not likely.

These were the things he told himself while his fingertips explored the soft flesh of her neck, the silken curls of her hair, the firm curve of her shoulder, the long line of her arm.

"What are you doing?" she whispered.

"What do you want me to do?"

The rise and fall of her breasts as she breathed became too much to merely witness. He needed to feel her against him. And whatever she might have said remained unexpressed as he pulled her to him and kissed her.

But this time…

This time he had no intention of stopping unless she told him to. This time, he felt a rush of need so strong he would not be satisfied until he had her against him, without the barrier of clothing between them.

"Marcus," she said breathlessly.

"Do you want this?" He shouldn't have asked, but he saw the signs.

He knew what she wanted.

And she melted into him. "The door," she said. "We should close the door."

Right. He led her to the edge of the bed, then went to do as she'd asked.

A moment later he was back, undressing her, exploring her with his hands and mouth, and before he knew it, they were both naked on the bed, a frenzy of desire propelling them forward without thoughts or words, only instinct.

Here a kiss, there a caress, and there a longing ache that needed satisfaction.

GINGER AWOKE WITH a start, her heart pounding at the sound of someone breathing next to her. Disoriented, she took in the fact that her bedside lamp was still on. And Marcus was lying in her bed, asleep.

She sat up and stared at him, catching her breath from the shock. Okay, so they'd slept together. They were adults. They could handle it.

Dear God.

She watched his chest rise with each inhalation, all smooth skin and sculpted muscle, and memories of every sensation from their lovemaking came back to her. She knew how he felt now, how he tasted. She could fill in all the blanks that used to exist in her imagination.

But her daydreams starring Marcus were about far more than sex. She'd fantasized about lying on a blanket with him, staring up at the clouds, the stars. Talking for hours, laughing, reading to each other—doing all the things they'd done in college as friends. Only this time with the added layer of intimacy that would come, she'd imagined, from being lovers.

Did it really work like that?

Or would that added layer of intimacy only ruin friendship, as some part of her had always feared it would? Bringing on jealousy, insecurity, hurt feelings and mistrust…

What had they just done?

And Izzy…

What if she woke up and discovered them here together? What if she'd already gone looking for Marcus and found his bed empty, and him in Ginger's?

That wasn't likely. They still had time to maintain appearances, to keep Izzy from experiencing the confusion Ginger felt right now.

"Marcus," she whispered, nudging his arm.

He stirred, rolling toward her, but didn't awake.

"Hey, wake up," she whispered, a little louder now, nudging a little harder.

He opened his eyes, frowning in confusion. "Hmm?"

"Wake up. We fell asleep."

"What's wrong?" he asked, then yawned.

"What if Izzy finds us here? You should go to your own bedroom."

He rose up on his elbows and looked around, still groggy. "What time is it?"

Ginger glanced at the clock on the nightstand. "One-thirty in the morning."

"I don't normally get up this early," he said with a wry grin.

"What if she goes for water or something?"

"Is there some reason she shouldn't know what's going on with us?"

His green eyes pinned Ginger with his question. He knew her weakness, and he was using it against her.

She wasn't sure if she had the will to resist him now any more than she had a few hours ago.

"Don't you think it will make a complicated situation even more confusing for her?"

He gave the matter some thought. "I don't like the idea of pretending in front of her. She's old enough to know what's really going on."

"Which is what?" Ginger blurted, before realizing she wasn't sure she wanted to know the answer.

"We slept together."

"I don't think it should happen again," she said, opposing feelings still battling inside her.

What *did* she think?

She needed time to sort it all out. Right now, she mostly felt grogginess and confusion…and fear.

"I'm only sorry it didn't happen sooner. I don't think we've made a mistake, Ginger. Didn't this feel as right to you as it did to me?"

"Of course it felt good. I mean…" She paused, blushing. "I mean, I guess my problem is we're both stressed out and confused, and I think we're just using sex as a distraction."

She could tell by his expression that he didn't buy a word of what she was saying. He had his own agenda, and he fully intended to pursue it.

He cocked one eyebrow, but remained silent for a few moments. "I'm sorry you feel that way," he said in a teasing voice that meant he didn't feel sorry at all.

But he rose from the bed and retrieved his clothes from the floor. He pulled on his jeans for the walk from her room to his, then went to her side of the bed and leaned down so that their faces were only inches apart.

"Night, Gin," he whispered, and kissed her gently on the lips.

When he was gone, she collapsed onto her pillow and sighed. Then she reached over and turned off the lamp.

She lay in the darkness as the minutes ticked past, turning into hours, but sleep wouldn't come to her. Instead her mind raced over the events of the night. Marcus confessing his desire to shrug off fatherhood. Her confessing her old feelings to Marcus, Izzy wanting to live with her… And then the grand finale of the night, this badly timed tumble into bed.

After the emotional turmoil of the evening, it wasn't hard to see why they'd sought refuge in each other's arms, but that didn't make what they'd done any less stupid.

She got up from bed, the clock having just flashed 5:02 a.m., and found a tank top and jeans to put on. After showering, dressing and pulling her hair into a ponytail, she slipped on a robe against the early morning chill and went to the kitchen to make coffee. No sense in wasting any more time waiting for sleep that wouldn't come. She might was well use the quiet to get a little work done.

Ten minutes later, coffee in hand, she sat in her office waiting for the computer to boot up. Her supervisor at the college was expecting her to turn in her syllabus for the summer class she'd start teaching soon, so she could work on that, or she could work on something fun.

Fun meant writing fiction. Unlike Marcus, her

own writing had never met with any great commercial success. She'd published in a handful of literary journals, and occasionally had stories picked up by national magazines, but as she'd told Marcus, her first novel had been a flop, judging by sales, in spite of her prestigious graduate education. If she'd been smart, she'd have done what Marcus had—taken off with a backpack for an education like no other. But she'd been safe, practical. She'd wanted a Master of Fine Arts degree, so she could get a teaching job to support her writing habit.

Classes at the community college would be starting in another week, and this would be her first time teaching Introduction to Writing Short Fiction. Since she needed to write the syllabus, and also develop lesson plans and decide on reading materials, she opted to be responsible and do the work she was getting paid for.

Once she'd started on her syllabus, using a template she'd developed for her other classes, she got lost in the work for a while and was surprised to hear hammering coming from the other side of the house.

Was Marcus up and working already?

She glanced at the small clock in the lower right corner of her computer monitor and saw that it was already past seven. Then she heard the sound of two people hammering at once, and she thought of Marcus's request of Izzy the night before.

No way was the teenager up already. Or was she? Ginger's office was located on the far side of the house from the bedrooms and kitchen, and she had turned music on, drowning out the little noises of an old house, which tended to distract her from her thoughts.

Ginger saved her document, then stood up and stretched, looking out the window for signs of life. Her office faced north, giving her a glimpse of the lake through the trees. The sun was just rising, and the forest and lake still had the misty, soft look of early morning.

She shrugged off her housecoat and grabbed a sweatshirt that lay discarded on the back of her office chair. Pulling it over her head, she hurried out to see what was going on.

Outside, she found Marcus instructing Izzy on how to properly use a hammer and nails. They were practicing on a piece of scrap wood.

"Be sure the nail is at least halfway in before you attempt to hit it that hard," he was saying.

A series of haphazardly bent nails littered the board.

"But you just use a nail gun. Why can't I use one?"

Marcus glanced up from their work when he

heard Ginger's footsteps. "Morning," he said, flashing a beautiful smile.

"Good morning. You two sure are up early." She couldn't see Izzy's eyes, but it wasn't hard to read the girl's posture.

Pure hostility—toward Marcus, or the task at hand, or both.

"I wanted to get out here while it's still cool," he said. "It's supposed to be a hot one today."

Ginger could smell the scent of a hot day coming in the air. She wasn't sure how, but it was a particular scent, indescribable but present.

"It's going to be too hot to work today," Izzy said, taking off the safety goggles she'd probably been forced by Marcus to wear.

"And I told you a couple of hours of work while the air's still cool isn't going to hurt us."

Ginger was impressed that he'd managed to get Izzy out here, and she figured she'd better keep at a distance so Izzy wouldn't be tempted to make her take sides again.

"Have you two eaten breakfast yet?"

"No," Izzy said, oozing sulkiness. "He said we'd eat *later.*"

"I could bring out some bagels and cream cheese for you to have while you work," Ginger offered.

Izzy shrugged.

"That would be great." Marcus sent her a meaningful smile.

She wasn't ready to exchange significant looks, so she turned and headed for the kitchen.

"Nail guns are dangerous, and you need to learn basic carpentry skills before you move on to convenience tools like a nail gun," she heard Marcus explain as she walked away.

"I'm taking a break," Izzy said. "This is stupid."

Ginger could hear footsteps following her. She paused at the door and turned to find Izzy right behind her.

"I'll help with breakfast," the girl said.

"I think your dad expects your help out there."

Izzy shrugged. "I'm tired. I'll go back out in a few minutes."

Ginger was still impressed that the teen had gotten out of bed to work so early without a fight. She wondered if deep down, and in spite of their conflicts, Izzy craved one-on-one time with Marcus, but was afraid to ask for it. Ginger made a mental note to test her theory next chance she got.

If true, it would be another piece of evidence that Ginger's presence in their lives could be a hindrance rather than a help.

"Why don't you fill these thermoses with orange juice," she said, taking two silver containers out of the kitchen cabinet.

Izzy went about her task while Ginger put bagels in the toaster.

"So what do you think of working as a carpenter so far?" she asked.

Izzy shrugged. "It's boring, and it's ruining my nails."

"I remember taking a wood-shop class in middle school when I was your age and totally loving it."

"Why?"

"I liked working with my hands, and I liked that at the end, I had something useful to show for my work."

"Oh."

"Just think—when you're done, your work will be a permanent part of this house. Every time I look at it, I'll think of you. That's pretty cool, right?"

"I guess."

Izzy was examining a broken fingernail that had been painted purple with little pink daisy accents.

"Maybe you could do that to your toenails instead of your fingernails. Then you wouldn't have to worry so much about your nails getting ruined."

Izzy cast a hostile glance at her but didn't argue the matter. "Did Marcus sleep in your bed last night?"

Ginger's face flushed, and her throat constricted. Did this girl miss nothing?

"Why do you ask?" she said evenly, as she removed the bagels that had just popped up from the toaster.

"I got up and found his bed empty. I was going to ask him if I could live with you after he leaves."

Ginger paused and turned to look at Izzy. "He was in my room for a while, yes."

"So you two are, like, sleeping together?"

"I'm not sure that's any of your business." She tried to use a joking tone, but the words came out sounding snootier than she'd intended.

"Well, whatever. I can figure stuff out. I'm not stupid."

"I know you're smart, Izzy."

"So you got what you wanted, huh? Are you guys going to be boyfriend and girlfriend now?"

Ginger was surprised by the snide tone. She'd been worried about Izzy getting her hopes up that the two of them would get together. Had she been mistaken? Was Izzy *jealous?*

"No, I don't think so. We spent some time together last night, but we're still just friends, okay?"

She blushed again, suddenly conscious of the fact that she was supposed to be a good role model for this girl. She was supposed to be modeling healthy, loving adult relationships, not playing a part in their own personal soap opera, complete with a game of musical beds.

But put on the spot this way, she didn't have a clue what to say or do. The issues of parenthood had been thrust on her by surprise, she was failing at every turn.

Izzy looked her up and down, flipped her hair over her shoulder and walked back out the door.

CHAPTER THIRTEEN

"SOMETHING'S DIFFERENT about you," Ruby said as she looked Ginger up and down.

"What do you mean?" Ginger stepped into the house, keys jangling in her hand.

They had a standing date for her to drive Ruby to the Thursday night ballroom dance at the Promise community center. Sometimes they had dinner beforehand, but Ruby had a date this week with a fellow who'd invited her to dinner before the dance.

Ruby cocked her head to the side, nearly knocking off the purple feather fascinator she wore.

"Oh, dear," she said, putting a hand up to steady the tiny hat. "Guess I'd better add a few more bobby pins."

She disappeared down the hallway and came back a minute later still fussing with her hat arrangement.

"I know what it is," she said. "You're falling in love."

Ginger blinked at this news. "No I'm not," she said too quickly.

Ruby offered her a sly look. "I'm old, but I'm not stupid, you know."

"Well, you're wrong." She crossed her arms over her chest, glancing at the ancient cuckoo clock on the wall. "Don't you have to meet your date at six? We should get going."

"A lady's always a few minutes late," her neighbor said, one of her oft-recited maxims.

As she got closer, Ginger could smell the cloying scent of flowery cologne that Ruby had applied liberally.

"Well, you look spectacular," she stated, hoping the topic of love would be dropped.

And Ruby did look amazing. She wore a beaded purple dress that swung dramatically about her legs and revealed her still-enviable décolletage. Her date was going to be floored.

But the very thought reminded Ginger of the way her own body had responded to Marcus's touch. Years of therapy and a small army couldn't have stopped her from falling into his arms.

They left the house, Ruby pausing to lock up, and crossed the yard to Ginger's driveway, where her little white Prius sat waiting for them.

Once they were in the car, headed toward town, Ruby said, "So tell me what's happened with your true love."

"I don't know what you're talking about," Ginger lied.

"You've got that delicious hunk of a man over there living with you, the only man you've ever loved, and you show up on my doorstep today glowing like a lightbulb and expect me to believe nothing's happened?"

"I told you I'm not in love with him anymore."

"Of course you are. True love never dies, especially true love that's never been consummated— or *has* it? Hmm?"

Ginger tried to stay annoyed, but she couldn't fight eighty years of wisdom. She laughed. "You're insufferable."

They rounded a bend in the road and passed the sign for Rainbow Farm. She'd been meaning to get out to Soleil's place for another visit, and made a mental note to take Izzy with her. She had a feeling the girl might even want to do a little volunteer work there now that she was used to getting her hands dirty.

"I imagine you finally stopped kidding yourself and took that gorgeous man to bed, didn't you?"

Ruby was relentless.

Ginger pursed her lips, unsure how much to reveal. "Things…progressed last night."

"Ah-ha! I knew it. You have the telltale glow."

"There's no such thing."

"Of course there is. Oh, maybe it's something about your posture or the lightness of your step or the way your face looks more relaxed— I don't know. But I can see it."

Ginger sighed. "It's a disaster, though. I never should have let it happen."

"You listen to your therapist too much. Tell me, does that woman have a happy love life?"

"I don't know. We don't talk about *her*. We talk about me."

"I'll bet you my fortune she doesn't. You can intellectualize your life all you want, but until you stop thinking about it and start living it with your heart, you'll never find out what's possible for you."

"Maybe I should be paying *you* to be my therapist," Ginger teased.

Ruby laughed, clearly liking that idea. "My Teddy died a happy, happy man."

"Have you ever thought about remarrying?" Ginger asked, deftly steering the conversation away from herself again.

"Oh sure, I've had offers. But I married young

and never got to sow my wild oats, so I figure I ought to spend plenty of time doing that before I settle down again—if I ever do."

Ginger smiled. "What do you mean, 'if'?"

"Most of these old geezers my age are looking for a nursemaid. Someone to take care of them and cook their meals."

"I see."

"It's hard to find anyone who can live up to the standard Teddy set for me. He was a rare find. I got lucky, and I don't expect to get that lucky again."

"You never know."

"So how was it?"

"How was what?" Ginger asked as they arrived at the main intersection in town and waited for the red light to change.

Ruby snorted. "The sex. With Marcus."

"Oh. Aren't you being a bit nosy?"

"I'm living vicariously."

"It was…great," she said, keeping herself in check. No sense in gushing about something that she knew for absolute certain was a disaster, no matter how toe-curling and way better than her wildest fantasies it had been.

"For the sake of that poor little girl, I sure hope you two can come to your senses and stick together."

Ginger had no comeback for that. Maybe in a perfect world, if she and Marcus could fall in love and stay together, they could all be a happy family. It wasn't likely to happen until hell froze over, but didn't Izzy deserve something that resembled a more perfect world after all she'd been through?

"How's she doing?"

"Izzy? She's okay, I guess. Not quite as volatile."

"I saw her out there working with her dad. That was a good idea—whoever thought of it."

"Marcus did. Yeah, I think it's giving her something else to focus on, and she's even starting to like it, now that she's getting better at handling the tools."

They pulled into the parking lot of the Trattoria Ginolina, where Ruby was scheduled to meet her latest beau.

"Thank you for the ride, my dear."

"You're welcome. Have fun."

Ruby paused halfway out of the car, the feathers on her fascinator brushing against the roof. "Just think about that girl, is all. Think about what she needs."

"She told me she wants to live with me."

"Of course she does. You two are kindred spirits. You have the same hole in your heart." Ruby reached out and patted Ginger's hand, then climbed the rest of the way out of the car.

"Oh, are we still on for you to drive me to my doctor's appointment tomorrow?"

"Absolutely," Ginger said.

"Bye-bye!" Ruby called as she entered the restaurant.

Ginger waved and drove away, her mind spinning. She knew, of course, how much it would have meant to her to have had an intact family while growing up. The ache was so deep she still felt it. Granny Townsend, loving as she was, couldn't replace what she'd lost.

And Ginger could never replace what Izzy had lost.

But she did know her pain. She knew it well.

And knowing it, she couldn't ever add to it. She knew Ruby was right—she had to do whatever she could to help Izzy grow into a happy, secure person. Everything in her life had been leading her to that very purpose.

OKAY, SO CARPENTRY wasn't quite as stupid as Izzy had thought it would be.

Sometimes it was even fun.

A week after she'd started working with her dad on the house, she was really getting into it. Sometimes she pretended she was one of those people on the reality TV shows, fixing up a house for some person who'd written in to ask the show for help.

She wiped her sweaty hands on the old jeans she'd bought with Ginger yesterday at the secondhand store, and went to the workbench to get her water bottle.

She and Marcus had spent the morning measuring and cutting wood, and now they were about to start demolition on the second window to be repaired—the one in Izzy's room. At least, she'd come to think of it as her own.

She believed Ginger really did want her to stay. She could tell when adults were lying, and Ginger was definitely telling the truth.

But she didn't know yet what Marcus thought about staying in Promise, and she was afraid to ask. Which was weird.

Izzy had never been afraid of asking questions. She'd been kind of famous at her old school for asking teachers questions that no one else would have dared to ask. Like "Mrs. Dupinski, why do you write the same comments on our papers, no matter what we say?" And "Mr. Floyd, do you really think no one knows you're having an affair with the vice principal?"

That second one had gotten her detention for a week.

The late-morning sun was just starting to heat up, and already Izzy's body ached from work. She was hot and tired, and she wore grungy clothes she wouldn't have been caught dead in a week ago. Her hair, pulled back in a ponytail, hadn't been washed yet today, and she wasn't wearing a spot of makeup. Not even concealer, which she used to be terrified of leaving the house without.

Izzy smiled to herself. This was what the country life was doing to her. Turning her into a sweaty, unstylish tomboy.

But the funny thing was, she felt better than she had for as long as she could remember. Maybe the last time she'd felt this good was when she'd been a little kid running around, getting dirty, not caring about anything but having fun.

Marcus came over and took off his work gloves, then grabbed his own thermos. "I'm hungry," he said. "What do you say we take an early lunch break?"

"Sure," Izzy said, shrugging.

She'd been pissed at Marcus for the first few days they'd worked together, but there was something about him that made it hard to stay mad.

He was nice. He wasn't like a lot of adults, who talked to kids like they were just dumb kids. He talked to Izzy like she was an adult. And he was patient when she screwed things up. Which she did pretty often.

And he made her laugh. Like when Lulu kept getting under his feet yesterday. Instead of getting mad at the dog, he'd picked her up and put the work goggles on her, then acted like he was teaching her how to level a window frame. Then for the rest of the day, he kept acting like he was teaching the dog carpentry lessons, when it was really Izzy he was teaching.

They went inside now, and Izzy got all the sandwich ingredients she could find out of the fridge. This had become their lunch routine. They'd put everything on the table and see who could make the most creative sandwich. That was the cool thing about Marcus—he could even turn fixing lunch into a game.

"Where's Ginger?" Izzy asked, wishing she was around to join them.

"She had to take Ruby to a doctor appointment in Santa Rosa. They're supposed to be back this afternoon."

"Oh."

"Didn't she ask if you wanted to go along and go shopping in town with her?"

"Uh-uh."

"She said she was going to, but I complained about her taking my assistant away. I guess she figured you'd want to stay and work." He flashed her a grin that said he knew she'd much rather have gone shopping.

Izzy rolled her eyes.

"Hey, I was wondering," he said as he sat down at the table and started opening a jar of pickles. "Did your mom ever get married or have a serious relationship?"

Izzy watched him closely, wondering how she felt about that. When she was younger, she used to fantasize that her dad would reappear and marry her mom and they'd all live happily ever after.

"She didn't get married, but she had boyfriends."

"Did any of them ever live with you?"

"Yeah, Jay did. For a few years."

"And then they broke up?"

"Then my mom got sick, and he didn't want to stick around to watch her die."

Marcus's face went hard. "That's pretty lousy."

Izzy shrugged. She'd been kind of relieved to see him go. She used to have her mom all to herself before Jay moved in.

"Yeah, I guess so."

"Did you get along with him?"

"I guess. He didn't really pal around with me or tell me what to do."

"He didn't try to be a parent to you."

"No." Izzy busied herself slicing avocado for an avocado, cheese and veggie sandwich.

"Will you make one of those no-meat sandwiches for me, too?"

"With pickles?" she asked, since all his sandwiches contained pickles.

"You decide."

She worked in silence for a minute. Then she said, "Why'd you ask about Jay?"

"I've been wondering if I'm one of a long string of guys who've come along and tried to be your dad."

"But *you* are my dad. You don't have to try, right?"

He shrugged. "It seems more like a right I should have to earn, don't you think?"

"No," she said without looking at him.

Something about this conversation was making her throat get all tight and her eyes burn. She didn't want him auditioning for the role of dad in her life, because that meant he could decide not to show up for the tryouts. He could just vanish if he didn't like the part. Like he'd already hinted he would.

"You think biology trumps performance?" he asked, his tone teasing now.

"I guess."

"How about social studies?"

"What?"

"Sorry, bad joke. I can't be on my game all the time. So what was this Jay guy like?"

"Are you sizing up your competition?"

"Absolutely."

Izzy finished making the first sandwich—whole-wheat sourdough bread piled high with avocado, Monterey Jack cheese, sprouts, lettuce, tomato, pickles and mayonnaise. She put it on a plate and pushed it across the table to Marcus.

"Now that's a work of art."

He picked it up and took a bite, while Izzy started assembling her own sandwich.

"Jay looked pretty different from you. He was small and kind of nervous. But he was a musician. He played jazz guitar, and he went on the road a lot, and my mom kind of didn't like that. They fought about it sometimes."

"Was he nice to you?"

"Yeah, I guess. But I thought he needed to, I dunno. Grow up?"

"Why is that?"

"'Cause he was older than my mom and still trying to be a rock star, you know? He didn't have a real job and didn't want to get married and didn't want to have kids, but just wanted to have fun."

She glanced up and caught Marcus looking kind of weird. As if he didn't like what she was saying, and then, in an instant, she knew why. Because Marcus was kind of like Jay.

Maybe her mom had liked a different type of guy than Izzy had thought—maybe she liked irresponsible guys who couldn't grow up. Marcus didn't want to get married or have kids or get a real job. He just wanted to run off and have fun, far as she could tell.

When she thought of it like that, she wanted to fling all the food off the table and break the dishes.

"How about your mom? Did she want to settle down and get married?"

"I guess. I don't know. She talked like she didn't, but she was always depressed after any of her boyfriends disappeared."

"Do you understand that if I'd known about you, I would have been a part of your life?"

Izzy blinked at this, trying not to tear up.

"You mean you would have married my mom?" she said, once she could speak again.

"I don't know about that. Your mom and I were young and fought a lot when we were together. I'm not sure how happy any of us would have been if we'd stayed together. But I definitely would have wanted to be a father to you."

"From Amsterdam?"

"No, I mean, I guess I would have moved closer—"

"You *guess?*"

He sighed. "I can't say what would have happened, but I'm here now, okay?"

"For the moment."

She placed a piece of bread on top of her sandwich, but she no longer had an appetite. She thought about what her dad had said about leaving Promise, about returning her to Nina and her perfectly stylish house in San Francisco....

"That's not what I meant."

Izzy picked up a stray bean sprout from the table and pretended to be interested in it twirling it between her fingertips. Under the table, Lulu was hovering near her feet, waiting for her to drop something interesting. Sprouts didn't count as interesting to the Chihuahua.

But Izzy was afraid to let Marcus speak to her. She didn't want to make him say something she didn't want to hear.

He bent down and came up with Lulu in one

arm. He placed the dog on the table, amid all their sandwich fixings.

"Shh, don't tell Ginger."

"That's gross. Her feet are dirty."

"Oh, right," he said, and scooped up the dog again, placing her on his lap. "Lulu, don't you know to wash your paws before you come to the table?"

He picked up his napkin and wiped the dog's front paws with it. Then he put her paws on the edge of the table as if she was waiting to eat.

"She doesn't like vegetables much," Izzy said.

"Oh? You haven't trained her to be a vegetarian, too?"

Izzy rolled her eyes. "She's a *carnivore*."

Marcus raised one eyebrow. "Are you sure? She doesn't look like she falls into the same category as a wolf or a lion."

"I think Chihuahuas were bred to hunt, like, rats and mice and stuff."

"Oh. I see. And you're not opposed to that, as a vegetarian?"

He was teasing her again, and she was kind of relieved to have them talking about something not so serious.

"I'm not going to make my dog be a vegetarian, okay? That's dumb."

He tried unsuccessfully to get Lulu to eat a piece of lettuce. But she went for the slice of avocado he offered.

Marcus looked up at Izzy. "I only meant earlier that I wish I'd known you as a kid. I wish I could have watched you grow up to be the kid you are today. I'm sorry I missed all that."

Izzy took a bite of her sandwich, because she didn't know what to say. And she kept her eyes on her plate, because she was afraid if she looked at her dad, she'd start bawling like a baby.

What he'd said… It felt kind of like something she'd been waiting her whole life to hear, and she didn't want to ruin the feeling by saying the wrong thing.

CHAPTER FOURTEEN

GINGER'S FIRST DAY of teaching at Promise Lake Community College was a success. Her students seemed eager and engaged, and her course load was light enough that she could still spend time with Izzy…and Marcus.

Nearly a week had passed since they'd slept together, and so far they'd managed to pretty much pretend nothing had happened. She didn't want to talk about it, and he didn't seem to care one way or the other.

Back at home, she put down her school bag and headed toward the sounds of life coming from the kitchen. Jazz was playing on the iPod speakers, and the scent of something garlicky and delicious filled the air.

"Hey," Marcus said, smiling when he spotted her in the kitchen doorway. "You're home just in time."

She took in the sight of the dining room table, bedecked in candles and set for dinner.

"Wow, what's the special occasion?"

Izzy placed a basket of bread on the table. "He's not telling. It's some big secret."

Marcus, looking ridiculously sexy in Ginger's green gingham apron, smiled. "Oh, just a little good news. I'll tell you when we're all sitting down."

With a pot holder in one hand, he removed a pan of lasagna from the oven.

Ginger inhaled and instantly felt hungry. "Anything I can help with?"

"No, just have a seat. Everything's ready."

Izzy sat down in her usual spot, put her elbows on the table and then, seeming to remember her manners, removed them again.

Marcus brought the lasagna to the table and placed it on a couple of extra pot holders he'd managed to unearth. Ginger had always liked the fact that Marcus knew his way around a kitchen, but this was his first time breaking out the domestic skills here at her house. He'd been so busy with the repair work, she imagined he hadn't had the energy to do more.

She eyed the bottle of champagne Marcus produced and began pouring, and her stomach flip-flopped. *Champagne?*

When he finished, he picked up his glass. "I'd like to make yet another toast, since that seems to be what we do around here." His eyes twinkled, but he offered no further explanation.

Ginger lifted her glass, and Izzy, looking as perplexed as Ginger felt, raised her own flute of apple juice.

"You have to tell us what we're toasting, you know," Ginger said.

"Okay." He paused, clearing his throat. "I got a call from my literary agent today. She said my publisher is offering me a big, big contract to write a memoir of my experience living with the death threats and being shot."

"Marcus, that's great! Congratulations!"

They toasted, and then Ginger thought to ask, "But wait, is this a book you didn't even pitch?"

He shook his head. "Me? Write a memoir? It's not exactly my chosen genre, but for the money they're offering, I think I can work up the enthusiasm to do it."

"Wow."

"It's great timing. I've been starting to wonder what my next project would be."

"You mean working on my house isn't satisfying your creative urges?"

"It does, actually—which scares me," he said with a wry smile.

Izzy was listening to their exchange quietly, and Ginger wondered what the girl was thinking.

Marcus continued. "They also want me to pick up my book tour for *Seven Grains of Sand* here in the U.S. now that I've recovered."

Finally, Izzy spoke up. "What does that mean?"

"It means I'll be traveling for a while, maybe six months."

Ginger stared at him, aghast. Did he understand what this meant for Izzy? He was smiling, clearly oblivious to the fact that his daughter shrank back in her chair at his words.

"But—"

"It's much safer to do a book tour here. I don't think we have to worry about a repeat—"

"What about Izzy?" Ginger blurted before realizing she probably should have asked this question in private.

"I don't know. We'll have to figure that out. You could stay with Nina while I'm gone, right? Or maybe here with Ginger?"

He didn't get it. He was so drunk on his good news, he really didn't get it.

Izzy glared at him, saying nothing. The only

sound in the room was Lulu's toenails clicking on the hardwood floor as she moved around.

Then, as if in slow motion, Izzy raised the hand holding her juice. The glass flew across the room and landed against the wall with a crash. Their second smashed drinking glass in a week. At the impact, time went into fast-forward. Izzy racing from the room. Marcus staring at her, stunned, a reprimand frozen on his lips.

And Ginger understood him perfectly in that instant as she rose and followed Izzy. He was frozen in terror, both literally and figuratively—afraid to assert his authority as a father, because doing so would make him one not just in name but in fact.

Running away on a book tour was by far the easier option.

The cowardly option.

The option he'd always chosen.

Izzy's door slammed just before Ginger reached it, and she heard the click of the lock.

"Izzy, please let me in," she called, but wasn't sure what she'd say if she was allowed in.

Yes, your father is an idiot. Yes, he's an ass. No, he's not really father material at all.

Your mother was right all along to have left him out of the equation.

Ginger pressed her forehead against the cool, grooved wood of the door frame, her hand resting on the knob. "Izzy?" she tried again.

Nothing.

Marcus came down the hallway and stopped beside her. "Open the door, Izzy," he said. "We need to talk."

But even Ginger could hear the uncertainty in his tone, as if he wasn't quite sure he belonged there, telling her to do anything.

First chance he had to return to his glamorous literary life, and he already had one foot out the door?

The writer in Ginger recognized the lure. Didn't every writer at times long to escape the complication of human interactions for the self-centered pursuit of one's own creative vision?

Over the years, Ginger had matured. She'd come to see her writing for what it was—one facet of her life, not more or less important than any other part. And in truth, it was often less important to her than the everyday, unglamorous act of helping a student find his or her own writer's voice.

Marcus tried to grab the doorknob, and she let her hand fall away. Who was she to interfere now? Doing so hadn't helped anything so far.

As he shook the door, she turned and walked

toward the living room. She went out the French doors onto the deck and leaned against the railing. Lulu followed her, so she scooped up the little dog and held her close.

"All this drama," she whispered. "You're the only one here who stays calm."

Marcus stepped outside a moment later.

"She's got to stop with these tantrums," he said, shaking his head as he sat down on an Adirondack chair.

Ginger bit her tongue. What did she know about raising a teenager, anyway?

When she looked at Marcus, her heart split in two. One part had always foolishly loved him, and one part, the wiser part, saw his ugly side and loathed his selfishness.

"So you're just going to *dump* her with someone and go on a book tour?"

She couldn't bite her tongue, after all.

Pure fury was rising up inside her. It was the fury of a mother bear protecting its cub.

He stared at her, shock registering in his eyes. "You think she's better off with me? Look what just happened. We try to have a nice dinner, and a glass gets smashed against the wall. She storms off and locks herself in her room."

"That's called having a teenager. A teenager who just lost her mother, by the way."

He shook his head, his shoulders slumped. "I'm not cut out for this. I thought I could handle her, but I can't, okay?"

Ginger wanted to shake him. She wanted to slap some sense into him. But she couldn't even find words.

He went on. "Besides, I have to earn a living, and the better my current book does, the better my next one will sell."

"Grow up, Marcus."

"What?" He blinked at her, incredulous.

"Grow the hell up! Stop thinking about your own damn ego and think about what's best for your daughter for once!"

Ginger hadn't meant to yell, but the fury had come bursting forth, and there was no stopping it now.

"Ginger—"

"You think the number of books you sell is more important than giving that child a chance to feel safe and secure and loved?"

"Of course not, but you can see that this isn't working. I'm not giving her what she needs."

"What happened to us becoming a big happy family? Wasn't that your idea?"

His expression turned darker. "Does this feel like a happy family to you?"

"I don't want you here anymore," she said. "Izzy can stay, but I think you should leave."

"Okay," he said evenly. "Should I leave tonight?"

"No," Ginger said, tears springing to her eyes. "Wait until tomorrow so we can talk to Izzy when she's calm."

How could she sit there and tell the girl she was about to lose another parent? How could Marcus?

She started to walk inside, but he stood and caught her by the arm. "Ginger, I'm sorry. I thought maybe this could work. I didn't want it to turn into something ugly."

And she understood then why he hadn't pushed the issue of what their lovemaking had meant. After the initial rush of excitement, the messy details of figuring out whether or not they could work as a couple were too much for him. He'd taken the coward's way out.

With that, she shook her arm loose from his grasp, turned and went inside. Lulu still in her arms, she went to her room and closed the door, lay down on the bed and cried.

CHAPTER FIFTEEN

IZZY HAD NEVER hitchhiked before. She'd seen other people thumbing for a ride on the side of the road, and of course her mother had told her to never, ever, ever do it because of bad people and all that. But her mom was gone now, and her dad didn't give a damn, so who was going to stop her?

She walked along the side of the road that led out of Promise toward the highway, making up a story for whoever stopped to pick her up. She would say she was sixteen, not thirteen, and that she'd been on her way to stay with her cousin in Los Angeles when her car broke down.

She carried most of her things in a backpack, and had tucked Lulu into the doggy travel bag with her head peeking out. No one would hurt a girl carrying a tiny dog, right?

She'd also have to tell the person who picked her up that her dad was abusing her and that she was going to stay with relatives who'd keep her safe. That way no one would try to take her back to Promise and hunt down her parents.

This time of morning, with the sun just about to rise, was an odd time for someone to be hitchhiking, but she couldn't have waited around any longer. She hadn't wanted to leave at night, so she'd slept for a while, then crawled out the window at dawn, a few hours before anyone would check to see if she was awake.

The cool morning breeze caused her to shiver, and she tried not to think about how scared she was. That would only cause her to shiver more. No, she wasn't going to be scared. It didn't really matter what happened to her anyway.

No one cared all that much, so why should she?

Once she did get to L.A., she wasn't sure what she'd do, but it seemed like the place to go if you were a runaway teenager. She remembered seeing what had seemed like hundreds of them in Hollywood when she'd visited there a few years ago with her mom. So at least she wouldn't be alone.

But she did worry about money—she had only forty dollars, left over from her last birthday—and food. How would she get any? She'd have to ask the other homeless kids. There were soup kitchens that gave away free food to them right?

What about Lulu? Would they feed dogs at a soup kitchen? It didn't seem likely, but she'd seen homeless people with dogs....

God, she didn't want to be on the street. She didn't want to go back to Nina's, either. Marcus would find her there, and then he'd get to be all smug that she was being well taken care of. Like he'd done the right thing, leaving her with her godmother.

The longer she walked along the side of the road, the more things Izzy could think of to worry about. But she wasn't going back. She wasn't going to give Marcus the satisfaction of leaving her behind. She wasn't going to let another parent abandon her.

She did feel bad about leaving Ginger, but Ginger would be fine. She could still adopt some cute little Chinese kid who wouldn't argue or slam doors, and it would be a lot more fun than having Izzy around.

A car approached, and Izzy raised her thumb, only her fourth chance so far to catch a ride. But the white car just kept going like the rest had; the driver didn't even slow down or give her more than a glance.

Memories of the night before invaded Izzy's thoughts.

It was easy to tell when adults had bad news, because they didn't want to look you in the eyes.

They started acting weird, too, but they figured you were too dumb to know something was up.

Izzy had known something bad was about to go down as soon as Marcus started making dinner, acting like he'd drunk too much coffee. He'd let her help when she offered, but he hadn't wanted to tell her why he was in such a frenzy.

For a short, foolish while, she'd kidded herself into believing maybe he was going to propose to Ginger. Or that he'd already proposed and they just needed to break the news to Izzy that they were getting married.

God, she could be so stupid.

So, so stupid.

But it hadn't taken long for her to realize that whatever was going on, it wasn't good news for her. If it had been, Marcus would have looked her in the eye. And he'd have told her what was happening. He wouldn't have kept her waiting.

Lulu whimpered, and Izzy stopped walking to cover the dog with the little blanket she'd wiggled out of.

From behind her came the sound of another car approaching. Then headlights appeared, rounding the bend in the road. She could see now that it was a truck, not a car. A big semi. As it passed, she stared at the driver and motioned with her thumb.

And something miraculous happened.

The truck slowed, then pulled to the side of the road ahead of her and stopped.

Izzy's heart pounded about a mile a minute. She wanted to puke. God, was she really going to do this? Get in that truck with some stranger?

What other choice did she have?

She jogged to catch up, and as she got closer, the truck's passenger door popped open. She climbed onto the step below the door and peered in at a gray-haired man with a beard and a big belly.

"Can I…um, have a ride?"

"Where you headed?"

"L.A."

"I'm going as far as Bakersfield. You're welcome to ride along."

Bakersfield. Where was that? North? South? Did it matter? She'd figure it out later. For now, this was the only chance she had to get away from Promise.

Izzy climbed into the truck and shut the door.

"Hi, I'm…Josie," she said, giving the name of one of her best friends from childhood. "And this is Lulu." She nodded at the bag. "You mind having a dog in the truck?"

"Don't suppose I do," he said as he pulled out onto the road again.

And that was it. She was on her way. Somewhere.

Away from Marcus.

Away from Ginger.

Away from everything that was never going to be.

"Have you seen Izzy?" Ginger asked.

Marcus was already packed, his suitcase standing next to the door, when Ginger found him putting on his shoes in the living room. Her heart sank for the second time in the past few minutes.

"I thought she was sleeping in," he said.

"Were you going to leave without saying goodbye to her?"

"Of course not. I just didn't want to wake her. I figured I'd hang around until she got up."

Hang around where? Ginger wanted to demand. *In your car with the engine on?* But she bit her tongue.

She was the one who'd asked him to leave, after all.

"She's not in her room. I just looked."

"Where is she then?" he asked.

"I was hoping you'd know. It looks like she left in a hurry."

"What about Lulu?"

"She's gone, too. Maybe Izzy took her for a walk, but Lulu's bag is missing, and I've got a bad feeling…."

"Her bag is missing?" He was a few steps behind Ginger in putting the facts together.

Already her hands were shaking, and she wanted desperately to pick up the phone and call the police—run out the front door and launch a search party. She needed to do something, anything, to make sure Izzy was safe.

"She wouldn't run away, would she?" Marcus sounded confused, as if he couldn't imagine a distraught, angry teenager ever thinking of doing such a thing.

"Why not?" Ginger nearly screeched, her voice rising. "Why would she want to stick around here?"

"She loves it here." He paused, seeming to consider the possibilities. "She said she wanted to stay here with you."

"Maybe she changed her mind."

Marcus expelled a ragged breath and ran a hand through his hair. "Okay, so let's start looking. I'll go down to the lake, where she likes to walk. You check around here?"

Ginger nodded, relieved to have a course of action. "I'll also check with Ruby to see if she's seen or heard anything. And I'll call Nina, too."

Marcus nodded. "If I don't find her by the lake, I'll circle back through the woods and look for her there."

"Bring your cell phone and call me if you find her. I'll do the same." Ginger headed back to Izzy's room to look for clues.

She had a strict policy against nosing around, and even now, under potentially dire circumstances, something in her rebelled against violating the girl's privacy. But necessity propelled her farther into the room, which was flooded with morning light.

The east-facing window stood partway open, but Ginger knew Izzy kept it like that to cool the room at night, since the house had no air-conditioning. The screen was still in place, so if she'd left in the night, she had to have gone through one of the doors.

The bed was unmade, its white sheets and flower-print quilt a tangled mess. That, too, was normal. Izzy didn't make the bed unless asked to do so.

Ginger went to the desk and rummaged around, finding nothing amiss. Then she looked in the closet and noticed that Izzy's jacket wasn't there. Also missing were several outfits, and the girl's purse, which she normally kept on top of the chest of drawers.

Ginger would have to check the laundry to confirm that the clothes were really missing, though, so she went down the hallway to the bathroom and searched the near-empty hamper, then went to the hall closet that housed the washer and dryer. Nothing in either place belonged to Izzy, except for one sweatshirt she'd spilled wood stain on while working with Marcus.

Back in the bathroom, Ginger checked for Izzy's toothbrush, but it was gone, along with the small pink bag of cosmetics she usually kept on the bottom shelf of the medicine cabinet.

Ginger's stomach felt hollowed out. Where would the girl have gone? And how had she intended to get there? As far as Ginger knew, Izzy had no money and no friends who drove.

Oh, God.

What if…

What if she intended to hitchhike?

Or what if she wasn't headed anywhere at all? What if she was suicidal?

The moment the thought formed in her head, Ginger tried to banish it. But she pictured the wide, cold expanse of Promise Lake. Maybe the idea of swimming until she grew tired might seem better than the other options Izzy faced. Ginger pictured the deep, dark sadness she'd seen more than once in Izzy's eyes, and cold fear shot through her.

She wouldn't, would she?

Ginger went to the phone and dialed Ruby. It was

just after nine in the morning, and her neighbor normally rose with the dawn light. If anyone had seen anything fishy, it would be her. She answered on the third ring with a friendly "Hello?" Ginger explained the situation, but Ruby hadn't seen Izzy.

Another phone call confirmed that Nina hadn't heard from Izzy, either. Her worried tone reminded Ginger that it was her fault—hers and Marcus's—that Izzy was missing now. Nina promised to let Ginger know first thing if she heard from Izzy, and she said she'd call around to alert any of Izzy's friends that she might run to for shelter.

After hanging up the phone, Ginger went out onto the front porch to watch for Marcus. He hadn't called, which meant he hadn't found anything. Maybe she'd be better off searching the woods, too....

Or was it time to call the Promise Police Department? Her throat tightened at the thought. God, what if…

No, she had to stop with the what-ifs. They weren't helping. Now was the time to remain calm and clear headed.

Wherever Izzy was, they would find her. Ginger had to believe that.

CHAPTER SIXTEEN

MORE THAN TWENTY-FOUR hours since she'd disappeared, and they still hadn't found Izzy.

Marcus jumped each time the phone rang, which was why he'd had to get out of his hotel room and do something. Almost every call had to do with his agent or his publicist, though. Schedules were being rearranged. People were upset with him. He was supposed to be starting his book tour with a reading in San Francisco tomorrow.

His whole life had turned into a surreal nightmare.

And the hours continued to tick by without any word from Izzy. No news of what had happened to her.

Ginger had been frantic to find Izzy, but she hadn't been willing to let Marcus stay. She'd insisted he had to leave, though she'd already called several times to check in and insist again that he phone her the moment he heard anything.

Marcus stood in front of the color copy machine

at the Promise Quick Copy shop and watched as flyer after flyer spat out.

This was what his stint as a father had been reduced to—making copies of a Missing Person flyer for his daughter.

He'd failed in an even bigger way than he could have imagined, and finally, he understood that this wasn't about him.

This wasn't about him.

It was about Izzy.

Too late he realized that parenting wasn't an interesting experience for him to partake in, to further round out his life and achieve personal growth. It was about raising a child as best he could, strictly for that child's sake, so that she might grow up and have something positive to contribute to the world.

Why couldn't he have understood that from the start? If he had, this might never have happened. Izzy would be safe, and Ginger wouldn't hate him for the selfish bastard he was. And he wouldn't hate himself.

He picked up the stack of five hundred copies, then went to the counter to ask if he could post one in the store window.

He almost couldn't look at the flyers, but

forced himself to read a copy one last time to make sure the phone numbers and contact information were correct.

Izzy's pretty, vaguely petulant face stared back at him. The photo was maybe a year old; it was the one she'd e-mailed to him before they met.

Isabel Grayson, aka Izzy, thirteen years old, missing from Promise Lake, California…

Tears welled up in his eyes, and he wanted to smash something, anything—smash everything into a million little pieces.

He loved that girl. He loved her, and if he got another chance, he'd do anything he could to make her happy.

The woman at the counter stared at the flyer.

"This your girl?" she asked.

He nodded, unable to speak.

"I'll be happy to post it for you, hon. And if you give me a little stack I'll make sure the rest of the businesses around here do the same, okay?"

"Thanks," he managed to croak.

"Such a shame," she said. "Poor thing."

He turned and left with the stack of flyers before he shouted at the woman. His daughter wasn't a shame. She wasn't a poor thing. She wasn't going to end up as a statistic, a face on the side of a milk carton.

He would find her, and she would be safe, and that's all he could allow himself to believe right now.

WHEN GINGER saw Marcus's car pull into her driveway with a thirteen-year-old girl alive and well in the passenger seat, she nearly passed out with relief.

The phone call hadn't been enough to convince her that Izzy was okay. She'd needed to see her in person.

And she still wasn't convinced. She needed to hug Izzy close, look into her eyes and sense with her gut whether there was any hidden damage, anything the girl might be afraid to tell them.

Ginger hurried out the front door and raced down the steps and across the grass. As soon as Izzy, looking tired and bedraggled, opened the door and got out, Ginger swept her into a big hug that went on and on.

"Thank God," she whispered into Izzy's hair. "Thank God you're okay."

Then she pulled back to look her in the eyes. "*Are* you really okay?"

Izzy, her expression self-conscious now, shrugged and stared at the ground. "Yeah, I'm fine. And I'm sorry for running away and worrying you so much."

"Is that what your dad told you to say?"

"I told her she owed you a year's worth of free carpentry work," he said.

Ginger looked up, almost shocked to find him there.

He looked tired, too, more tired than she'd ever seen him. As if he hadn't slept in days.

And if he hadn't, good for him. He deserved some sleepless nights.

Okay, maybe she was being a bit unfair, but she wasn't about to make any more excuses for Marcus.

"I'll be able to…I mean, I could keep helping with the house if you want me to, because we're going to stay in Promise," Izzy said, smiling tentatively.

"You are?" Ginger looked from her to Marcus for confirmation.

We? Did that mean both Izzy and Marcus?

"I canceled the book tour. Told my publisher I have more important things going on in my life right now that need me to stay put."

Ginger blinked. She knew better than to take such an about-face as the final word on the matter. Surely he'd change his mind once the reality of having to live the small-town life as a single father caught up with him. The glamour of the literary world would tug at him, and he'd find a way to escape.

"He really did cancel his tour," Izzy insisted.

Ginger saw the girl's hopeful expression, and

knew she had to banish her cynicism for Izzy's sake. The girl needed something to hope for.

Ginger looked at Marcus then, really looked at him. His face was so familiar, yet unfathomable now.

"Why don't we go inside and drum up a celebratory lunch?" she suggested. "I've been missing your avocado sandwiches."

There'd be time for questions and explanations later.

"Um, actually, I'm kind of tired," Izzy said. "I haven't slept in two nights. I was hoping I could lie down for a bit and take a nap." She glanced at Marcus as if to get his approval.

But her words had the feel of rehearsed lines, and Ginger's instincts went on alert.

"Okay," she said. "Let's get you settled then."

She picked up the carrier that held Lulu, and they went inside to Izzy's bedroom.

What she'd come to think of as Izzy's bedroom.

But now she would live somewhere else with Marcus. Ginger had allowed herself to hope that Izzy really would be hers. Whatever that meant. She'd let herself believe she would finally have the child she'd always wanted.

When she watched Izzy climb into bed and settle under the covers, her heart ached.

Marcus bent and gave Izzy a kiss on the forehead, then picked up the dog and left the room.

Ginger went to the side of the bed and sat down on the edge. She met Izzy's gaze with a gentle smile.

"Wherever you go, I want you to know you can always come back here, okay? This is your room, and this is a place you can always call home."

Izzy nodded. "Thanks," she said. "I promise I won't run away again."

"I love you." Ginger bent to give the girl a hug. "Now get some rest."

She left the room and found Marcus in the kitchen, looking tense and nervous. Lulu was on the floor devouring a bowl of dog food. When Marcus saw Ginger, he sighed.

She raised her eyebrows in a silent question.

"Can we go for a walk?" he asked.

He looked as if he hadn't slept in years, not days. And some lingering bit of tender feeling caused her to want to reach out and smooth the tension from his brow, but no. She knew better now.

"Sure," she said.

At least they had Izzy back. That was probably what he wanted to talk about. Far enough away that Izzy couldn't overhear.

He'd learned his lesson.

They went outside and walked along the path toward the lake. It was a clear, warm day with a soft breeze sweeping over the water. Sandal weather, Ruby called it.

And Ginger was wearing sandals, a pair of brown beaded flip-flops that didn't do well on the uneven gravel path. Her yellow sundress blew in the breeze, and as she walked, she tried not to be so conscious of Marcus's presence.

He was here, and she had to be okay with that for now. For Izzy's sake.

"So she was picked up for shoplifting?" Ginger asked, unable to control her curiosity any longer.

"Yeah. But I told the police her story, about losing her mom and just having met me, and they let her off with a dire warning. The owner of the 7-Eleven she tried to steal from agreed not to press charges."

"Sounds like she got lucky."

"Very. She was a wreck when I got there, crying and scared half to death."

"But…Bakersfield?" Ginger asked as they scrambled down the drop-off that led to the beach. "What was she doing there? How did she get there?"

"She hitchhiked with some trucker who was headed that way."

"Oh my God."

"By the time I got to her, she'd already had the life scared out of her by the cops about all the bad things that could have happened to her while hitchhiking."

Ginger paused once she reached the beach, and tried to get her equilibrium back. "The thought of her climbing into a truck…with some strange guy…"

"I know. I can't even think about it right now."

Marcus took Ginger's hand in his, and she resisted the urge to pull away. He led her toward the water's edge, where the sand was flat and wet. They took off their shoes and walked toward the wide stretch of beach that headed east around the lake.

"Where did she plan to go?"

Marcus told her everything he knew about Izzy's ill-thought-out scheme. The driver of the semi who took her to Bakersfield warned her not to do any more hitchhiking when he let her out at the bus station. Paralyzed with fear, she'd spent what little money she had on the cheapest ticket to L.A., but the bus didn't leave until the next day. She wandered around Bakersfield and spent the night in a park. By the following day she'd gotten hungry enough to steal, which had led to her getting busted in a convenience store for trying to shoplift a bottle of apple juice and a box of cereal.

"Wow," Ginger murmured when he finished talking.

Her anxiety over the girl's ordeal hardened into a solid knot in the pit of her stomach.

They walked in silence for a few minutes, until a piece of driftwood blocked their path. Rather than going around it, Marcus stopped walking.

"I couldn't go," he said. "I couldn't go on the book tour now. I mean, I won't go."

"Good," she said quietly. "Izzy needs you after what happened. She needs things not to change."

"You were right about me." He looked into Ginger's eyes, and she saw a depth of pain that had never been there before.

The water lapping at their feet was cool and brought with it the sensation of washing their troubles away, or their past, or both.

"What do you mean I was right?"

"I need to grow up. Needed to grow up."

"Needed?"

"I've made a few vows to myself. I'm going to be a good father to Izzy. And I'm going to make sure the people who matter to me know how I feel."

Ginger said nothing.

"That means you," he continued.

"Marcus, please…" She tried to turn away.

She didn't want to hear that he needed her because Izzy needed a mother. Much as she wanted to fill that role, she knew it wasn't a solid foundation for a relationship.

"I love you, Ginger. I've always loved you."

"That's not enough, Marcus. You know it isn't."

"I don't mean I love you as a friend. That's how I used to feel, but everything's changed. You're not the girl I used to be friends with. I've fallen in love with the woman you've become."

She wanted to brush off his words, but they rang true. Because it was exactly how she felt about him. He wasn't the man he used to be.

He wasn't running away now. He was here, trying to be a father to Izzy. He'd faced some of the most challenging circumstances a parent could imagine, and he hadn't buckled. He'd stuck with the job.

And he was telling Ginger he loved her.

He loved her.

Unlike other times in her life when she'd heard those words, now they resonated deep down in a part of her that hadn't been touched in too long.

"I love you, too," she heard herself say, before reason could jump in to stop her.

But she didn't want to stop herself. The words

felt right on her lips. She knew she meant what she'd just said.

She loved him. It was true. And it wasn't the silly, unrequited love of her college days. This was something more.

Something real.

"You do?" he said, his eyes sparking with the slightest bit of hope.

"I do."

In his eyes she could see something she'd never seen before.

Humility. It was what grief had left behind—the evidence of his trial by fire.

"I'll make it worth your while," he said.

She smiled. "I'll bet you will."

* * * * *

2 FREE BOOKS
AND A SURPRISE GIFT

We would like to take this opportunity to thank you for reading this Mills & Boon® book by offering you the chance to take TWO more specially selected books from the Cherish™ series absolutely FREE! We're also making this offer to introduce you to the benefits of the Mills & Boon® Book Club™—

- **FREE home delivery**
- **FREE gifts and competitions**
- **FREE monthly Newsletter**
- **Exclusive Mills & Boon Book Club offers**
- **Books available before they're in the shops**

Accepting these FREE books and gift places you under no obligation to buy, you may cancel at any time, even after receiving your free books. Simply complete your details below and return the entire page to the address below. You don't even need a stamp!

YES Please send me 2 free Cherish books and a surprise gift. I understand that unless you hear from me, I will receive 5 superb new stories every month, including two 2-in-1 books priced at £5.30 each, and a single book priced at £3.30, postage and packing free. I am under no obligation to purchase any books and may cancel my subscription at any time. The free books and gift will be mine to keep in any case.

Ms/Mrs/Miss/Mr _____ Initials _____

Surname _____

Address _____

_____ Postcode _____

E-mail _____

Send this whole page to: Mills & Boon Book Club, Free Book Offer, FREEPOST NAT 10298, Richmond, TW9 1BR